# THE PATH TO VIHAAN

DANIEL J. LYONS

The Path to Vihaan

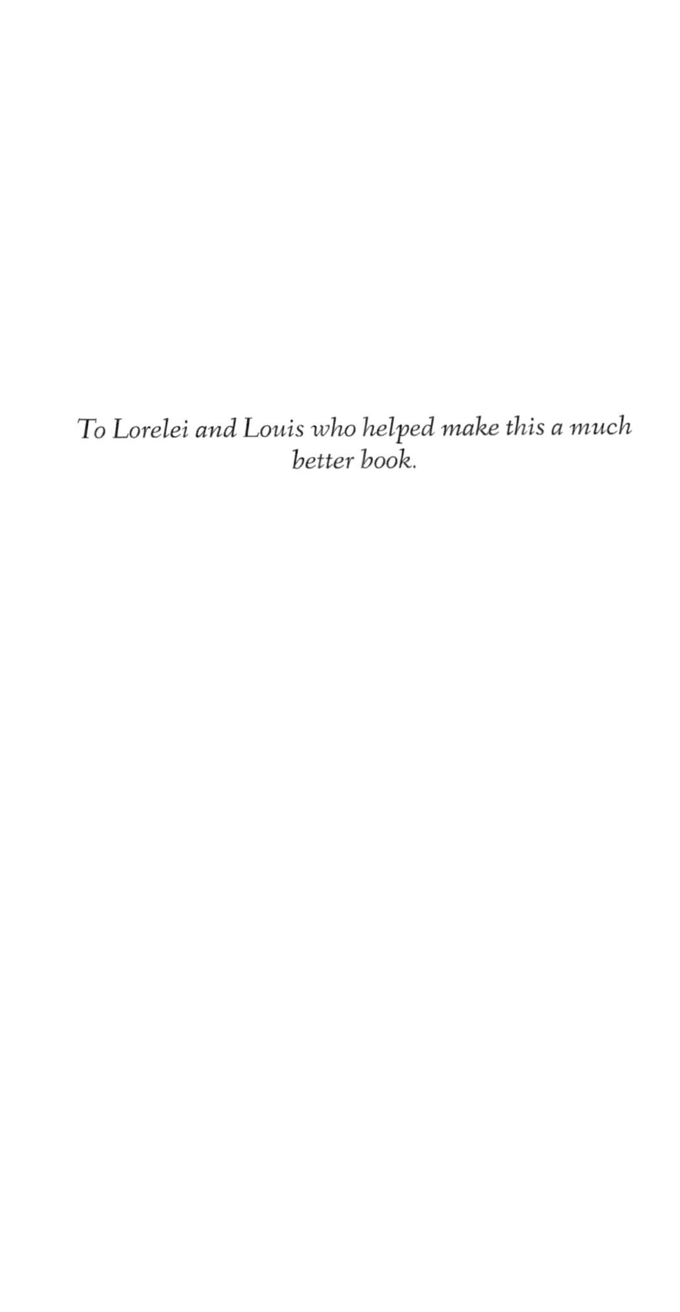

*To Lorelei and Louis who helped make this a much better book.*

# FOREWORD: WHY A TRANSGENDER HERO?

There is a very legitimate concern about a cis man writing the story of a transgender man, so I want to be very up-front about my cis status.

To everyone reading this, thank you for taking an interest in my novel.

Causing offense with this novel is, quite literally, the last thing I wanted to do. (Well, upon reflection, I suppose I'll be okay with offending bigots.)

To be completely honest, my character's gender snuck up on me—and scared me to death!

I can't speak for other writers, but I don't create my books in a linear fashion, and most of the large-scale construction happens within my subconscious.

When I started this one, I knew that the main character was being referred to with female pronouns—so I made an assumption.

That assumption was shattered when I saw him declaring that he could no longer live as a female, then physically transitioning to male.

I immediately realized that I would need to further educate myself in order to portray this character properly.

At the same time, I was extremely concerned that unconscious biases might skew the story away from my original intent.

So, as soon as I completed an initial draft (it contained the main plot moments—and far too many typos—but lacked most of the side plots and the majority of the world-building), I reached out to a transgender friend for her take.

She helped this book more than I could ever have imagined—both with her feedback and by starting an online discussion with her friends to recommend resources to advance my education.

We agreed that I still had a lot of work left to do, but I felt confident that I had a solid foundation to build upon.

Once I finished the first draft, I reached out to a member of the transgender community that I met through the online discussion for a sensitivity read. His insights helped me to refine how this world talks about transgender, or *partite*, people and their transition, or *alignment*.

I don't claim any special right to tell a story about a transgender man and I certainly don't believe that the transgender community needs me to tell their story.

I do, however, feel a need to tell the stories in my head. But, in doing so, I must acknowledge that I have an obligation to portray these characters as accurately, and with as much respect, as possible.

If I have succeeded, it is, in large part, due to the generous guidance described above as well as members of the transgender community who have shared their own stories, like Jamison Green (*Becoming a Visible Man*) and Skylar Kergil (*Before I Had the Words*).

DJL, 22 September 2022

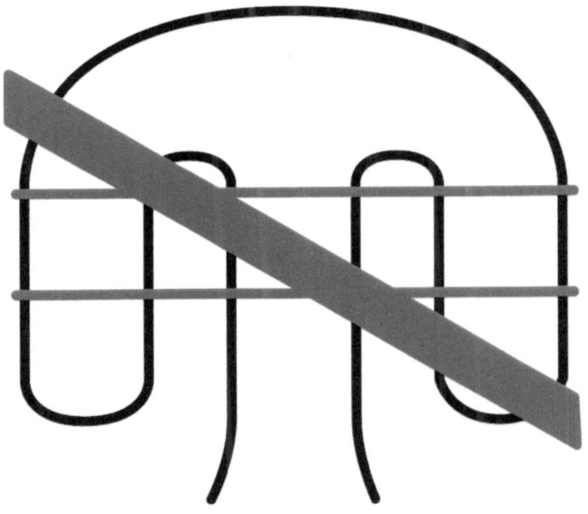

Rumetre (cc. 7 BL): elvish familial crest

# PART ONE: THE PAIRING

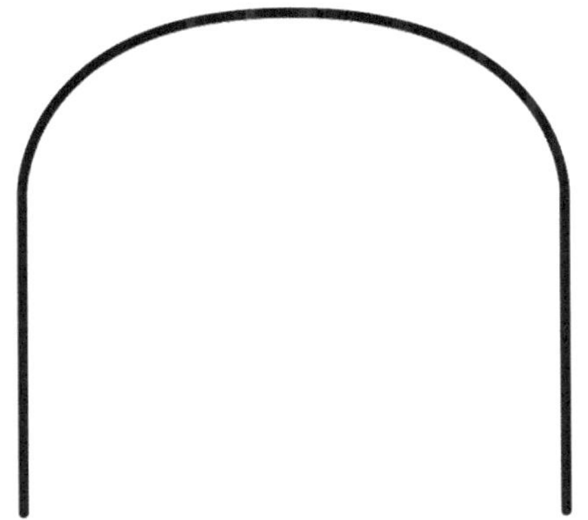

**Ru (base): ground, soil**

# SIBLINGS

The chipped and faded red doors of the Hinter Consolidated School building burst open seconds after the student body was dismissed by the deep gonging of the school's preprogrammed tocsin talisman.

The excitement of being freed from school was clear on the dark-cherry-red faces of the elvish children.

Among the exiting students was a group of five male elves, aged fourteen through sixteen, who gathered at the edge of the school grounds on top of a waist-high stone wall.

One of the other students stumbled.

"Nice move, dragon feet!" the group's de facto leader, Gondefle Rumetre, shouted.

His friends laughed.

"Yeah, are you still breaking them in?!" Chotu, the youngest member of the group, added.

"You're so immature!" Treowe, Gondefle's oldest and closest friend, said as he punched Chotu hard in the shoulder.

"That's right!" Chotu said with pride, childishly flicking the tips of his pointed ears. "School-certified!"

The group laughed again.

Chotu had been held back two years before when the school had declared him—in writing—"too immature to advance."

Behind them, peering through a thin section of the school's decorative hedge wall and desperate to join in but staying hidden to avoid the group's routine rejection, was Gondefle's ten-year-old sibling, Aadima.

Aadima was hiding because, even though Gondefle's friends didn't want Gondefle's "weird sister" around, he still longed to rejoin their group.

Neither of the brothers dared reveal that, although he had been born into a female body, Aadima had always known he was a boy.

Chotu had been the first of the group to object. "It's... uh... she's just creepy and weird!" he had shouted, not meeting Aadima's eyes.

His adamancy had quickly convinced the others, forcing Gondefle's hand.

But, soon after he had publicly told Aadima to keep away, Gondefle had privately started passing along any clothes he grew out of—much to their mother's chagrin.

"A Rumetre shouldn't be wearing secondhand clothes," their mother had said the first time Aadima had proudly appeared at breakfast in one of Gondefle's old jumpsuits. "What will people think?!"

"That I'm not naked?" Aadima had offered, to displeased parental glares.

"They're just clothes," Gondefle had told their

parents. "No one will care. They know who we are."

The boys ran out of targets as the last of the students disappeared down the lane that led back towards the interior of the village.

They went quiet.

"How'd you do on your monthly evaluation?" Chotu asked, eager to fill the silence.

Gondefle scoffed. "It doesn't matter."

"Sure," Treowe said with a laugh, "I bet your mother would *totally* agree with that!"

"*She* doesn't matter either."

Aadima had to fight back an exposing gasp.

*He sounds so angry!*

He knew that Gondefle and their parents hadn't been getting along lately for some reason but also knew it couldn't last long. Gondefle had always been their parents' favorite.

He calmed himself so he could focus on the conversation.

"...with what I've found, I'll be so powerful that no one will matter!"

"Not even us?" Treowe said with a feigned hurt expression.

"Of course *you'll* matter!" Gondefle laughed, then adopted a severe expression. "I'll need you to help me finally give the humans what's coming to them!" His friends' laughter turned uncomfortable as his expression moved to anger. "We'll make them suffer *twice* the pain that they've put us through!" Seeing their discomfort, Gondefle forced a smile. "Don't worry, there will be *plenty* of power to go around..."

There was a howling from Treowe's pocket.

With a practiced motion, he pulled out the flat metallic oval, speaking while his arm was still in motion and before looking at the name displayed across the front of it. "Invoke."

His face fell when his mother's angry visage appeared on the chatter's dull surface.

"I need you to pick up some butter on the way home," she said without preamble. "That pet of yours just stole the last stick and I can't make dinner without it!"

"I'll be right there," he said, his face flushing as his eyes darted away from those of his friends. "Done!"

His mother's face disappeared as the chatter went idle.

He cleared his throat and hopped off the wall. "I was about to leave anyway."

"Yeah, yeah," Chotu mocked, "no other reason."

Treowe scowled as he turned and rushed down the path.

It wasn't long before the other members of the group found their own excuses to leave, partly to make sure that they didn't get their own embarrassing calls.

Aadima waited until Gondefle had turned the first corner before following.

As he walked down the path, he moved through the commercial district, which constituted almost half of the outer ring of Hinter. The school was near the edge of the district, only a few paths away from the industrial district that filled the rest of the ring.

Soon he reached the residential district, which wrapped all the way around Village Centre, where the business and government facilities were located.

It was not a long walk; the oval-shaped village was on the smaller side of average, and the school was located on one of the long sides.

Most cities and villages in the country of Timor used a standard circular plan, but the Inviol Valley, where Hinter was located, was too narrow to allow for it.

Hinter's modified village plan had been tested several times in the past century and a half and had proven itself sufficient to minimize the damage of the periodic demon-attacks that struck every community on Feracio.

Halfway through rounding a corner, Aadima quickly, and with strained casualness, crossed to the opposite side of the path.

He was avoiding Ealdgyd Confut, who was currently standing on the pathside, glaring at Wafi Innoxi, who, unaware of her attention, continued with his yardwork.

Manager Innoxi had been in charge of the Hinter Blood Bank for as long as Aadima could remember, but he was human. Cuisinier Confut had run one of the fanciest eateries in Hinter until her retirement a few years earlier.

While most human Hinterites were young government employees who didn't have the grades to start their careers in a more respectable location and left after a year or two, a few, like Manager Innoxi, stuck around long enough to become mostly accepted as part of the community.

"This is a proud planned elvish community, one of the first founded after the Nekane Rule freed us!" the first of Cuisinier Confut's multiple lectures that he could remember had begun. "It's bad enough that we have to put up with them running everything! They should at least have the good sense to stay in the overly fancy neighborhood set aside for them!"

Aadima rolled his eyes at Cuisinier Confut's outdated attitude and wished he had a recondite talisman so that he could make himself invisible.

As he did so, he thought about the rest of that lecture. It had been one of the short ones, but it was also before he had learned that she wasn't actually looking for a discussion.

"But they changed those laws fifty years ago," he had said in exasperation.

Cuisinier Confut had given him a pitying glare. "The so-called *Equitability Era* was a misguided fringe attempt to mix species that even fools know need to be kept apart!"

"But why?" Aadima had asked with genuine curiosity. "What's wrong with a few humans in Hinter?"

"Hinter is *our* village!" she had shouted. "Humans *always* have an ulterior motive. They don't trust us! That's why they won't let us run our own affairs!" she'd sneered. "And we don't need humans with red-fever sniffing around our children!"

Aadima still didn't know what a red-fever was and, considering the source, didn't dare ask.

The hateful look on Cuisinier Confut's face had made Aadima even more uncomfortable than enduring the berating lecture.

"I need to get home," he remembered saying. "My mom is waiting for me."

Cuisinier Confut had looked him over, as if seeing him for the first time. "And why aren't you in a dress?"

"I don't like dresses."

"Life is full of things we don't like. Being part of a civilization means acting in the prescribed fashion! You're a Rumetre, you need to set an example for our people! And to do that, and be part of society, you have to dress properly!"

Aadima's disdain must have shown on his face because Cuisinier Confut had grown angry. "Mark my words! If you don't start dressing like a proper woman soon, you won't get anywhere in life!"

"Okay," Aadima had said, trying to sound sincere.

"If you're not careful, you'll end up like that pervert Konnyr!" She was fuming now. "That worthless little wannabe doesn't even have the sense to know when it's not wanted."

He had fled from the angry words, but they had chased after him.

"There's one right way of doing things!" she had shouted after him. "If more people paid attention to that, the world would be a better place!"

*No lecture today*, Aadima thought with a sigh of relief as he rounded the next corner.

Two turns later, he arrived onto Balefire Way and caught sight of home.

Instead of his usual smile at the respectable but midsized house located in the last elvish neighborhood before the human section, Aadima frowned in confusion.

Gondefle was working ardently in the front border garden.

*It's not even Restday afternoon!*

Aadima stopped to watch him for a few minutes to see if his normal procrastination would return.

*Is he in trouble?* he wondered. *Is that why he was so mad at school?*

Finally Aadima shrugged and untucked his hair, kept long at his mother's insistence, from inside his shirt, where he stuffed it to keep it out of the way when his teachers and parents weren't there to stop him.

He finished his walk home, and as soon as the front door clicked shut, Jabeza Rumetre, Aadima's mother, called him into the living room.

Jabeza was holding up his brother's monthly evaluation. "You got your evaluation today?"

Even from across the room, Aadima could see that there were no red failure marks, nor even any orange bases, on his brother's evaluation.

Her mother seemed normal.

*Why isn't she mad if Gondefle is in trouble?*

"Yes, Mother."

"How did you do?"

"Two primaries in history and mechanics."

"That's my little girl!" his father, Samael, said from the other side of the room, his attention momentarily pulled away from the news feed on his divulgate.

As usual, Aadima felt a mix of pleasure and discomfort at his father's favorite nickname.

"And...," his mother prompted.

"Three secondaries and"—Aadima nervously brushed his hair behind the points of his ears—"one base in social studies."

A look of angry disapproval filled his mother's face. "Another base?!"

"Just one! It's not like I failed!"

"Your brother wasn't getting bases at your age."

His brother.

Aadima couldn't remember a time when he hadn't wished he could be more like him.

*No one ever told Gondefle he wasn't a boy!*

Sometimes Aadima told himself that he only envied his brother because of his mother's constant comparisons.

But, in more reasonable moments, he reminded himself that he *could* remember a time before his mother had started regularly assuring him that he never quite measured up.

When Aadima didn't speak, his mother grunted. "Then I guess you should get upstairs and get started on your homework."

Aadima fled to his room but, when he got there, left his school-issued divulgate in his schoolbag and invoked his personal one instead.

Aadima's tocsin started ringing at ten minutes to five that evening.

The small rectangular stone changed from red to gray with each ring, only stopping when he lifted it off his nightstand. When he put it down, the ringing stopped and the stone remained gray.

"Done," he said with resignation. The command stopped the latest episode of the long-running, and his all-time favorite, divulgate show *The Rajveer Chronicles*, just as Cal had pulled his human partner, Rajveer, aside to share what he had learned about their quarry.

"*We'll finish this later,*" Aadima said to the now-blank divulgate in his best Rajveer impression before rolling off the bed.

It was time to set the dinner table, a chore that he had inherited from his brother once Gondefle had been old enough to move on to yardwork.

Gondefle burst into the house just as Aadima reached the bottom of the stairs.

"Hey!" Aadima shouted as he leapt aside.

Gondefle paid him no mind. He was covered

nearly head to toe in grime and took the stairs two at a time to minimize the possibility of leaving any of that filth in his wake.

The front door didn't fully close, so Aadima, after an irritated glance up the stars, went to shut it. As he did, he could see that the garden was neatly trimmed.

*He's actually finished?! What is going on?*

"Are you just going to stand there or are you going to set the table?" his mother said from the dining room.

"Sorry." Aadima nearly jumped. "On my way!"

As soon as dinner was on the table, Gondefle started gulping his down.

Aadima was so fixated on his brother's behavior that he barely noticed what he was eating.

Gondefle was abnormally quiet. Gone were his usual bragging recollections about his day.

Aadima almost missed them.

*Gondefle must have found something really great! I need to know what it is!*

A plan started to form in his mind.

"How was school today?" Samael asked.

Caught by surprise, Aadima said, "One of the other boys—"

"*Other* boys?" his mother said with an angry glare.

Aadima cursed himself. He had learned early on that mentioning his gender in front of his parents was a mistake and knew better. "I meant to say one of the boys at school."

His mother's glare hardened. "Have you been talking to that Konnyr?"

"No, of course not!" Aadima said.

"Good," Jabeza said frostily. "I don't want you associating with mentally unstable degenerates like that. You need to remember that anyone who *chooses* to live like it does forfeits the right to remain in decent society. If people want to live like that, they need to do it somewhere else, somewhere away from normal families like ours." She snorted in disgust. "It's disgraceful that the village manager won't do anything about it!"

*But I never chose to be a boy*, Aadima thought, not for the first time.

An uncomfortable silence followed, broken only by the uninterrupted clanking of Gondefle's utensils against his rapidly emptying plate.

*I need to know what he's found!*

"I'm going to go to the library tomorrow!" Aadima blurted. "I might be there all day... so I can study up on social studies... and do better next term."

"If you paid better attention to your homework instead of those childish divulgate shows, you wouldn't *need* to spend extra time at the library," Jabeza said flatly.

"Well, I think it's a great idea!" Samael said. "My little girl knows what's important."

Aadima squirmed internally but forced a smile onto his face.

Across the table, Gondefle rolled his eyes and took a final bite of his meal.

Later, on his way to bed, Aadima knocked hesitantly on his brother's bedroom door. "Gondefle, is everything okay?"

"Open the door," Gondefle's muffled voice answered. "I'm not naked or anything."

Aadima opened the door and then repeated his question as Gondefle slowly rolled over and sat up.

"Why wouldn't it be?"

"You were so quiet at dinner and I... I thought you might be in trouble... or something."

Gondefle smiled. "No, if anything I'm in safety" —he winked theatrically—"perhaps for the first time ever."

Aadima frowned. "I don't understand, are you planning something?"

"Nothing you need to be concerned about."

Aadima brightened. "But maybe I could help?!"

"Don't you worry, squirt," Gondefle chuckled, "I'll take care of—"

Aadima's chatter began to buzz. He pulled it out of his pocket and looked at it. "It's Wafaee, I have to get this. You're sure you're okay?"

"Yeah, no problems here, squirt," he said with a kind grin as he waved him out of the room. "You're bothering me anyway."

"We missed you again after school," Wafaee said as soon as Aadima invoked his chatter.

"Sorry, I—"

Wafaee chuckled, "Don't worry, I'd spy on your brother's little group if I had the chance. Although I'd be looking at your brother, not Chotu."

Aadima scoffed. "I *do not* like Chotu!"

"Suuure you don't," Wafaee said, rolling her eyes, "and I guess he *haaates* you!"

"He does!"

"Suuure, that's why he doesn't even *look* at the rest of us." Wafaee sighed loudly. "Did you *at least* see something good?"

"No... yes... Gondefle is acting weird—"

"Don't boys *always* act weird?"

Aadima cringed inwardly. "I guess—"

"Aadima!" his mother shouted from downstairs. "It doesn't *sound* like you're in bed."

"I'm going!" he shouted over his shoulder before turning back to the chatter and whispering, "I'll talk to you tomorrow. Done!"

*We'll make them suffer twice the pain that they've put us through!*

It didn't make sense—Gondefle's words had been so full of hate, but he had seemed so happy when they had spoken.

*He was just trying to impress his friends,* Aadima told himself as he lay in bed. *Gondefle's perfect! After all, what have humans ever done to him?*

*I'll be so powerful that no one will matter!*

Aadima was so confused. He had never heard him talk like that.

*Maybe he just means he'll be rich! What could he have found that would make him rich enough not to care about his grades?*

His thoughts eventually drifted to the Bokor family.

It had been the first chain store in Hinter and Aadima had been hugely excited.

After days of begging, and getting inexplicably subdued responses from his parents, they had finally given in when Gondefle had agreed to support Aadima's plea.

The new Ameliorates was twice the size of the dilapidated apothecary just a few doors down the main path.

"They even have Hale recharge potion!" Aadima had squealed. "Just like Rajveer uses!"

Their father hadn't been impressed. "We can't stay long. Just find what you need and let's go."

"Aww," Gondefle had replied.

Aadima smiled and whispered to him, "It's so close that we can stop here anytime and get whatever we need!"

"Stop sharing secrets and get moving!"

Aadima ran out of the store with his Hale potion clasped to his chest and waved it at the first people he saw. "Look what I got! It's what Rajveer and Cal use!"

It was Aster and Bosa Bokor. Aster placed a steadying arm on his wife's shoulder as she backed away from Aadima on her spindly artificial legs. They looked at him with sad expressions.

"Don't bother people with that," his father said as he followed him out of the store.

Samael's face went ashen.

"Samael, what's wrong?" Jabeza said from behind him. "Oh."

"The kids, you see...," his father said.

"They just opened!" Gondefle added, holding up his own prizes. "Have you checked it out yet?"

"Gondefle, quiet!" their mother whispered

harshly before forcing a smile. "We'll be over at your place on Restday for the important stuff."

"Of course," Apothecary Aster responded. "See you then."

They moved past without another word.

"That was weird!" Aadima said when they were out of earshot.

"Aadima!" Jabeza whispered angrily.

"They're weird," he continued. "They're older than you, why don't they have any kids?"

"You're being rude," his father said. "Whether they can have children or not is none of your business."

Jabeza had roughly taken Aadima's hand. "Now be quiet and come along."

Less than a year later, and without prior notice, the Bokors were gone and the Bokor Family Apothecary closed.

"They went bankrupt and had to move out-loop to Wove!" Aadima had overheard one of the village gossips saying to another.

"What's bankrupt?" he had asked.

"Mind your business," his mother had replied sharply.

Aadima hated minding his business, especially when he didn't know what it actually was that he was minding.

The true reason for their departure came up on Aadima's divulgate news feed a few weeks later.

## Local Family Auctions Off Pilate Seedlings, Moves In-Loop

Beneath the headline was a full-color image of

two potted plants sprouting delicate blue leaves with bright silver veins.

*So beautiful!*

He had to read halfway through the story before it finally explained what the plants were:

> Pilliate is used in almost every healing potion but produces seedlings irregularly—often only once every few generations. Once the root system is fully established, they are impossible to transplant to factory farms. The bidding for these seedlings was fierce, ending at an undisclosed amount well into the millions of units.

Aadima hadn't known what bidding was, but he did know that millions of units was *a lot of money.*

*That must be it! He found the Bokors' source! He found more pilliate!*

Aadima grabbed his chatter from his nightstand, where it was bathing in a recharge potion that he had invoked just before lying down, and flipped it over to look at the picture from that story.

It had taken three weeks of allowance to pay for it to be transferred onto his chatter, but it had been worth it!

The pilliate plants were still the most beautiful things ever!

Despite their beauty, the picture was also tinged with disappointment. He had always been sad that they had been so close but that he hadn't gotten to see them in person.

For a while he had even pondered venturing out to find the patch of pilliate that had spawned the seedlings. But the story had said that they were found in the forest, and the fear of being eaten by a demon had more than outweighed his desire to see them.

*If Gondefle is after another seedling, there's no way I'm missing out this time! He may not want my help, but there's no reason I can't be there just to see the pilliate!*

He smiled into his pillow, remembering his clever plan from dinner, and picked up his tocsin from his nightstand. "Invoke, wake me at dawn."

The small rectangular stone changed from gray to red as it acknowledged his instruction. He set it back down, snuggled under the covers and closed his eyes.

The rhythmic sound of rain against his bedroom window lulled him into a sleep filled with dreams of spinning happily in an endless field of pilliate.

The next morning Aadima's tocsin rang three times before he finally lifted it off the nightstand to silence it.

As much as he hated mornings, he was happy to be awake when he heard Gondefle talking with their father downstairs.

He rushed into the body-launder, then back to his bedroom to throw on the tunic and pants that were on the top of each respective pile. Dressed, he hurried downstairs.

His mother grunted in surprise. "You're up early."

"I don't want to waste any time," Aadima said,

imagining that it was exactly what she wanted to hear. "Gotta get started on my studies."

"Good," his mother replied without conviction.

Aadima gathered the quickest breakfast he could think of and watched his brother closely as he ate.

"I'm going to Treowe's for the day," Gondefle announced as he roughly tossed his dishes into the kitchen-launder. "I'll be back by dinner."

He left, slamming the door behind him.

Aadima waited an entire painful minute before stuffing the last bit of food in his mouth and jumping up from the table to add his own dishes to the launder. "I should get going too!"

Confident that it hadn't been long enough for Gondefle to get past the end of the path, he slung his schoolbag over his shoulder and hurried out of the house.

# DISCOVERY

After years of practice, Aadima had become very good at not being seen while shadowing his brother.

He had learned early on to always keep an eye out for anything that he could slip behind whenever Gondefle glanced in his direction.

He was proud of his skill, sometimes imagining himself to be an undercover constable tracking a dangerous fugitive.

Gondefle made his way through one of the industrial districts without slowing and, after a furtive glance that sent Aadima flying behind a hedge, stepped beyond the village limits and into demon-land.

From his position behind the hedge, Aadima quaked in fear.

Outside of the protected speedways, there was no safety in the countryside. More importantly, there would be no one to rescue you when you met up with the demons who lived in the otherwise-unoccupied lands between settlements.

Aadima saw an image of himself surrounded by

demons, Gondefle already fallen to their horrible advance.

He took a deep breath, filled his mind with images of pilliate leaves, and forced himself onwards.

He didn't get far. The grassland in this part of the valley offered no protective cover, and he ended up waiting impatiently behind the border fence. Fortunately, Gondefle wasn't being careful and left a trail of crushed grass behind him.

Once he was out of sight, Aadima followed as quickly as he dared—keeping a constant lookout for incoming demons.

The grass started to thin as they approached the base of the eastern line of the Inviol Range.

*How will I track him now?!*

As he cautiously peered through the last few stalks of the tall grass, Aadima smiled and thanked the sky for the previous night's rain.

Gondefle's trail continued through the muddy ground.

As they closed on the foot of the mountain and the ground grew rockier, his brother's trail shifted to muddy footprints. Aadima smiled at the sight, but then his smile faltered and he looked up at the mountains—Gondefle's trail was heading straight for them.

*But Pilliate only grows in the forest!*

He glanced back towards Hinter and beyond it to the forest surrounding the departing stretch of the Boon Loop Speedway on the far side.

*Where is Gondefle going? What could he have found out here?*

His determination wavered.

"Perhaps it's some other magic plant."

Despite being a whisper, the sound of his own voice made his goal real again.

Eventually, Gondefle's muddy footprints led to a narrow crevice within an old rockslide.

Aadima glanced into the opening. The passage turned sharply just a few feet in.

*What if it's a demon-lair?!*

*No, Gondefle said that he had* discovered *something! He's been here before. It must be safe!*

Mostly reassured, he stepped into the crevice and moved into the mountain.

As he turned the corner into a deepening darkness, his bright dreams of seeing some beautiful magical plant evaporated.

*What could he have found in here?*

So distracted by trying to figure out what his brother was after, Aadima took a wrong turn and found himself at a dead end.

He retraced his steps until he found the larger set of muddy footprints again.

*Pay attention!*

He was thankful for his acute night vision as he focused on the trail, but his fear was growing.

Eventually Aadima paused, feeling tears welling in his eyes.

He traced the logo on his shirt. It was for a band that he didn't really know much about, but it had belonged to Gondefle and that was comforting.

But it wasn't comforting enough.

Aadima turned and retreated a few steps towards the entrance before he heard the sound of Gondefle's footsteps echoing in a large chamber behind him.

With great relief, he spun around and rushed towards the sound.

His fears vanished altogether when the cave brightened with a flickering yellow light.

"Gondefle's torch!"

Aadima covered his mouth.

*I hope he didn't hear!*

His brother had picked up the potion-wood torch from their favorite swap meet, the one they kept going to despite their parents' disapproval, when he was Aadima's age, and Gondefle had been enamored by the old-fashioned light source ever since.

Aadima headed towards the light and it wasn't long before he squeezed his way between a very smooth stone wall and a more uneven stone leaning against it.

*It's getting dark again!*

He looked around in panic before realizing that the light was disappearing into a corridor at the back of the large chamber.

He headed quickly towards it, not wanting to be caught in the dark and have to use his own lucent, which might give him away.

Out of the corner of his eye, he saw a very familiar rune carved into the wall.

His curiosity drew him over.

The wall was no longer featureless like it had been at the entrance. Beside him there was a recessed area hung with vaguely familiar items. Each one was the same shape and size, either gray or bronze, and had a thick disk on top with a narrower cylinder hanging beneath. The disks were resting on pairs of posts carved out of the wall, and a single rune was engraved above each one.

Aadima giggled as he realized that the carvings were all secondary runes.

*They all have names!*

He took a closer look at the rune that had caught his attention. It was rume—the secondary version of rumetre, the base of their family crest.

There was a smaller inscription beneath the rune that he hadn't noticed before, but the torch-light was nearly gone and he couldn't make it out.

Now intensely curious, and less worried about being discovered, he pulled out his lucent case.

Aadima unfastened the dark leather cover on one end of the small, tubular case. Very carefully, he opened it the tiniest bit.

A narrow beam of bright silvery light poured out.

The lucent talisman was a family heirloom that had been willed to him by his grandfather when he was seven.

He moved it closer to the wall.

As the light reflected off the rune carved into the wall, Aadima used his finger to wipe away a curving strip of dust—drawing in the extra stroke that converted it into the primary, rumetre.

The sight reminded him of the previous year's Yielding, when his cousin Oroitz, on a dare, had re-cited all of the family heroes starting with the family's first heroic death, which had elevated their surname from Rume to Rumetre.

He looked down at the smaller inscription but was still unable to read it, so he started wiping away the accumulated dust to reveal:

## 302-13-19

*It's a date!*

It was written in the same format as the ones in some of his older history books. He ran his right pointer finger over it as he mentally converted it into the modern form, 19 Teivelan 302.

*Over two thousand years ago!*

The thrill of discovery was shattered by a painful cry that echoed through the chamber.

"Gondefle!" He turned towards his voice, ready to rush to his brother's aid.

As he did, his fingers dropped onto the disk of the item hanging beneath the inscription and his world went white.

Aadima's entire body felt like his feet did when he sat cross-legged for too long. But this time, he couldn't move to shake the needles away.

Finally the tingling started to subside and he stumbled blindly backwards, eventually landing hard on his bottom when his calves struck stone.

It was some time before his sight returned and the painful tingling subsided enough to allow him to think again.

*What did I land on?*

His lucent was still in his left hand, so he pointed it beneath himself and panned the light along the stone.

He was on the end of a long, curving bench carved out of the floor that stretched halfway across the chamber. A matching bench, just one of several rows, stretched to the wall on the other side of the open aisle down the center of the room.

He panned the light around and saw that the

benches at the back of the room were partially crushed beneath the rockslide.

Aadima put his hands down to push himself up and realized that they were both curled into fists.

With surprise, he saw that his right hand was clenched around the dark gray item that had been hanging on the wall.

He puzzled at it for a moment before the memory of his brother's pained scream flooded back into his mind.

"Gondefle!"

He jumped up. With a practiced one-handed move, he slid more of his lucent out of its case as he ran towards the back of the room.

At the point of the wedge-shaped room was a small platform with a central pedestal. The corridor, now illuminated by a pulsing orange light, was immediately behind it.

Aadima ran into it in a panic.

"Gondefle!"

He passed two doorways on either side and leapt over a collapsed section of ceiling as he ran.

Aadima followed the light to an open doorway.

"Gondefle!"

He ran into the silent room.

Gondefle's potion-wood torch lay on the floor, its flickering flame burning without heat.

The flame's yellow light was mixing with a throbbing red one from the other side of a long table that filled the middle of the room.

Aadima moved fearfully towards the unfamiliar light and gasped as he saw his brother's form on the floor beyond the table.

"Gondefle!"

He dropped his lucent and kneeled down beside his brother.

Gondefle was in a section of floor that had been mostly cleared of dust. The clearing looked disturbingly like the demon-prey traces that kids made in the snow every winter by tossing themselves down and thrashing about.

He recoiled in horror when he saw Gondefle's face.

Gondefle's usual complexion, the same cherry red as his own, was now a ghastly pink—so light that it was nearly white. His face looked surprised and his unblinking eyes stared through Aadima.

"Gondefle?" Aadima said with trepidation as he shook his brother's shoulder with his left hand. "Gondefle!"

He didn't respond. Aadima reached out with both hands to shake his brother harder, suddenly realizing that he was still holding the item from the wall.

His brother was holding one too.

It was the source of the red light and, in between flashes, Aadima saw that it was bronze and flecked with green.

Aadima looked down at the gray object in his hand, then back to the glowing bronze one in his brother's.

Gondefle's hand, still tightly clinging to the object's handle, was its normal shade of red, but it was quickly fading to match his face.

Aadima felt tears in his eyes.

"Gondefle!"

The last of the color drained from Gondefle's

fingertips and his hand fell open. The now-dark object rolled away.

Aadima shook Gondefle again. His head lolled towards the wall. Aadima recoiled in horror, staring at the object in his right hand.

*They're Hilts!*

The magical weapons that had been made famous during the Demon Wars.

He fell back against the table and tears poured down his cheeks.

"How could I have been so stupid?!"

His cry echoed around the room, taunting him.

It was so obvious. This was a Hilt foundry. The items in the main room had been the warning display of exposed Hilts always found in a foundry's showroom.

His brother was dead, killed by an exposed Hilt!

He glanced at the Hilt in his own hand again.

*But I'm alive.*

It didn't make sense.

*Why did he come all the way back here? Why would he want an exposed Hilt anyway?*

He looked up at the wall in front of him. There were several shelves carved into it, filled with glass canisters. The intact canisters contained different-colored powders.

*This is some kind of workroom! That's why Gondefle was here—he was after an unbonded Hilt!*

Aadima looked down at his brother's motionless body. "Then why are you dead?!"

He was about to shake him again in desperation when he remembered the previous day:

*We'll make them suffer twice the pain that they've put us through!*

As he remembered his brother's expression of hate for humanity, his last glimmer of hope died.

Aadima knew that Gondefle was dead —and why.

His brother had tried to claim the Hilt while his spirit was in turmoil, exposing it.

Looking again at the green patina, he realized absently that it must be a blood-copper Hilt.

He squeezed his eyes shut.

Just like in the stories, when Gondefle had exposed it, the Hilt had drained his blood into itself.

Opening up his eyes and blinking away tears, Aadima looked again at the Hilt still clutched in his own hand.

"How am I alive?!"

It was certainly an exposed Hilt; otherwise it would never have been put on display.

He lifted his hand to throw it away, but something stopped him and he pocketed it instead.

He began to sob and continued to do so for a long time.

Finally, gulping for breath and batting away the last few tears, he dug into his schoolbag for his chatter.

He needed his parents. He needed help.

He sobbed again when he couldn't find it and realized that, in his rush that morning, he had left his chatter in its pool on his nightstand.

Aadima looked back at Gondefle's body.

In his front shirt pocket was his chatter, its oval outline pressing against the fabric. He started reaching for it before remembering.

Gondefle had forbidden him from touching it after he had accidentally called one of his friends while playing with it. To make sure, he had used up his allowance and added a phylactery talisman to it.

The chatter wouldn't work for anyone but Gondefle.

*Now what?*

# CONSEQUENCES

Aadima faced a choice: abandon his brother's body here in the cave or try to bring him home.

He thought about the conditioning class the previous spring when he had finally been able to lift twice his body weight. It was a proud moment for a young elf when their strength finally started kicking in, the unofficial transition from child to young adult.

His thoughts turned to the narrow, rocky entry to the foundry.

*Difficult, but not impossible.*

Aadima was sure he would be able to get him out of the cave.

*But can I make it all the way back?*

A chill ran up his spine as he realized how much longer the trip back to Hinter would take carrying his brother's body.

*What if I run into a demon?!*

Abandoning Gondefle to become a demon-feast would be so much worse than leaving him alone in a cave!

*Could* he leave him alone in a cave?

*If only I had my chatter!*

It was a useless wish and Aadima shook it away.

Finally, he made a decision.

Wiping the last few remaining tears from his eyes, he took hold of his brother by the arms and began to drag him out of the room.

Aadima leaned Gondefle's body against the rockslide and mopped sweat off his face.

*I didn't think I'd ever make it out!*

He sat his aching body down next to his brother's and rested his head back against the stone.

"Ugh, it's already afternoon!" He closed his eyes. "I'll never make it!"

Aadima closed his eyes. *Okay, you've always wanted to create your own episode of Rajveer—now's your chance. What would you have him do in this situation?*

"I need a litter!"

Aadima pictured the litters that Rajveer and other divulgate heroes like him always made out of their own shirts to get wounded comrades back home.

He rushed over to the largest bush he could see and quickly pushed aside its branches to examine the trunk.

"Useless!"

The trunk would be less than half his height even if he could somehow straighten it out.

Aadima racked his mind for a moment, then remembered Cal sprawled in the desert unconscious, his red skin cracked and torn after an ambush deep in demon-land, at the start of the episode "A Worthwhile Burden."

Aadima nodded to himself.

Just like Rajveer, he would welcome the burden and carry Gondefle home.

Picturing the scene in his head, Aadima took hold of Gondefle's wrists, hefting his arms over his shoulders like the straps of a backpack, and pulled until his brother's chest was pressed against his back.

Gripping Gondefle's arms tightly, he started back towards Hinter, following the two sets of dried mud footprints.

The rocky ground turned to soil and Aadima groaned as he realized that the loose mud had filled their tracks before drying out in the sun.

He felt a tear on his cheek and wiped it away angrily against his brother's shirtsleeve. "No, I'm a Rumetre! We don't give up!"

He knew where he was going; he wasn't wandering around. *Just go straight!*

Aadima moved towards the grassland in the distance, his brother's trailing feet lifting a small cloud of dust behind them.

He almost collapsed in relief when he finally saw the broken stalks of grass from their earlier passage.

He stopped for a short rest, then moved into the grass.

The regular sound of Gondefle's feet knocking against the tall stalks on either side of the trail filled Aadima's ears as he plodded on.

~

Aadima's eyes snapped open and he attempted to jump to his feet. But, still groggy, he ended up face-down in the grass, two thicker-than-average stalks pressed against his forehead.

He had fallen asleep!

"Inutile!" he shouted at himself. "No more stopping, no matter what!"

He lifted his brother back onto his shoulders and resumed his slog back to Hinter.

Dusk soon arrived and brought rain with it.

*Ah, that's nice!* he thought as the heavy rain soaked through his tunic, soothing his aching muscles.

Aadima continued on, the ground getting softer and softer as the rain pounded down.

He whimpered as his teeth started chattering—the cold rain now chilling him to the core.

He kept moving forward.

Soon, he had to slow his pace so that he didn't lose sight of the path through the rain and his fatigue-blurred vision.

His entire body was shaking violently by the time he saw the lights of Hinter.

He pressed on, now shouting for help.

He heard something ahead of him.

Voices!

"Please!" he shouted raggedly. "My brother!"

Aadima collapsed and his world went dark.

Aadima awoke to a world of pain and a tightness across his chest.

He touched the tightness and realized that it was a strap.

His world went dark again.

"I don't understand it any more than you do…"

The voice was familiar.

Aadima struggled to open his eyes, to focus on the voice.

"I need to know whether she *killed him with that thing*!" His mother's voice was angry.

"That's out of my area of expertise," the first voice replied.

Aadima opened his eyes, but everything was blurry.

"Jabeza," his father said in a calm voice, "we don't even know that she used the Hilt, just that it was in her pocket."

Aadima reached into his pocket and, with a surge of panic, realized that the Hilt was gone.

"Brandr will be here soon to retrieve it," the first voice said.

Aadima shot up at the thought of the Hilt being taken away, unconsciously clasping a hand to his heart.

His hand landed on a cold stone embedded into the leather strap around his chest. Absently, he recognized it as a physic talisman, part of a standard healing strap.

His vision finally cleared enough to reveal that the other voice belonged to Reselda Ianuaria, Hinter's chief healer and director of the Healing Complex. She was sitting at the far side of a desk, dressed in her usual white jumpsuit with its large pocket in the front and thick administrative-black trim, and his parents were on his side, seated with their backs to him.

Between his parents, he could just see the dark gray Hilt sitting in the middle of the desk. Somehow he knew it was the same one despite the fact that it looked slimmer than he remembered.

At the sound of movement, his mother spun around and stood, her chair falling away beside her and banging into a cabinet. The bottles inside of it clattered together as the chair loudly scraped its way to the floor.

Aadima recoiled from the hateful expression on his mother's face.

"How *could* you?!" She lunged towards him. "You never cared enough about us to be a *normal* child and *now* you take my only son from me?!"

Samael wrapped his arms around his wife, stopping her advance. "This isn't helping...," he whispered into her ear.

Healer Director Ianuaria stepped out of the room and shouted down the hall.

*"It's your fault!"* His mother moved forward angrily, dragging her larger and stronger husband with her. "How could you let him die?! Why do you keep humiliating us like this?!"

Aadima cowered and retreated to the far edge of the examination table.

*Rajveer was welcomed as a hero when he got home!*

"Please, Jabeza, get control of yourself!" Still struggling with her, Samael turned his head to face two large elves in white jumpsuits who were rushing into the room. "Please, take her to another room so that I can talk with our daughter!"

The orderlies struggled with Jabeza but finally managed to move her through the doorway.

"No!" his mother screamed from the hallway. "She killed my only son!"

Aadima curled into a ball as his father approached the examination table.

Samael took hold of his arms, pinning them painfully to his sides, and pulled him forward until he was seated on the table's edge.

"Aadima," he said softly, looking directly into his eyes, "we need to know what happened to your brother."

Shaking from fear, pain and horror, Aadima couldn't collect his thoughts enough to form words. After a few false starts, he started picking at the medical strap instead.

His father started stroking his arms, knowing from experience that it would calm him. It did, but this time mostly because it relieved the pain in his arms.

After Aadima finally stopped shaking, his father stepped to the side, squeezed his shoulders, and pointed towards the desk.

"Did that Hilt kill your brother?"

Still unable to speak, Aadima shook his head.

"Did it come from the place where your brother died?"

He nodded.

"Where did it happen?" he asked forcefully.

Aadima finally managed a croak. "Cave."

"Why did the two of you go to a cave?"

"Followed," he whispered hoarsely.

"Did the two of you follow someone in?"

Aadima shook his head.

"Did you follow *him*?"

He nodded, picking at the strap again.

"Do you know why he was going there?"

He nodded again.

After a moment of silence, his father softly prompted, "Can you tell us?"

"I think...," he started shakily. "I think he knew it was a foundry..." He stopped to wipe tears from his eyes.

"A foundry?!" His father stiffened. "Were there *more* Hilts there?"

Aadima nodded.

Healer Director Ianuaria gasped from the other side of the room.

"You said you thought he knew it was a foundry." His father was insistent and his look was piercing. "Why do you think that?"

"I overheard him talking to his friends." Aadima started crying hard and couldn't continue.

His father's gaze was almost physically painful. Aadima looked down at his shirt.

Samael calmed himself, then took Aadima's face in his hands, wiping tears away with his thumbs. "Please, Adi, this is important. What did you hear him say?"

After a few more sobs and false starts, Aadima whispered, "He said he had found something, something powerful." He fought for control. "He said he would use it to hurt the humans the way they hurt him."

His father gasped, a brief look of understanding crossing his face before shifting to anger. He shook him. "Why didn't you *tell us* about this?"

"I didn't believe him," Aadima sobbed again. "I

thought he had found more pilliate." More sobs. He tried to lower his face again, but his father held it tighter, painfully tight.

"Pilliate?" his father asked with a confused expression.

Aadima was embarrassed. His pilliate fantasy seemed so foolish now.

"Or maybe some other magic plant," he said softly.

"You know that magic plants are dangerous even when you *know* what they are!" His father was squeezing his face even tighter. "Didn't we teach you better than that?! You should *never* have gone after it without telling us about it first!"

"I wanted to see it." He broke down completely as an image of his brother's pale face filled his mind.

His father released him, and he curled up on the table, squeezing his eyes shut in a futile attempt to stop the tears.

Samael Rumetre looked down at Aadima and shook his head in disappointment.

# INVESTIGATION

The next morning, two humans arrived at the Rumetre home, flanked by four elvish constables, each clad in constable-yellow protective armor.

The first human was Brandr Fortier, Hinter's Armourer. His armor was trimmed with thick gray lines. The other, whose armor was trimmed in equally thick black lines, was Ikhtiar Torin, the chief constable. They both had elaborate leather Hilt-holsters attached to the right faulds of their armor.

Samael guided Aadima to the front door. Jabeza hadn't left her bedroom since they had returned from the Healing Complex.

Aadima's eyes were downcast, allowing him to notice that the plating on Chief Constable Torin's right calf was far narrower than that on the left.

*He must have an artificial leg.*

Chief Constable Torin addressed his father. "Is she ready to show us what happened?"

"She is." Samael squeezed Aadima's shoulders roughly. "Aren't you?"

Aadima nodded but didn't look up.

"The other half of our protective detail will meet us where your daughter was found." Chief Constable Torin gave Aadima a stern look. "I trust you can get us to the foundry."

Aadima made an affirmative noise but didn't meet his gaze.

Chief Constable Torin grunted. "Let's get going, then."

When they reached the edge of the village, they met up with five constables waiting beside a heavily laden handcart painted bright constable-yellow.

"Okay, standard demon-land protocols," Chief Constable Torin said with a nod to the only waiting constable not wearing armor.

Aadima recognized the human, in his usual constable-yellow jumpsuit with the thick silver trim that marked his area of expertise, as Nityam Mean, the constabulary's practitioner.

Practitioner Mean opened up a large canister at the front of the cart and scooped a Hilt out of the potion within. Unlike the ones from the newly re-discovered foundry, this Hilt was a squared-off, flat T-shape—the standard output of modern mass production.

"Hilts for everyone," he said, handing the first one to the closest constable.

Aadima recognized her too—Khloe Aasim, a young elf who had graduated the previous year.

Constable Aasim took the Hilt and Practitioner Mean directed her to a covered basket on the back of the cart. "The lucents are charged, invoked and ready."

She collected a lucent from the glowing selection within the basket, inserted it into a purpose-built brass receptacle in her breastplate not far beneath her chin and slid it shut.

She stepped aside and with a hungry expression said, "Invoke!"

While Practitioner Mean fished out another Hilt, her face scrunched in concentration as she willed the potion-steel Hilt to bond with her for the day. After a moment, the sharp edges of the Hilt's handle softened as it conformed to her hand.

With a smile, she tested the bond, willing the Hilt to extrude a double-sided blade, then retracting it several times.

Satisfied, she slid the Hilt into a loop in the waistband of her armor, then fastened a securing strap over it.

Nearby, Armourer Fortier and Chief Constable Torin tested their more powerful, and permanently bonded, blood-steel Hilts in a similar fashion. Once satisfied, the two returned the Hilts to elaborate leather holsters.

Once the other armored constables had received and tested their standard-issue Hilts, they secured them with the simple Hilt-loops that were part of their armor's belt.

Four of the armored constables selected packs from the center of the cart and helped each other clip them to loops built into the shoulder and lower-back plates of their armor.

They rejoined the group and formed the back

of a diamond-shaped protective formation around the armourer, the chief, Aadima and his father.

"All right," Chief Constable Torin said as he finished a brief inspection turn.

He looked down at Aadima.

"Just point and we'll get moving."

He did, and the group moved out of Hinter and into demon-land.

Aadima was surprised when they arrived at the rockslide, having no memory of the trip.

"Constable Wileen." Chief Constable Torin waved forward the constable at the front of the diamond, whose armor had the thin gray trim of a squad leader.

In a well-practiced move, Constable Wileen rotated open the brass cylinder embedded in his chest plate that contained his lucent. The lucent's pale yellow light poured out, and he stepped up to the crevice. "Footprints are still here, just like she said."

Chief Constable Torin nodded. "Take Aasim and Ritza with you and make sure that the main chamber is clear."

Two constables from the back of the diamond moved forward.

The three elves hunched over and moved into the mountain. Constable Wileen invoked a scribe talisman and used it to leave regular glowing marks along the right side of the passage.

A few minutes later, Constable Ritza returned. "All clear. No sign of any new intrusions."

Except for two constables tasked with guarding the entrance, Chief Constable Torin waved each member of the party, one at a time, into the narrow crevice and the foundry beyond.

When Aadima arrived, the last one besides the chief himself, the chamber was illuminated by four light-platforms. The platforms were scattered around the room, each floating at shoulder height above its now-empty carry pack. Each platform was composed of a large yellow industrial lucent strapped to the top of a buoyant talisman.

Constable Wileen and his two companions accompanied Chief Constable Torin, Aadima and Samael into the back corridor to confirm that they had located the correct room.

Standing in the doorway once again, Aadima nodded silently. It was the room where he had lost Gondefle, and the exposed Hilt that had taken him away lay where it had fallen.

An intense sadness filled Aadima when he saw Gondefle's torch, long out of potion and extinguished, sitting on the floor.

*Gondefle would want me to bring it back to him.*

But Aadima couldn't make himself enter the room.

"Ritza," Chief Constable Torin said, "escort the girl out of the cave and have the rear guard watch her while we finish here."

Aadima managed one last glance at Gondefle's forlorn torch before Constable Ritza nudged him back along the hallway.

On their way out, they passed Armourer Fortier, who had paused to evaluate the warning display in the main room.

In the three days since the death of Gondefle, the town gossips had spread countless theories about his demise, the current favorite being that he had walked stupidly into a demon-lair. Some even passed along, or perhaps unknowingly guessed, the truth.

Aadima heard none of it.

Immediately upon his return from the foundry, his parents had blocked him.

Once removed from the household phylactery, he couldn't even close the door to his bedroom or the privy for fear of getting locked in.

His parents had also taken away his chatter and divulgates—he was utterly cut off from the world.

He wasn't even allowed to go to school!

Today was the first day he had been outside since being blocked, and it was to answer a summons from the Hinter Village Council.

Now he stood at the front of the Council Room of the Village Hall, the sole target of the council's gaze. Each councilmember was dressed in the same black jumpsuit with thick white trim.

Aadima took a deep breath.

*Maybe now I can finally get some answers!*

"Aadima Rumetre?" the head of the council, an elderly elf who Aadima had never seen before, asked from the highest chair.

"Yes," he squeaked.

"We've read your statement and have a few additional questions."

"Do you—"

He ignored Aadima and continued, "Can you tell us how your brother knew the location of the foundry?"

"Um… no… he never said. Do you know if—"

"And do you know whether he planned on arming just himself," another member of the council asked angrily, "or some other group?"

"What group?"

"*Any* group."

"I don't know about any—"

"Was your brother involved in any elvish protest organizations?!" a third member asked.

"No! Of course not!"

"And you're certain that he found it himself and wasn't led or directed there by anyone else?" yet another councilmember asked.

"Yes… pretty sure. Who would have—"

"Did you ever hear your brother talking about self-harm?" the head of the council asked in a bored voice.

"No!" Aadima's head was spinning. "Can you please tell me if he hurt? If Gondefle suffered?"

"Do you believe her?" the head of the council asked the elf beside him.

"I think it's the best we're going to get."

"Um…," Aadima said, "about my brother?"

The head of the council looked back at him. "Thank you for answering our questions. You can return to your parents."

He looked away.

"But—"

There was a hand on Aadima's shoulder. It turned him around and firmly guided him out of the room.

*What* was *that?!*

His head still spinning, he walked across the

hallway to the bench where his parents were waiting.

His mother looked angry.

"We have to go to the constabulary for a meeting with Armourer Fortier," his father said.

Aadima felt a surge of hope. "Is he going to tell us more about what happened to Gondefle?"

"He's not telling *you* anything!"

"We'll be dropping you off at the village traject," his father said stiffly.

"But—"

His mother scowled him into silence.

"Just come along," his father said.

Even more frustrated than before, Aadima allowed himself to be led outside and across the square to the public traject booth.

Samael inserted his adit talisman into the exterior slot in the booth's front wall and rested his hand on the traject talisman immediately beneath it.

Aadima groaned.

The adit meant that he was sending him directly to his room instead of to the path in front of their house like a normal person!

*Not that I could even get into the house while I'm blocked!*

Samael gestured for Aadima to enter and he reluctantly complied.

"You're to stay in your room until we get home for dinner," he said before picturing Aadima's bedroom in his mind and willing him there.

Aadima quickly squeezed his eyes shut to block the blue-and-red flashes that always accompanied a traject-powered voyage.

He groaned again as he opened his eyes to see that his bedroom door was closed.

The stool that he had been using to prop it open was lying on its side nearby.

He rushed over and shoved against the door; it remained firmly shut.

"I can't even go to the privy?!"

He flopped down on his bed to brood until his parents came home.

# CONCLUSIONS

A very young constable met Samael and Jabeza Rumetre at the door to the Armoury. "Armourer Fortier is just finishing up a meeting with the chief constable and will be with you shortly. If you would follow me."

The constable led them to the armourer's office. Despite the fact that it was unoccupied and the door was open, it was filled with a thin haze of smoke.

"I apologize for the smoke, but there's nothing to worry about," the constable said uncomfortably. "I'll make sure that Armourer Fortier knows you're here."

The Rumetres looked at each other in confusion, then settled into the two well-worn desk chairs in front of the battered desk.

Jabeza squealed as a wisp of smoke escaped from between the doors of the cabinet next to her. It was quickly sucked up towards a vent in the ceiling.

"Perhaps we should swap," Samael said.

They swapped seats and waited uncomfortably

for the armourer to arrive, Jabeza pointedly ignoring the cabinet and its occasional puffs of smoke.

"Sorry to keep you waiting," Armourer Fortier said as he stepped into the room. "And for the atmosphere in here—I'll explain that in a minute."

He walked over to the smoking cabinet and opened the doors. A large cloud of smoke escaped and languidly rose towards the vent in the ceiling. The armourer coughed and attempted to hurry the smoke on its way.

He removed a metal tray from the cabinet; there was a dark gray Hilt lying on it.

Jabeza hissed painfully. "I presume that this will be the last we see of *that*."

A wisp of smoke rose from beneath the Hilt as Armourer Fortier carried it around the desk. "That's what we need to discuss."

"What is there to discuss?!" Jabeza shouted. "Just *get rid* of it!"

"Jabeza, please." Samael ignored her angry glare and addressed the armourer. "Please go on."

"This is a soul-iron Hilt," Armourer Fortier explained as he lowered the tray down in the middle of the desk and sat behind it. "We found an empty slot in the exposed Hilt display; it was labeled as having claimed one of your Rume ancestors. We think that's why Aadima picked it up in the first place. But we're having trouble understanding—"

"That's not possible," Samael interrupted. "The Rumetre family *founded* Hinter, so there never were any 'Rume ancestors' here, and the post-Liberation laws would never have allowed us to build weapon factories!"

"I understand that," Armourer Fortier said patiently. "It looks like the foundry predates Hinter, but that's not where the problem lies."

Samael frowned but motioned for him to continue.

"The problem is that, if the Hilt your daughter found was truly exposed, it would have killed her, like the blood-bronze Hilt killed her brother."

Jabeza hissed again and hunched down in her chair.

"I can't explain why it was in the warning display," the armourer said, focusing on Samael. "And if the evidence weren't so conclusive, I wouldn't be able to accept that it even was the same Hilt."

"But how do we get *rid* of it?" Jabeza said impatiently. She grabbed her husband's shoulder and looked at him pleadingly.

With a grimace of pain, Samael removed his wife's hand. "We'll just put it back where it belongs and be done with it."

"I'm sorry." Armourer Fortier shook his head. "That's out of the question. It has to be returned to your daughter or—"

Jabeza jumped up as she shouted, "I'm not having that *thing* in my house!"

Only her husband's quick action prevented her from launching herself across the table. "Jabeza..."

"I'm sorry... we're... we're *decent* elves!" She started crying, then flopped bonelessly back down. "How could something like this happen *to us*?!"

Samael put an arm around his wife and gestured for the armourer to continue.

Armourer Fortier rested his hands on the edges of the tray as another wisp of smoke rose from beneath the Hilt.

"However it happened"—he glanced uncomfortably at Jabeza, who had begun keening softly—"this Hilt is bonded to your daughter now."

Jabeza went quiet and doubled over in her chair.

Samael began stroking his wife's back and gestured again for the armourer to continue.

With an uneasy expression, Armourer Fortier said, "If it was a blood Hilt, we could lock it away and hope she never figures out how to summon it. But this is a *soul* Hilt."

He paused for a moment to let his words sink in. Samael stared back at him blankly.

"As you know," Armourer Fortier continued, "bonded soul talismans are proactive."

*Crack!*

Armourer Fortier winced at the sound from the tray. As a wisp of smoke rose from it, he continued, "As you just heard, this Hilt will not be kept apart from its bond partner."

Jabeza moaned and started rocking back and forth in her chair.

Fortier's discomfort increased and he glanced sideways towards the door.

Samael tightened his grip on his wife to hold her still and motioned again for the armourer to continue.

"We need to return it to her as soon as possible, today if possible, Freday at the latest."

The Hilt sizzled softly, as if emphasizing the armourer's point.

"It's just warning us right now. But the longer they're separated, the more aggressive it will get."

"How aggressive *can* it get?" Samael asked quietly.

"Very," Armourer Fortier replied. "It's not just the anti-soul-harvesting laws that keep us from making things like this anymore. If we keep it from her, it will make its own way to her, going straight through anything, and *anyone*, in between."

There was a moment of silence while they absorbed the news. Samael's head drooped and Jabeza sat up again.

"But where did it come from?" Jabeza said. "How could it be older than Hinter?! This was all just demon-land before the village."

Relieved by her calmer demeanor, Armourer Fortier replied, "Some of the markings we found in the foundry indicate that it was part of Antedil."

"We've found Antedil?!" Samael asked with surprise.

"An outskirt at least," Armourer Fortier clarified. "We always knew it had been located in Immure County but never imagined it was so close to here. I would guess, by the orientation of the lobby, that our village was built over Antedil's foundations."

"But Antedil was destroyed *thousands* of years ago," Jabeza said plaintively. "How could something so dangerous have been left *lying around* for that long?"

"They say that Antedil was destroyed by a cataclysm during Demon Rule," Armourer Fortier said. "No doubt the foundry survived due to its eccentric location."

"Do you think the founders knew?" Samael asked.

"I doubt it." There was a dark anger on the armourer's face. "I can't imagine the humans who sent us here would have exiled their former slaves to such a historic site."

❧

That night, Hinter Village Manager Quinn Dufort held a gathering in the Village Centre Square to present the findings of the investigation.

Almost the entire village showed up and clustered around the base of the granite steps leading up to the ornate First Hall building, the traditional home of the village manager.

Manager Dufort, a human like all of the civic leadership of Hinter, came out and descended the steps to the usual fanfare. He was dressed in the professional black jumpsuit that was the official uniform of administrative workers throughout Timor. Over that he wore his managerial vest. The traditionally cut vest was almost pearlescent white with gold trim and was open to show that his jumpsuit lacked the pocket found on the ones workers wore. Dufort's name was embroidered on the right breast in midnight blue just above "Hinter Village Manager," which was embroidered in a reflective silver. Hinter's village seal, in the same shiny silver, was embroidered on the opposite breast.

Waiting for him, beside a podium that sat on a temporary stage, was Chief Constable Torin, his jumpsuit crisp and spotless as if just received from the clothier. Armourer Fortier stood on the ground just beside the small platform in his usual gray-trimmed constable jumpsuit.

Manager Dufort stepped up to the podium and, after acknowledging the crowd's anxious welcome, motioned for silence.

"I have gathered you here this Wodnesday evening to inform you about the circumstances surrounding the death of Gondefle Rumetre." Dufort's practiced voice was just loud enough that the entire crowd could hear him while he still sounded calm and in control. "After an investigation by the constabulary"—he nodded towards Chief Constable Torin—"it has been determined that this was a death by misadventure."

A sound of dismay from the crowd forced him to pause and gesture again for quiet.

"The dangerous area where the tragedy occurred has been sealed," Manager Dufort declared. "It will never have the chance to take another life again."

# OBSEQUIES

"For the funeral," Jabeza Rumetre said as soon as Aadima opened the door to step out of the body-launder.

"Mom!" he cried as he grabbed his robe from one of the hooks attached to the side of the launder.

Covered, Aadima's anxiety over his female body was suppressed for the moment, allowing him to realize that his mother was holding a frilly white dress.

"Mom, I can't!"

"You will." She grabbed him by the arm and pulled him across the hallway to his room.

He looked up at his mother with a plaintive expression as she carefully laid the dress on the foot of the bed beside a pair of underwear and some white tights.

Aadima tried to think of something, anything, to dissuade her. "But..."

"Put it on," his mother said crossly, folding her arms across her chest.

Aadima hated dresses in general, but this one, on this day of all days, felt disrespectful—like a

Yielding costume. He opened his mouth to protest again.

His mother's eyes widened with anger. "You will honor your brother's memory by dressing *properly!*"

Aadima's eyes welled with tears. He waited a moment, hoping that she would at least let him dress in private.

She glared at him.

He removed his robe, flushing again with embarrassment.

He yanked on the underwear but had to go slower with the tights for fear of tearing the lightweight fabric. Finally, with a mixture of relief at finally covering himself again and disgust at being forced to wear the distasteful garment, he pulled on the dress.

His mother inspected him as he stood there fidgeting in a futile attempt to shift the dress into a comfortable position.

A single tear slid down his cheek.

"Save the tears for the funeral where they belong," his mother said angrily as she straightened the collar. "We leave as soon as your father is ready."

The Hinter Ossuary was on the forest side of the village, filling the narrow end beside the out-loop section of the speedway.

The Rumetre family memorial was opposite the speedway with an unobstructed view of the valley and was separated from the rest of the ossuary by an ornate stone wall. A gilded version of the family crest was carved into each of the support columns that held up the archway over the entrance. At the very top of the arch was a gilded engraving of the rune pu, itself a shallow arch, that symbolized peace.

Like Aadima, his parents were wearing traditional funerary white as the trio sat quietly in the ossuary's family room until the last of the guests had settled into place.

"It's time," said an ossuary assistant wearing an administrative-black jumpsuit with thin support-white trim as she held the door open.

By tradition, the mother went first, followed by her spouse and children from oldest to youngest.

Aadima stared at his father's back as they walked solemnly along the narrow path through the middle of the burial grounds, only glancing briefly at the guests as they passed through the entrance arch.

Interments were normally a private affair, limited to those closest to the departed, but the Rumetre family was large and Gondefle's interment had drawn over two dozen attendees. His friends shifted uncomfortably in their rarely worn but bright white funeral suits as they stood with their parents in the front row. Behind them, in various states of shock and grief, was nearly every Rumetre relative that lived within a day's travel.

Hinter's mortician, Nye Than, dressed in the traditional white jumpsuit of his profession (and all of those who helped people through the difficult chapters of life) with its thick gray trim, was waiting for the family beside the shrouded Departed Pillar.

The Departed Pillar was attached to the end of a curving half-height section of the outer wall that extended a short distance into the memorial from the right column of the entrance.

As the Rumetre family stepped up to the pillar, Mortician Than removed the white shroud to reveal the skin-red cube that contained Gondefle's prepared remains. The sides of the cube were completely smooth and slightly translucent, as if made out of fine crystal. Embossed on the top were Gondefle's name and their family crest.

Mortician Than carefully folded the ritual fabric and gingerly placed it into the large pocket in the front of his jumpsuit.

Jabeza moved ahead while Samael clasped the mortician's shoulder and nodded thankfully. Mortician Than nodded back, then formally departed, walking slowly through the entranceway and back along the ossuary's main path.

Samael reverently lifted the cube containing his son, then silently followed his wife, with Aadima trailing a few steps behind.

A funerary coffer had been set up just beside Grandfather Jehan Rumetre's marker, a gray rectangle with his first name and the family crest engraved into it as well as a golden disk bearing the village seal that proclaimed Hinter's gratitude for his sacrifice while defending the village from a demon-attack.

The gray funerary coffer came in two parts: a base that had been placed into a shallow, freshly dug depression so that its top was level with the ground around it, and a tall hood with a handle on each side, which was sitting on the grass nearby.

Jabeza kneeled down beside the coffer-base and waited for her husband to arrive with the remains of their eldest child.

Samael handed the cube to his wife, who took it in her trembling hands and held it to her chest for a long moment before holding it out over the coffer-base.

"Dear Gondefle," she said in a shaky voice, "I brought you into this world, now I pass you along to the next, to your eternal reward."

After a brief hesitation, she lowered the cube into the base, making sure that Gondefle's name was properly oriented so that it could be read by someone walking through the entrance of the memorial. It fit loosely in the base's slightly wider top.

With her left hand on her heart, she placed her right over her son's name on the cube and gently pushed it down into the coffer-base until its top was flush with the closely trimmed grass around it.

"May you have peace," she said unsteadily.

After a short moment, she stood and gestured to Samael and Aadima. The pair moved to the coffer-hood, one on either side. They took hold of the handles and lifted the heavy piece half a foot off the ground.

One formal step at a time, they moved towards the coffer-base until the hood was positioned directly above it.

They waited.

After a minute, Jabeza nodded reluctantly and they lowered it onto the base. With a soft scrape, the hood settled resolutely into place.

Samael took Aadima's hand and they stepped back.

Jabeza took hold of the coffer-hood and rested her forehead on it, her tears making dark streaks down its smooth gray side.

Finally she sat back and put her left hand over her heart again, leaving her right on the hood. "Invoke. Inter my son and be a marker of his time in our world."

The coffer halves sealed together, then sank into the ground until the only thing visible was the rectangular blank gray top of the hood. Gondefle's name slowly sank down into the surface, followed by the family rune immediately below it.

Jabeza's tears turned into sobs and she covered her face. Samael stepped forward, put his arm around her, then led her out of the memorial, gesturing with his other hand for Aadima to follow.

The burial made Gondefle's loss real to Aadima, and he wanted desperately to find somewhere to hide from it. But obligation and tradition didn't allow for that, and he followed his parents as they walked silently from the ossuary all the way to the Second Hall in Hinter Village Centre. The funeral guests followed, also in a respectful silence, the traditional twenty paces behind.

Second Hall was formally known as Hinter Public Hall, the official location set aside for public gatherings. The nickname had arisen because of its traditional placement on the opposite side of the Village Hall from the village manager's First Hall.

As soon as they arrived in the function room, Aadima retreated to a corner and sat there with his dress tucked between his thighs. He closed his eyes and tried to tune out the buzz of conversation, grief and reassurances that filled the room.

"Ugh," he said to himself shortly after noon when the pressure in his bladder got too strong to ignore.

He crossed to the privy room as quickly as he dared, not wanting to attract attention.

Aadima's stomach growled loudly as he stood from the privy-launder. He pulled up his uncomfortable tights and exited, intending to check out the lunch buffet.

He never got there.

A hand clasped unexpectedly onto his arm before he made his third step towards the food.

"What did you do to my nephew?!" his aunt Danya whispered harshly.

"I didn't do anything!" Aadima tried to pull away, but Aunt Danya's grip on his arm was solid and painfully tight. "I just followed him." He struggled. "If I hadn't, we would never have found him!"

"So, I guess we should thank you for that," Aunt Danya sneered. "Is *that* it?"

"No!"

"You little—"

Aadima slapped the hand around his arm as hard as he could. Aunt Danya released him with a shocked expression.

He managed to avoid his aunt's attempt to resecure him and started to flee back to his corner.

He skidded to a stop when he saw that the entire room, including his father with a disappointed look and his mother with a furious one, was watching him.

His face heated, he dodged past his aunt's still-grasping hands and ran for the exit.

Just before he reached it, and after there were too many tears in his eyes to identify the source, he heard, "Look at her! I hear that they won't even be able to claim the blood insurance after what she did to him!"

# REUNIFICATION

Aadima ran all the way home and sat on the front steps to wait for his parents.

It was a long wait.

He felt a rush of relief when he finally saw them turn onto Balefire Way, glad to no longer be alone with his thoughts.

His father was carrying a stack of three covered plates.

*Takeaway food!*

Aadima almost smiled when they got to the house. "Did you...?"

Jabeza silenced him with a glare.

"Inside," Samael said flatly as he pushed the door open.

Aadima went directly to the dining room.

"Eat." His father removed the fitted cover from one of the plates of food and set it at Aadima's usual spot.

Aadima started to open his mouth again, but his father just glared at him, so he sat and focused on his plate.

*What did you do to my nephew?!* His aunt Danya's words filled his head again.

They had been living there all afternoon. Not even the memories of his favorite *The Rajveer Chronicles* episodes had been able to chase them away.

Aadima squeezed his fork hard as he stuffed a chunk of meat into his mouth, barely tasting it as he chewed.

*The funeral was supposed to give us closure!* he thought. *But things just keep getting worse!*

*What did you do?!* the voice in his head asked.

*I didn't do anything wrong!*

The ache in his heart made him wonder.

*Why won't they talk to me?!*

His parents were at the head and foot of the table, as usual. Not as usual, neither of them had looked up from their plates.

Aadima looked at his mother. She seemed to be just as angry as she had been back in the Healing Complex.

He turned to his father; he looked even more upset!

*Why won't they look at me?!*

Aadima scraped the last bit of food off his plate.

*Please look at me!*

Resigned, he picked up his dishes and brought them over to the kitchen-launder.

"Aadima," his father said.

Aadima turned, hope filling his chest.

*Finally!*

"We need to talk to you about that Hilt," he continued, his mother hissing painfully at the word, "that you found in the cave."

"Oh, okay." Aadima sat back down at the table. The flare of hope in his heart sputtered.

He had been so upset about Gondefle that he had nearly forgotten about the Hilt. Suddenly he felt a deep longing for it.

His father looked into his eyes. His mother's gaze was still locked on her barely touched meal.

"You know that some Hilts bond with the person that first uses them. Yes?"

"Yes," Aadima said, fighting against the urge to add one of the multiple facts about them that he had learned from the history books, the good Delphi Press ones that they never assigned for class.

"And that some," his father continued in a tight voice, "once bonded, cannot be safely kept apart from their wielder?"

His mother actually growled as she finally looked up and glared angrily at her husband.

"Yes," Aadima said quietly, the longing growing stronger.

"I can't!" his mother shouted simultaneously.

She stood and tearfully stormed out of the room.

"Don't worry about your mother," Samael said with an unconvincing smile. "She'll come around."

Aadima nodded silently.

"The Hilt you found has bonded with you," his father said, his expression unreadable.

Aadima forced himself not to betray his growing excitement.

"The village armourer will be bringing it over this evening."

There was a crash from the other side of the house, followed by angry sobs.

Samael winced, his control faltering.

When he continued, it was at a much-quicker-than-normal rate. "Your mother and I need to make sure that you understand just how dangerous it can be. We need to know that you will treat it with the proper respect."

"I understand," Aadima whispered.

"Do you?" he said with heat. He banged his fist on the table. "Hilts are *weapons*! They shouldn't be in the hands of *children*!"

Aadima forced himself not to correct him by pointing out that Hilts were designed to be tools first and weapons only as a last resort.

"I know," he said instead. "I'm sorry."

Samael calmed himself with a visible effort. "You can't bring it to school, but the armourer assures us that being separated for a few hours a day won't create any problems from it."

Aadima nodded.

"He's putting together a special case to keep it safely contained during the day."

"Okay," Aadima said softly.

"If we *ever* catch you using it to hurt or threaten anyone"—his anger welled and his face went red—"we *won't stop* until we've found a way to destroy it! *Understand?!*"

"Yes."

"Clean up and go to your room." Samael closed his eyes and rubbed at his temples. "We'll call you down when Armourer Fortier arrives."

Aadima walked calmly upstairs, but his control faltered at the landing. He ran to his room—careful not to knock over the stool that was propping the door open—tore off his clothes, grabbed his robe, then rushed across the hall to the privy room, where he leapt into the body-launder.

As the launder magicked the day's grime from his skin, he tried to remember how the Hilt had felt in his hand.

It wasn't until he was out of the launder and fixing his too-long hair in the mirror that he remembered the angry look on his father's face.

Pain and guilt overwhelmed him.

After a moment he steadied himself.

"They blame me for everything!" he hissed at his reflection.

He started to tear up.

*Maybe they should*, he thought, *I'm always making trouble!*

"No," he said aloud. "I didn't do anything wrong! They're just being mean!"

A horrible thought occurred to him:

*What if they take it away again just to hurt me?*

He wiped away a tear with a corner of the towel wrapped around his torso.

*I won't let them!* he thought to himself with an assured smile. *I won't give them the satisfaction! I'll never let them know how much I want it!*

And he *did* want that Hilt. He wanted *his* Hilt more than he had ever wanted anything, except perhaps to have Gondefle back.

He saw his own eyes widen in the mirror.

*No*, he thought, *I don't want it, I* need *it! It's part of me like Dad said.*

He made his way back to his room, quietly this time. Quiet enough so that no one would even know he was there.

～

"Aadima, it's time," his father finally said from downstairs.

Despite having been hiding at the top of the stairs since hearing the household portend ring, Aadima descended the stairs slowly, focused on his vow.

*I'll never let them know!*

His father and Armourer Fortier were standing together near the front door when he arrived.

The armourer was holding a metal box under his arm and had a half-smile on his face. Samael looked nervous and kept glancing towards the back door.

As he reached the bottom of the stairs, Aadima finally figured out why.

He heard his mother's muffled voice from the back porch and the sounds of her pacing back and forth.

Relieved that he couldn't make out her words and eager to reunite with his Hilt, Aadima walked calmly to the center of the room and took up a position a short distance in front of Armourer Fortier. He looked at the armourer's feet as he waited in silence.

There was a pressure building behind his heart—like someone was trying to push it through his sternum.

He remained silent.

After a long moment, Samael nodded reluctantly.

Armourer Fortier lifted the box, and Aadima focused on it.

As the lid opened, a dark puff of smoke was released.

The inside of the box was heavily scorched, and lying in the center, within a warped and partially melted metal basket, was Aadima's Hilt.

The pressure in his chest turned warm as a sense of relief filled him, and he finally felt the belonging that he had been missing at dinner.

Aadima reached out for it.

When his hand was above the Hilt, it leapt up into his palm. He automatically closed his fingers around it—it felt right.

Armourer Fortier stepped back in surprise, slamming the box shut as he fumbled with it. He managed not to drop it but did spill ashes onto the floor.

Beside him, Aadima's father gasped.

Aadima felt something warm touch the skin of his wrist. He looked and saw that a thin band was growing out of the flat base of the Hilt and snaking around his arm.

Everyone gasped in shock, including Aadima.

A moment later the band completed its trip and the end fused back into the handle to form a loop.

Aadima was so focused on the loop's progression that he barely noticed that the disk on the top was also changing into a narrow cross guard, the same depth as the handle but three times the width, the tips bending down slightly.

Aadima forgot his vow and smiled.

His father's shocked expression changed to one of fearful anger.

Armourer Fortier looked curious but quickly

switched to a neutral expression when he noticed Samael's reaction.

Aadima forced the involuntary smile off his face.

As he did, he felt the Hilt tug very slightly away from his palm.

He released it and it pivoted on the loop until it was pressed snugly against the underside of his forearm.

It felt warm against his skin.

They were complete together.

He looked up and saw his father's face for the first time.

He had to say something!

"I promise that I will never use it as a weapon. This will never be more than the tool that Hilts were originally meant to be."

# DENIGRATION

"Aadima," Samael Rumetre shouted up the stairs. "Come down here!"

Aadima, happy to be allowed out of his room, quickly complied.

"I need you to run to the store and pick up a few things for dinner." He handed him the oldest divulgate in the house and the family specie. "Here's the list. Go and come directly back."

"I will!" Aadima said, taking the divulgate and specie and rushing out of the house for the first time in nearly two months.

Gerst Provenders was on the outer edge of the commercial district. Aadima paused out front to savor his partially restored freedom.

"Is that Aadima Rumetre?" a departing customer asked her companion in a stage whisper. "I thought they sent her off to Wove!"

Aadima cringed, his happy mood shattered.

He looked around and saw that the few other customers that were meeting his gaze were unfriendly at best and disgusted at worst.

He suddenly wondered if he had missed similar looks during his blissed-out walk to the store.

Aadima headed into the store and focused on the divulgate shopping list.

The collector, who was usually far too chatty, only grunted at him as she gestured for Aadima to hand over the family specie. She didn't even glance at him when she returned it.

Aadima tossed it in the box with the groceries and headed home, careful this time to pay attention and avoid people as much as possible.

The front door was propped open with a bucket when he got there. He carefully moved it aside with his foot to allow the door to close.

"Put them in the kitchen, then go back to your room," his father said from the family room. "And don't disturb your mother."

His mother didn't acknowledge him as he placed the box onto the counter immediately behind her.

Samael opened the door to Aadima's room shortly after bedtime a few days later. "Set your tocsin, you're going to school tomorrow."

"Really?" Aadima said excitedly, but his father was already gone.

*At least I'll get to see my friends again!*

He snuggled back beneath the covers. Rehearsed reunion conversations with his friends filled his dreams that night.

But the anticipated conversations didn't stay in his dreams and monopolized his thoughts during breakfast, even pushing away thoughts about his Hilt.

As he finished his meal, his father turned towards him with a serious expression.

"You are to come home immediately after school. Understand?"

"I do."

"If you behave, your mother and I have decided that you can have your chatter and divulgate back when you get home."

"I'll be good."

"You'd better be—the administrator will be watching." He paused and looked at him hard. "Show me your arm."

Aadima didn't have to ask which one. He lifted his bare right arm and said, "It's upstairs in the case that Armourer Fortier gave me."

His father held out his open palm. In it was a rectangular gray stone with a swirl rune engraved into it.

The household phylactery.

Aadima pressed a finger against it.

"Invoke, grant child access to this individual."

When the phylactery pulsed red, Samael closed his fist around it.

"Now go on," he said, waving Aadima towards the door. "You don't want to be late."

The Hinter Consolidated School's hallways were a blur as Aadima rushed directly to the classroom dedicated to his year.

*I must be earlier than I thought*, he thought when he found the room nearly empty.

None of his friends were there yet, but they would be soon. They always gathered first thing so they could catch up before class.

His anticipation turned to anxiety as the start of the school day grew closer and closer.

That anxiety turned to disappointment when all of his friends arrived together in the last-second rush to beat the start-of-day gong of the school tocsin.

Unable to catch their attention before the educator arrived, he reluctantly turned his attention to the lucubrate at the front of the room.

Unlike its smaller cousin, the divulgate, the wall-sized lucubrate was only useful when paired with a formulae, or other data talisman, that could provide content for it to display.

It was every schoolchild's fantasy that their educator would forget theirs and be unable to teach.

No fantasies were fulfilled as Mackinley Lehrer, the school's social studies educator, pulled his formulae from the large pocket in the front of his academic-green jumpsuit and placed it into the matching slot along the base of the lucubrate. The words "Lesson Thirteen" appeared across the top.

It was forever until the tocsin announced morning break.

Aadima rose to follow his friends, who were at the front of the line exiting the room.

"Aadima Rumetre," Educator Lehrer called out.

Aadima reluctantly turned back to the educator, who motioned for him to join him in the front of the classroom. When Aadima arrived, he reached for his school-issued divulgate.

Aadima let him take it, and Educator Lehrer pulled another formulae with a built-in consociate out of the pocket in the front of his jumpsuit and tapped it against the matching consociate embedded into the side of the school divulgate.

After a moment, he handed the divulgate back and pointed to Aadima's desk. "You will need to spend your breaks here if you are to make up for the time you lost."

Aadima reluctantly sat back down and invoked the divulgate. There was now a long list of makeup work added to his assignment list.

*This will take forever!*

The next class for his year was history, and he let himself get swept up in it, his growing anxiety held at bay until a food worker arrived and placed a tray of food on his desk just before the lunch gong sounded.

"Wafaee!" Aadima tried to catch his best friend's attention as the room emptied out.

Educator Hodzic tapped a formulae against his school-issued divulgate as he left the room.

Aadima groaned. His assignment list was now more than twice as long.

"At least these will be almost interesting," he grumbled to himself as he took a bite of lunch and tapped the first new assignment.

Aadima, knowing by now what to expect, rushed up to the front of the room as soon as the tocsin's gong announced the end of the school day.

He fidgeted while Meghan Garnett, the mechanics educator, added the last batch of makeup work.

The instant that his divulgate vibrated to signal that it had associated with the new information, Aadima rushed out of the room.

Educator Garnett looked after him with a grin on her face; he had forgotten to say goodbye.

Aadima caught up with his friends just short of the main entrance. "I missed you all *so much!*"

They all looked uncomfortable. Even Wafaee was silent.

Finally Merari spoke up. "Things have... changed."

Aadima's face fell.

"Uh," Merari continued, "my parents are... worried about demon-attacks and need me to come straight home."

The entire group nodded in unison.

"Mine too!"

Aadima was crestfallen. As the group started to depart, he grabbed Wafaee's arm.

Wafaee shook it off and looked away from the door. "Sorry, I have to go to the administrator's office."

She hurried back into the school.

Aadima stood there in shock, jostled occasionally by the last few departing students rushing by.

Finally he remembered his father's instructions and reluctantly headed home.

When he arrived, no one was there, so he went

straight to his room—only momentarily distracted by the thrill of being able to open the doors by himself again—put on his Hilt with a sigh of relief, and let himself cry.

After he had cried himself out, he realized that his chatter was sitting in its recharging pool on his nightstand.

He squealed with delight as he grabbed it. "Invoke, get me Wafaee."

The chatter vibrated for a moment, then displayed the rune for lost.

Aadima was dumbfounded.

Slowly the meaning dawned on him and he angrily tossed the chatter away.

Wafaee had disassociated their chatters!

After sobbing for a while, he got up and retrieved his chatter from where it had landed under his bureau. He dusted it off and sat on the edge of his bed.

He went through his association list and his eyes got wet again as he realized that most of the associations were marked with the same rune that Wafaee's was.

"Invoke, clear all lost associations!"

He fell back, rolled over to bury his face in his pillow, and let the tears flow again.

Aadima got to school early the next day and lay in wait to catch Wafaee as she arrived.

It wasn't long before he saw his oldest friend enter the school and look furtively down the central hallway before hurrying towards a side corridor.

Aadima followed and grabbed her by the shoulder.

"Wafaee!" he said with tears in his eyes.

Wafaee looked terrified.

"We've been best friends since we could walk!" Aadima said in a harsh whisper. "How could you disassociate me?"

"I..." Wafaee swallowed. "You can't be here!" She glanced around nervously. "I can't be seen with you!"

"Why?"

"I can't." Wafaee glanced down pointedly at Aadima's right wrist. "I won't. *Just leave me alone!*"

Aadima watched his former best friend rush away and wondered how he could survive without her.

~

Aadima's thoughts turned morbid as he made his way home at the end of the day, imagining a dark and lonely life before finally dying alone in the Healing Complex's charity ward.

He stopped in front of Ameliorates.

He had planned on stopping there on the way home to get more renewal potion for his chatter.

*Should I bother? Who am I going to chatter with?!*

After a moment of indecision and a deep sigh, Aadima went in to get the potion.

He was oblivious to his surroundings until just after he got to the renewal section and heard someone say "Rumetre family" in the next aisle.

Curious, he leaned closer to the shelf to listen.

"Yes," a different voice said, followed by a tutting noise, "it's so awful about Gondefle."

Aadima recognized the voice of Assistant Teagan, who worked with his father. They hadn't met, but her office was right next to his father's, and he had heard her talking loudly into her company chatter almost every time he had visited.

"I know, but I was talking about their disgrace of a daughter, Aadima."

He recognized the second voice as Manager Jessop, Chotu's mother. He must have told his mother some nasty lies about him.

"Which one is that?"

"The weird one."

"Oh yes, *now* I remember. Always was an awkward child, never quite grew into herself, if you know what I mean. I assumed she was just slow."

Aadima teared up and nearly stopped listening.

"She is, I'm sure. But I hear she got her dirty little hands on an *actual* soul Hilt."

"Wait," Manager Jessop gasped, "I heard that Gondefle was killed by a Hilt. Did *she* do it?"

"They *say* she didn't, but I'm *sure* they're covering for the family." She laughed derisively. "Wouldn't want to *sully* one of Hinter's founding families and the descendants of our great Demon War heroes."

Manager Jessop snorted. "How the mighty have fallen."

Their laughter faded as they moved on down the aisle.

Aadima dried his eyes, grabbed a bottle of potion, and hurried towards the checkout at the front of the store.

# DOUBT

Aadima tried to act normal as he arrived at the checkout and hurriedly handed the recharge potion and his specie to the collector, who was wearing a heavily worn and baggy gray worker's jumpsuit.

"Did you find everything that you were looking for today?" she asked cheerfully.

Aadima recognized her as one of Gondefle's classmates but couldn't remember her name.

"Yes," he answered impatiently.

The collector took his specie and placed it carefully into the fitted slot in the ledger embedded into the top of the counter between them.

Then, painfully slowly as far as Aadima was concerned:

The collector picked up the bottle of potion and her store-issued formulae talisman.

Holding the bottle in front of her face, she spoke clearly into the formulae. "Hale brand recharge potion, one bottle."

She then gently placed the bottle down on the counter and positioned the formulae into its own fitted slot in the ledger.

Aadima could barely stand still as they waited *forever* for the ledger to display the total charge.

Then they had to wait *again* for it to transfer the units from his account to the store's.

As they waited, Aadima could hear Manager Jessop and Assistant Teagan, mostly Assistant Teagan, getting closer.

He glanced nervously over his shoulder to make sure they couldn't see him.

*Why is it taking so long!*

The ledger buzzed to confirm that the funds had been transferred.

"Have a nice—"

"Thank you!" Aadima grabbed the bottle and his specie and bolted out the door.

Where he collided with Meghan Garnett.

As Aadima bounced off his mechanics educator, the recharge potion slipped from his grip and landed in the path. He was able to keep from joining it, but only just.

"Watch where you're going, boy!"

"Sorry," Aadima said over his shoulder as he chased down his retreating potion. He caught it and turned back to Educator Garnett. "I'm *really* sorry…"

"Aadima Rumetre!" Educator Garnett shouted, her face flushing brightly with anger.

Aadima was confused. It was just a little bump!

"Girl, you need to start dressing properly!" Educator Garnett said in a disgusted tone. "I'd think, after everything you've put them through lately, that you'd try to show a little more respect for your family's reputation!"

Aadima looked down at himself. He was wearing what he usually wore.

Today it was a blue casual jumpsuit that had been Gondefle's favorite when it had belonged to him. His hair was tucked under his collar so that it wouldn't get in the way, as it usually was when he wasn't at home or in school, where it wasn't allowed.

Some of his happiest memories were of times when people recognized him as a boy. He knew that his parents didn't approve, but he had never considered it to be disrespectful.

Aadima loved being a Rumetre—being part of a lineage of heroes.

Seeing the blank look on his face, Educator Garnett rolled her eyes. "Well, girl, just go away, and pay attention!"

*Well, girl!*

The phrase reverberated within Aadima's head.

He saw Manager Jessop through the store window and decided to take Educator Garnett's advice.

The memory of Educator Garnett's voice chastised as he rushed away. *Show more respect for your family's reputation!*

*Is thinking I'm a boy* really *disrespecting the Rumetre family?*

Educator Garnett certainly thought so—and she was Aadima's second-favorite!

Remembering their reactions whenever the subject came up, he suddenly realized that his parents did too.

*Her parents?*

Were they really just trying to teach Aadima the right way to be a Rumetre?

*Am I really a girl after all?*

The thought hurt, but the body Aadima occupied was certainly female.

Aadima thought about the village freak, Konnyr, who claimed to be a man despite being born a woman. He had never really made the connection between them before.

Jabeza Rumetre's hate-filled voice shouted in Aadima's head: *It belongs someplace like Wove that will put up with its perversions!*

Everyone *knows Konnyr's sick!*

Aadima nearly collided with someone else but barely noticed and continued on without apologizing.

*Am I sick?*

Aadima started crying and looked around for somewhere to hide the embarrassment, finally settling on a heavily shadowed section of the closest alley.

Aadima rushed into the concealing darkness and leaned against the wall.

*Am I stupid?*

Aadima thought about a naked boy and put his hand down there.

That *feels like a girl.*

Aadima's eyes squeezed shut, and the tears continued unabated.

*But I hate girls!*

Not for the first time, Aadima wished that there was someone to talk to about these things, someone who could understand.

School would just call Aadima's parents.

Aadima's parents would just yell.

*Who am I? What am I?*

Gondefle would have listened.

*But I let him die!*

Gondefle couldn't listen anymore, but he did answer: *Don't let other people tell you who you should be.*

The conversation had happened a few weeks before they had gone to the cave. His brother had found him crying after an upsetting day at school.

"What's wrong, Adi?" Gondefle had asked, settling down onto the corner of Aadima's bed with a reassuring smile.

In between sniffles, Aadima had explained, "Mom made me wear *that dress* to school today."

"The new one?"

He had nodded.

"With the flowers?"

He had nodded again.

"And?"

It came out in a rush. "Everyone kept telling me that I looked *so* good, that I should dress like that *every* day."

"That doesn't sound so bad," Gondefle had said softly. "What else did they say?"

"That I *finally* looked like a *proper girl!*"

Aadima had barely stopped himself from sobbing. It was all embarrassing enough without crying like a baby!

"Ah, the boy thing."

"I *am* a boy!"

"I know." Gondefle looked nervously towards the open bedroom door. "But be quiet about it. You don't want Mom to hear you!"

Aadima had looked up at him in surprise and, before he could stop himself, said, "Am I just a stupid girl like Mom says?"

"No," his brother said gently as he patted him on the shoulder. "You need to trust yourself." He paused. "Look, I never said this but"—his voice had become angry and pained—"don't let other people tell you who you should be."

Aadima had been surprised again. He had never heard that tone from his brother before.

"*Be who you are!*" Gondefle had closed his eyes tightly, as if to block out the world. "Not who society tells you you're *supposed* to be."

The memory warmed Aadima's heart, and the longing to speak to Gondefle again burned hotter.

*What if Gondefle was right and Mom and Dad are wrong?* Aadima sobbed. *They're not!* Everyone *says it's wrong! I need to stop being a foolish girl!*

Through the painful thought, Aadima suddenly remembered Neander Rumetre:

"Today, Aadima is going to tell us about one of her most famous ancestors!" Educator Hodzic had announced to the class.

Eight-year-old Aadima had tried to smile but only managed a nervous grimace.

After a painfully long pause, Educator Hodzic gave Aadima a nudge.

"Neander Rumetre was not just a founder of Hinter," he remembered himself saying in a rushed monotone. "He was a true elvish hero even though he never raised a weapon."

"Quiet, please," Educator Hodzic said in response to the class's murmur.

Aadima continued, "Neander Rumetre was

nineteen years old when the Nekane Rule was made a law. Even though he was only nineteen, he had already become a leader for the other elves he had been property with."

After a short pause, Aadima swallowed and continued, "Neander Rumetre fought against the corrupt politicians trying to pass laws to keep elves suppressed even after slavery ended. Everyone told him he was wrong, that elves had to know their place. Neander Rumetre never stopped fighting, but they passed the laws anyway. We elves never forgot him. But we finally made humans listen during the Equitability Era. Neander Rumetre's fight was the foundation of the Equitability Era and his speeches were shown at every rally. That was how Neander Rumetre earned the Rumetre family their fourth honor slash even though he had been dead for a hundred years."

*They were wrong about Neander, but what if they're right about me?* Aadima could feel the stream of hot, shameful tears. *I'm not a hero!*

The doubt faded as Aadima's mind filled with memories of being forced to act like a girl and how wrong it always felt.

After a moment, Aadima shook away the tears and stepped away from the wall.

"Stop it! You *are* a Rumetre! Being a Rumetre is about being brave! It's about standing up for what you know is true *no matter what*!"

Aadima started walking towards the mouth of the alley.

"I *know* I'm a boy, no matter what anyone says."

Aadima wiped away the last of his tears as he stepped out into the path.

# RETREAT

Merari's voice echoed through the Hinter Consolidated School's main hallway. "I finally figured out why Aadima killed her brother!"

"Why?" an eager chorus asked.

"Jealousy!" Merari laughed. "We've all seen how much her parents favored Gondefle. She couldn't stand not being the center of attention!"

"Disgraceful!"

"I don't even want to think about that freak!"

Wafaee snorted. "I can't believe that we were ever friendly with trash like that!"

Aadima was shattered by the raw hate in his former best friend's voice.

*They're doing it on purpose!*

They were punishing him for not saving his brother, just like his mother was!

Just like his mother.

Aadima suddenly realized what was happening: they were laying the groundwork to push him out, just like everyone in Hinter did with anyone who didn't fit into their preconceived notions of propriety.

He hurried down a side corridor to hide his pain.

*Is that it?! Will they just ship me off to Wove?*

He leaned back against the wall and found himself longing for his old, happy life.

*Happy?! Was I ever* really *happy?*

Outside of his small group of friends, he had always felt awkward and out of place.

A confusing encounter filled his mind:

He had been walking through Village Centre, happy to be wearing a pair of Gondefle's old clothes. He had tucked his hair into his shirt and was pretending that he *was* his brother.

He imagined himself as a perfect, confident boy strutting through his territory.

"Where are you going, little boy?" an older boy had asked.

He was one of a group of boys that, lost in his fantasy, Aadima hadn't noticed.

Suddenly back to reality, he had meekly answered, "I'm just going home."

"It's a girl-boy!" one of the others shouted.

"Don't be mean," the first boy answered. "We need to be supportive of the next generation!"

They had all laughed. Aadima joined in nervously, which made them laugh harder.

"Want to play catch, little boy?" the first boy asked.

Confused, Aadima answered, "But we don't have a ball."

"No problem." He stooped and picked something up off the ground.

He threw it.

"Ow!" Aadima cried as it struck his shoulder.

It was a rock.

Soon, all five of the laughing boys were scooping up rocks and throwing them at Aadima.

He fled.

They kept laughing but didn't follow.

His old life hadn't been happy either, but now he was alone.

"Aadima Rumetre, the murdering weirdo!" a voice called out at him as he walked home one night three months later.

There was a group of older kids laughing nearby.

"Who said that?!" he demanded.

"Who said that?!" the group chorused back.

"Get out of here, freak!" one of them shouted. Aadima recognized him as having already graduated but didn't know his name.

With tears in his eyes, Aadima focused on the path in front of him and increased his pace.

"Freak!"

The taunt haunted him as he ran home.

He felt worthless.

He *always* felt worthless.

It wasn't even the first time he had been called that today, but something snapped inside him.

"I'm sick of it!" he shouted once there was no one else around.

What little sleep he got that night was filled with dreams of running free.

He awoke before his alarm and stared at the tocsin, willing it to go off.

*I'll run away! No*—he paused, remembering a passage from one of his books—*I'll go on a hegira! Once I'm away from the familiar, my spirit will guide me to where I need to be!*

When his tocsin finally did go off, Aadima skipped his morning launder and gathered his most treasured possessions into his schoolbag. His Hilt, packed away in its case, went in last.

Like most mornings, there was no conversation with his father over breakfast aside from the perfunctory wrist check.

As Aadima left his house, he glanced back.

*The very last time!*

He headed out into the world.

Halfway down the path, he stopped.

"It's Wodnesday, there's a test in history today! I can't miss my history test!"

Aadima stood there. History was fun, but life was awful. He compromised.

*I'll run away* after *school!*

Aadima smiled at the end-of-day tocsin gong.

*My last day of school ever!*

After he had walked blissfully out of the Hinter Consolidated School building, he glanced back with satisfaction.

*The very last time!*

He thought about history class.

*I slayed that test!* He smiled to himself. *Better than anyone else in class I'll bet!*

Before long, he found himself at the Hinter exit of the Boon Loop Speedway.

A speedway exit was little more than an archway cut through its otherwise continuous protective cover. The tube of the speedway disappeared in the distance in either direction.

He put on his Hilt, drew courage from it, and walked under the arch.

He looked both ways and wondered which was best. Out-loop led to the mysterious village of Wove before starting back inwards again. In-loop led towards Akin, the center of Immure County, capital of Timor, and one of the few fully integrated urban communities in the country.

"In-loop it is," he said finally. "Everything's better in-loop!"

The in-loop paths were on the far side of the speedway. Beyond them was the fenced-in area used by vendors during the daily commute that extended outward from the other side of the arched speedway exit.

He stopped at the first in-loop path. There were two, as there were on the out-loop side, divided by a thick red line. The red line, and the fat red arrow painted on the ground beyond it, marked it as the ultra-fast cargo-only lane.

It was his first time on the speedway without his parents and he suddenly felt nervous.

*A Rumetre isn't afraid of a speedway!*

He turned to align with the large but thin white arrow painted along his selected path. After a moment, he walked up to the white line at the edge of the archway that marked the edge of the accelerated path.

*Life will be better in-loop!*

Aadima started walking and smiled.

*I'll* never *come back!*

The path this far out was poorly lit and he kept imagining that he saw demons lurking in the blurred scenery visible through the speedway's translucent cover.

After an hour he reached the next exit and stopped to rest.

He sat on a bench just behind one end of a yellow line that marked the start of the more modern "quick passage" section of the speedway.

*Stupid politicians! If they actually cared about Hinter they'd have modernized the entire loop!*

Aadima stood and headed back to the in-loop paths.

Halfway through the exit, the pedestrian path split, a double white line separating the two. The arrow painted on the closer path was the same as the one at the Hinter exit, but the new lane's arrow had a dashed line instead of a solid one. The dashed arrow marked the express path that everyone just called the "rush path," which accelerated walkers twice as fast as the standard lane, itself twice as fast as the standard lane he had used from Hinter.

By habit, he followed the solid arrow as he stepped over the yellow line.

As he walked, he kept finding himself looking over at the double white line.

*It would get this over with so much faster.*

But he was nervous. A few years previously he had been running ahead of his parents and accidentally stepped over the white double dividing line onto the high-speed path. He had been separated from his parents for what seemed like ages, shaking and alone, before they'd finally caught up.

*I'm going to do it! The faster I get away from Hinter, the better things will be!*

Just as he was moving towards the double lines, something flashed past in the cargo lane, moving so fast that it was an unidentifiable blur.

He lost his nerve and casually moved back to the center of the standard path.

Rattled, he felt his fears multiplied, finding more ominous shapes among the rushing scenery outside of the speedway.

He stepped across another yellow line and into the next exit. Aadima felt a moment of relief from the imagined dangers outside the path, but it faded quickly as he realized that the open exit left him exposed to those same dangers.

He rushed across the exit and crossed the next yellow line, back into the speedway's acceleration.

*Just relax, you're on the path and moving quicker than the fastest fulgent.*

Imagining the pretty golden dragons racing through the air all around him helped calm his nerves. He pictured their long, narrow wings flapping slowly with their four little legs folded neatly beneath them as they swooped nearly close enough for him to touch.

As the sky darkened towards dusk, Aadima found himself exhausted and hungry and left the speedway at the next exit without even bothering to read the sign to find out where it led.

The first thing he saw as he stepped through the speedway's exit arch was the friendly and brightly colored front wall of a Pabulum.

*Civilization! They'd never open a Pabulum in lousy old Hinter!*

His stomach growled and he headed towards the chain's signature "Quick Eats!" sign, which spanned across the top of the main entrance, fishing his specie talisman out of his schoolbag.

As he waited in the queue, the dining room began to fill with noise.

"Who let that little red-tip in here?" a harsh voice cut through the angry grumble. "I have my kids with me!"

*They mean me!* Aadima thought after a moment. *Should I leave?*

His stomach growled louder than before and he remained in line.

After a moment a woman came up behind him. "This is a respectable village. You don't belong here!"

Aadima's fear and hunger fought for dominance.

"I just need something to eat, then I'll leave right away!"

He was turning back towards the counter when something struck him in the back of the head.

He spun around to find the source of the projectile and another one struck him in the lower back.

He spun around again, and his Hilt slapped into his hand, forming into a large round shield just in time to block the splash of some hot beverage.

The grumbling was replaced with a collective gasp of shock.

"It's a bandit!" someone shouted fearfully. "Call a constable!"

Aadima took a step back, trying to comprehend what was happening.

"We won't let you corrupt our children!" a man his father's age shouted. He gestured towards the counter. "How can you let this in here?"

Aadima's Hilt gave a little tug. He spun in that direction—just in time to block an empty mug that shattered against his Hilt-shield. It tugged again—a balled-up napkin with something hard in the middle. The tugs became constant as the number of projectiles increased.

Just as they were starting to arrive too fast to block, they abruptly stopped.

A man with an angry red face wearing a worker-gray jumpsuit with Pabulum's "Quick Eats!" logo embroidered on the front stepped up to him. "Your kind isn't welcome here. You need to leave."

He started for the door with tears in his eyes when a strong tug brought his shield up again. A porcelain serving tray burst into jagged pieces against it.

"Good riddance!"

He ran out the door, stopping a short distance away on the sidewalk to regain control over himself.

"Keep going!"

Aadima looked up to see that several of the Pabulum customers, and a few of the staff members, had followed him into the path and were gesturing at him angrily.

Several had projectiles in their hands and were getting ready to throw them.

He turned and ran. Most of the group followed, shouting angrily. He released his Hilt and it swung madly from his rapidly pumping arm.

Aadima jumped onto the speedway, going

straight to the out-loop lane, and ran until he could no longer hear the angry crowd behind him.

He collapsed in a heap in the middle of the path, trembling uncontrollably.

"I did nothing to them, but they still *hated* me," he shouted through his tears. "How can there be so much hate in the world? I'll show them!" He wiped at his eyes angrily. "I'll learn how to fight and *kill them all!*"

His right wrist was broiling hot. He absently reached over to wipe whatever it was off but pulled away when his hand touched the searing surface of his Hilt-loop.

"Are you against me too?" He glared at the Hilt, fury changing to dismay.

Suddenly his mind was back in the foundry, watching his brother die.

His Hilt wasn't against him at all. It was guiding him back towards rationality, away from hate.

As his anger cooled, so did his Hilt.

He took hold of the Hilt and patted the loop around his wrist. "I'll find some other way to fight them."

Sad, lonely and defeated, Aadima picked himself up and headed home.

# PART TWO: THE JOURNEY

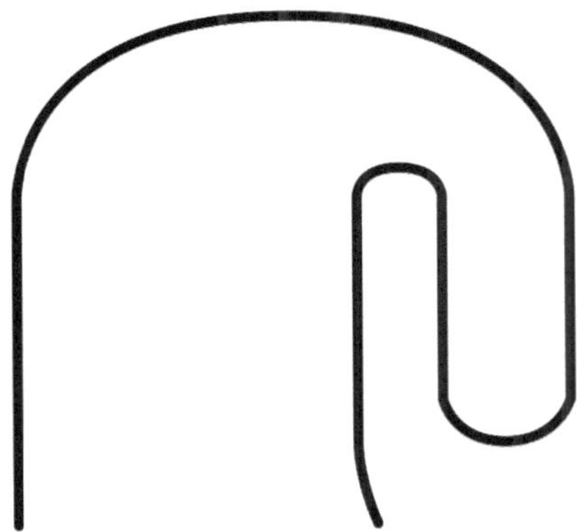

**Rume (secondary): an edible mushroom that grows alongside rumetres**

# LINEAGE

Aadima smiled as he pulled the oversized brown leather work jerkin over his head.

The lightly used jerkin was a birthday gift to himself that he had purchased at his favorite swap meet the previous Restday.

He looked at himself in the mirror, proudly tracing out the large Rumetre family crest that he had spent the past week carefully carving into the front panel.

He turned to the side to make sure that the tight old undershirt beneath his tunic was keeping his small but unwanted breasts flattened against his chest.

The compression that his "tight-shirt" offered had not only helped Aadima feel more normal, it also prevented some of the increasing number of glances from men of all ages that made him feel dirty and wrong.

He turned back to the mirror and examined the slightly tapered bottom of the jerkin—it could be wider, but it still covered what he needed covered.

Aadima happily traced the crest again.

Not only would this maintain his privacy, but it would show off his pride in being a Rumetre!

He pulled at one of the self-sealing flaps for the large pocket built into the back of the jerkin's front panel. It opened smoothly, releasing the scent of cured leather. Aadima closed it, then repeated the process with the seal on the opposite side.

He smiled. The feel of the two edges snapping magically together was oddly reassuring, as was the thought of such an intimate and secure place to keep important possessions.

It would be quite the upgrade from his school-bag, where everything got battered by the school-issued divulgate and all of the formulaes that rattled around within it.

Aadima looked down at the items spread out on his bed in a neat arch: his specie, Grandfather's lucent, some tissues and a travel bottle of recharge potion.

*Did I forget anything?*

He tapped each of the four items, internally reciting his list.

"My chatter!"

He retrieved it from the recharge pool on his nightstand and, with a smile, stuffed it into his jerkin pocket. The items from the bed quickly followed.

After sealing the pocket, Aadima turned to examine himself in the mirror.

He turned back and forth a few times before nodding.

*You can't even tell there's anything in there!*

After one last proud glance at the crest on his chest, Aadima headed downstairs for breakfast.

He had been so excited to wear the jerkin to school that he had awoken nearly an hour early. In his excitement, he had also lost track of time and forgotten his family's unwritten breakfast schedule.

Two-thirds of the way down the stairs, he saw his mother step out from the dining room. She was dressed for work in her administrative-black pocketless jumpsuit.

He started to turn, but it was too late.

"What is *that*?" His mother was glaring unhappily at him.

"It's a jerkin!" Aadima said with a smile as he descended the last few steps, his pride overwhelming his sense of caution. "I carved the crest myself! It's just like the ones our family wore on their armor during the Demon War!"

"It's a disgrace!"

Aadima felt foolish for letting his guard down.

"You're not going out in public wearing that, are you?"

Aadima opened his mouth to reply.

"Of course you are." Jabeza rolled her eyes. "Foolish girl!"

Aadima wanted to scream in frustration but just looked down at the floor.

*There's really no point.*

"I don't want to look at that thing!" his mother said after an uncomfortable moment. "I may not be able to stop you from making a fool out of yourself *out there*. But you *will not* wear that in this house!"

"Yes, Mother," Aadima replied flatly.

Jabeza pushed past him, averting her eyes, and rushed up the stairs.

Dejected, Aadima gathered a cold breakfast and dropped into his usual chair.

He absently rubbed the wide gray cuff around his right wrist, dreading the fact that he would have to take it off again soon.

The original Hilt-loop had expanded over the past few years into the far more comfortable cuff that covered most of his forearm. Plus, the new Hilt-cuff was able to hold the main Hilt in place even during the most vigorous arm movements.

The Hilt-cuff was decorated with an intricate pattern of engravings that was replicated on both the cross guard and the half-dome pommel that had formed a few weeks after they had been reunited.

The Hilt's handle was still the same shape, but now it matched the red of his skin and felt like padded silk while still providing a solid, slip-proof grip.

His hand touched an unexpectedly smooth section of the cuff. Aadima looked down to see that there was now a plain raised disk in the center of the top side of the cuff.

*What is that?*

As he watched the smooth surface, it began to change, filling with the Rumetre family crest.

He raised his wrist to get a better look.

"Wow!"

The crest spun within the disk, remaining upright as the Hilt-cuff angled upwards.

"Cool!" he said as he moved his arm around.

The crest remained upright.

"I can't wait to show everyone!"

Before the words were even all the way out of his mouth, he knew how foolish they were.

He had fallen into the same trap that he had with his jerkin, imagining the crest as the gesture that would finally convince his family to accept his Hilt.

*It's been years. Have they ever brought it up or called it anything other than "that thing"?*

He sighed, quickly finished his breakfast and went to wait in his room until the very last minute before packing his Hilt away for the day.

Aadima took a deep breath as he ran out of side paths and had to step out in view of the large crowd of students gathered in front of the school.

He was pleased that the looks he got were not the ones that made him feel dirty, just ones of disapproval, and he was well used to those.

*At least one part of my plan actually worked.*

"What is she wearing?"

"Does she think she's an iron-worker now?"

They were the same voices that taunted him every day. They just had a new topic to focus on.

"Look, it's the last of the great Rumetres!"

His step faltered for a moment.

*No,* he thought firmly, *I am not disgracing the Rumetre name, I am living up to the Rumetre legacy!*

He tuned out the voices with the theme song for *The Rajveer Chronicles* and was soon taking his usual seat in the back corner of his year's classroom.

"You need to take off your coat in class," Educator Lehrer said.

"It's a jerkin."

"Whatever it is, take it off when you're in my class!"

Reluctantly Aadima did, thankful that his tight-shirt was doing its job, and carefully draped it over the back of his chair.

Despite his exposure, he was able to draw comfort from the feel of the leather behind his back as the class went on.

When the tocsin gong rang, he slipped back into his jerkin for the duration of the break.

At lunch, Aadima took his regular seat in the darkest corner of the cafeteria and ate his meal without tasting it.

"Look, it's Aadima the metal-working boy!"

He smiled inwardly. *At least you got one part right!*

# REVELATION

"Aadima, dinner," Samael Rumetre shouted up the stairs.

"Be right down," Aadima shouted back as he paused the latest episode of *The Rajveer Chronicles*.

He set his divulgate on his nightstand and, on his way out, ran a hand over the crest on his jerkin as it hung on the back of the door.

His father was already seated at the table when Aadima arrived.

"I hope you're enjoying your birthday," he said without looking up.

Aadima sighed silently, wishing that he would look up and greet him as "my little girl" again. Despite the discomfort, he missed the sense of belonging that the nickname had conveyed.

He sat in front of the only other plate of food on the table.

His father looked up. "Did you get your gift?"

"Yes, thank you both."

The units transferred into Aadima's account

that morning had been much less than the year before.

His father nodded and continued with his meal.

They ate in routine silence.

"Enjoy the rest of your birthday," his father said half-heartedly when Aadima headed back upstairs.

Once in his room, Aadima watched the end of his episode and, to cheer himself, rewatched his favorite episode from the first season before going to bed.

But sleep was elusive.

Aadima's mind kept dredging up the memory of every incident that had ever made him feel guilty or sad.

Eventually he nodded off.

Much later, he slipped into a dream.

Thousands of elves were somehow crowded around Aadima in Hinter Village Centre.

"Hail the conquering hero, home at last!"

It was Manager Dufort's voice from somewhere behind him.

Being below average in height, Aadima couldn't see the hero through the silent crowd surrounding him.

He advanced, frequently needing to elbow his way between the throngs.

As he worked his way forward, he saw a bright light ahead of him and heard the sound of solid footfalls.

He doubled his efforts, squeezing through the unyielding and faceless masses.

Aadima burst through the edge of the crowd and into the light.

He stood in a circular opening. It was empty except for a pink ribbon at his feet.

The ribbon blew away and Aadima looked around in confusion.

The crowd started to cheer.

Aadima looked back to see Gondefle step confidently into the opening from the other side.

His heart leapt into his chest, then dropped just as fast.

*But that can't be Gondefle!*

Not-Gondefle smiled and looked at him knowingly.

He was Aadima's father's age and clad in classic Demon War armor. On the breastplate, the lines painted skin-red, was a deep engraving of the Rumetre family crest.

He wasn't Gondefle, but the hero *was* family.

But who was he?

The crowd started chanting.

It was just an indistinct sound at first, but as it grew louder, Aadima was slowly able to understand it.

"Vihaan!" the crowd shouted. "Vihaan!"

The hero was *Vihaan* Rumetre!

Vihaan, now at the center of the circle, started to spin slowly, waving appreciatively to the crowd.

As he turned, Aadima could see the engraved crossbar of a Hilt resting in a slot built into the top of the armor's faulds.

He racked his brain but couldn't remember anyone in the family named Vihaan.

In fact, he couldn't think of *anyone* named Vihaan.

Suddenly the dream's viewpoint changed and

he was the returning hero: confident, humble and completely at ease.

He was alone in the circle and everything felt right.

The dream ended with a start, but the feeling remained, even stronger as the revelation sank in.

He was Vihaan.

Everything fell into place; his name as a man was Vihaan.

Now that he knew what to call himself, he knew that it was time to live the gender he had always known he belonged to.

But the joy of naming his true self was short-lived.

This would be so much worse than bringing home a Hilt.

He got up early the next morning to make his parents breakfast, hoping the gesture of kindness would be reciprocated, just getting it onto the table as they came down the stairs.

His mother looked at him with a mixture of surprise and suspicion. "Why are you up this early?"

Also caught by surprise, his father exclaimed, "Did my little girl make us breakfast?"

Vihaan's daydream came back to him, but the exclamation didn't feel like acceptance—it felt like correction.

"I'm not your little girl."

"Of course," Samael added quickly as he sat and started scooping up some of the scrambled eggs.

"That's actually what I need to talk to you

about." The end of the sentence came out in a squeak as an uncomfortable lump grew in his throat.

His mother took her chair and frowned. "What is it now?"

"I realized something last night." Vihaan paused to steel himself.

"Which was?" Jabeza said after the pause went on too long.

"I can't live as a girl anymore."

"Don't be foolish!" she exclaimed.

"I'm a man and my name is Vihaan." It came out in a rush.

A great weight lifted off his shoulders.

It crashed back down as his parents' faces flushed with anger.

"That is not funny," his father said stiffly, jamming another forkful of eggs into his mouth.

"I'm not joking," Vihaan said quietly. "I'm a partite man and can't live this lie anymore. I've always known I was male, and despite how painful that knowledge has been, I've never been more certain. This is who I was meant to be."

"That's it!" his mother exploded. "You've put us through *enough*! I won't put up with you *playacting* in this house, Aadima!"

"That's my point—I can't *pretend* to be a girl anymore!" Vihaan said through the ache in his heart. He suddenly remembered one of his Delphi Press history texts. "Back before Liberation, people like me were accepted as part of society. One of Timor's founders was a partite man!"

His father snorted. "That's a fringe fantasy!"

"Back before Liberation," his mother quoted

him with a sneer, "we let ourselves be ruled by amoral demons! That *alone* should tell you that anything that was *acceptable* back then is *evil!*"

"It's *not* evil! *I'm* not evil!" Vihaan felt an overwhelming sadness. "I'm just a man born into the wrong body."

"The body of *my daughter!*" Jabeza sobbed and ran upstairs.

"Look what you've done now, you stupid girl!" Samael brushed both plates of food onto the floor. "I'll have none of this depravity! *None!* Do you hear me!"

Vihaan didn't answer; he was struggling to keep from rising to meet his father's anger.

Finally his father snorted. "Clean up this mess and get to school!"

He stormed out of the room.

Vihaan let the tears flow as he kneeled down and started to gather the widely scattered chunks of egg.

The next morning, Vihaan paused just as he was about to remove his robe and step into the body-launder.

He returned to his room and came back wearing his Hilt.

*It's time to get rid of Aadima's hair.*

He hung his robe on the closest of the hooks built into the side and stepped into the launder, closing the door behind him.

With great satisfaction, he formed his Hilt into

a sharp curving blade and cut off his hair just at the base of his skull.

With a smile he watched the severed hairs land on the floor of the launder and disappear.

He released his Hilt. It returned to neutral and the cuff slid up to his bicep so that the launder's magic could reach his forearm.

*Time for the next hurdle*, he thought as he stepped out of the launder and slid back into his robe.

"What was the importance of Declivity and what happened to it?" Gathin Hodzic asked at the start of Vihaan's first class of the day.

As usual, when no one volunteered the answer, Educator Hodzic turned to Vihaan. "Aadima, do you know the answer?"

Vihaan steeled himself. "Please call me Vihaan."

"What?" Educator Hodzic said over the class's amused murmur.

"I'm not a girl. I was born in a female body, but I am male."

Laughter filled the room.

"Quiet, please." Educator Hodzic glared angrily at him. "If you're bringing this up *during class time*, I assume that your parents have already filed the appropriate paperwork and notified the administrator?"

"Well..." Vihaan squirmed. "Not quite yet."

"Well, until they do, you will answer to your

*legal* name," Educator Hodzic said with a frown. "Now, Aadima, do you know the answer?"

Vihaan's newly found identity battled with his love of history and the embarrassment of losing the support of his favorite teacher in front of the entire class.

With a sigh, he recited the obvious. "Declivity was the first capital of Timor. It was leveled during a demon-attack in the year 350. There were no survivors and it was never resettled."

"Very good, Aadima."

Vihaan fumed, reminding himself once again that being a Rumetre meant standing up for what you knew was true no matter what.

# REACTION

The news of Vihaan's new name and gender declaration spread fast, and the Hinter Consolidated School became an even more unwelcoming environment than it had been since he had bonded with his Hilt.

To give his classmates time to come up with some other topic to focus on, he had begun avoiding them, to the point of collecting his lunch and bringing it outside to eat.

The uncomfortable days passed slowly.

On the Tewesday after his declaration, Vihaan had just finished lunch and was following his new routine of cutting through the storage corridor that ran along the demon-land side of the building.

He was halfway to class when, from the corner of his eye, he saw something move in an open doorway beside him.

He started to turn towards it.

"Freak!" The voice was quiet but angry and full of hate.

Something struck him hard in the chest, knocking the wind out of him.

His lungs were on fire!

Someone else shoved him from behind.

Vihaan's forehead hit the corridor's stone wall hard enough to tear his thick elvish skin and blur his vision. The rest of his body followed, slamming against the wall as blood flowed down his face and into his eyes.

"I'm sorry, did you trip?" a second harsh voice whispered.

Confused, frightened and desperately trying to fill his empty lungs, Vihaan was only able to squeak weakly.

He reached up to wipe the blood from his eyes.

Something struck his wrist, knocking it away from his face.

This time whatever it was shattered and Vihaan could feel the small but sharp pieces of it spearing into his face and neck.

"How dare you prance around pretending to be a boy, you little murderer!"

Vihaan was punched in the stomach. He felt the seam of his tight-shirt split as he doubled over, falling to the floor.

"Yeah," the second voice hissed. "Did you think we wouldn't know who you really are, *Aadima!*"

A series of kicks followed.

After one struck him hard in the head, he belatedly put his arms up to protect it.

The kicks continued, focusing on his torso. Vihaan vomited.

"Disgusting pervert!" the first voice shouted.

The kicks resumed, more frantic this time.

Vihaan's world was growing dark when he

heard a deep voice booming out, "What's going on in here?"

The kicking stopped and he heard two pairs of feet scramble away.

Another set approached just as quickly.

"Are you okay?" the deep voice asked.

Vihaan wiped the blood from his eyes and was finally able to draw a deep, unsteady breath.

There was a large, dark-haired and square-jawed human leaning over him, eyes full of concern.

"You're...," Vihaan croaked with all of the breath he had managed to gather, "the new chief constable's son."

"Daughter, actually," she said, looking extremely nervous. "Not that I've been brave enough to tell anyone." She smiled. "Not like you."

The ringing in Vihaan's head made her words difficult to understand.

He inhaled. His lungs were still burning and his chest ached, but it was getting easier.

"Like me?"

"Yes." Her eyes were damp. "It's something that I've struggled with for years, but when I saw you, and how sure you are about yourself, it helped me accept myself for who I really am—a partite woman. Please call me Amineh."

Vihaan's sluggish mind processed her words as his breathing became more regular, each inhalation accompanied by sharp pains.

"Thank you, Amineh," Vihaan said weakly before being overcome by a fit of coughs.

"We need to get you to the healer!"

"Not yet." Vihaan wiped a piece of vomit from

his chin and saw that it was mixed with blood. "I need a minute." He started shaking. "I'm not feeling brave enough to face anyone else right now."

"I'm never brave," Amineh said sadly, lowering her wide, muscular form to the floor beside his slender one and effortlessly lifting him up into a sitting position.

Vihaan winced but found that, after the initial burst of painful motion, the pain in his chest became slightly more bearable.

Without realizing it, he started sliding slowly sideways, back towards the floor. Amineh placed a strong and comforting arm around his shoulders and held him in place.

"You sure sounded brave to me," Vihaan said with a shaky laugh, unaware of his averted lean. "Certainly those inutiles were convinced. They couldn't get out of here fast enough."

"They just saw Durmad Kamali, the chief constable's son," Amineh said bitterly. "They're more afraid of my dad than they are of me."

"I doubt that." Vihaan reached up and weakly squeezed her thick wrist. "Besides, I couldn't see a thing and you sounded brave enough to me."

Amineh smiled gratefully. "I've been watching since you announced your aligned name. Watching and wishing that I could be true to myself like you are."

Vihaan didn't know what to say and just stared blankly back at her.

"Ready?" she said after an awkward moment.

Vihaan nodded and she lifted him to his feet.

He squealed in pain and swayed for a moment before finding his balance.

"Ready?"

He nodded again, leaned against her, and let her guide him out of the room. "I'll understand if you need to get clear once other people are around."

"No!" Amineh said. "Never again! From now on we watch each other's backs."

"You're sure?"

"I am right now." She took a deep but uncertain breath. "We'll see how I hold up when I try to tell my parents tonight."

"Do you need backup?"

"No." She squeezed his shoulders and glanced at the tip of his ear. "One surprise at a time."

They laughed together, Vihaan's ending early in a rattling cough.

Late that night, Vihaan's chatter buzzed for attention. He saw Amineh's name on it and whispered, "Invoke, low volume."

He propped it up against his pillow as Amineh's face appeared. "How did it go?"

A look of relief filled her face. "Better than I hoped."

Vihaan smiled. "You humans have all the luck."

"Not all of it!" She smiled back. "My father was 'very disappointed' but my mother was supportive. She *really* surprised me—I always thought she was the old-guard one! It took a while, but we worked out a compromise. No girls' clothes but they'll call me Amineh. My father couldn't help adding 'until you grow out of this,' but I still feel better, lighter."

"That's how I felt when I first chose my name,"

Vihaan said wistfully, "like I had been in the dark all my life and suddenly was surrounded by lucents!"

"Exactly!" A serious look crossed her face. "Thank you for helping me find the courage."

"I didn't do anything," Vihaan laughed, then winced in pain. "Okay, I guess I fell down a lot."

Amineh laughed uncomfortably.

"But remember," Vihaan said with mock severity, "it's just this once. Next time you need a nudge, let someone else take the beating."

Amineh's answering smile did not displace the concern in her eyes. "You're really going to be all right?"

"Yeah." Vihaan put on a disgusted look and twanged the leather medical strap around his chest. "Potions for breakfast every day for a week and I have to wear this style-choice, but I'll be fine."

They ended their chat several hours later.

Vihaan was cleared by the healer to return to school the next Wodnesday.

When he did, he wore his Hilt.

The start-of-day gong was still ringing in his ears when he was summoned to the administrator's office.

"You can't have *that* in this school," said Administrator Baston, in her pocketless black jumpsuit with its academic-green trim, as soon as Vihaan appeared in her doorway.

"I'll leave it at home if *you* can guarantee that I won't be attacked by any of *your* students again."

She appeared nervous for a second, then turned angry. "From what I hear, you fell down the stairs. This fight story is just another of your attention-seeking ploys! You will go home immediately, leave that thing there, and come directly back!"

"I will not."

"I'm not giving you a choice."

"Then I'll give you some." Vihaan grinned darkly. "You have three options: kick me out, take it from me yourself... or leave me alone."

Her forehead beaded with sweat. "I'm calling your parents."

Vihaan leaned against the door frame and folded his arms in front of him, making sure that the family crest on his Hilt-cuff was facing her.

She pulled a chatter from her desk. "Invoke, Samael Rumetre!"

"Administrator Baston," Vihaan's father said flatly through the chatter. "What has she done now?"

"Your daughter has brought a weapon to school!"

"She promised us she wouldn't."

"Well, she broke that promise." Administrator Baston was seething. "Are you surprised? What are you going to do about it?!"

"She's a teenager now. I've given up trying to control her." His father sounded annoyed. "I don't care what you do—kick her out, let her keep it, whatever. Just don't bother me about this again! Done!"

Administrator Baston slammed the chatter down on her desk.

"So, which is it?"

"You know I can't be seen expelling a Rume-tre!" She looked disgusted. "Get back to class and keep that *thing* stowed!"

"Sure thing." Vihaan started to leave. "I promise I won't *start* anything."

Amineh was waiting for him in the hall. Vihaan grinned but decided not to ask how she had gotten herself out of class. He nonchalantly walked past her.

"Will they let you keep it?" she asked, falling into step beside him.

Vihaan tapped on his cuff. "Did you really think Baston had the reach to take it away from me?"

They laughed together and returned to class.

# OUTCASTS

It was Saterday afternoon, the end of the school week, but Vihaan and Amineh didn't head towards home after being released by the tocsin's gong.

"You have the address?" Vihaan asked once no one else was around.

"You know I do," Amineh answered. "Don't tell me you're getting nervous *now*?"

Vihaan was embarrassed. "I keep hearing my mom's disapproving voice in my head."

"So, nothing new or different."

Vihaan laughed. "But today I keep hearing her say 'stay away from the freaks and the lazy down there.' Have you ever been to that part of Hinter before?"

"To *Shant*?!" Now Amineh laughed. "Can you *imagine* my dad letting me into the bad part of the village?"

"No, I guess not." Vihaan thought for a moment. "He doesn't have any family here anymore. Why do you think he stays?"

"Habit, my father says." Amineh grinned. "But I think he's just too stubborn to give in."

"Seeing a bit of yourself in him?"

"I hope so."

Vihaan nodded. "Me too."

It wasn't long before the pair arrived at the address on Fray Avenue that Amineh had liberated from her father's files.

It was a shabby pale yellow house with one of the two front windows boarded over. While it wasn't the worst-looking structure on the block, it was certainly in the bottom half.

"My dad would be *so* furious if he knew where we are!" Amineh whispered as they stood uncertainly in front of the yellow house.

"He's the only partite man in Hinter," Vihaan whispered back. "I can go alone and fill you in later if that's what you want."

"*Now* you're brave?" Amineh smiled and continued adamantly, "When we first met I said that we'd always watch each other's backs and I meant it."

Vihaan nodded gratefully.

They walked to the door together and Vihaan knocked. A scruffy elf wearing a heavily worn gray jumpsuit trimmed, where it wasn't worn away, in white and an angry expression opened it. He was well past his prime but not quite elderly, and he silently glowered at them each in turn.

"Cuisinier Konnyr?" Amineh said with a tremble in his voice.

"Just Konnyr," the tall man answered gruffly. "Is this general curiosity or are you working on a report about failed morality for school?"

"No!" Vihaan blurted. "We're..."

When Vihaan's silence had stretched to the

point of discomfort for everyone, Amineh said, "We're like you."

Konnyr looked them over with an incredulous look. "Are you sure about that?"

"We are," Vihaan said, finally finding his voice. "I've always known I was male."

"I've thought of myself as female for the last few years." Amineh looked at Vihaan nervously. "But I sometimes have doubts. Especially when I catch my father looking sad and he hides it when he sees me looking."

Vihaan put a reassuring hand on his friend's arm.

Konnyr's face softened, not quite to happy, but no longer angry. "It took me years to accept my spirit-gender," he said, looking at Vihaan. "Most of those years I hated the thought of being different, of being wrong in the eyes of society." He looked at Amineh. "Being partite is not an easy path. We all figure ourselves out at our own pace."

Konnyr looked unfocused for a second, then said, "Sorry, I'm not used to guests and I'm being rude."

He reached out and clasped Amineh's hand.

"Amineh Kamali."

"Like the chief constable?"

"My father."

Konnyr nodded. "I've met him. He seems to be a good, fair-minded man."

"He is," Amineh said with a smile.

Konnyr clasped hands with Vihaan.

"Vihaan Rumetre."

"I've heard about you but never knew that you were partite."

"I only recently started to openly express my spirit-gender."

"Please come in," Konnyr said, stepping back. "I apologize for the state of the place but, as I said, I'm not used to guests."

Amineh entered first, followed closely by Vihaan.

Konnyr removed a large divulgate from the wide couch along the front wall, just below the boarded-up window, and motioned for them to sit.

"Let me see if I have anything suitable for visitors," he said as he headed into the kitchen.

Amineh and Vihaan examined their surroundings.

The small house had three rooms: the main one, which filled the front half of the structure, and two more that evenly divided the back. The room on the left was an open-plan kitchen/dining area. The room on the right was walled off and the door was closed. In the corner of the main room, against the front wall of the partitioned room, stood a tall body-launder.

"Do you think the privy is in the bedroom?" Vihaan whispered.

"No one puts a privy *inside* a bedroom," Amineh whispered back.

"Then where is it?"

"Maybe he uses the body-launder?"

"Gross!"

"Just because you sit on it doesn't make a privy-launder work any differently than a body-launder!"

Vihaan didn't get the chance to respond as Konnyr came back from the kitchen at that moment, balancing a box of Salubrity flax crackers, a large bottle of green juice and three mismatched glasses in his arms.

"Do you like pique juice?"

They both nodded. The cheap juice was always served with their school lunches.

Konnyr filled a glass for each of them, murmuring, "It's been a while."

"Why don't you tell us about yourself?" Amineh said as she picked a cracker from the proffered box. "All we know is what the stupid gossips made up."

Konnyr sneered, forgetting for a moment to offer the box to Vihaan.

"At least you're willing to hear the truth," he said, finally holding the box out to Vihaan. "That's not exactly common around here."

Amineh took a bite of his cracker, scrunched up her face and looked down at it for a moment before she reluctantly continued chewing.

"Well," Vihaan said, "we know the types of lies they say about us, so we know better than to trust them."

"I guess you would at that," Konnyr chuckled. "Well, where do I start?"

Vihaan took a bite of his own cracker, frowned for a moment, then chewed.

"How about where you work?" Amineh suggested.

"I'm at Blotch Brews right now." He winked. "A place I certainly hope the two of you never find yourselves. It's a rough crowd, but the owner is willing to put up with me as long as I stay in the kitchen. He even pays me a bit extra on the side to stay after closing on Restday so he can overcharge the drunks for snacks."

"I've never been much good at cooking," Vihaan admitted. "I can make eggs but that's about it."

"I've always wanted to learn," Amineh added.

"Maybe someday I'll teach you a few things." He glanced towards the small kitchen. "I don't usually do any real cooking at home." He looked back with a smile. "But I imagine that you have more pressing questions than how to prepare a nice fresh prosy."

"We were hoping that you might be able to tell us how to find out more about... people like us," Amineh said.

"I've never even met anyone else like us before!"

"Neither of us have."

"I can tell," Konnyr said. He looked over at Vihaan. "And, despite that top, I can also tell that you're not binding."

"Binding?"

"Your breasts."

"Oh." Vihaan had never heard the term before. "I, uh, usually wear a tight-shirt... I mean an old undershirt that's too small... but the side seam on my last one split last week."

"Clever boy, I never thought of that!" Konnyr laughed.

Vihaan was inordinately pleased and felt a wide grin fill his face.

"I used to wear so many layers to hide mine that I was drenched with sweat even in the winter," Konnyr continued. "I solved my problem with a clandestine trip to Wove."

"Alignment?" Vihaan asked.

"No, cosmetic spell-work was more than I could afford at the time." Konnyr got up. "I want to show you something, if I can find it."

He went into the walled-off room. As the door opened, they could see that it was a bedroom, mostly filled with a large bed. There was no privy inside.

He moved to where they couldn't see him, and for several minutes they could hear him moving things around.

When he returned, he was holding a slightly tattered but very heavy-looking sleeveless half-shirt. He handed it to Vihaan.

"That's one of my old binders," he said as he settled into his chair. "In fact, it's the one that I wore the day I was finally able to afford my alignment." Konnyr smiled and rubbed his chest. "It hurt like demon-fire, but it was such a relief!"

Vihaan held the binder out in front of him, looking for a tag. "Is this custom-made?"

"Has to be," Konnyr said. "You won't find them in the usual divulgate catalogs."

"From Wove?" Amineh asked.

Vihaan was looking at the binder with a wistful expression.

"Yes," Konnyr said. "If I thought that would fit, I'd let you have it. The man who made me that one is long gone, but I have a good friend in Wove that makes them."

Vihaan looked up with an excited expression. "Can your friend make one for me?"

"His name is Mosegi," Konnyr answered with a smile. "And I'm sure he can. He specializes in adaptive clothing for aligned men." He looked over at Amineh. "But his business partner, Mbaziira, could put something together for you too, if you're interested."

Amineh looked surprised. "For me?"

"Well," Konnyr said with mild embarrassment, "I don't know too much about it, but I'm sure you'd feel more feminine with some... uh... shapewear."

"I've dreamed of looking more feminine but didn't think it would be possible"—Amineh looked embarrassed as she ran her hands up her sides—"considering my size."

"I'll admit, you're a bit... taller than most. But I've seen partite women nearly as... tall who could blend easily even without alignment." He stood and started back towards the bedroom. "I've got one of Mosegi's consociate cards here somewhere."

"They must be *good* friends," Amineh whispered with a wink over the sounds of searching. "You don't hand off something *that* expensive to just anyone who's not an official sales rep!"

"Well, he's my sales rep now!" Vihaan gave her a wry grin. "I'm placing my order as soon as possible!"

# COMFORT

Vihaan smiled and quickened his step when he saw Amineh waiting for him in front of the Hinter Consolidated School with a package tucked under her arm.

She was wearing her favorite shirt, a flowing bright yellow one that her mother had given her. It had been the most feminine thing available in Panopoly's men's section and was part of her mother's strategic wearing down of her husband's resistance.

"Is that it?!" Vihaan asked in a squeaky voice.

Then he came to a stop, cleared his throat and, in a normal tone, repeated, "Is that it?"

"I didn't open it." Amineh shook the package. "But I'm not expecting any other packages from Aligned Attire in Wove for..." She held it in front of her face and squinted at it. "Vihaan Kamali."

"And your parents won't tell anyone?"

"No, you know my mother will make sure of that."

"I wish I had your mother."

"Well, I'm not willing to trade."

"Nor would I recommend it!" Vihaan continued in a gently accusatory tone. "Why didn't you say anything last night?"

"I wanted it to be a surprise!"

"Well, it is." Vihaan gestured impatiently. "Now may I *please* have my order?"

Amineh handed it over. "Let's go where you can try it on!"

Vihaan tucked the package under his own arm and they headed into the school. "What about yours?"

"Mbaziira walked me and Mom through how to take the measurements so I could place my order last night," Amineh said with a laugh. "Now that my parents saw that you weren't just donating your units to a hollow rep."

"Glad that I could help calm their minds!" Vihaan said as he opened the doorway to the school's basement. "Did you get to order the full set?"

"Yes!" Amineh said, following Vihaan's lead and taking the stairs two at a time. "I can't wait to try them on and finally look as feminine as I feel! Dad grumbled a bit, but I ordered three sets of bras and gaffs and a corset to see if I can handle it."

At the bottom of the stairs was a door labeled "Maintenance Staff Only." They went through it without hesitation.

They both waved at the janitor in his perpetually grimy gray jumpsuit. He nodded back as they headed straight to the single-seat privy room in the far corner.

"Your private privy, sir!" Amineh said with a flourish.

"Oh, the novelty," Vihaan said with a shake of his head.

He stepped into the small room, for once not caring that school policy now forbade them from using the student privy rooms on the main floor.

Vihaan tore open the package: inside were two heavy padded binder tops just like the one Konnyr had shown him.

"I could only afford to order one, but there are two in here!" Vihaan shouted through the door.

"I hope it's not someone else's order," Amineh shouted back. "Look for a packing list or a note!"

Vihaan picked up the first binder and saw that there was indeed a folded note between the two garments:

Vihaan,

Since this is your first and you're a friend of Konnyr, I've made you a second binder. Everyone should have a spare and I'm certain that you'll feel better in these than your old tight-shirts!

Yours in alignment,

Mosegi

"Mosegi is the best!" he shouted. "He made a second for free!"

"You have all the luck!"

Vihaan was smiling widely as he removed his jerkin, tunic and undershirt so that he could slip into the binder.

"Is everything all right in there?" Amineh asked after he banged into the door for the third time.

"It's tight!" Vihaan shouted through the binder, which was currently stuck over his head.

"Let me know if you need a hand," Amineh answered.

"I think I've got it," Vihaan replied through the fabric over his face.

He worked his way deeper into the binder until it was finally in place.

With a sigh of relief, he stood on his toes so that he could see his chest in the chipped and frosted mirror above the sink.

Vihaan rewrapped the second binder in the remains of the packaging and stuffed it and his tight-shirt into his schoolbag.

He pulled on his tunic and, after a long hesitation, opened the door and stepped out.

"How do I look?"

"Turn," Amineh instructed.

Vihaan did, feeling extremely self-conscious.

"Hmmm," Amineh said.

Vihaan looked over at her, saw her smile, and relaxed.

"You look great!" she said, meeting his eyes. "Guess you won't need that worn-out jerkin of yours anymore."

"I've never *needed* it," Vihaan replied with a grin. "It's useful and I've come to think of it as my *style*."

"More like lack thereof," Amineh said as she watched him pull the jerkin back on.

Vihaan rubbed his hand over his chest. "Ready for class!"

"Are you sure?" Amineh teased. "It's spell-work."

"And there hasn't been an elf practitioner since slavery," Vihaan said, quoting the first day of class.

"I know, but it's still fascinating to see how it all works."

"You're such a sponge, you should be an educator when you grow up."

Vihaan laughed. "Who in their right mind would listen to me?"

Amineh joined the laugher as they rushed upstairs to beat the start-of-day gong.

When the end-of-day gong sounded, Vihaan found that he was disappointed.

"No one even noticed," he said to Amineh.

"Does anyone ever *really* notice us?"

Vihaan laughed. "I guess not. But I *feel* so different!"

"You weren't really that big yet," Amineh said. "And with that jerkin, the difference is hard to see."

"I guess."

"Still," Amineh said, putting her hand to her own chest, "I wish we could just trade."

"Let's do the next best thing!"

Amineh looked at him quizzically.

"Let's go into the Centre and celebrate!" Vihaan said. "With my units!"

Amineh smiled. "Free celebrations *are* the best celebrations!"

"Then come on!"

A passerby sneered at them as they ran past.

"Do you think people do that in Wove?" Vihaan asked.

"I doubt it," Amineh said. "I hope we get to see it someday."

"Right after graduation," Vihaan said eagerly. "Let's promise each other!"

They stopped and clasped hands.

"A promise it is!" Amineh said cheerfully.

"Can you imagine being able to just walk into Aligned Attire?!"

"Even better"—Amineh grinned—"being able to talk to other partite people!"

"I'm getting boring," Vihaan said mournfully. "I knew it had to happen someday."

Amineh punched him in the shoulder, and he staggered.

"That hurt!"

"It was *supposed* to!"

"You may be a little slow," Amineh said with a laugh, "but you're never boring."

Vihaan laughed and rubbed his shoulder. "Where do you want to go?"

"Is there *really* a choice?"

"There's *always* a choice."

"And you *always* choose Delectables."

Vihaan sighed theatrically. "If you want to go somewhere else, I won't complain."

"I guess there really isn't anyplace else nearly as good."

"So *you* choose..."

"*I* choose Delectables!"

"I'll have the recherché swirl," Vihaan said to the collector at the Delectables front counter.

"Sweet cacao, please," Amineh said when the collector turned in her direction.

"Be right up," the collector said cheerfully as he walked back to the cold-cabinet.

"How can you eat that stuff?" Amineh asked for the umpteenth time. "It's just a spell. It doesn't taste anything like the real thing!"

"It tastes close enough to *remind* me of the real thing!" Vihaan smiled. "It was Double Sync Day and I was four..."

"Skip the story," Amineh said. "I've already heard it. Besides, here they come."

Vihaan had his specie in the ledger before the collector arrived with their frozen treats.

"It's nice today," Amineh said after the ledger buzzed. "Let's eat outside."

"Then we had better hurry—there's only one table free!"

They rushed towards it.

"Vihaan, Amineh!" Konnyr said from nearby. "How're things?"

Vihaan flushed with pleasure. It was the first time that anyone other than Amineh had used his chosen name in public.

He glanced over at her and saw that she had a huge smile on her face too.

"Come eat with us!" Vihaan shouted. "My treat!"

"Thanks, but I have early dinner plans," Konnyr said as he joined them. "But I can stay for a while to chat if you're willing to be seen with me."

"If you're willing to be seen *with us*," Amineh said, pointing at the available table, "you're more than welcome."

The trio moved to claim the table.

"We're celebrating!" Vihaan said as he took a

chair facing back at Delectables. "My new outfit from Mosegi arrived today!"

Konnyr smiled. "How does it fit?"

"Perfectly!" Vihaan put a hand to his chest. "Your measurements were just right. And Mosegi even included a second one for free! I'm going to chatter him as soon as I get home to say thanks."

"Mosegi always clears the extra acre." Konnyr nodded and turned his attention to Amineh. "And what about you? Your parents going to let you order *your* outfit now?"

Amineh smiled. "I placed my order with Mbaziira last night. I can't wait to actually *look* like I feel inside!"

She took a big bite of her perfectly priced treat.

"You'll never be the same again," Konnyr said with a knowing smile.

# PRODUCTIVITY

"Why can't you ever do better than bases?! You are an embarrassment to the Rumetre name!" Jabeza Rumetre said with disgust as she crushed Vihaan's most recent monthly evaluation in her hand.

Vihaan started to protest that he did, actually, get secondaries in both history *and* mechanics. But self-preservation prevailed, mostly.

"I'm trying as hard as I can!" he retorted. "But even when I get *all* the questions right, they won't give me more than a secondary!"

His mother gave him an ugly look. "Your teachers tell me that you *still* can't even spell your own name!"

"That's not fair!"

It was an old argument but one she knew always hurt.

"You wouldn't lose twenty points every time if you would just put down your *real name!*"

"I *am* putting my real name! My name is *Vihaan*! If one of you would just sign the paperwork—"

"Aadima!" As always, the idea of confirming his

chosen name enraged her. "Go to your room until I tell you you can come down!"

Vihaan stomped his way upstairs.

The next day was Restday and Vihaan rushed through an early breakfast, hoping to avoid his parents.

His head was inside his jerkin when he heard his mother's voice.

"Where are you going?"

"I'm going to work," he said once his head was free again.

"After the grades you just got, don't you think you should be studying?"

Vihaan had to struggle to keep his anger from showing on his face. "With those grades, don't you think it's better that I learn how to earn money as soon as possible?"

She looked at him with disgust, both for disappointing her in general and for cutting her rant short. "Just go."

Amineh met him halfway down Balefire Way.

"Good morning, Laborer Rumetre! You're going to *really* like this one," she said, bouncing as she moved in-step beside him.

She was wearing a fitted red casual jumpsuit that emphasized her enhanced bust.

"We're clearing land for Old Man Aldenkamp," she continued. "Plenty of opportunities to use your Hilt for what it was *meant* to do!"

"Aldenkamp is *the worst*!" Vihaan was shocked. "I can't believe that he would hire *us*."

"My father and I ran into Old Man Aldenkamp last night." Amineh grinned. "Dad reminded him that he had been receiving complaints, so I *happened* to mention that we could take care of it for him."

"Leveraging the lawman," Vihaan said with genuine appreciation. "Nice work!"

When they arrived, Vajran Aldenkamp was standing on his front porch, looking unhappy.

He pointed toward the side of the house and grumbled, "You know what I want."

"We do," Amineh said cheerfully. "And we promise you will be happy with the results!"

They walked around the well-kept house.

"I still don't understand why it got this bad," Amineh said as they surveyed the overgrown greenery filling the backyard. "And why only back here?"

"Seriously?" Vihaan laughed. "They've been at this longer than I've been alive!"

"They?"

"Aldenkamp and his neighbor."

"Come on," Amineh said impatiently. "Out with it!"

"Ashmatee Jamarreon was his schoolyard sweetheart, but it didn't end well and they've been butting heads ever since." He gestured towards the yard. "This part of their feud started when Educator Jamarreon was foolish enough to complain about Aldenkamp's hedges being 'unkempt.'"

"But the hedge was fine."

"It is *now*." Vihaan grinned. "But after her complaint, he stopped trimming them. When she finally had enough and called the village manager,

Aldenkamp blamed it on old age and started trimming them immediately. From then on, he kept the hedge perfectly trimmed but didn't touch the grass. The backyard is just the latest item that he's 'accidentally' neglected."

"Well," Amineh laughed, "at least we'll get some units out of it!"

"And I owe you one for that!" Vihaan agreed. "My binders are getting tight and I still need another thirty to buy the next set."

"You could always take it out of that big savings account of yours."

"You know I can't." Vihaan frowned. "I'm going to need every single unit someday. You know my parents won't help if things ever get tight."

"Sorry," Amineh answered guiltily. "I wasn't thinking."

"Don't worry about it," Vihaan said cheerfully. "But we should probably get started."

Amineh went over to the back of the house and collected a barrel and a rake. Vihaan willed his Hilt into a scythe.

Out of the corner of his eye, he saw Aldenkamp through a back window. The old elf flinched as he watched the Hilt-blade form.

Vihaan sighed.

"You saw?" Amineh asked.

"No matter how many times, or how patiently, I explain it," he said in frustration, "people like Old Man Aldenkamp can never seem to accept a soul Hilt as something that a *proper* elf would be associated with."

"You know the truth," Amineh said evenly. "Why worry about it?"

"I *try* not to."

"Let me know if you ever succeed." Amineh rolled her eyes and brandished her rake. "You cut, I clear?"

Vihaan smiled. "As always."

He and Amineh quickly settled into their work and the yard was cleared by lunch.

Vihaan's fifteenth birthday was a few weeks, and two similar jobs, later. Fifteen marked his moil-majority, the first step towards the full majority of adulthood. It also meant that he could finally separate his specie, and the units associated with it, from his parents' accounts—and their control.

As soon as school let out, they headed into Village Centre so Vihaan could open his first account at the Hinter Blood Bank.

"Name?" the teller, in a gray jumpsuit with blood-red trim, said coldly when it was his turn.

"Vihaan Rumetre."

"I'm sorry, I don't have any records for a Vihaan Rumetre." She looked back at him with a tired expression. "You can't open an account without proof that you are at least fifteen years of age."

Vihaan groaned inwardly and reminded himself how much he needed this.

He felt Amineh's supporting hand on his arm and heard her whisper, "Just think about the birthday lunch that Konnyr's preparing!"

He gritted his teeth. "I was born with the name Aadima."

"Ah." She looked at him with distaste. "Aadima

Rumetre, I've heard about you." She glanced back at her divulgate. "I do see an Aadima Rumetre here, and she *did* turn fifteen today. If *she* wants to make a deposit, I could certainly help with that."

She looked at him expectantly.

Vihaan held back an angry retort.

The odd jobs that they had been able to find over the past few years had helped. But, if he was ever going to escape Hinter, he needed the small-but-steady income that his own blood bank account could provide. Blood was, after all, money. Plus, if the interest wasn't enough to get by, he could always sell the blood-credit to a practitioner.

He swallowed his dignity and choked out, "Okay, fine."

She adopted a smug expression. "Name?"

"Aadima Rumetre," he growled.

"Now, that wasn't so hard, was it?" Her smug expression was replaced by one of superiority and achievement.

Vihaan didn't respond, working hard to keep his face neutral. Amineh's hand squeezed his arm.

The teller smiled back at his obvious anger.

"Do you have your specie with you today, dear?"

Vihaan handed it over while fighting against the urge to roll his eyes.

The teller took it and set it into an indentation in the counter between them.

"Okay, dear, I have opened your account, transferred your credits and connected your new account to this specie." She smiled insincerely as she handed it back. "I have to inform you that you can only make *one* blood-deposit every *other* month."

Vihaan had to fight harder to control his anger. Everybody knew that! She hadn't "had" to inform anyone in the line in front of him.

Amineh squeezed his arm again.

"I understand," Vihaan said shortly.

"Good." She pointed towards the waiting room as if there was no other way he could find it. "Now you two dears go take a seat and someone will call Aadima in for the blood draw shortly."

∼

"Why didn't I listen to you?" Vihaan fumed as soon as Konnyr opened his front door. "I knew what to expect, but it still caught me by surprise!"

"Hinter never changes," Konnyr said gently as he waved his guests inside.

"Then why do you stay?" Vihaan asked. "If I were you, I'd have left for Wove ages ago."

A sad look crossed Konnyr's face. "It is a temptation but"—he paused as he closed the door—"my parents died defending this village and, despite the vitriol, it's always been *home*."

"I... ah..."

"What is that smell?" Amineh asked as she closed her eyes and inhaled dramatically.

Konnyr smiled widely. "I was able to get some saftec steaks from Blotch's supplier at wholesale. They're a bit heavy for lunch"—he winked—"but it *is* a special occasion. Now grab a seat at the table while I finish up."

Soon Konnyr returned to the table with three plates precariously balanced on one arm. With barely a wobble, he distributed them around the table and took a seat.

"Thank you so much for this," Amineh said after a short moment of silence while nudging Vihaan under the table.

"Yes!" Vihaan said quickly. "I really appreciate you going out of your way just for me."

"Hardly just," Konnyr said. "It's been a long time since I had friends—local friends, that is, that I could spend time with. Even if you're unbelievably young and ignorant."

Everyone laughed.

"So," Konnyr said while cutting his meat, "have you given any thought to your majority career?"

"I guess I could become a scribe," Vihaan said with a shrug. "I used to think I would write drama, but now, I suppose, I'd probably write about history." He cut a piece of steak and lifted it partway to his mouth. "Or I could be an educator. Or both." He pulled the steak off his fork and chewed slowly.

Amineh rolled her eyes. "That's our Vihaan, the great planner!"

Vihaan frowned theatrically before shaking his head and helping himself to another bite of his steak. "This is very good!"

Amineh winked at Konnyr. "Don't worry, I'll make sure he doesn't end up in the charity ward."

"And," Konnyr said with a good-natured scowl at Vihaan, "I know every cretin in this village and will drag you back to your parents if I ever catch you with any of them!"

They laughed together, then the table went silent as the trio consumed their meals.

"That was fantastic!" Amineh said after she finished chewing her last piece of roll, which she had used to clean her plate.

"As usual," Vihaan agreed just before placing his last bite of steak in his mouth.

"Thank you," Konnyr said with a grin. "It's nice to make a proper meal. I don't often get the opportunity at work considering the menu."

"I was thinking," Vihaan said after he finished chewing, "that we could finish fixing the siding on the back wall this afternoon."

"Absolutely not!" Konnyr shook his head and stood. "As much as I appreciate all the work you both do for me around here, this is a *social* visit." He shook his finger at Vihaan. "*Only* a social visit!"

"I told you!" Amineh laughed and poked Vihaan hard in the ribs.

"But that does remind me..." Konnyr walked over to his bedroom door and opened it just wide enough to retrieve a small parcel. "I had Mosegi double your order and convinced him to let me hand-deliver it as a moil-majority surprise."

Vihaan found himself holding back tears as he accepted the package. "I don't know what I'd do without you. Either of you."

# LOSS

Vihaan was awoken before dawn by his chatter rattling around in its now-empty charging pool.

"Invoke," he mumbled as he grabbed for it.

"Please turn the chatter around," Amineh's shaking voice said.

Vihaan was fully alert by the time he had spun the chatter around and saw Amineh's red, puffy eyes.

"Wha...?"

"They've murdered Konnyr!"

Vihaan was shocked. In the past few years, Konnyr had become both friend and confidant—the parent he wished he had at home.

"Who? How?" he asked with tears in his eyes.

"A group of drunks followed him home." There was a cold fury in her voice. "They scampered when a constable arrived, but it was already too late."

"Do they know *which* drunks?"

"Yeah, the remembrance in front of Blotch recorded them harassing him as he left the bar, then following after him." Her anger eased slightly. "Dad just took six of his best and headed out to Shant to round the worthless orts up. I just hope he gets there before they slip into the weeds."

"He will," Vihaan said. "With the lawman on the case, they'll get what's coming to them! Does Mosegi know?"

"Yeah, he's down as next-of-kin, so Dad chattered before he left," Amineh sighed. "I'll miss his laugh."

"I'll miss his advice," Vihaan replied sadly. "I was *so* happy when we met that I finally had someone to talk to who had actually gone through the same things that I am."

"But I won't miss his crackers!"

Vihaan laughed despite himself. "They *were* awful, weren't they!"

"But healthy!"

"Salubrity flax crackers," Vihaan said, quoting one of their old divulgate ads, "the healthiest, tastiest snack you can buy!"

They laughed together.

"I don't know what I'll do without him," Vihaan said, wiping away a tear and putting his hand to his chest.

Amineh unconsciously did the same. "He didn't deserve to die like that."

"No one does."

"His murderers do."

"Amineh," Vihaan said with concern in his voice, "what would your father say if he heard you talking like that?"

She grunted. "I'll ask him when he gets home."

Vihaan had barely gotten home from school the next day when his chatter vibrated for his attention. It was Amineh.

"Invoke," he said, blindly tossing his schoolbag behind him as he sat on the edge of his bed.

Amineh didn't wait for Vihaan to speak. "Dad hasn't come home yet." Her face was drawn and her lips were trembling.

"Do they—"

"No, they haven't heard anything from anyone on his team or any of the suspects." She started sobbing.

"Amineh, I'm sure—"

"People saw them head into demon-land…," she managed to get out between sobs.

All of Vihaan's childhood fears came back to him.

His own tears started flowing. "I'm so sorry."

"Search parties from the county constabulary arrived this afternoon and are tracking them now."

"They'll find him," Vihaan said with as much confidence as he could muster.

"I know," she said softly, with far less conviction.

The next day, partly to keep their minds off the search for Amineh's father, they went to Hinter Ossuary to find out about Konnyr's interment.

"How can I help you through your loss?" an ossuary assistant greeted them as they walked into the main office.

"We're inquiring about the interment for Konnyr, who was... who died a few days ago," Amineh answered.

The assistant checked his divulgate.

"I don't have any information about that. Let me check with the mortician."

He stepped into the next room, closing the door behind him.

The walls were thin enough that his words were audible:

"There are some people here inquiring about the Konnyr interment."

"Who would care about that?" they heard Nye Than reply.

"It's *them*."

The other room was quiet for a moment, then Mortician Than came out.

"I'm afraid that Cuisinier Konnyr's remains have not been released by the constabulary yet."

Amineh hmm'd. "It's usually standard procedure to provide the mortician with a timetable so that they can schedule the proper reception."

"Uh." He looked nervously at her. "Probably tomorrow, they said."

"So," Vihaan said, "would the interment be on Restday?"

Mortician Than cleared his throat. "I'm afraid that there will not be an official interment."

"Why not?" Amineh asked angrily.

Mortician Than's eyes darted between them. "His funerary fund did not have enough to cover a full ceremony." He cleared his throat again. "I'm afraid that he will await his eternal reward in the charity crypt."

"No marker?!" Amineh asked.

"No," Mortician Than replied. "But I assure you that his remains will be prepared to the highest standards."

"Can we be there when he's warehoused?" Vihaan asked, torn between grief and anger.

"I'm afraid not." Mortician Than looked at Amineh again. "As I'm sure you know, only ossuary staff are allowed in the crypts"—he paused—"for the safety of the departed."

Vihaan looked at Amineh, who had absorbed the answers to most legal questions from her father. She nodded reluctantly.

"Thank you for your time," Vihaan said.

The pair departed.

Mortician Than rolled his eyes and returned to his office, evicting the assistant back to his usual place at the counter.

As the ossuary disappeared around the corner behind them Vihaan shouted, "I can't believe that we won't be able to say a proper goodbye!"

Amineh put her arm around him. "I think the last thing Konnyr would want is a *proper* anything! We'll stop at Delectables and send him off to his eternal reward over glasses of pique juice!"

"But *no crackers!*"

Vihaan was in the front yard doing his chores when his chatter started to vibrate.

He pulled it out, then frowned when he saw Amineh's name.

"Invoke!" he said as his Hilt retracted to neutral.

Amineh's face appeared. She was upset, but that wasn't unusual these days.

"Are you all right?" he asked.

"We're leaving," she answered through tears.

"What? When?"

"Tomorrow."

"Why so soon?"

"They've declared Dad..." Amineh broke down completely.

Vihaan swallowed hard. It had been six weeks since her father had disappeared in pursuit of Konnyr's killers.

"Take your time." Vihaan tried to sound comforting but knew it wouldn't be enough—that it *couldn't* be enough. "I'm here."

She put down her chatter. The bouncing picture changed to one of a cobweb on the ceiling of her bedroom. Vihaan could hear her blowing her nose.

There was silence for an uncomfortably long time.

Finally, she picked up the chatter again.

"They've declared him a demon-loss," she said quickly.

"I'm so sorry."

The searches were over. Amineh's father was gone.

The looked at each other silently through the chatters, the grief too much to bear.

"I almost killed Assistant Teagan this afternoon," Amineh said casually after a moment. "The demon-spawn was telling everyone who would listen about what a fool my dad was for *wandering* out into demon-land!"

Vihaan scowled. "Demon-spawn is too kind for her."

"He was doing his job!"

"I know," Vihaan said calmly. "Every *sensible* person knows. Those inutiles say that every time."

Amineh smiled darkly. "Had her pinned against the wall before my escort even saw me move."

"Who was it?"

"Wileen—he's temporary chief until they bring in someone new."

"I don't envy him." Vihaan forced a smile. "You could take him out with one arm cut off."

Amineh smiled again, kindly this time, but didn't reply.

"So, tomorrow?"

"Yeah, our place came with Dad's job, so we can't stay." She paused. "Mom says it's for the best —it will let us get away from the memories."

"Will you go back to Akin?"

"No." Amineh's face flushed with anger. "They're holding up Dad's salary and pension until they finish their *investigation,* so we couldn't afford Akin even if we wanted to! Besides, the only opening my mom's company has right now is in Wove."

"Well," Vihaan said, "at least you'll finally get to see what Wove is like."

"Yeah," Amineh agreed weakly. "I'll look Mosegi up for you."

They went quiet again.

Finally Vihaan asked, "Will there be a Sending?"

"No, my family doesn't believe in them—it's interment or nothing," Amineh said sadly. "And with nothing to inter…"

"Is there anything I can do?"

"You're doing it already."

Vihaan shuddered as he stepped into the Hinter Consolidated School building two days later. With Amineh in Wove and Konnyr gone, he felt completely alone.

"I hear your bodyguard got shipped out to Wove," Merari said from the front of her current group of friends. "Who'll protect that soft back of yours now?"

The weeks of pain and loss got the better of him. Vihaan stalked over and planted himself immediately in front of Merari. He held his right wrist hard against his former friend's cheek.

"My back is fine," he hissed. "But yours will be in shreds if you try anything!"

Merari swallowed hard, desperately trying to focus on Vihaan's Hilt-cuff in the hopes of getting a moment's warning before it lashed out at her. Her followers were silent; no one moved.

"I didn't mean us!" she whispered, her followers nodding in unison. "We… we've always been on your side! That… that's why I wanted to warn you! There are… bad people around…"

"Then I apologize for my misunderstanding."

Vihaan lowered his arm and stepped back, still glaring. "By all means, keep me informed of any *bad people* that you hear about."

Merari nodded eagerly, and Vihaan stomped off.

After a moment of confusion, the shaken group retreated in the opposite direction.

# EXILE

When Vihaan came downstairs on the morning of his eighteenth birthday, he was surprised to find both of his parents seated side by side at the table.

"Is this for me?" Vihaan asked, looking at the meal laid out at his regular spot at the table.

"Of course," his father said. "Enjoy your birthday."

Vihaan sat and looked at his parents. The three of them hadn't eaten breakfast together in years, and even having everyone together for dinner only happened once or twice a month.

His parents didn't meet his gaze, looking down at their plates as they slowly ate their meals.

Vihaan shrugged.

*At least I don't have to make my own food this morning!*

As he worked his way through his meal, he watched his parents closely. They seemed to be taking turns looking up just enough to see how much was left on his plate.

"Thanks for breakfast!" Vihaan said brightly when he was finished.

He picked up his dishes and took them over to the kitchen-launder. When he turned back, his parents were both looking intently at him.

"Aadima, you're eighteen now. That means that you've reached your full majority and that you are now an adult," his mother said stiffly. "We're giving you one last chance to stop pretending. If you're not willing to face reality, you're no longer welcome in this house."

Vihaan looked at his father. He seemed slightly uncertain, but his eyes offered no support.

Vihaan sighed. The day was finally here. "I'm not the one who isn't facing reality."

Samael put his arm around his wife's now-shaking shoulders.

"I can't be the girl you want me to be," Vihaan continued. "If I said that I was, it would be a lie. And it's a lie that I can't live with." Vihaan's heart began to ache and he tried one final plea. "If you could just accept me as I am..."

"Aadima!" his mother shrieked, her eyes going wide.

All three of them fell silent, his mother still shaking, now with rage. Vihaan fought to remain calm.

His father shook his head, the uncertainty in his eyes fading. He locked those now-determined-and-focused eyes with Vihaan's.

"You have one week to find somewhere else to live."

A lump welled in Vihaan's throat, making it difficult for him to answer. "I'll be gone before lunch tomorrow."

He turned away from the angry stares, grabbed his schoolbag, and started out of the house.

"Leave *our* chatter and divulgate when you go," his mother shouted after him.

~

Vihaan found himself standing in the utility corridor where he had first met Amineh with no memories of his walk to school.

He yanked out his chatter. "Invoke, get me Amineh."

"Hey there, my technically adult friend!" She stopped and her smile faded. "What's wrong?"

"My parents are throwing me out..."

"Come to Wove!" Amineh said through an angry expression. "You can stay with us until you get your own place."

Vihaan sighed. "I probably will, eventually."

"Eventually?"

"I need some time to myself," Vihaan said, surprising himself. "I need a hegira. Some time to figure out who I am outside of Hinter."

"You *know* who you are."

"Maybe." Vihaan hesitated. "But I still feel lost and incomplete."

"You always knew this day would come."

Vihaan nodded. "I did, but it still hurts."

"You shouldn't be alone."

"Probably not." He shrugged. "But I really feel like I need to spend some time in the world before I can settle down again."

"I'll go with you!"

Vihaan laughed. "I appreciate the gesture and

would love spending time with you. But your mother would never let you leave school so close to graduation, and you know hegiras need to be solitary."

"Is there such a thing as a group hegira?"

"When I get back, we'll invent one."

Amineh laughed sadly. "But you'll keep in touch, we'll still talk every day, right?"

"They're not letting me keep my chatter."

Amineh's face rushed towards the chatter as she said, "Then just *take* it!"

"No," Vihaan said quietly. "I don't want anything that ties me back here."

"But it ties you to *me* too!"

The images on the chatters were shaking for both of them.

"I know." For the first time that morning, Vihaan had to fight back tears. "I promise, as soon as I'm where I need to be, who I need to be, I'll get a new chatter and visit you in Wove. We'll associate again and then never be disconnected again."

"How long will that be?"

"I don't know."

"Please don't let it be too long."

"I won't," Vihaan said over the school's gonging tocsin. "I've got to go. We'll talk at the usual time tonight."

After a long and bittersweet final chatter with Amineh, Vihaan settled on the floor next to his preserval trunk. He opened it and looked inside.

It was filled with books, all with the red D embossed over the book-like erudit rune that formed the Delphi Press logo at the bottom of the spine— his precious collection of history, the result of countless begging trips to the local bookseller and a few lucky swap meet finds.

It was too heavy to carry very far.

*I've put too much into this to lose them now.*

He closed the trunk and headed to the privy to wash up.

He undressed, carefully avoiding catching sight of his naked body in the mirror, tucked his only binder under his arm, and stepped into the privy-launder.

"Stay where I can see you," he said to the binder, half in jest and half covering his lingering anger at his mother.

Ever since Vihaan had come out, he had been responsible for buying and washing his own clothes. He didn't mind the extra work but often missed the nicer fabrics that were now beyond his meager budget.

He had been careless the last time he had done his laundry, getting lost in a rare Delphi Press book he had found after years of searching.

Once he'd realized that the launder cycle was long over, he'd rushed downstairs, but it was too late.

His laundry had been stacked on top of the clothes-launder, which was green, indicating that it was in the middle of a cleaning cycle.

His binder had been nowhere to be found.

Back in his room, he packed his most durable clothes into his schoolbag and stacked his two divulgates on the edge of his chatter's charging pool on his nightstand.

He knew it was petty, but he had deliberately failed to mention to anyone that today was his last day at school and had brought the school-issued divulgate home so that his parents would have to break the news when they returned it.

His tocsin woke him at midnight. He stuffed it into his bag, hefted his trunk of books, then left his childhood home behind.

Vihaan's first stop was a small park in his neighborhood where he had played as a child. His path illuminated by a tiny sliver of his grandfather's lucent, he went to the least-visited corner, where the grass was always brown, and used his Hilt to lift up a large section of sod directly in line with the two oldest trees. He set it aside and quickly reformed his Hilt and sank it into the exposed ground. When the hole was large enough for his trunk, he willed his Hilt into a platform and lifted it off the ground beside him.

*The talisman will protect it*, he thought to himself as he lowered his treasured collection into the hole, *as long as no one disturbs it.*

Once the hole was filled in and the sod pressed firmly back into place, Vihaan found himself with a large Hilt-full of dirt. He walked around the neighborhood, scattering the excess dirt in the front gardens of every house that he passed until he ran out.

With his Hilt stowed, he headed to Provenders, the ever-open shop on the edge of Village Centre closest to the speedway exit.

He grabbed a basket and went straight for the snack aisle.

*I'll only be able to fit a few in my jerkin*, he thought as he gathered up a selection of trail bars, *but I should be able to fit at least a dozen in my bag.*

When he put the basket onto the counter at the front of the store, the collector gave him an odd look.

"Midnight craving?"

"No, I'm... camping with some friends and forgot to pick up the snacks."

"A Rumetre is going *camping?*"

"Just me"—Vihaan cursed himself—"and some friends."

"Of course," the collector said insincerely as he started reading the labels into his store formulae.

The trail bars packed away, Vihaan soon found himself at the Boon Loop Speedway exit.

Without looking back, he walked over to the in-loop path and started towards Akin.

He walked down the speedway in a daze, eventually passing Akin and following it back out-loop on the other side.

Someone flashed by on the other travel lane, causing Vihaan to look up.

The sky was brightening in the east.

*Almost time for the morning commuters*, he thought, *time to get off the speedway.*

He took the next exit, thankful that it was still empty and he didn't have to deal with anyone.

He let himself through a gate in the vendor area of the exit and onto the maintenance path that ran along the outside of the barrier. Then, like a bandit on the divulgate, he began following the trail to the next exit, keeping an eye out for work crews.

Although isolated from the increasing traffic

within the speedway, the path was still within the influence of the string of aegis talismans positioned at the top of the path's cover to protect travelers.

It was nearly dusk when Vihaan spotted a rumetre ahead. He smiled to himself.

*How appropriate that the shelter tree is here when I need it most.*

From the outside, the rumetre looked like a solid tangle of branches that arched out from the top of the tree before drooping almost all the way to the ground.

Vihaan lay down in front of the tree, rolled under the bottommost branch tips and into the inner cavity. He stood up and brushed some loose soil off his jerkin.

He took a deep breath, enjoying the smell of the moist dirt, the fragrance from the leaves he had crushed during his roll, and the slightly musty odor of the rume mushrooms that grew in clusters all around the base of the tree.

With another smile, he knelt down and cleared away rumes until there was a space large enough for him to sit and lean back against the trunk.

After wrapping the extras in one of his shirts, he made a meal out of the flavorful rumes and thought about his family. Not just his parents, but all of the Rumetres.

*Will I ever be welcome in any of their homes again?*

As he ruminated, he started to trace his family crest in the dirt with the tip of his finger.

He started with the tall arch of ru, the base rune that, fittingly, meant soil.

Next he added another, tighter arch within the

right side of the first one, connecting one side to the first, making it into rume.

He popped one of the mushrooms that the secondary rune represented into his mouth and was lost in thought for a moment.

Ever since he was a child, he had thought that the runes were backwards. Sure, he understood; a simple shape for a base, an adornment on one side for a secondary and mirrored adornments for a primary, but he had spent a lot of time pondering the family crest and the rumetre rune it was built on.

Every rumetre he had ever seen, even the one that was currently sheltering him for the night, had a thin mat of interwoven branches nowhere near as thick as what the rune depicted. The fat lobes on the rune were a far better match to the cap of the rumes.

He filled in the opposing side of the rune and extended the two inner edges of the tight arches to make the complete rumetre rune.

As he prepared to convert the rune into his family crest, he recalled his cousin Oroitz drunkenly singing out the names of the family heroes to win a bet during Yielding so many years before.

Family lore, and Oroitz's slurred recitation, claimed that it was Yeong Rume that had earned the family their primary rune. Unfortunately, since she had died fighting very early in the Demon War, there were no surviving records to confirm it aside from the elevation of the family name.

The family's two hero bars had been earned at the cost of two more family members fighting in the later years of that same war. Vihaan carefully drew them across the middle of the rune, making sure that they were respectfully straight, parallel and properly spaced just like his father had taught him.

He finished the crest with the honor slash, working as best he could with the materials at hand to get it exactly five times as wide as the rest of the line-work to properly honor each of the recipients.

Vihaan leaned back against the trunk of the tree, absently tracing the crest carved into the front of his jerkin as he fell asleep.

A few days later, Vihaan approached the next exit of the speedway.

He stepped onto the in-loop path and made a few backwards steps so that he could read the name of the village on the exit sign:

## Deadfall

*Ominous but appropriate,* he thought ruefully. *I am dead to my family after all.*

Before setting out, he had memorized the names of every elvish or mixed community along the Boon Loop Speedway to make sure that he didn't repeat his experience from the last time he had fled Hinter.

Deadfall had been on that list as a mixed village but it wasn't anywhere he had ever heard of before preparing to leave home.

A shudder passed through him when the first thing he saw as he stepped out of the other side of the exit was a Pabulum franchise.

He crossed to the other side of the path and

headed towards an inn a few doors down along the gently curving central path through the commercial district.

There was a human woman in gray at the counter, her attention focused on a show playing on her divulgate.

Vihaan cleared his throat and held out his specie. "I'd like a room for the night."

She looked up and started. Her hand moved below the counter. "Sorry, we don't have any rooms available."

"But the sign." Vihaan looked through the window at the vacancy sign that had drawn him here; it was no longer lit.

"Sorry." She shrugged theatrically and gestured towards her divulgate. "Rented out the last room a while ago but was so caught up that I forgot to turn it off."

Vihaan smiled. "Sorry for disturbing you, then. I'll let you get back to your show."

He wasn't far down the path when something behind him caught his attention. The vacancy sign was illuminated again.

"Specist inutile!"

He wanted to go back and confront her but knew it would be futile.

The next two inns that he passed had no vacancies either, at least according to their signs.

Vihaan was starting to despair that he'd end up walking all the way around the village before finding a place to stay when he caught sight of the familiar yellow jumpsuit of a constable ahead.

*Finally, someone who can help!*

He headed directly towards the constable, who

turned towards him as soon as they saw him coming.

"Where did you get that Hilt?" the human constable said gruffly as Vihaan got close.

Taken aback, Vihaan stammered, "I've had it since I was a child."

"Likely story—who would give a Hilt to an elf like you?"

"It wasn't given," Vihaan said, trying to project confidence. "I discovered it and it bonded to me."

"More likely you stole it."

Vihaan couldn't keep a look of shock off his face. "You can't *steal* a bonded Hilt."

"You elves always find a way."

"Look, I'm not doing anything wrong," Vihaan said with forced calm. "I'm a visitor to Deadfall and just need a place to stay."

"Why aren't you in Redtown where you belong?"

"Redtown?" Vihaan wondered if it was a nickname or if the humans here had actually given such an offensive name to a real place. "I'm not sure I like the sound of that."

"No one cares what you *like*."

"I'm not looking for trouble, just for a place to stay." Vihaan suddenly realized that it would be better to spend the night in demon-land than to continue this conversation. "I'm sorry I bothered you."

He started to walk away.

"Where do you think you're going?" the constable said angrily. "I haven't dismissed you!"

Vihaan stopped.

"That's better. Now, I've got a place where we can keep a troublemaker like you."

Vihaan couldn't help himself. "I haven't *done* anything!"

"I think you're acting suspicious." The constable pointed to his wrist. "And you're armed with a deadly weapon..."

"I've never used my Hilt offensively."

"You *have* it. That's offensive *enough*. *And* you're acting belligerent." He pulled a chatter from his belt. "Invoke. Backup requested at this location, I have an armed and aggressive elf."

"Wait...," Vihaan sputtered.

The human face on the chatter nodded. "Dispatching backup now."

A blue flash announced the arrival of more constables. They were in full armor and had their Hilts ready, each formed into long batons.

Vihaan was still in shock. "But I haven't *done* anything!"

"We are authorized to use force if you resist arrest," one of the new constables announced from behind his protective mask.

"I'm not resisting," Vihaan pleaded. "I just don't understand."

"Understanding is not required," one of the others said. "Just do as you're told!"

Seeing no alternative, Vihaan allowed the constables to escort him into the middle of the path.

"Prisoner acquired," the first constable said into his chatter, "ready for recall."

There was a double flash and Vihaan found himself standing in the center of a fenced-in fieldstone patio attached to the back of the local constabulary.

The two constables behind him prodded him in the back with their Hilt-batons towards the only door, which led to a large room. They roughly guided him into one of four side rooms.

The room was empty aside from a chipped wooden table with a box on top.

"Remove your weapon and empty your pockets."

In his terror, Vihaan removed his Hilt, the cuff flattening as it came off his arm. He placed it reluctantly into the box.

Silently he emptied out the large pocket behind the front of his jerkin into the box as well, the constables watching closely.

After one last feel in the pocket to make sure he hadn't missed anything, Vihaan stepped back and looked expectantly at the opaque face mask of the nearest constable.

"The coat too," she said.

Vihaan removed his jerkin, folded the tough leather neatly, and placed it into the box.

The constable pulled the box to her side of the table, then said, "Arms over your head and spread your legs."

The second constable stepped behind Vihaan and put his hands in his armpits.

"There's something under his tunic," he said, slowly moving his hands down over Vihaan's binder. "It's a girl in disguise!"

"I'm not a 'girl,' I'm a partite man," Vihaan said without thinking.

There was a snort from behind him.

"Attempting to disguise your identity will result in additional charges being brought against you," the female constable said with contempt.

Vihaan forced himself to stay silent.

"Take it off," the constable behind Vihaan barked.

"Can I have some privacy?"

"This is private enough," the female constable answered.

Vihaan reddened with embarrassment as he pulled off his tunic, then squeezed out of his binder. He tossed the binder into the box with the rest of his possessions and quickly pulled his tunic back on.

His breasts pulled uncomfortably on his chest as he put his hands back up and spread his legs.

The constable behind him finished the search, ending by squeezing both of Vihaan's breasts and whispering, "You shouldn't hide them like that."

The other constable pointed to the doorway. "Out."

Vihaan fumed as the constables guided him back into the main room, where an older constable was waiting.

The waiting constable, yet another human, shook his head. "I'm already late for dinner. All I want is the property so I can log it and go home." He looked at Vihaan and jerked his thumb over his shoulder. "You'll be processed in the morning."

Two Hilt-batons prodded Vihaan in the back and he moved out into the hallway. With more jabs, the constables guided him to a small jail on the other side of the building.

"Okay, *fella*." The male constable placed his hand on Vihaan's back and pushed. "Into the cell!"

Once he calmed down, Vihaan realized that he could feel his Hilt nearby. He drew thin comfort from the connection, but he was angry at his naivete.

*How could you just wander into a village without knowing if it was elf-friendly or not?!*

He had trusted the first list he had found on his divulgate and hadn't even thought to do any further research!

"I can't believe they've got me locked up with an elf," a male voice from the next cell said in a disgusted tone.

Vihaan jumped at the sound.

"Sorry, red-tip, I didn't mean to frighten you."

Vihaan saw that the voice was coming from a well-muscled, middle-aged human man wearing heavy traveling attire that was worn but functional.

"Don't call me that."

"Sorry again," he said flatly, "force of habit. I was brought up that way." He stood and watched Vihaan through the bars that separated their cells.

"You grew up here?" Vihaan said coldly.

The other man laughed. "Absolutely not! I'm Dugal Valdis"—he bowed grandly—"public menace no longer at large."

"Vihaan Rumetre, innocent bystander."

Dugal laughed darkly. "And I'm sure you've learned by now that no elf is an innocent *anything* in Deadfall."

"I've never *seen* constables like these!"

"You haven't *been* many places, have you?"

Vihaan flushed a darker red at the pointedness of the observation.

"What kind of 'public menace' are you?"

"The kind that associates with the wrong people." Dugal sat down on the bench at the back of his cell. "I needed some gear for my quest and the only place that had it was the black market. What made the constables doubt your 'innocent bystander' status?"

"They disapproved of my Hilt."

Dugal's eyes widened. "*You* own a Hilt?!"

"I take it that's rare around here."

"Rare and *valuable* to the right people."

"I'm not a criminal."

"Neither am I." He paused with a self-conscious grin. "Well, I suppose that the point could be contested." He leaned towards Vihaan with a curious expression. "Is it true what they say? That a Hilt-wielder can summon their weapon to them from anywhere?"

Vihaan almost didn't answer, still embarrassed to be here and stinging from Dugal's words, but at least the conversation was a distraction.

"I think so," he said. "No one at home even wanted to touch mine, so I haven't had an opportunity to try."

"Well, try it tonight!" Dugal said a bit too loudly. "There's only one guard and they're usually asleep in the office."

"If I escape, I'll be the criminal they think I am."

"To the Deadfall daisies," Dugal sneered, "you'll *always* be the criminal they think you are."

"They don't have any evidence against me." Vihaan was adamant. "I'll be gone in the morning once someone with a level head looks at the facts."

"Dream on," Dugal laughed. "If you help me escape I'll show you the quickest way out of the city. We'll be long gone before they even start searching for us." He thought for a moment. "I'll even throw in some gems that I have left over from my shopping trip!"

"No," Vihaan said firmly, "I have faith that they'll do the right thing."

"Sure thing, girlie. When you come around, let me know."

"Don't call me that!"

"Whatever, you'll come around."

# ESCAPE

A few days later, a human constable—there didn't seem to be any elvish ones—that Vihaan hadn't seen before slid his dinner through the slot at the bottom of his door.

"Excuse me," Vihaan said, "do you know when I'll be able to speak with someone about my arrest?"

The constable impassively slid Dugal's dinner under his door.

"Constable?" Vihaan said, slightly louder.

The constable left, slowly closing the door behind him.

Vihaan picked up his tray, then sat on his bed, facing the other cell.

"Is your offer still good?"

Dugal smiled as he sat on his bunk with his own dinner. "I've got nothing planned for tonight."

"First, I need to know what you're going to do if I let you out of here."

"Afraid that I'll tear through the village raping and pillaging?"

"Something like that."

Dugal's smile vanished. "I won't be staying. I have a demon to hunt."

Vihaan scoffed. "You're mad!"

"No, I'm *angry*." Dugal paused. "My parents were taken during a demon-raid when I was a teen and I've been looking for the one who did it ever since."

Vihaan was flabbergasted. "But how could you expect to *survive* against a demon, let alone actually *kill* one?!"

"I've been training for this every day since I was orphaned." Dugal clenched his hands into fists. "The only thing I didn't have was the right weapon for the job."

"Is that what you were looking for in the black market?"

"That's what I *found* in the black market." He grinned conspiratorially. "You're not the only Hilt-bearer in the room."

"If that's true, then what do you need me for, *Hilt-bearer?*" Vihaan snorted. "Just summon yours and do it yourself!"

"After weeks of bribes and cajoling, I finally had the box with my Hilt in my hands." Dugal glowered as he held his hands around an imaginary box. "I was halfway back to my room in the inn when I found myself surrounded by daisies." He closed his hands together into a double fist. "If I'd been able to bring my sword into the village without raising suspicion, they wouldn't..." He sighed. "I never even got the chance to use it."

"And you actually think you'll survive going to go up against *a demon* with a Hilt you've *never even used?*"

"Look," Dugal said with annoyance, "I've trained with swords for over a decade. I won't have a problem using it once I get my hands on it."

"Do you even have a plan?" Vihaan said, reconsidering. "How does one go after a demon anyway?"

Dugal grinned. "Last year I finally found her. They call her Leah, the Beast of the Mountain."

"Sounds like a pushover."

"How would anyone know?" Dugal replied sharply. "The authorities are too afraid to even try!" He grew angry again. "I know, *I asked*! They laughed me out of the constabulary despite the fact that the beast has been doing this for *generations*! I am going to stop her because *no one else will*!"

"So," Vihaan said, impressed, but not convinced, by his single-mindedness, "you'll just chatter and set up an appointment?"

Dugal laughed weakly. "No need, I have an invoked lodestar in my pack."

"Okay, then how did you track her down?"

"*I* didn't." Dugal smiled. "But remember, I know some of the wrong kinds of people, the kind that prefer not to travel on protected speedways."

"Fine," Vihaan said, coming to a decision. "It doesn't matter anyway. They've already held me longer than the law allows and I'm *done with it*."

"So you'll do it?"

Vihaan stabbed one of the irregularly sized pieces of meat on his tray. "I will."

As soon as the lights went out, Dugal was at the bars between their cells. "Do you think you can summon it quietly? We'll need a head start even with my shortcuts."

"I'll try. But *you'll* need to be quiet so I can concentrate."

Dugal retreated to his bunk, sat on it, and stared at Vihaan impatiently.

Vihaan lay back on his cot with his right arm straight out beside him and started thinking, *Come to me quietly*—repeating it to himself like a mantra.

It was quiet for several minutes, then there was a soft popping sound, followed quickly by a louder thunk. There was a gasp from Dugal, but Vihaan ignored him.

*Come to me quietly.*

There were several quick, soft taps, then something landed on the bed beside his outstretched arm.

With an overwhelming sense of joy, Vihaan opened his eyes to see his Hilt. He slid it on, and the Hilt-cuff quickly cinched itself around his forearm.

*Never again!*

He stood and walked quietly to the door of his cell, feeling Dugal's eyes following him every step of the way.

As he reached the door, he could see a square Hilt-cuff-sized hole in the opposite wall, the cutout portion lying on the floor beside it. Shelves filled with boxes were visible through the opening.

Vihaan flipped his Hilt into his hand and willed it to form a short, thin post. He slid his arm through the bars and inserted the post into the cell door's lock. As he pictured an animation of tumblers he'd seen during a mechanics lesson back at school, it expanded and started manipulating the real ones. After they clicked softly into place, his Hilt returned to neutral. He released it and it folded back beneath his wrist with a soft clink.

Vihaan let himself out of his cell and, after a very slight pause, repeated the process on Dugal's cell door.

As Dugal sipped out, Vihaan whispered, "Our stuff is in the next room."

"Obviously." Dugal gestured at the hole in the wall. "Do you think you can teach me that?"

"If we don't get out of here fast, you won't be learning anything!" Vihaan whispered back.

Dugal nodded and waved him on.

They moved silently down the hall and, with Dugal watching out for the night constable, Vihaan used his Hilt to unlock the storeroom door.

Vihaan easily found the box with his possessions. It was the only one of the mostly identical boxes with a hole sliced in the side. He threw it open. Scattered across the top were the shredded remains of his binder.

*Lousy orts!*

As he began removing his possessions from the box and stuffing them into his schoolbag, his heart sank again as he realized that his jerkin was missing.

*I'm surprised those thieves left this alone,* Vihaan thought angrily as he stuffed his lucent into his bag. He paused, took a calming breath and looked around. *Maybe they just misfiled it.*

Dugal had finally located his box and hastily carried it over to a large backpack leaning against the far wall. He quickly started returning the box's contents to the appropriate parts of the pack and scowled as he noticed Vihaan rushing around the room, pulling the lids off all of the other boxes.

His jerkin wasn't in any of them.

Frustrated, Vihaan turned away from the shelves and started rolling his shoulders to relax and let himself think. But before he formed a thought, he saw the worn leather of his jerkin hanging on the wall in the room across the hall.

He smiled until he realized that, by the number of fresh scrapes and punctures, the constables must have used it as the target in a knife-throwing contest.

Vihaan fumed as he headed towards the door.

"Where are you going?" Dugal hissed as he shoved his last possession into his pack. "That's where the daisy is! We need to get out of here!"

"I need my jerkin."

"Is it worth getting caught?" Dugal hefted his large pack onto his back. Some of the contents clinked loud enough to make him wince.

"To me it is."

Vihaan crept across the hall and into the constables' lounge. He returned a moment later, relieved to be wearing his jerkin again.

"Not very flattering."

Vihaan frowned. "It's not decoration, it's functional."

"It hides all of your best features."

Now he glared. "In *your* opinion."

"And others', I'm sure." Dugal winked.

Vihaan patted his Hilt-cuff warningly.

Dugal sobered. "Let's get out of here." He gestured towards the back of the jail. "If you would do the honors."

# OPPORTUNITY

Dugal led Vihaan confidently through the twisting back paths of Deadfall, pausing only twice to avoid nocturnally active residents. Before it seemed possible, they were standing at the edge of the pool of light cast from the Boon Loop Speedway exit.

Dugal stepped into the light. "Good riddance," he spat back into the darkness.

"Well, this is where our agreement ends," Vihaan said as he joined him in the light. "I thank you for your help. I couldn't have gotten out of the city so quickly without you."

"It's where our *original* agreement ends," Dugal said smoothly. "But I couldn't have gotten out without *you* either. It would be simpler, and safer, to finish my quest if I had someone watching my back."

"Even an elf?"

"In this case, *especially* an elf." He jerked a thumb over his shoulder. "You proved yourself back at the jail. Besides, there's a reason why there's always an elvish regiment at the front lines—you're known for your strength and endurance. You were, after all, made for hard labor…"

"You expect me to help you when you spout *specist* lines like that?"

"Sorry, I didn't mean anything by it," Dugal said with apparent sincerity. "I'm a product of my upbringing—it's what they taught us in school."

"I thought you hated elves."

"I suppose I do, but sometimes you have to put personal prejudice aside for the good of the mission. So, girl, are you with me?"

"Don't call me girl."

"Okay, woman."

Vihaan choked down his anger. "I am a man, a partite man. The fact that I was born into a female body does not change that."

"I'd say it changes it a little."

"If you can't accept me as I am, this isn't going to work." Vihaan turned and started walking towards the speedway.

"I'm sorry." Dugal rushed out in front of Vihaan. "I just don't understand elvish culture."

"This isn't 'elvish culture,' this is basic spirit-identity!"

"I'm sorry! I'll try, I really will!" Dugal pleaded, retreating slightly from Vihaan's anger. "I really do need your help and I *am* trying. It's just that my upbringing makes accepting new ideas difficult for me."

"Dealing with someone who tries to deny my identity is *more than difficult* for me."

"Look, I'm sorry. I understand, or at least I'm trying to." Dugal forced a smile. "You're my guy!"

Vihaan groaned. "If you can't get it right, stick with Vihaan, no pronouns."

"Deal," Dugal said with relief. "Vihaan, are you with me?"

"I'm not sure I'm ready to throw my life away just yet."

"I honestly need your help." Dugal's grin returned. "Besides, if I fail, you should have plenty of time to run away while the demon consumes me."

"Assuming there's only one."

"And that it's hungry!" Dugal said with a laugh. "Besides, did you have something better planned? Another village you're hoping to get arrested in?"

*Is this why my spirit led me here?*

"I guess not," Vihaan said, then thought about his list of "safe" villages, now probably useless. "Do you know the area?"

"Like my own feet!"

"Okay, fine," Vihaan said with resignation, holding out his hand. "If you can keep my gender straight and your specist comments to yourself I could use the distraction of a quest."

"I'll do my best." Dugal's smile widened as they clasped hands. "But if I unconsciously stray, you'll need let me know so that I don't accidentally terminate our partnership with my own ignorance."

Vihaan rolled his eyes. "Okay. So, what's your plan?"

"First, we need to travel to the Catechi Valley," Dugal said, fishing in one of the side pockets of his pack.

"Never heard of it," Vihaan admitted.

"It splits the Agee range," he said, searching another pocket and mumbling, "Nothing's where it's supposed to be!"

"Sorry, I'm not familiar with Agee either."

"It's on the far side of Commix County." Dugal made an affirmative noise and pulled something out of his pack. "It marks the border with Acclivity County. The specific spot that we're looking for is near the base of the tallest peak in the mouth of the valley on the Commix side."

"You still haven't explained why you think you won't be killed instantly."

"I have something in my quiver that will make that the Hilt of the job, so don't worry. We just have to get there without crossing paths with overzealous constables... or the wrong demon." He lifted his hand and opened it with a flourish to reveal a green talisman. "But this lodestar will keep us on track and away from prying eyes."

"Will it matter if we're on track if we get caught out in the middle of demon-land?"

"You worry too much, especially for someone with their own Hilt."

"My Hilt is a tool, not a weapon."

"That's absurd, how can a Hilt *not* be a weapon?"

"Hilts were not designed to be weapons," Vihaan said, knowing the argument by heart. "They were designed to be multipurpose tools." He finished by quoting a favorite passage from one of his off-curriculum history books: "They only became weapons out of the dire necessity of the Demon War."

"That doesn't sound right to me."

"It doesn't need to 'sound right,' it's fact."

"Okay." Dugal rolled his eyes. "I guess I'll just have to take your word for that."

"Or you could do the research and confirm it yourself. I can even recommend a few good reference books to start with."

"Yeah… research isn't my thing." Dugal swung his arm as if brandishing a sword. "I'll stick with action!"

"Speaking of action," Vihaan said, grinning despite himself, "what *action* are you going to take against a demon?"

"I'm going to keep that in my quiver for now," Dugal laughed. "I don't want you stealing my plan and going after Leah yourself!"

"That's not *my* thing."

"Either way, we'll cover that when the sun is high."

"Whatever," Vihaan sighed. "How many exits do we need to pass before we get to Agee?"

"None." Dugal grinned, tapping on the lodestar. "We'll be following this cross-country. The speedway gives the daisies too many chances to do Deadfall a favor and return us to the welcoming arms of the local constabulary."

"Demon-hunting wasn't bad enough, so you're heading there through demon-land?!" Vihaan groaned. "Did you forget that, even if we don't end up as demon-loss, we won't have anyone to pull us out of the mud if we get into trouble?"

"Relax!" Dugal snorted. "Always the dark side with you! Speaking of darkness, do you have a lucent?"

Vihaan reached into his schoolbag and, after fishing around for a moment, found his grandfather's lucent. He opened the case and slid the talisman out just a bit.

"What an odd color," Dugal said as the silvery light lit his face. "But it works, and I'm out of recharge for mine."

Dugal reached into his pack and eventually pulled out a dark leather wristband, nearly as wide as Vihaan's Hilt-cuff. There was a copper cylinder attached to the top with matching bands that connected the cylinder to the leather with rivets. He opened it and pulled out a dull-yellow lucent.

"Wear this on your nondominant arm." He handed the wristband to Vihaan, then stuffed his depleted lucent back into his pack. "You'll need both hands free where we're going, especially at night."

While Vihaan transferred his lucent from its case to the wristband, the entire exit was bathed in bright silver light. The lucent fit perfectly.

"Not bad." He closed the rolling brass cover over it. "I can see how this could be handy."

"Now you can watch my back *and* be able to see it!" Dugal winked. "Lucky gi... guy!"

Vihaan rolled his eyes, then patted the pocket in his jerkin. "Let me just repack a few things, then we can get going."

Dugal nodded and took the opportunity to rearrange his pack while Vihaan loaded up his jerkin pocket. Once they were both satisfied that everything was in its proper place, Dugal pulled out his lodestar, held it clenched in his fist and whispered softly to it.

"I've invoked it to use the safest route and to keep us away from other people." He started walking down the maintenance path beside the speedway. "This should be an uneventful trip, but it will take a few weeks."

Vihaan opened his lucent-band a sliver, releasing just enough illumination to light their way but not enough to draw too much attention, then followed.

"What about supplies?" Vihaan asked, looking over at the lights of Deadfall. "I have some trail bars but that's about it."

"Not a problem," Dugal chuckled as they moved out of the light from the exit. "Most of my pack is filled with provisions. I had enough to cover me there and back before the daisies took their share. Assuming we eat off the land as much as possible, it should be enough to get us to our destination."

"And when we get there?"

"There are villages nearby where we can resupply." Vihaan could picture his grin. "Besides, there's an even chance that *we'll* be the provisions at that point."

Vihaan shook his head and continued along the path.

They walked in silence for nearly an hour before Dugal grunted.

"Just got a nudge," he said, stepping off the paved path and onto a narrow dirt one. "Time to head cross-country."

Vihaan took a deep breath, then followed him into demon-land.

As he emerged on the other side of a hedgerow, his lucent-light revealed several gray-skinned fruit at their feet.

"What are these?" Vihaan said, focusing the light on one.

"Piques," Dugal said dismissively.

"Should we gather some?" Vihaan asked. "You said that we should eat off the land as much as possible."

"No point, they're too tough," Dugal said as he kicked the fruit away. "Besides, if we do get desperate enough to eat them, they grow everywhere. So why drag any around with us?"

Vihaan nodded, thinking wistfully about long talks with Konnyr and Amineh over crackers and pique juice.

"I guess that makes sense."

They headed on into the night.

# PROPOSITION

As dawn broke, Dugal smiled into the sunlight. "There's nothing better than sunrise in the open country!"

"But is it really worth risking demon-land travel for?"

"With the right company it is."

Vihaan scowled.

"Besides," Dugal continued unabashed, "despite its colloquial name, there are actually very few demons wandering around out here." He reached out and plucked a leaf from a tree, then waved it over his head. "I've spent years traveling beyond the speedways and have never encountered one face-to-face."

"And now you're seeking one out. Are you *really* sure that's wise?"

"Maybe not," Dugal said with a grin, dropping the leaf and watching it fall to the ground, "but it is something I *need* to do."

Vihaan shrugged. He knew all about doing what you had to no matter how foolish others might think it was.

A few minutes later, Dugal stopped and motioned Vihaan to be silent.

Very slowly, he reached into one of the pockets on the right side of his pack and pulled out a small slingshot and a perfectly round stone.

With great caution, he loaded the slingshot and aimed it at something Vihaan couldn't see in the foliage hanging over the path in front of them.

He fired.

There was a pained squawk and a bird fell into the path in front of them. It twitched a few times, its head at an odd angle, before going still.

"That's a prosy!" Vihaan said.

"A small one." Dugal grinned. "They are curious creatures and can't help themselves when there's something new in their territory. They hide pretty well, but I learned how to spot them when I was just a boy."

"You were allowed in demon-land when you were a child?!"

"My dad ran the village butchery." Dugal smiled at the memory. "He never saw the point of maintaining a captive flock when it was so easy to collect them from the wild."

He retrieved the dead prosy. "Do you know how to process one of these?"

"Yes." Vihaan smiled. "Thanks to an old friend, I do."

"Then by all means." He handed it to Vihaan. "I never did like dealing with the mess."

Vihaan quickly drained, plucked and gutted the carcass, the memory of Konnyr's lessons guiding his movements.

"Wow!" Dugal nodded with approval. "Most of

my father's apprentices couldn't have done it that well!"

"My friend was a cuisinier," Vihaan replied proudly as he held up the offal.

"We're not that hard off yet," Dugal said with a shake of his head.

Vihaan tossed the offal into the woods.

"He must have been a good one," Dugal said. "Dad always said that you could tell the quality of a cuisinier by how well they break down a carcass." He turned his back to Vihaan. "There are clips along the bottom of my pack. Clip the legs into one of the smaller ones and we'll get going. I plan on stopping for breakfast in about ten minutes, so it will be fine there for now."

Vihaan did as instructed and they started walking. The prosy swung back and forth—draining away a few last drops of blood.

"I was nine when Dad first took me out on a hunt," Dugal said over his shoulder. "We went out before dawn. My dad must have taken down a hundred before he saw one easy enough for me."

Vihaan made a noncommittal sound.

"It was the first time I used that slingshot," Dugal continued, excitedly holding his hands up as if holding a slingshot at full extension. "I took my brand-new slingshot in my tiny little hands, pointed it just where Dad said, pulled back on the pouch as hard as I could"—he mimicked the movement with his hands—"and let fly!"

Dugal went silent.

Eventually Vihaan felt obliged to ask, "And?"

"Missed it by a mile!"

He laughed; Vihaan groaned.

~

"We'll camp here for the night," Dugal said, stepping into a small clearing beside the path as the light started to fade. He sniffed the air. "Smells like rain, so we'll need the tent. Do you want to pitch it or would you rather dig the fire pit?"

"Uh... I'm not sure how to do either."

"Haven't you ever gone camping before?"

"A little bit on my way to Deadfall."

"And what did you do at night?"

"Looked for a rumetre or just sat up against a tree."

"But how did you keep warm?"

"My jerkin keeps me pretty warm."

"Fine." Dugal rolled his eyes, smiled, then winked. "Come over here and I'll show you how to pitch a tent."

He pulled a cylindrical bag out of his pack.

"It's primitive, not nearly as nice as a harborage, but much cheaper," he said as he dumped out the bag's contents.

The fabric bundle rolled open to reveal two pieces of string with a loop on each end and a variety of sticks, some short and some long.

"We'll trade off, one on watch and the other in here."

Vihaan looked at the pile and thought about half a dozen humans huddling in a tent on a demonland survival drama he had once watched.

Dugal picked up two sticks, each with a short, blunted spike on one end.

"The supports go together like this." He flipped them so that the spikes were in opposite directions.

One of the sticks had a narrow post on the end, which he fitted into the other one.

He handed the assembled pole and two more of the same sticks to Vihaan, who slotted them together and, at Dugal's gesture, set them aside.

"The crossbar slots together the same way with two ends"—he handed Vihaan two sticks with flat rings on one end, one having a post on the other end —"and two of these." He offered two more sticks with posts on one end.

Vihaan slotted the crossbar together as Dugal shook out the tent itself.

Unlike the one he had seen on his divulgate, this one was tiny and the fabric was transparent.

"Why is it see-through?" Vihaan asked. "Shouldn't it be camouflaged or something?"

"In demon-land you don't want privacy, you want to be able to see if anything is coming for you." Dugal spread an opening at the top of the tent. "The crossbar goes through this sleeve."

Vihaan inserted it until the ring came out the other side.

"Now the supports."

Vihaan picked up the two support poles and handed one to Dugal.

He inserted it into the closest loop. "You hold this side."

Dugal picked up one of the strings and half of the smaller sticks, then walked to the back of the tent, where he attached the second pole.

"Now, keep it vertical and the top tight like this." He pulled his side tight. "Don't catch the tent fabric, but stick the base spike into the ground."

Together they forced the spikes into the hard ground.

"Hold it up while I spike it down and set the straps." He dropped two of the three small sticks and held up the string. "These lines will keep the top up."

Dugal hooked the string onto the top of the support, then, not letting the top of the tent sag, he pulled the string tight and staked it into the ground with the small stick. Next he pulled each corner of his side of the tent taut, slid a spike through an attached loop and pressed it into the ground with his boot.

He moved back to the front of the tent and took hold of the support. "Now you take care of this end."

Vihaan picked up the remaining sticks and string and repeated Dugal's actions. When Dugal nodded, they both stepped back.

"It's rated for two people," Dugal said with a smile. "Two *friendly* people."

Vihaan ignored the comment. "And the fire pit?"

"I'll collect some rocks for the containment ring if you dig a twenty-four-inch bowl in the exact middle of the clearing. Don't dig the center more than four or five inches deep. When you're done, gather some wood. Make sure it's dry and that you get some small, medium and large pieces."

Dugal headed into the forest as Vihaan formed his Hilt into a spade.

He made quick work of the fire pit, then headed into the forest on the opposite side of the clearing from where Dugal had gone.

By the time he had returned with a Hilt-full of wood, Dugal had built a stone ring around the hole with two taller stones leaning against each other on either side. The stones were supporting a long straight stick stuck through the large prosy he had killed shortly after lunch. In the middle of the pit was a small pile of dried leaves, and just outside the ring of stones was a pot full of water.

"Put a few of the smallest sticks in a loose pile over the leaves," Dugal said as he took the spit off the stones and leaned it carefully against his pack. "Hand me a few of the others, not the really big ones, and I'll show you how to build a proper fire."

After depositing the small sticks, Vihaan handed over a bundle of midsized ones.

Dugal stacked the sticks so that they supported each other over the pile of kindling in the middle, then pulled a red stone from his pack.

"Never go into the wilderness without an enkindle!"

He pressed it against the leaves. "Invoke."

The leaves ignited. Soon the small kindling followed, then the leaning pieces of wood.

Dugal set the pot next to the fire, pulled out a packet and emptied it into the pot

"A nice hot broth is the best thing to keep you warm on a damp night like this one." He winked. "Well, the *second*-best thing."

He returned the spit to its position over the fire and applied all of his focus to it, regularly turning it to let the heat cook the entire bird and occasionally requesting specific pieces of wood from the pile to feed the fire. When it was done, he proudly split it in half and handed one half to Vihaan.

They ate. It wasn't nearly as good as Konnyr's prosy roast—lacking any seasoning as it was—but it was filling nonetheless.

"I'll take first watch," Dugal said as he finished his share.

"Thanks," Vihaan said and went to the tent.

He pulled the tent's flap. It hesitated for a moment before separating.

*Just like my jerkin!*

Once inside the tent he struggled out of his jerkin, realizing that he should have removed it before climbing into the small shelter.

Vihaan was just sliding beneath the blanket that Dugal had provided when he noticed through the tent wall that Dugal was watching closely, a look of approval on his face.

"I'm open for some entertainment if you're interested," Dugal said with a confident grin. "I'd be happy to show you what it's like to be with a *real* man, a *human* man."

Vihaan felt just as dirty as he had as a teen when he had begun drawing unwanted leers from older men.

*If only I had my binder!* he thought, not for the first time that day. Aloud he said, "You would lie down with an elf?"

"As I said before, elves have their uses." The flickering firelight cast ugly shadows on Dugal's leer.

Vihaan unconsciously pulled his jerkin over the blanket.

"I've been with several elf girls," Dugal continued confidently, "and *none* of them left disappointed."

"I'm sure none of them left *uncompensated* either."

"In some cases," Dugal acknowledged while running his hands over his hips, "but in others they just couldn't help themselves."

Vihaan rolled his eyes. "Well, sorry to disappoint, but I don't like men, and certainly not *human* men." He put on a disgusted look. "And you're so pale that you look like a corpse to me." He paused as a thought occurred to him. "If that was what you were looking for from me on this trip, we need to go our separate ways in the morning."

"No." Dugal shook his head and leaned back. "I meant it when I said that I needed you to watch my back. I was just hoping for a bit of a bonus. But I need your strength and your Hilt far more than I need entertainment." He shrugged, turned away from the fire, and continued to himself in a tone that he might have thought Vihaan couldn't overhear, "I'll be able to get plenty of red-tip ass after I come home with the head of a demon."

Vihaan grunted in disgust.

*Is this* really *where I should be? Was jail* that *bad?*

A few hours later, a damp and towel-clad Dugal shook the tent to wake Vihaan for his watch.

As soon as Vihaan's eyes opened, Dugal pulled the towel off with a flourish.

Vihaan closed his eyes tightly. "I thought we agreed that you would keep *that* to yourself!"

"I just thought I'd let you gather more *detailed*

information." Dugal flipped the towel over his shoulder. "In case you might want to change your mind."

"I won't," Vihaan said tightly as he awkwardly struggled into his jerkin and aggressively yanked open the flap of the tent. "And if you try to force the issue again, I will turn you into the corpse that your pasty body reminds me of."

"Don't worry," Dugal said, pulling on a clean pair of underwear from his pack, "I need you watching my back. I won't do anything else to encourage you to put a knife into it." He chuckled as he untwisted the waistband. "You can't fault a man for trying."

"I can if he does it again," Vihaan said darkly as he moved over to the fire pit.

"Your loss," Dugal said as he sealed himself into the tent.

Vihaan kept his eyes averted until Dugal started snoring.

When he finally glanced back, he was disgusted to see that the leer was back on Dugal's sleeping face.

Vihaan shuddered at the thought that he might be part of Dugal's lustful dream.

The disgust turned to anger, and he suddenly found himself picturing his Hilt smashing the leer off Dugal's face over and over again.

"I hope my sprit knows what it's doing," he mumbled to himself, shaking the image away and unconsciously rubbing his slightly warm Hilt-cuff.

# PRACTICE

Vihaan awoke to soft sounds of movement nearby. He reflexively flipped his Hilt into his hand as he opened his eyes just enough to look for the source of the sounds.

Dugal was crouched over one of the stones at the edge of the still-smoldering fire pit.

Vihaan's Hilt returned to the underside of his arm, but he kept his eyes open just enough to watch.

On the stone sat a Hilt.

Vihaan hadn't gotten a good look at Dugal's Hilt before but could now see that it was made of copper and, by the heavy green patina, appeared to be rather old.

As he watched, Dugal poured a blue potion onto it and softly said, "Invoke."

Vihaan must have made a noise because Dugal began to turn his head towards him. He quickly closed his eyes.

*It must be a potion-copper Hilt.*

He had assumed, based on the lengths that Dugal had gone through to acquire it, that it was a more permanent type—blood or perhaps even soul like his own.

The realization gave Vihaan pause. According to the history books, potion Hilts were useless against demons. The only recorded kills from the Demon War were from a soul Hilt or a coordinated attack by multiple blood Hilts.

What could he possibly have in his quiver that would make a potion Hilt deadly to a demon?

*Everyone knows that the best way to manage demon-attacks is to minimize the damage,* Vihaan thought. *That's why it's been centuries since anyone's been foolish enough to provoke them.*

But Dugal seemed so sure. Perhaps there had been some private research that Vihaan just hadn't heard about. Some secret weakness that had been discovered.

Vihaan sat up and opened his eyes. The Hilt and potion were gone—as if they had never existed. In their place were two ration bars and a canteen.

"Ready for breakfast?" Dugal said with more brightness than usual.

"Let me rinse off first."

"Need someone to wash your back?"

Vihaan's Hilt snapped out and formed into a large club.

"A joke!" Dugal said quickly. "Just a joke!"

Vihaan released his Hilt, which retracted to neutral and slapped back against his cuff in a single motion, and shouldered his towel.

When he returned, one of the bars was gone. Dugal offered him the remaining one.

"Thanks," Vihaan muttered as he took it and the canteen, which was half-full of stream water.

Dugal smiled and headed back towards the stream that flowed parallel to the path they had been following.

Vihaan took a swig of the water, his finger absently stroking the edulcorate that kept it clean. Reluctantly he opened the ration bar. They reminded him of Konnyr's crackers, nutritious but barely palatable.

Dugal returned with his Hilt in his hand just as Vihaan was washing down the last crumbs.

"Before we break camp, I'd like to get some practice in with this." He tossed up his Hilt and caught it on the way down. "Care to spar with me?"

Vihaan hesitated. "I've never used my Hilt as a weapon."

Dugal gave him an appraising look. "I wasn't sure whether to believe you when you said that before."

Vihaan stood, his Hilt snapping into the palm of his hand. He smiled as the old passages came back to him.

"A Hilt is a tool, more versatile than any other." His Hilt extruded a long post with a flat square plate on the end. Vihaan placed the plate on top of the last few embers of their fire. As the embers sizzled beneath it, the plate grew, its edges digging into the ground as it formed into a large cylinder around the coals. The cylinder rotated 180 degrees before flattening back into a plate. Vihaan pressed the plate down to firm up the disturbed soil. The plate then split into a rake, which he used to spread leaves and other forest debris over the buried fire pit. The Hilt retracted to neutral, then folded away.

The fire pit was nearly invisible.

"I see," Dugal said with a shocked expression. "I never even imagined that a Hilt could do something like that!" He looked at Vihaan with dawning realization on his face. "When you used it to open the locks in the jail, you didn't just stab through the mechanism, did you?"

"No, I picked the lock." It was Vihaan's turn to grin. "If not for the hole in the wall where my Hilt passed through, there would have been no trace of how we got out."

"I do need to get used to using this as a sword," Dugal said, looking thoughtful. "But, if you don't mind, perhaps we can exchange knowledge. Weapons in the morning, tools at night?" He was truly excited now. "You could show me how to pitch camp with my Hilt."

Vihaan looked down at his own Hilt. "I guess that I should learn more about the *secondary* uses of a Hilt. It could come in handy if your demon plan goes awry."

"It won't," Dugal said with complete confidence.

"It doesn't seem like an even trade, though," Vihaan said with a grin. "Perhaps I could show you a few things if you take care of pitching and breaking down camp."

Dugal tossed his Hilt in the air and caught it before responding. "Deal. You weren't really much help last night anyway. Let me just stow the tent and we'll get started."

Once the tent was in its carry bag and the bag back in his pack, Dugal held up his Hilt. It extruded a cylindrical practice blade. "Ready to start?"

Vihaan's Hilt snapped out again and formed a

matching blade. "As ready as I can be without actually knowing what I'm doing."

"To start, just try to block my attacks."

He took an unnaturally slow swing.

Following the gentle nudge of his Hilt, Vihaan moved the practice blade quickly into position to block the blow.

Dugal looked surprised and repeated the attack on the opposite side at twice the speed.

Vihaan obeyed the nudging and blocked again.

Dugal's attacks increased in speed and strength, but Vihaan had little trouble blocking them. Finally he couldn't help himself and he started fighting back, carefully copying Dugal's moves.

"You're a natural," Dugal said, surprised and panting with exertion. "If not for your complete lack of form, I'd say you were lying about never using it as a weapon."

"My Hilt is guiding my actions," Vihaan said as he blocked another blow. "It has never done that as anything other than a shield before."

Dugal's Hilt retracted to neutral. "I've never even *heard* of a Hilt doing that." He held up his own. "This one certainly doesn't guide *me*. If I hadn't spent years studying, I doubt I could have held you off." He watched Vihaan's Hilt retract to neutral. "What kind is that anyway?"

"It's a soul-iron Hilt."

Dugal's surprised look was quickly replaced by one of considerable awe. "I didn't think they made those anymore. At least not anywhere where someone with a conscience like yours could get one."

Vihaan shrugged. "I don't know whether they do or not. This one is kind of a family heirloom."

"Now I know you're lying," Dugal said with a sneer. "How stupid do you think I am? Everyone knows that bonded Hilts die with their wielder."

"It's a long story," Vihaan said, "but, to summarize, I'm the first one who bonded with it."

Dugal grunted, only partially satisfied. "Making off with the family trophy, eh? Your parents must not have been too happy."

"I wouldn't call it a 'family trophy,' but they were certainly not happy about me having it."

"There's more to you than I thought, red..." Dugal paused and made an apologetic gesture. "Sorry, force of habit."

"We should get going," Vihaan replied to hide his annoyance. He retrieved his schoolbag from beside the fire and slung it over his shoulder.

"You're probably right—I'll think up a more advanced training session for the morning." Dugal shouldered his much larger pack, pulled out his lodestar and pointed into the forest. "That way to the mountain."

# WILDERNESS

After two days of travel, Vihaan still found himself awed by the wilds of demon-land and was gawking at a large flower hanging from a tree when his ankle turned unexpectedly beneath him.

He fell hard, barely catching himself before his face struck the ground. His right hand was burning.

"What happened?" Dugal asked, turning back.

"I didn't see that rock," Vihaan said, gesturing to the freshly overturned stone that had interfered with his balance.

"And you cut your hand."

He looked and saw that he had stopped his fall by placing his hand over another, very sharp stone, which was now red with his blood.

"Do you have a healing kit?"

Vihaan shook his head.

"You're *really* not prepared for this, are you?" Dugal rolled his eyes. "Let me get mine."

Dugal fished in his pack and pulled out a healing strap and a white stone.

"Put the prophylaxis right on the wound," he said, handing Vihaan the stone.

Vihaan silently complied, watching as the dirt and blood disappeared. When his hand was clean, he handed it back.

"Now hold this against it for a while."

"Thanks," Vihaan said, pressing the strap's physic talisman against the fresh blood welling up out of his wound. "I think I'm okay to get going."

It was only a few hours after lunch when they came to the edge of a prairie.

"We should make camp here," Dugal said. "I can't see the other side and don't want to get caught out in the open at nightfall."

Per their agreement, Dugal set up camp and Vihaan walked him through digging the fire pit with his Hilt.

After a brief sparring session, which started at first light, they set out into the prairie.

Dugal looked back over his shoulder. "This all used to be forest, you know."

"Really," Vihaan said noncommittally, thinking to himself, *Not* another *story!*

"It's true." Dugal looked forward and spread his arms. "It was the greatest battle of the Demon War in Timor. Thousands of warriors on either side exchanged so much magic that the entire area was leveled."

"Uh-huh."

"And not just leveled," he said, swinging his arms out to encompass the countryside. "*Scorched.* Scorched so badly that experts doubt anything more advanced than grass will *ever* take root here."

"Tell me more," Vihaan said unconvincingly.

He did.

As the day progressed, a stiff wind began to blow, and as afternoon drew towards evening, the sky filled with heavy clouds. When the day finally faded to dusk, they still couldn't see the other side of the prairie.

"Last time I came this way it was deep into the wet season, so I didn't come through here," Dugal said in frustration. "But we're just going to have to keep going. This wind is too much for my tent and I'm none too excited about sleeping out in the open during a rainstorm."

"I have a thought about that." Inspired by the worsening weather, Vihaan had, in between stories, been pondering the issue. "If we work together I think we can make a burrow for the night."

"I don't see how digging a pit will help." Dugal pointed up at the clouds. "It would be a pond by morning."

"Not a pit," Vihaan said, his Hilt snapping into his palm. "A *burrow*." He lifted his Hilt to eye level and stamped on the ground. "The soil is hard-packed and the grass looks to be deeply rooted. If we work together, we can lift it up and make a shelter beneath it."

"A sod house!" Dugal smiled. "You're pretty impressive for a... a man your age."

Vihaan ignored the stumble and formed a wide, thin blade from his Hilt. It extended on a post, then angled down. When the leading edge met the ground, it sank in easily.

"I was right." Vihaan nodded a moment later. "I just felt the tip of my blade cut through the last of the root mass."

He willed his Hilt-blade to bend and extend forward parallel to the surface. The slight rise in the ground caused by the blade was now slightly longer than Dugal was tall. The rise widened until it was just past shoulder width.

"Get your Hilt ready," he said. "When I start lifting this end, I want you to dig out a chamber and pack the displaced soil into supports on either side. Don't worry about digging down if you need to. When the sides are up, we'll dig out another piece of sod to raise the floor far enough that you don't end up drowning in that pond you were picturing."

"Me?" Dugal said. "Does that mean you're staying out in the rain?"

"No," Vihaan laughed. "I'm planning on separate accommodations for the night."

"Got it," Dugal laughed, and he extended a long post from his Hilt, the tip angling parallel to the ground just behind where Vihaan's blade disappeared into the ground.

Vihaan's blade arched upwards, creating an opening, and Dugal shaped a cylindrical chamber beneath the disturbed sod.

"You're getting good with that," Vihaan said as they stepped back to inspect their work.

"Thanks," Dugal said with pride. "I have a great teacher."

"Speaking of teaching," Vihaan said as the first

drop of rain struck the top of his head, "let's switch roles for the next one."

It was raining hard by the time they had the second burrow completed, and they both retreated into the claustrophobic shelters.

After two more days on the prairie, they spent the night on the edge of a forest and, after their usual morning training session, they found a game path and followed it into the woodlands.

They had barely settled into their stride when the foliage at the edge of the path exploded into motion.

His Hilt in his hand, Vihaan looked around for the source. Eventually he caught sight of a small brown six-legged animal fleeing up a tree.

"Was that a dragon?" Vihaan said as his Hilt folded away.

Dugal snorted. "Just a braken."

"A brush dragon!" Vihaan smiled. "I've never seen one in person."

"Well, as you saw, they're skittish, so they don't get too close to civilization." Dugal grinned. "Nothing to worry your pretty little head about."

Vihaan's smile faded. He rested his hand on his Hilt-cuff and gave him a warning look.

Dugal sobered, cleared his throat, then quickly moved past the still-swaying bush.

Vihaan took one last glance into the trees. The little dragon was perched on a branch, watching him intently. He gave it a little wave and moved on.

As they walked, he found his gaze snapping

around to follow every sound and motion on either side of the path, hoping to see another braken or other wildlife.

~

The next morning, just after snuffing out their breakfast fire, Dugal extruded a blade with rounded edges from his Hilt.

"This morning," he said, swinging the blade in front of him, "let's move on to something a bit more realistic."

Vihaan willed his Hilt to create a matching blade.

It felt odd as he made a few practice swings. The blunted blade was so much more aerodynamic than the posts they had been using.

Three hits later, he finally adjusted to the change and was able to hold his own against his far more experienced teacher.

Returning from washing up afterwards, Vihaan found Dugal sitting against a tree, holding a metal clip out in front of him within a beam of sunlight.

Every few seconds, he would change the clip's position and redirect the sunbeam into his eyes. As the light struck, he smiled.

Vihaan's curiosity overwhelmed him. "What *are* you doing?"

Dugal slipped the clip into a pocket, looking embarrassed for a moment, then smiled again. "You caught me fantasizing."

"About what?" Vihaan laughed. "An illuminated whore?"

Dugal joined in the laughter. "Now there's a

thought!" He was quiet for a moment, as if saving the image in his mind. "No, I was imagining a demon-flare."

It took a moment for Vihaan to connect the term to one he knew. "Ah, the death-light. Giving yourself a little preview of success?"

"I've fantasized about it ever since I found out that she killed my parents!" Dugal's grin got wider. "I can't wait to watch the Beast of the Mountain's supernatural spirit flare away!"

"We have to get there first."

Dugal nodded and was still smiling to himself when they headed out for the day.

After another two weeks, the forest began to thin and they could see the head of a valley in the distance.

"Reminds me of home," Vihaan said wistfully, "or at least what used to be home."

"You've never mentioned home before," Dugal said as he came abreast of him.

"I try not to think about it."

Dugal nodded sympathetically. "Yeah, I was like that for a while after I first left."

"Have you been back?"

"Not yet," he said with a shake of his head. "Not until I have justice for my parents."

"We're nearly there."

"Yes, I'm actually starting to look forward to it."

It was late in the day when Dugal guided them into a clearing. "We'll camp here."

He slid out of his pack and pulled a folded paper map from a hidden pocket built into the padding that usually rested against his back.

"This is the map that I got from my source," Dugal said, spreading it out on a large rock.

Vihaan was surprised. "I thought your source gave you the lodestar."

"No, I scouted the area out to make sure it was accurate before setting the lodestar myself." He tapped on a handwritten circle. "There's a symbol carved into what appears to be a door at the back of this cave, which I have identified as Leah's personal rune."

Vihaan tapped on the map. "So, we're about here, then?"

"Exactly there."

Vihaan looked down the valley. "Looks like we can make it by dusk."

"No, we'll start off fresh at dawn."

Vihaan examined the map again. He tapped on

a dark circle marker beside the line of the speedway. "Is this the closest village?"

"That's just Feeb," Dugal said. "Just a little brickbat, I wouldn't bother with it."

Vihaan grinned. "Just trying to figure out where to run to while you're being consumed."

Dugal groaned flamboyantly. "Well, take it from a corpse who has been around for a while—if you do go to Feeb, stay off the speedway. It only works right once a year, immediately after the municipal aerosol carts come through with whatever watered-down recharge potion they have left after finishing with all of the more important routes. I nearly broke a leg after running into a depleted section the last time I came through there."

"What else is around here?"

"Two more minor villages, both several days' walk cross-country." Dugal paused. "And home"— he tapped on where the line of the speedway extended off the edge of his map—"a few exits this way."

"What's it called?" Vihaan asked. "I'll make sure to stop by and let them know about your passing."

"Okay." Dugal started folding the map. "If you're not going to be helpful, I'm going to make something to eat."

He got out his Hilt and started digging a fire pit to prepare an early dinner.

Just as Vihaan was finishing with his dinner, Dugal gestured with his Hilt. "One last sparring session?"

"Why not?"

Their Hilts formed the blunted practice blades

as the pair took their starting stances.

"I'm not holding back anymore," Dugal said. "If you need to stop, just say so."

"I will," Vihaan said, moving his Hilt-blade into position.

Dugal's face went blank and he burst into motion.

Even with his Hilt's guidance, Vihaan could barely block the fierce blows and was forced to retreat nearly to the edge of the clearing.

"You were holding back more than I realized!" Vihaan said.

Dugal responded with a lunge.

As their blades met, Vihaan felt his confidence slipping. Dugal was so much better than he had thought! How could he keep up with him? How could he keep up with anyone?

Vihaan slashed his practice blade towards Dugal's torso, pulling back as he felt his opponent's blade moving to disarm him.

Before he even realized it, his Hilt was pointing towards Dugal's feet and the tip of Dugal's blade was resting lightly against the Rumetre family crest on his jerkin.

Vihaan knocked the blade away and went on the offensive.

They traded blows for a while, then Vihaan's confidence left him entirely when he stumbled over a rock and began to fall.

As his Hilt retracted to neutral, Dugal's in-process stroke caught him hard on the upper arm.

"What happened?" Dugal asked, reaching down to help him up.

Vihaan tried to laugh it off while rubbing his

sore arm. "I guess you were too much for me and I lost focus."

"Well, if we survive this, remind me to tailor your training towards concentration exercises."

Vihaan continued to rub his arm. "For now, why don't you tell me about that move you used earlier—the one that got through my defenses so easily?"

Dugal smiled. "It's a modified helix riposte that I came up with to get back at one of my more aggressive sword masters."

"How does it work?"

"Make a blade," Dugal said while forming his own. "Now hold it like you just finished a lateral slash."

He did, and Dugal slowly brought his blade against Vihaan's.

"You start with a standard helix." He started moving his blade around Vihaan's. "When your opponent recognizes it, they'll make the standard counter. You'll feel them shift their balance back to center and start retracting their blade." He started pushing downward. "When that happens, drop their blade out of position and thrust forward." The tip of his blade stopped just before contact. "Their own defensive move clears the way for your blade to strike."

Vihaan looked down at Dugal's practice blade. "Is it always this effective?"

"It never fails, especially against an arrogant opponent." Dugal swung his own slow lateral slash towards Vihaan. "Now you try."

❧

After breakfast the next morning, just as the sky was beginning to brighten towards dawn, Dugal set his Hilt on the same stone they had used to review his map and gave Vihaan a confident grin.

Still chilled from the morning's cold snap, Vihaan watched him pull a heavily padded bundle from the same pocket where he kept the map. When unwrapped, it revealed a small wax-sealed bottle filled with dark red liquid.

He handed it proudly to Vihaan. "This is what I couldn't get anywhere else but the Deadfall black market." Vihaan swirled it around in the bottle, not really knowing what he was looking at, then handed it back. "It took the majority of my life's savings and, according to the proprietor, four souls to make this bolster potion."

Dugal held up the potion and smiled at the sun through it.

"It only lasts from dawn to dusk, but while it's active, my Hilt will be *much* more powerful than yours." He broke the seal and pulled on an embedded string to remove the stopper. "More than powerful enough to take care of the beast."

He carefully poured the viscous red liquid over his Hilt, pausing occasionally to let the accumulation soak into the copper before adding more.

After a few minutes, he shook out the last drop.

As it landed, he reverently said, "Invoke."

The Hilt glowed bright orange for a moment before returning to normal.

"Now I'm ready." Dugal smiled widely and his eyes gleamed as he lifted his Hilt over his head. "Now it's time to finish this!"

# OBJECTIVE

After a short hike, Dugal stopped at a cave and smiled as he pointed out its arching top. "See how smooth the mouth is? Like it was carved rather than formed naturally."

Vihaan was filled with terror, suddenly realizing that he hadn't been in, or even near, a cave since Gondefle's death.

Dugal looked back at him, a questioning look on his face.

Embarrassed, Vihaan said, "You sure this is it?"

"Absolutely," Dugal said impatiently. "Leah's door is at the back. Now come on, victory is at the tip of my blade!"

Vihaan opened the copper cover on his lucent-band just enough for a thin beam of silvery light to escape. He held it out in front of his chest, then moved into the cave with Dugal following closely behind.

The cave wasn't very deep, and Vihaan stopped in surprise only a few steps in.

Illuminated by the lucent-light was a door—it was wide open and the room behind it was dark.

Vihaan looked nervously at Dugal, who nodded confidently in response and motioned for him to follow before stepping over the threshold.

As Vihaan began to move, there was a scraping noise in the darkness.

Vihaan's Hilt snapped into the palm of his hand and formed a large round shield in front of him. Dugal lifted his own Hilt and formed a blade with a wickedly barbed tip.

Vihaan stepped through the doorway and was reaching over to expose more of his lucent when a calm female voice said, "Illume."

The room brightened to reveal a human-looking woman with red eyes.

Part of a childhood rhyme flashed through Vihaan's mind: *Beware the one with skin-red eyes; where demons gaze, someone dies.*

They had found their prey!

The demon Leah was dressed in a dark blue old-fashioned shirt with voluminous full-length sleeves. The matching trousers fit loosely and had a slit up the front of each calf, nearly to the knee. She was wearing a necklace made up of large unmatched beads, with a similar bracelet on each wrist and a heavy ring on each finger.

Dugal rushed forward and slashed at the demon's torso.

Leah's shirt was torn, but there was no mark on the skin underneath.

Dugal stared, dumbfounded.

"You ruin my vintage handmade shirt with a *potion* Hilt?" Leah laughed derisively, picking at the tear. "You could barely kill *yourself* with that."

"But the bolster..."

Leah barked a laugh. "Let me guess, a potion that makes any Hilt stronger than a soul Hilt?" She continued giggling at Dugal's horrified expression. "And I bet there was a pretty orange glow when you invoked it. Right?"

Dugal opened his mouth to answer her taunts with a challenge, but nothing came out.

She continued mirthfully, "That glow-casting con was old when *I* was a child! I can't believe that fools still fall for it."

The little remaining color drained from Dugal's face and he started shaking.

After a moment, he dropped his Hilt, turned and ran back towards the entrance.

Leah tapped on one of the beads on her necklace and Dugal froze, his panicked eyes locked onto Vihaan's.

Vihaan watched in horror as Dugal's feet snapped together and he rose onto his toes. He squealed in pain as his arms lifted parallel to his shoulders and his entire body bent backwards. He hung there for a few seconds, gasping in pain, until his sides collapsed inwards with a loud crunch.

Dugal gurgled once. His head fell forward, then his body fell bonelessly to the floor.

Vihaan watched him land, the torso twisting unnaturally and the face turning away from him. He tore his eyes away from the sight and focused on the demon, realizing far too late that he should have fled.

The demon was looking back at him with an unreadable expression. "Well, aren't you going to finish your master's quest?" Leah stepped closer and began to study him.

Vihaan was terrified and took a step back towards the door, raising his Hilt in front of him so that she could see it flowing back to neutral.

"I'm not looking for trouble," he said shakily. "I'm just a hired hand, I didn't realize..."

Her eyes glinted as she watched his Hilt shaking with his hand. She gestured towards Vihaan, tapping another bead on her necklace. "What type of Hilt is that?"

Vihaan flinched, expecting a painful death like Dugal's.

The door to the chamber scraped shut behind him.

"Why does it matter?" he asked, still backing away.

"Answer me!"

"I just want to leave!"

Vihaan took another step back, pressing himself against the door.

Leah roared in fury and rushed towards him, grabbing at his Hilt-cuff with her left hand.

Without thinking, Vihaan knocked her hand away. As he did, the Hilt's guard scraped against her skin. The scrape immediately turned black.

"Finally!" Leah cried, her eyes fixed on the black mark on her palm. "A soul Hilt!" She focused greedily on Vihaan.

Leah reached out again and Vihaan knocked her hand away, more forcefully this time.

But instead of letting her hand be pushed aside, Leah shifted so that her palm struck hard against the edge of the Hilt's cross guard. This time the guard slashed her palm wide open. No blood came out but the cut immediately turned black.

The black began to spread across the rest of her palm.

Leah's hand clenched shut around the wound just as the black spread past her palm. She watched as her fist changed color, stopping just above the wrist.

She smiled and poked the petrified hand with a finger from her other hand. It crumbled.

A hand's worth of black dust, as well as five rings, fell into a pile on the floor. Leah watched in fascination as the dust liquefied, spreading out into a puddle while the rings settled down through it onto the floor before the former hand evaporated around them, rising as silvery steam.

"A *strong* soul Hilt!"

She grinned madly and focused back on Vihaan.

Vihaan flinched. "I'm not looking for trouble!" He pressed even harder against the closed door behind him.

"Neither am I," Leah said softly, her expression becoming serene. "I'm looking for release."

She reached out for him again. Vihaan slid sideways along the wall, then took several uncertain steps into the room.

The demon followed and started circling Vihaan. He spun in place so that she couldn't get behind him.

"If not for the cullings, I would have run out of things to live for *centuries* ago."

"This is a misunderstanding." Vihaan forced himself not to look at Dugal's twisted body as he stepped over it to stay out of her reach. "I don't mean you any harm. All I want to do is leave!"

"The only way you're leaving here is *after* I'm dead!"

Vihaan unconsciously formed his Hilt into a shield again.

"Almost." Leah smiled and advanced towards him. "But I need you to use that Hilt as the weapon as it was meant to be!"

*It's not a weapon!* Vihaan thought desperately as he retreated deeper into the room.

She stepped towards him again.

"Please," Vihaan said shakily as he kept his distance, "I've never used this Hilt as a weapon and I don't intend to start now."

"I don't care about your *intentions*! Acuminate!" A jewel in her necklace flared white and the demon's arms morphed into blades, the left one blunted at the tip.

Leah leapt towards Vihaan.

He was able to sidestep the attack, but she struck again and again, her arms blurring with speed.

He let his Hilt guide his defense, barely able to keep from closing his eyes to the inevitable.

A shift in her attack caught him by surprise and her right blade-hand sliced his left shoulder open.

Vihaan reeled from the blow, blood flowing hotly down his arm.

He overcompensated, centering his Hilt-shield in front of his wounded arm as if to ward off the searing pain.

Leah took advantage and sliced open his unprotected right side.

Vihaan retreated. The second wound was much

deeper, and his shield expanded to wrap around him and cover his entire body.

Leah repeatedly pummeled his shield as he continued to retreat. Soon he found himself wedged into a corner of the room. The shield surrounded him almost like a cocoon, flexing inward with every blow, its edges clattering against the stone walls.

Panic filled Vihaan's mind when he saw Dugal's body and the sealed exit on the far side of the room through the gap between the shield and the wall as the shield bounced back from another series of blows.

*I'm not going to die huddled in a corner!*

He gathered his aching body's remaining strength and retracted one side of the shield just enough to leap through the gap.

Leah's blade-arms cut deep gouges in the wall as the shield followed him.

Vihaan's Hilt reshaped itself into a copy of Dugal's barbed blade. He held the blade out in front of him, forced to use both hands to minimize the wavering.

"Please, it doesn't have to be like this!"

"Oh, yes, it does!" Leah shouted as she leapt towards Vihaan. "Obtuse!"

Her arms converted back to flesh—the left hand still missing—and she spread them wide.

She landed, impaled on Vihaan's blade.

There was a hissing sound as the wound started turning black.

"Thank you," Leah whispered, a look of bliss on her face.

The black spread quickly until there was a blinding flash.

Through the afterimages, Vihaan saw Leah's body crumble to dust, leaving behind a motionless translucent gray image of her. Her beaded necklace fell with the dust, landing on Vihaan's blade as he retracted it, sliding down to rest around his wrists. The remainder of her jewelry bounced musically around the room.

Her clothes, now crumpled on the floor, rustled and darkened as the dust that still filled them began to melt.

The gray version of Leah wavered for a moment before brightening to silver.

The silver image, a look of relief still frozen on its face, began flowing like smoke into Vihaan's Hilt.

As the last wisp of Leah's no-longer-immortal form was absorbed into his Hilt, Vihaan released it. It returned to neutral and snapped back against his cuff.

With his vision still filled with afterimages, he slid down to the floor and put his face into his hands.

# SHELTER

Vihaan awoke an unknown time later, Dugal's physic clutched tightly against his chest.

He gingerly checked his wounds. They had both stopped bleeding but were still an angry red, several shades darker than his skin—the pain continued unabated.

After three clumsy failures, he managed to get the physic's strap around his chest, then squealed in pain as he cinched it tight.

The prophylaxis was sitting on the floor beside him. He picked it up and pressed it gently against each wound until the caked blood was gone, then placed it into his jerkin pocket.

Fighting the knowledge that it was still strapped to his twisted remains, Vihaan fished a ration bar and a canteen out of Dugal's pack.

He wolfed down the bar and took a long swig from the canteen before crawling a short distance away and passing out again.

When he awoke again, he choked on the thick air. After retching for several minutes, he realized that Dugal's body had begun to decompose.

His stomach growled insistently despite the odor and its recent heaving.

After examining his wounds, now closed but still rough, puckered and painful, he removed the healing strap and exchanged it with a blanket from the pack and a few ration bars.

After making the bar into a quick, steadying meal, Vihaan moved over to the remains of his companion.

"Sorry," he said as he awkwardly removed Dugal's pack and leaned it against the back wall of the cave.

He rolled Dugal onto his back, arranged him in as peaceful a position as he could, then wrapped him tightly in the blanket.

"I'm sorry you didn't make it home," he said to his companion.

He laughed mockingly at himself.

*Home? I don't even know where you called home!*

Vihaan returned to the pack and dug through it. Only a few full days' worth of rations remained.

*At least the canteens are full*, he thought. *And if I ration, the bars might even last a couple of weeks.*

He looked over at the sealed door, then down at his Hilt.

"I could probably break that down," he said halfheartedly before curling up beside the pack and falling asleep.

~

"I need a plan," Vihaan told himself, as he had every morning since he had awoken almost two weeks before.

He picked up a chunk of ration bar from where it sat on its wrapper beside him and choked it down with the last of his water.

*Leah's silver shape flowing into his Hilt-blade.*

He shivered, rattled by the image and the low temperature of the cave.

"Cold night," Vihaan said as he stood and started pacing the room, "or morning. Not that it matters."

*How long does it take to starve to death? Is it longer than it takes to freeze to death?*

He stuffed his stiff-fingered hands into his jerkin pocket.

As his hands regained sensation, he felt something unfamiliar.

He pulled it out—it was Leah's necklace. He must have shoved it there out of habit.

He held it up in front of him, the beads clanking against his Hilt-cuff.

After her performance in the cave, he knew that at least some of the mismatched beads were actually talismans. He stuffed his left hand into his jerkin pocket to keep it warm as he paced the room, inspecting each bead.

He finally got to the one that she had touched to kill Dugal—he didn't recognize the rune carved into it.

His fingers were getting stiff, so he wrapped the necklace around his left hand and put his right into his jerkin pocket to warm it.

Only one of the other seven beads had a recognizable rune, the one for door.

"I think it's the same one she used," he mumbled to himself as he held the bead in his palm. "Maybe if it closed the door, it could open it too."

He tapped at it with his index finger several times before giving up and putting the necklace back into his pocket and letting his hand warm back up.

Vihaan closed his eyes and resumed his pacing, but he was still shivering despite the activity.

It wasn't long after that when he stumbled and nearly fell.

He opened his eyes and saw that he was standing in front of the door in the back of the cave.

He rested his right shoulder against it as he waited for his light-headedness to pass. Before it did, the door swung open and Vihaan fell through.

A burst of warm air flooded out to greet him.

After a moment to steady himself, Vihaan lifted himself up—and his jaw dropped.

Behind the door was a parlor far plusher than anything he had ever seen—even in the most fabulous divulgate shows. There was a large couch just a few steps away. He rose unsteadily to his feet and stumbled towards it, the door closing unnoticed behind him.

His shivering subsided as the heat began to seep into him.

With a bemused smile, Vihaan dropped into the couch facefirst and slept.

∾

Vihaan awoke with a loud groan, echoed by an equally loud growl from his stomach. He sat up and looked around the parlor.

"If you're going to die," he said to the empty room as he got unsteadily to his feet, "you might as well do it somewhere *nice!*"

The room was as large as his childhood home and had the same two stories. The second story here was marked by a balcony bordered by an ornate half wall. He could see that all of the walls, where they weren't covered with paintings or other hangings, were of unnaturally smooth stone.

Along the right side of the room was a staircase leading up to the balcony.

Directly opposite the door to the cave was another, more ornate one.

He headed slowly towards it, clutching his left hand to his empty stomach.

At the door, he put his right hand against it and pushed. After a brief hesitation, it swung open to reveal a dark corridor.

Vihaan looked into the dark for a moment, wondering whether he should proceed.

*Does it really matter if it's safe or not?*

He stepped through the doorway.

There was a soft scraping noise above him and the corridor filled with bright white light.

He looked up towards the sound to see a panel sliding to a stop beside a lucent embedded into the ceiling.

Several identical panels were opening along the length of the corridor.

Vihaan examined the closest panel and, after squinting to focus his vision, realized that there were three stones embedded in a line along the center of the panel—each with a flattened side that was pressed against the next.

"A *real* catena talisman?!" Vihaan exclaimed as he recognized the three runes as the same ones that had featured in an episode of *The Rajveer Chronicles* where the catena had chained together a descry and a locomotion talisman to automate dropping a boulder to block the entrance of an ancient temple when the descry had sensed that Cal was at the center of the room.

His awe faded to confusion.

*If Leah put that much into the lights, why didn't she have a phylactery to keep out riffraff like me?*

His stomach growled again and pulled him from the contemplation.

There was a door on either side of him. He pushed his way through the one on the right.

The room brightened with the same soft scraping sound from the hallway to reveal a large kitchen.

Vihaan's stomach growled yet again.

He threw open the nearest cabinet. It was filled with cakes and pastries. If his mouth wasn't so dry, he would have drooled.

Vihaan grabbed the closest one, a medium-sized cake, dropped down to the floor and messily ate the entire thing.

His stomach pleasantly full but his mouth painfully dry, he hurried over to the largest sink he had ever seen.

*It's even bigger than the one in Merari's family's restaurant!*

He pulled the lever with the white spiral and put his mouth into the stream from the faucet.

He gulped down the clear, ice-cold water until he began to feel almost normal again.

*Water has never tasted so good!*

He shook his head—both to express his disbelief and to shake off the water dripping down the side of his face—and watched the water stream between the faucet and the drain. Back in Hinter, the water was always lukewarm and tasted like the metal walls of the rain collection cistern beneath the roof of the house.

He turned the water off, then, out of curiosity, pulled the lever with the orange spiral.

The hot water was just as clear as the cold.

"I'll just assume that it tastes the same," he said as he swiped his hand through the column of steaming water.

His needs met and his curiosity awakened, he started opening random cabinets and marveled at the neatly organized contents. Finally he came to the largest cabinet in the room, a full-height one directly opposite the entrance. A burst of cold air greeted him as he pulled open the double doors.

The cold-cabinet was stuffed full of food!

Vihaan squealed when he saw two plump, full-bodied recherché sitting on the second shelf from the top—he grabbed one and examined it closely.

"They're so much fresher than the ones Dad got!" he said in surprise. *No sense letting it go to waste, it'll be rotten by tomorrow.*

As he bit into it, the flavor brought him all the way back to that Double Sync Day when his father had received a big bonus from work and brought home four of the expensive fruit to celebrate. They had already started to shrink in on themselves, well into their twenty-four hours of edibility after being picked, but the flavor had been exquisite.

He wandered around the room as he reduced the fruit to its pit, savoring both the taste and the happy memory, especially the one of Gondefle's smiling juice-covered face.

Vihaan had forgotten just how sweet the recherché were and headed back to the cold-cabinet, where he had seen an old-fashioned jug of milk.

*Ugh, I'll have to admit to Amineh that she was right!* he thought to himself as he reached for the cabinet doors. *They're so much sweeter than the recherché swirl I...*

His thoughts came to a halt as he opened the cabinet—there were two recherché on the shelf.

He grabbed one, closed the cabinet, and opened it again—two recherché.

Vihaan stared into the cabinet in awe. "Leah has a satiety!"

He recalled an episode of *Timor Lore* shown during history class: "The satiety—a unique but un-documented creation of a rogue practitioner," the narrator had said, "predates Demon Rule and is used to maintain the menu of the National Muse-um's café..."

He put the recherché he was holding on top of the two in the cabinet, then closed and reopened the door.

Two recherché.

"If the entire larder is like this," he said, grab-bing the jug of milk, "I'll *never* have to leave!"

He took a long drink of milk, returned the jug,

then started back to the pastry cabinet to see if the cake he had eaten had returned.

His smile evaporated after a few steps as he remembered, "Dugal!"

*How could you forget?!*

Ashamed of himself for getting so caught up in the luxury of Leah's lair that he had forgotten his traveling companion, he rushed back to the cave.

"I'm sorry," he said quietly to the bundle beside the front door. "I truly thought I'd be joining you. I don't know how to get you home, but I do know a place where you can rest. Assuming I can get the door open."

Vihaan examined the door with both hands. As he pushed against it, it swung open with no resistance.

*Inutile, you could have walked out anytime!*

He paused and glared at the open door.

*What if it closes behind me?*

After a moment's pondering, he turned and collected Dugal's pack, which he leaned against the door.

Then, still fuming at his shortsightedness, Vihaan carefully lifted Dugal's body and carried it back to their final campsite.

"I'm sorry I don't have a coffer," he said as he set the body down at the edge of the clearing. "I hope you'll be satisfied with an old-fashioned grave."

His Hilt flipped into his hand and a large spade formed from it.

He worked in silence until the deep oval grave was finished, then stepped back to Dugal's tightly wrapped body and willed his Hilt into a platform beneath it.

With great care, he lifted the body and brought it over to the grave.

"Well, Dugal," Vihaan said awkwardly as he deposited Dugal into the ground, "I avenged your parents."

He paused with tears in his eyes.

"I'm sorry that you never saw your demon-flare!"

He smiled through the tears at the memory of Dugal sitting at the base of that tree.

It had been so much brighter than that polished clip!

As Dugal came to rest at the bottom of the grave, Vihaan saw Gondefle's dead eyes staring at him from that day in the foundry.

"I'm sorry I couldn't save either of you!"

Vihaan wiped his eyes and sobered. "All I can do now is pass you along to the next world"—he thought of his mother's words at Gondefle's funeral—"to your eternal reward.

"May you have peace," he said softly before re-forming his Hilt into a spade and filling his companion's grave.

# PART THREE: THE QUEST

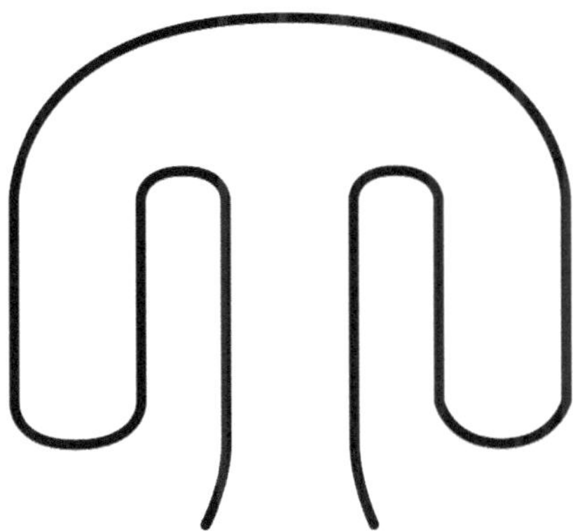

**Rumetre (primary): a tree in the complect family; (colloquial) "the shelter tree," referencing the internal cavity formed beneath the primary branch mat**

# EXPLORATION

*It's time to explore this palace that I'm squatting in,* Vihaan thought as he finished breakfast the morning after Dugal's burial.

He started to get up, then something he had read about in one of his Delphi Press books about the Demon War flashed through his mind.

*No, not squatting.*

He stood and folded his arms across his chest.

"I claim victor's right of ownership on this place and all of its contents," Vihaan said formally before smiling widely. *Now, let's see what wonders await me in my new domain.*

He started with the room across the hall from the kitchen.

*How have I not opened this door before?* he thought. *I've even been in both of the supply closets on the sides of the parlor.*

He threw open the door dramatically—it was a large supply closet filled with a variety of travel gear neatly arranged on shelves along either side.

*With a place like this, who needs to travel?*

He headed to the stairs at the end of the hall but paused on the landing.

*Up or down?* Vihaan nodded to himself. *Let's rise to the occasion.*

He ascended to the second-floor landing, which led to a single door. He closed his eyes as he pushed it open with his Hilt-hand.

He opened his eyes to see another door and a corridor heading off to his right.

*Okay.* He stepped up to the door. *What wonders await?*

The door opened to reveal a small dining room with seating for four. He glanced around the room. The walls were blank except for a mural dominating the wall immediately to his right.

He focused back on the table. It was ornately carved and had a smooth, mildly reflective top with an inlaid trim around the edge. The chair on the mural side was equally ornate, with thickly padded arms and a raised headrest. The other three chairs, one on each remaining side of the table, were smaller; they had similar carvings but lacked armrests or headrests. Each was connected to a leg beneath the table so that they swung out for seating. The backs, which rose only a few inches above the tabletop, curved partway around the round seat and sat with one edge snugly against the table.

Vihaan turned back to the mural and after a moment recognized it as depicting the entire Agee range with large, faceted gems at the peak of each mountain. The seams for four sets of cabinet doors were just visible, the hairline fissures barely interrupting the flow of the mural as they traveled from ankle height to shoulder height.

Vihaan crossed to the far side of the mural and opened the set of doors there.

Behind the left door was a cold-cabinet filled with juices and cold breakfast items; behind the right was a hot-cabinet with a variety of premade breakfasts.

He rearranged a few of the shelves and closed the cabinet doors.

When he reopened them, everything was back in its original position.

"I'll never go hungry here!" he said with a laugh.

He moved over to the next set of cabinets. Inside was more hot/cold storage, this time populated with luncheon fare.

*And I'll never have to cook again!*

The third cabinet was cold on both sides, containing a wide variety of drinks, salads and desserts.

"And for our entrée!" Vihaan declared as he opened the final cabinet.

A breathtaking variety of preprepared dinners filled the hot-cabinet.

Vihaan glanced over at the table and the single seat on each side.

*Even for demons, that's a lot of food for four people.*

He shrugged and left the room, walking down the short corridor until it made a hard left turn.

"Wonders?" he said as he turned the corner.

At the end of the long, featureless corridor he arrived at the balcony around the main parlor.

*Leah must have kept the rest of the wonders on another floor.*

He returned to the stairwell and ascended again.

After a brief pause, Vihaan pushed at the entry to the third floor, his Hilt-cuff clicking against the stone door, which swung back to reveal a lounge.

The style was different from the parlor, and it was filled with a variety of comfortable-looking chairs and short tables. A long corridor with regularly spaced doors extended away on the other side of the room.

"Better," he muttered to himself as he walked over to the corridor, "a little mundane but better."

He stopped at the first door on his right. In the wall beside it was a round indentation. Looking down the hall, he could see that every door had an identical indentation on the side opposite the lounge. He poked at it with his finger, but nothing happened.

With the fingertips of his right hand, Vihaan pushed gently against the door. It resisted for a moment, as if unaccustomed to opening, then swung inward.

It was clearly a guest room, like you could rent in any inn, with a large bed, writing table and separate privy.

He crossed the hall diagonally to the second door down on the left and pushed it open. It was the mirror image of the first.

*Great, a secret inn.* Vihaan shook his head. *I'm the proud owner of a demon vacation spot.*

He headed back to the stairs and ascended another floor.

"I'm betting on demon office space," Vihaan said as he pressed his left hand against the door.

It wouldn't budge.

He put his left shoulder into it, to no better result.

*It was good while it lasted!* Vihaan thought, resting his left cheek against the cold door. *I guess you wouldn't want just anyone barging into your secret office.*

Vihaan braced his right hand against the door to push himself away.

The door swung open.

*Must have been stuck*, he thought as the scent of leather filled his nostrils. "Oh my!"

Behind the door was a library.

It took all of his willpower to step back from the door. "I *will* be back, but I'll bring provisions because I might never leave!"

Vihaan drank in the sight of his own private library and continued to do so after releasing the door and until it closed, blocking his view.

He looked back at the stairs, then at the door again.

*The rest of the place will still be here tomorrow.* He started back towards the door, stopped, shook his head and sighed. *So will the library. One task at a time.*

He ascended the stairs again to find another stuck door. He groaned and pressed his weight against it until his left shoulder ached.

Vihaan was about to give up and try the next floor when a thought occurred to him. He put his right hand against the door and pushed gently.

The door opened easily.

Vihaan looked at his hands. *Who would invoke doors so that they can only be opened by your right hand?* He chuckled to himself. *Maybe Leah's nemesis had just the left!*

Behind the door was a corridor just like the one on the third floor.

*More guest rooms?*

He pushed open the first door with his right forearm, his Hilt-cuff clicking softly against it. It opened to reveal a plain room with a square island in the middle.

"Not a guest room, then."

His mind finally registered the sound of his Hilt-cuff against the door.

*Maybe it's not invoked for a hand after all.*

Vihaan did something he hadn't done willingly in years—removed his Hilt entirely.

He paused for a moment, nearly overcome by memories of being Hilt-less in Deadfall.

*It's only for a moment. I just need to know if I'm right.*

He took a breath, stepped back and watched the door to the not-guest-room close. Next, Vihaan walked a short distance down the corridor and gently placed his Hilt on the floor. He walked back, put his right hand against the door and pushed—it wouldn't budge. He put his right shoulder against it and pushed with all of his might, with the same results.

Vihaan looked over at his Hilt on the floor. "That doesn't make sense."

He put his Hilt back on.

*Leah didn't even have a Hilt.*

"Why would the doors be invoked to open only if there's a Hilt present?"

Suddenly he pictured Leah's silvery form flowing into his Hilt-blade.

Her *soul* had been absorbed into his Hilt.

He felt stupid.

Her lair *did* have a phylactery—and as far as the phylactery was concerned, his Hilt *was* Leah.

The next few floors passed in a blur as Vihaan struggled with the idea that his Hilt had harvested a demon's soul.

He focused on his task again as a door opened to reveal a comfortable sitting room decorated in the same style as the main parlor.

*I guess, if this palace is a vacation spot, this would be where the proprietor goes for some privacy.*

He smiled at a duplicate of the couch he had spent his first night on as he walked to the only door in the room.

*Private bedroom?* Vihaan pushed the door open. *I guess not.*

It was a dining room, just like the one on the third floor, but with only two cabinets and no gems in the mural.

*How many places to eat do demons need?!*

He opened the cabinet on the left. It was cold and had three sections, one for each meal. The one on the right was hot, with the same divisions.

Shaking his head, Vihaan ascended the final flight of stairs.

He pushed open the last door and it exposed a platform with a view of the entire surrounding countryside, currently bathed in the late-afternoon sunlight.

Dazzled by the scenery, he stepped through the

doorway, expecting to feel the cold mountain breeze against his face.

The air was still and just as warm as in the stairwell.

Something out of place caught his eye, and Vihaan looked down in confusion.

In the middle of the platform were a large bed with a low wood-paneled headboard and two stone nightstands, one on either side.

He blinked. Beside each nightstand was a faint rectangular outline rising from the floor, not enough to block his view, but enough to let him know that something was there.

"What are those?" Vihaan said, stepping closer to the one on his left.

He stopped, realizing that there was no wall or door behind him.

He was standing on the top of the mountain!

He turned to look behind him and saw a third rectangular outline right where the entrance had been.

With his right hand, he pushed on the center of the outline. It swung back to reveal the landing behind it.

He stepped through and was surrounded by the stone of the mountain again.

Vihaan pressed his hand firmly against the solid granite of the wall beside the door.

As he stepped back into the room, he slid his hand along the outer wall, through the doorway and onto the inner wall.

He could still feel the smooth, solid stone of the wall but found himself looking past his hand to the countryside again.

The walls were invisible!

Vihaan watched as the landing disappeared behind the door as it swung shut.

"No wonder there's no wind, I'm still inside!"

Amused, he turned back to the bed—it was covered by a plush black quilt.

He sat on the corner and bounced heavily to test the mattress.

"Oh, I am definitely sleeping up here tonight!"

Vihaan reached into his jerkin pocket and pulled out his old tocsin, tossing it onto the nightstand on the left side of the bed before lying on his back.

It was the most comfortable bed he had ever been on!

*I may never leave!*

Luxuriously comfortable for the first time in weeks, Vihaan watched the sun go down.

*CRACK!*

Vihaan awoke with a start.

Rain pounded against the invisible walls of the bedroom, flowing in odd shapes and collecting in eddies and puddles at apparently random locations as it snaked its way down the mountainside.

A flash of lightning filled the room.

Vihaan was out of bed, his Hilt in his hand, running for cover before he realized he was moving.

"Invisible walls!" he shouted before dissolving in laughter.

Still chuckling at himself, he lay back down on the bed and watched the storm rage around him.

# RAPPORT

The light of dawn woke Vihaan the next morning. He threw off the covers and savored the warmth of the morning sun.

*Now that I know there's a phylactery here some-where, it's time to take proper ownership of this place.* He paused. *If I were Leah, I'd want my assemblage somewhere close, somewhere private.*

He looked around.

"Somewhere like an extravagant bedroom that already has conveniently invisible walls!"

He started by running his hands over the invisible outside walls of the room, finding them to be completely smooth and featureless until he reached the first invisible bedside door and pushed it open.

Behind it was a closet filled with clothing in a variety of antiquated styles, all appearing to hang on unsupported bars floating on either side of him.

Vihaan looked down at the unwelcome swell of his breasts, then back at the clothing.

*She* was *a bit smaller than me.*

He sorted through the clothes until he found a

thick sleeveless top. He took it down and pulled at the fabric.

*It feels strong enough.*

He slung the top over his shoulder and continued through the selection. After he found another one just like it in a different color, he returned to the bedroom and tossed them onto the bed.

Vihaan pulled off his tunic and tossed it on top of his jerkin, which had been laid over the nightstand on the far side of the bed the night before. He pulled on the first of the tops.

*It's tight enough but too long.*

He took it off again, formed his Hilt into a long sharp blade, then sliced off the bottom third of the garment.

Vihaan put it on again and smiled.

*Not quite as good as one of Mosegi's binders, but it will do until I can get to Wove.*

He repeated the process with the second shirt.

Comfortable for the first time since Deadfall, he put on his tunic, then his jerkin, and resumed his search with the walls of the closet.

They were just as blank as the walls of the bedroom.

The opposite outline opened to reveal a privy with an oval-shaped black counter hanging in midair and a tall triangular mirror rising from the back of it.

After another fruitless examination of the walls, Vihaan realized that he needed to relieve himself.

He looked down at the privy-launder, then out at the countryside with consternation.

"I looked at this peak from outside," he said to himself firmly. "No one can see me here."

He took off his jerkin—hanging it on a barely visible hook attached to the back of the invisible door—then pulled down his pants and sat atop the privy-launder.

Nothing happened.

*This is just wrong!* he thought, looking out at the countryside.

He closed his eyes and tried to relax. After a few minutes he finally felt relief.

He hurriedly dressed and returned to the bedroom.

He started checking the wall behind the bed and noticed that one of the panels in the low headboard didn't quite match the others.

"Wonders?" he said as he pressed his Hilt-cuff against it.

There was a scraping sound above him as a round section of the invisible ceiling began lowering into the room.

A huge assemblage was sitting on the visible side of a large buoyant platform.

*That's some pine cone,* Vihaan thought with a smile.

Despite the resemblance, the dark brown assemblage was made of stone and, instead of seeds, held talismans nestled atop most of the scales.

As it descended, Vihaan realized that it contained more talismans than he had ever seen gathered in a single place.

*I hope that the phylactery is marked!*

As the platform came to a stop just above the bed, he could see the familiar swirl rune that marked a phylactery on the talisman at the peak of the assemblage.

Vihaan removed it and carried it over to the nightstand on the right side of the bed.

He placed his Hilt against one side of the talisman and his left pointer finger against the other.

Remembering how they did it on the divulgate, he recited, "Invoke, remove all current access and set this new individual as the household primary."

The phylactery pulsed red once, grew warm against his finger, then cooled.

He placed it back into the assemblage, then tapped on the secret panel.

As the assemblage rose back into the ceiling, he removed his Hilt, placed it on the nightstand next to his tocsin, and walked over to the closed door that led to the stairs.

*Let's just make absolutely sure that it worked.*

Vihaan pushed on the door with his left hand and it opened without resistance.

He smiled and retrieved his Hilt.

Now fully in control, Vihaan headed downstairs to see what else his new home contained.

On his way down, he stopped in the kitchen for breakfast.

Unable to help himself, he pulled out the smaller of the two recherché and started munching on it as he walked slowly around the room, glancing into the few cabinets that he hadn't examined the day before.

After his third luxurious bite, Vihaan stopped and nearly dropped the fruit.

*How much blood did it take to create this palace?*

He closed the cabinet he was examining. It had

been stuffed with an infinitely refilling selection of dry foodstuffs.

He felt sick.

*How many souls?!*

He pushed the thought from his mind.

"No one else will be harvested by Leah!" he shouted. "I made sure of that!"

He felt another pang of guilt as he looked up at the lucents in the ceiling—each was the bright white of blood-lucents.

He found himself thinking about the odd but comforting silvery light of his grandfather's lucent and felt a surge of lonesomeness mix in with the guilt.

*Not another drop. But I'll put what's already here to good use.* He looked around. *The only thing missing is companionship.*

Vihaan's mind filled with the thought of Dugal, buried in his unmarked grave in demon-land. Wafaee and his childhood friends, happy that the bad memories he represented were finally gone from Hinter. His parents, probably pretending that he never existed. Finally he saw Gondefle lying lifeless in the foundry.

*Maybe solitude is for the best.*

Scraping the last bit of flesh from the pit of his recherché, Vihaan headed back to the cold-cabinet and retrieved the bottle of milk. Grabbing one of a dozen identical glasses from a nearby cabinet, he filled it and took a sip.

*This would go nicely with some of those pastries!*

With a stack of pastries balanced precariously on his arm, he picked up his milk and headed into the hallway.

Unfortunately he forgot that, unlike his parents' house, the doorways in his new home all had thresholds.

Vihaan stumbled and flung his arms out to steady himself.

The pastries dropped, their flaky crusts bursting and spreading their contents across the floor. The glass shattered against the opposite wall, milk streaking its way down to collect in a puddle on the floor.

*Inutile!*

Vihaan rushed back into the kitchen and to a cabinet filled with neatly stacked cloth napkins and place settings.

He hurriedly grabbed a fistful of napkins and turned back to the hallway.

The hallway was perfectly clean.

He puzzled for a moment, then went back to the cabinet with the glasses. It was full again, so he grabbed two of the largest ones, turned and threw them into the hallway.

They shattered, the broken glass spreading throughout the hallway and past the threshold back into the kitchen.

He went to the door to watch, being careful not to step on any shards on the way.

Nothing happened.

He waited for several minutes before turning back to the counter where he had dropped the napkins. Broken glass crunched under his foot.

As he turned back, napkins grasped in his fist, he saw that the hallway was clean all the way up to the kitchen threshold.

He smiled, dropped the napkins on the floor, and walked into the hallway.

Keeping his eyes forward, he took several steps before turning back.

When he returned, the kitchen was clean—the glass and napkins were gone.

With a smile, he started regathering his breakfast.

*Where should we begin today?* Vihaan thought before popping the last piece of his last pastry into his mouth.

*Well,* he thought as he finished chewing, *I did promise that library that I'd be back!*

Vihaan returned to the fourth-floor landing and stepped into the spacious library. No longer over-whelmed with surprise, he took a closer look at the room.

Directly in line with the door was a free-standing three-quarter-height wall with a large lu-cubrate hanging on it.

Between the door and the lucubrate was a selection of differently sized, heavy wooden tables arranged in a large, loose square. There was a plush straight-backed chair neatly tucked under two sides of each table, one on the inside of the square and the other on the outside.

In the center of the square was a four-sided half-height cabinet with a thick marble top.

On one of the smaller tables, on the right corner near the lucubrate, were six faceted black gems with a large smooth surface on either side.

"Muster talismans?" Vihaan said as he read the rune on the closest one. "Did Leah have *children?*"

He shuddered at the thought of Leah's wild demon-children popping up behind him, looking for revenge.

To distract himself, he took a closer look at the lucubrate. It was much nicer than the ones at school and had a dozen formulae slots along the bottom.

He stepped into the square and pulled open the closest side of the cabinet. It was filled with a selection of baked goods, each plated with a cloth napkin.

Astonished again by the lair's bounty, Vihaan walked over to the head of the closest passage and looked down the stacks.

"Wow!"

It was longer than the parlor was wide.

*Just this aisle could hold more books than the entire Hinter Village Library!*

He walked down the passage for a minute, then plucked out a book at random, glancing excitedly at its cover.

The title on the cover looked like no language that he had ever seen.

Disappointed, he put it back and examined the books around it. He recognized a few of the languages from museum exhibits, but none of them were written in common.

He couldn't read *any* of them.

Vihaan silently cursed the Hinter Consolidated School for not offering language classes like schools in more affluent villages.

He kept moving down the shelves until he reached a cross passage and saw a small desk a few passages over with an open book sitting atop it.

As he approached, he saw that there was a thin silver chain nestled in the gutter of the book.

"Finally!" he shouted when he got close enough and saw that the book was in common.

He quickly shut the book and lifted it up so that he could read the title.

It was gibberish or, to be fair, another language he didn't know.

Disappointed, he flipped through the pages, none of which were readable until he got back to the pages marked by the chain.

He looked closer. The text detailed an experiment to determine whether an animal had a soul that would be compatible with spell casting.

Vihaan was shocked. He had never even heard about animals having souls, let alone that anyone had ever tried to use them to power spell-work.

He sat down and dropped the book back onto the desk. As he did so, something caught his eye.

There was a small green pendant within a silver mount attached to the chain.

He picked it up but couldn't identify the rune carved into it.

As the chain lifted off the paper of the book, the text at that level changed from common to the language found on the rest of the pages.

He lowered it down again and watched the words change back to common.

It was an elucidate talisman!

He pulled the entire thing away and the common writing vanished.

Gripping the chain in his fist, Vihaan stood and smiled, wondering where the history section was.

# TREASURE

After spending a deeply disappointing day in the library—all the books he found were reference works or fiction—Vihaan found himself staring up at the lucents in the ceiling during his next breakfast.

*So much magic!*

He took another bite of his pastry and chewed it thoughtfully.

*So much wealth! But demons can't use species, so they must have something to barter with.*

He remembered the stairway down from the parlor, the one he hadn't yet bothered to descend.

"Inutile!" He slapped himself in the forehead. "*Everyone* knows that the most secure vaults are underground! It probably leads to her own private loot-room! *My* own private loot-room!"

After tossing his breakfast dishes back into the pastry cabinet, he headed to the stairs.

The stairwell at the back of the lair's first floor went down a single level, ending directly across from a padded workout room with a variety of unfamiliar pieces of equipment hanging on the walls.

"Well," he said to himself in disappointment, "if *I* were a demon, I wouldn't keep *my* treasure in a gymnasium!"

He looked down the hallway on either side. On each side he saw a selection of apparently randomly located doors along the wall opposite the landing and single doors at either end.

*If anything leads down to the vaults, it's got to be behind the doors at the end.*

He turned to his right and headed to the end of the corridor.

Behind the door was a stairwell that led him down another level before continuing on.

He smiled as he pushed open the door to the first room in the subbasement. A lucent in the ceiling uncovered automatically and filled it with light.

It wasn't filled with precious metals or jewels, but it was nearly as impressive.

At the back of the room in one corner stood an imposing set of jet-black armor, an unfamiliar rune engraved on each piece. A selection of matching bladed weapons hung on display along the back wall beside it.

The lower two-thirds of the side walls were covered by chests of drawers. The chest drawers varied in size, from small to medium, except for two chests on either side of the very back of the room, which had three large drawers each.

Atop the chests along the right side was a line of displays, each holding a beaded necklace.

*Talisman jewelry for every occasion!*

Vihaan glanced around and caught sight of a

divulgate in a pocket just inside and to the left of the door. He picked it up.

"Invoke."

A picture of the room appeared on the face of the divulgate.

Vihaan tapped on the suit of armor, and the image zoomed in on it. A label appeared along the bottom. "Recondite armor, acquired Banteer-Offis-Peregria/5729-2-2."

*Is that what I think it is?*

He tapped on the description, which changed to read, "Renders the wearer imperceptible to any creature or magic other than a transfix. Deterge installed. Porter pack enclosed."

"Wow! Self-cleaning stealth armor!"

He tapped on the unfamiliar word, transfix.

The screen image spun around to focus on one of the small drawers on the right side of the room. The image drawer opened to reveal a clear talisman labeled, "Transfix, acquired Ingres-Cinch-Timor/8497-1-27."

He tapped again. "Enables the invoker to see through any magical illusion or camouflage."

*This is going to be easier than I thought!*

Vihaan tapped on one of the medium-sized drawers shown on the divulgate.

The image zoomed in on an image of the drawer sliding open. Inside was a small, shallow leather bag with a wide mouth. The loop of a handle stuck out from beneath it and there was a clip attached to one end. Across the front of the bag were three stones poking out from beneath a darker leather strip. Vihaan recognized the phylactery in the middle by its familiar rune, but the other two were unknown.

He tapped on the first one. "Incessant, acquired Wausau-Chippewa-Timor/5722-12-1." Still no wiser, he tapped again. "Infinite, zero-heft, indexed storage."

He hadn't even known such a thing was possible!

He tapped the last stone. "Perdurable, acquired Chary-Acclivity-Timor/6172-3-14."

He didn't need clarification on this one. It made things indestructible!

Rajveer used them all the time to protect precious items that they needed to use as bait to draw the villain out of hiding.

He looked closer at the rune and realized that it was the same one he had seen on the divulgate, just with a few added flourishes.

"That could be handy." Vihaan patted the front of his jerkin. "No more groping around for what I need!"

Vihaan tapped on the image of another drawer.

"Quintessence, acquired Asomatous-Agrestal-Uberus/5702-01-25."

He tapped and a description appeared. "Glows in the presence of a spirit other than the invoker's. Intensity equivalent to proximity or, when in contact, the spirit's strength."

Disinterested, he moved on to another drawer.

"Anneal, acquired Loughlea-Offis-Peregria/5728-13-5."

Vihaan sighed and tapped. "Renders any non-solid item solid."

He laughed again. *Each one more useful than the last.*

He tried another drawer.

"Aegis, acquired Augury-Chippewa-Timor/5723-2-9."

And another.

"Annul, acquired Chary-Acclivity-Timor/6172-3-14."

*A spell-breaker! Another trusty tool from Rajveer's arsenal!*

He tapped another.

"Bulwark, acquired Herm-Acclivity-Timor/5813-12-29."

He tapped on the description. "Projects an impenetrable crystal shield around the wielder or chosen target."

He tapped another drawer. "Traject, acquired Wausau-Chippewa-Timor/5722-12-3."

Vihaan gasped, almost dropping the divulgate as he rushed over to the location of the physical drawer and yanked it open.

Inside was a gold pendant on a chain. The pendant was a fixture holding an unassuming brown stone.

Vihaan picked it up excitedly, put the chain around his neck, pressed his left hand over it, and whispered, "Bedroom."

There were two flashes, first red, then blue, in rapid succession that left him blinking. When his vision cleared, he was standing in the bedroom at the top of the mountain.

"My own *personal* transport talisman!" he shouted. "I'm going to keep this close!"

He put his hand over the talisman, remembering to close his eyes this time, then whispered, "Storeroom."

After the flashes subsided and he had opened his eyes, Vihaan spun around in the storeroom with a giddy grin before forcing himself back to the task at hand.

Reluctantly, he tucked the traject beneath his tunic, where he could feel it against his skin.

"What's next?"

Vihaan dragged his finger across the divulgate. The picture spun to follow it, eventually changing to a picture of the hallway as his finger passed over the doorway. It changed again when he dragged it through the doorway on the other side of the hall.

His jaw dropped.

*The vault!*

He rushed across the hall, pushed into the room, then stood in awe for several minutes.

When he was finally able to tear his eyes away from the bins overflowing with precious metals, gems, and jewelry, Vihaan gazed to the left of the door.

There was another divulgate there.

*Is there one in every room or just down here?*

He crossed the hall again and put the first divulgate away.

Closing his eyes, he pulled out the traject. This time he simply pictured the bedroom.

His giddiness returned when the blue flash faded and he opened his eyes to the bedroom's commanding view.

With determination, he headed to the nightstand where his tocsin sat. The nightstand had a built-in cabinet, which he hadn't thought to open yet.

He pulled it open. The cabinet was filled with nightclothes and there was a divulgate in a pocket attached to the back of the door.

He pulled it out and closed the cabinet.

Out of curiosity, he opened the cabinet again—the pocket was empty.

*So, not everything replenishes.*

"Invoke."

The divulgate vibrated softly but did nothing else.

"Show me an inventory."

A picture of the bedroom appeared.

"Show the inventory as a list of rooms."

The picture faded and was replaced with a list starting with "Main bedroom."

"Re-sort by floor."

The list shuffled. "Main bedroom" was still near the top but now beneath the heading "Peak."

He spent the rest of the day working his way through the list, tapping into each room to view the map.

"An entire sword-fighting ring?!" he said as he tapped the image of a door in the basement.

As with several of the rooms, it took all his willpower not to immediately rush down and check it out in person.

He had reached the list for subbasement three, the lowest level, and there was no response when he tapped on the first room.

*Another room without a map?!*

"Three more?!" he said after the next two rooms

failed to react to his tap. *I guess I'll just have to discover what's in those in the morning.*

The first unmapped room was located behind a hidden doorway in the kitchen that was covered in hooks holding large pots and pans, thoughtfully highlighted on the map.

As he pushed open the no-longer-secret door, a cloud of humid air escaped. He stepped in quickly and closed the door behind him.

The room was filled with raised plant beds, some within their own enclosures. As he looked around at the plants, he realized that he couldn't identify any of them.

"Whatever these are, they look healthy," Vihaan said with awe. "It must be self-managing."

He walked deeper into the room, wishing that he had studied agriculture, until he saw blue leaves veined with silver in the next aisle.

*Pilliate!*

The plant brought back bittersweet memories.

After a few more minutes in the greenhouse and finding nothing else he recognized, Vihaan used his traject to transport himself down to the subbasement where his original exploration had stopped. Having never been to the third subbasement where the other three mapless rooms were clustered, Vihaan was unable to traject there and had to take the stairs the rest of the way.

When he stepped into the first mystery room, Vihaan saw that it was filled with floor-to-ceiling shelves, all of which were packed to the edge with glass bottles. Each bottle was filled with a softly glowing silver substance and had a neat label attached to the front.

He picked up the closest one:

## Stead, Acclivity, Timor/8479-7-15

Vihaan sloshed the substance around in the bottle, marveling at how pretty it was until he remembered a passage from history class.

He dropped the bottle back onto the shelf and leapt backwards, slamming into the shelf on the opposite side of the room. He jumped forward, with marginally more control, horrified as the bottles clanked loudly together.

He stumbled into the hallway, shaking.

They were souls—*bottled* souls!

It was like something out of the worst divulgate horror show!

The passage from his school-issued history book filled his head:

Researcher Pax Salmon proved decisively that end-of-life reaping captured both the soul *and* *spirit* of the donor almost twenty percent of the time. He warned that, with the individual so close to the brink of death, the spirit was often too weak to separate themselves. Since the prevention of even one spirit from ascending to their eternal reward was unacceptable, the practice was forever banned in Timor and all civilized countries.

Vihaan doubted that demons would be too concerned about whether a spirit got its eternal reward or not. It wasn't like a spirit impurity would interfere with their spell-work.

He pictured himself trapped in one of the bottles and fought to keep his breakfast in place.

He lost that fight repeatedly and continued losing the struggle long past the point where there was nothing left to expel.

After the heaving finally began to subside, Vihaan stumbled out onto the landing to let the hallway clear away the mess.

It was nearly two weeks before Vihaan was able to return to the third subbasement, and that was only after he remembered the quintessence listed on the inventory divulgate.

With the talisman clutched tightly in his fist, he braced himself and stepped back into the soul room.

After a steadying breath, he lifted his arm, opening his palm to reveal the glittering gray talisman, and said, "Invoke."

The quintessence glowed faintly, and Vihaan's heart sank.

*There* are *spirits trapped here!*

His stomach churned and he was very thankful that he had decided to skip breakfast.

Vihaan swung his arm back and forth while watching the quintessence's glow—it was brighter towards the left side of the room. It brightened again as he stepped into the center of the room. He lifted the talisman to the level of the top shelf and the glow faded slightly. As he lowered his arm, it increased again. The glow continued to increase until his hand passed the second shelf from the bottom. With a sigh, Vihaan got down on his knees and placed the quintessence on the edge of the second shelf, then slid it to the point where it shone the brightest.

The stone was sitting between two bottles, so he moved them to the floor against the bottom of the shelves along the right wall. He slid the talisman again and left it where it was brightest, then removed the bottles around it. The process was repeated as Vihaan started burrowing into the deep shelf.

Finally, after he removed a bottle labeled "Bantam-Nim-Timor/6145-3-28," the stone's glow faded.

Vihaan picked up the quintessence and held it against the bottle—the glow intensified.

Vihaan reverently carried the trapped spirit down the hall and carefully set it down just past the landing doorway.

The quintessence went dark as he walked away from the bottle. Vihaan closed his fist as his dread intensified but sagged with relief when he opened it as he reached the center of the soul room—there was no reaction from the talisman.

He stuffed the quintessence into the pocket of his jerkin, then went to retrieve the bottle from the landing. The divulgate map had indicated that there was a workroom in the center of the level, so he took the trapped spirit there.

*Do I just pull the stopper?* Vihaan wondered after placing the bottle in the center of the central worktable of the room.

He glanced over at the wall beside the door where a set of heavy work clothes, all marked with the small red X that indicated that they were magic-proof, hung on a selection of hooks.

*Just to be safe*, he thought as he retrieved a pair of gloves and put them on, then hesitated. *Should I really do this?!*

As he waffled, he suddenly imagined himself looking out of the bottle, knowing he was trapped.

*How can I not?*

Vihaan pulled the stopper.

The silver contents burst out as if they had been under pressure.

Vihaan leapt back, nearly dropping the bottle.

The expelled contents hovered above the table and contorted randomly as their color began to shift from silver to gray. Eventually the contortions became more deliberate and the substance took on a bloated humanoid shape. The shape coalesced, and details began to emerge.

*It's a human woman!*

Soon the cloud was gone and a blurred gray woman was floating above the table, canted at an angle as if leaning casually against the back of a chair.

The unseeing eyes on the still-blurry face snapped open and she was suddenly wearing an old-fashioned suit—like what they used to wear for important events.

Her eyes fixed on Vihaan in confusion, and her mouth opened and closed silently.

By this point, her form was slightly translucent but just as distinct as Vihaan's.

She began to croak, then managed to weakly say, "Where?"

At least, that was what Vihaan thought she said

—her accent was odd, the word coming out more like *way*-air.

"We're inside of a mountain just at the edge of Commix County."

Her brow furrowed for a moment—apparently Vihaan's accent was as strange to her as hers was to him.

Finally she said, "Commix?"

"Yes." Vihaan spoke as slowly and clearly as possible. "On the Acclivity side."

"I don't know Commix." Her voice was stronger but still reedy.

Vihaan assumed that "doey-tent nay" meant "don't know" based on the context.

"Commix is the local county."

"Last I remember, I was in Nim County." Vihaan had less difficulty understanding her this time.

"I don't know Nim..." Vihaan remembered the bottle. "But does Bantam mean anything to you?"

"We're in Bantam?"

"No." Vihaan stopped and muttered, "Actually, I don't know where Bantam is, so I can't say for certain."

She gave him a puzzled look.

"Sorry," he said at normal volume, "I don't know."

She nodded, then, realizing that she was looking down at him, settled down to the floor just beside Vihaan.

"Who is in charge?"

Vihaan shrugged. "I guess I am. We're well into demon-land out here."

She jumped back, lifting off the floor again and floating into the table. "You work for demons!"

"No, no!" Vihaan instinctively reached out to reassure her, but his hand passed through her arm and came out ice-cold.

She flinched backwards, staring at her insubstantial arm in surprise.

"That's just what they call the unprotected land between cities and villages," Vihaan said while rubbing warmth back into his own arm. "It's where the demons roam."

The woman looked down, realized that she was floating in the table and moved forward to resume her place beside Vihaan. "How did you hear about Bantam?"

"It was written on the bottle I found you in." He started to hand it to her but, remembering her arm, set it down on the table beside her instead.

She bent down and examined it. A look of sadness crossed her gray face. "I remember... I remember the demons coming at me with a talisman." She swiped her hand through the bottle. "I thought I was dead."

"Your body was, but that talisman must have been a reaper. Your spirit was harvested with your soul and remained with it until I found you."

"How long has it been?"

"I don't know, the bottle only has a location and a serial number. My name is Vihaan Rumetre." He held out his hand for a moment before looking sheepish and retracting it.

"I am Theia Ilham." She looked around. "Is this your laboratory?"

"I guess. It's part of the lair of a demon that I defeated."

Theia floated off the floor again. "Then the rebellion is happening! Then it was all worth it!"

"Wait, are you talking about rebellion against Demon Rule?"

"Yes, what else?" She settled back down. "You're a soldier?" Then, excitedly, "How *is* the war going?"

"The Demon War ended thousands of years ago."

Theia floated up again. This time her form grew less distinct for a moment.

She returned to the floor. "I've been dead for thousands of years?"

"I guess." Vihaan sat down. "Let me give you a quick timeline. The Demon War began in 7 BL..."

"BL?"

"Sorry, Before Liberation."

"It only lasted seven years? I expected it to be longer." She stopped herself. "Wait, you said that you defeated a demon? How many are still around?"

"No one knows," Vihaan said. "We mostly stick to our villages, where we can better protect ourselves from their attacks."

Theia shook her head. "How long exactly has it been since... Liberation?"

"This is the year 2371 After Liberation."

"I think that's all the history that I can take right now." Theia was quiet for a moment. "How did you find me?"

"By accident," Vihaan admitted. "I claimed victor's rights here after the former occupant died and was looking around when I found your bottle."

Theia looked indignant. "They kept me as a trophy?!"

"I don't think so." Vihaan felt a pang of guilt. "I found it in a storeroom."

Theia lifted off the floor. "Was I alone?!"

"You were the only spirit there."

She was furious. "How could you know?!"

"I had a quintessence!" Vihaan fumbled in his pocket, then pulled it out and invoked it. It glowed brightly between them.

She calmed and settled back down to the floor. "I need to see."

"It's just down the hall."

Vihaan paused at the door to the soul room.

"This might be a shock. I, uh, emptied my insides the first time I saw it."

He pushed open the door, held the quintessence out in front of him where she could see its soft glow, then moved to the middle of the room. The talisman grew fainter as he walked in, then brighter again as Theia followed.

"Are these my friends?" Theia asked softly.

The look of horror on Theia's face cut into Vihaan's spirit. "I'm going to destroy all of them!"

"What?!"

"Harvesting souls has been illegal for hundreds of years! Even if no one else is trapped, they're tainted!" His Hilt snapped into his hand and formed into a club. He drew back for a swing.

"Wait!" Theia stepped in front of him, but he was already moving, so she passed right through him.

Vihaan shuddered, releasing his Hilt, which returned to neutral.

"I'm sorry!"

"No." Vihaan was shivering hard. "It's okay. They need to be disposed of safely. It would be disrespectful to just smash them."

"Do they *need* to be disposed of?"

"I can't *use* them!"

Theia tried to calm him with a gesture, making sure not to intersect him again. "You said you killed a demon."

"I said that she impaled herself on my Hilt."

"You didn't... that's not important." Theia's voice was full of emotion. "I was *harvested* by a demon."

"I know, I'm sorry. That's why I *need* to get rid of these!"

"You don't understand. That's why you *can't*!"

Vihaan was shocked into silence.

Theia looked determined. "If it was my soul in one of those bottles and I knew that it had been liberated from the demons who harvested it, I wouldn't want it to be tossed aside *like garbage*! I'd want it used *against* the demons, or at least for something *worthwhile*!"

"Well," Vihaan said, remembering a passage from one of his Delphi Press history books, "technically, it's not illegal to *use* them, just to *harvest* them. Practitioners demanded the loophole when they were passing the law, and it was never repealed."

"There you have it." She crossed her arms and looked around the room.

They were quiet for a while.

"And that talisman tells you that there's no one else trapped here?"

"It does." Vihaan swung the talisman past the shelves on the opposite side of the room from Theia; the soft glow never changed. "It would get brighter if it passed close to another spirit."

"And you've checked the entire room?"

"I have," Vihaan said softly, putting the talisman away. "If you weren't here, it wouldn't be glowing at all."

Theia nodded and they went quiet again—eventually she turned and exited the room. Vihaan followed.

Theia stopped a few steps down the hallway. "What do I do now?" she asked in a plaintive tone.

"You're welcome to stay here with me. There's way more room than I need." He looked appraisingly at her. "Assuming you need room. Or, I suppose, you could go out and explore the world. Find out what's changed while you've been... uh, away."

Theia passed her arm through the wall beside her. "Is there an exterior wall nearby?"

"I think that the stairwell at the end of the hallway is as far as this palace extends, but we're underground."

She put her head into the wall beside her, waited a few moments, then pulled it back out again. "It doesn't seem like that will matter."

Vihaan followed her as she floated down the hall.

"I'm not sure what I'm going to do," Theia said, settling down onto her feet at the end of the hall, "but I want to see the sky."

Theia stepped into the wall and bounced off it.

She floated quickly backwards, passing through a nearby wall and into the room on the other side.

Vihaan followed her in through the doorway. "Are you all right?"

"Yes." Theia ran her hands over her insubstantial body. "I'm not hurt, just surprised."

"I'll bet that Leah has an occlude in her assemblage and that it has the same effect on you as it does on someone trying to traject." Vihaan pulled out his traject. "I'll try to traject outside."

Vihaan focused on the clearing in the valley where he had buried Dugal.

Nothing happened.

"Are you sure that is actually a traject?" Theia asked. "I've never actually seen one outside of pictures in history books."

"Yes, I've used it to move from room to room but never to actually go outside."

They both moved back out into the hallway.

"Perhaps this is a sign that I should stay around for a while," Theia said.

"I certainly wouldn't mind the—" A thrilled expression crossed Vihaan's face. "I just thought of something!"

Vihaan flashed away.

"I guess it *is* a traject," Theia said, surprised that she needed to blink the red light's afterimage out of her eyes.

With a blue flash, Vihaan returned.

"I saw this in the inventory but didn't know how it could be useful." He held up a dark brown talisman. "It's an anneal—it makes things solid."

"Things like ghosts?"

"Only one way to find out." Vihaan bounced the talisman in his hand. "Want to give it a try?"

Theia shrugged. "What's the worst that can happen?"

Vihaan held it out towards her. "Invoke, solidify this ghost."

They looked at each other for a moment.

Theia passed her hand through the wall. "Well, that didn't work."

"Done. Perhaps you have to invoke it," Vihaan said, holding his hand out with the talisman in his palm.

Theia put her finger onto the anneal. "Invoke, make me solid." She pushed her finger into it and repeated herself, then dropped her arm. "Maybe it's a situational talisman?"

Vihaan thought for a second. "What if I toss it into you?"

"Couldn't hurt."

He did.

As soon as the talisman intersected with Theia's form, she turned solid. She was still gray, but when she tapped on the wall, they both heard the contact.

Theia took a few steps. "Ugh, is this what it was always like?"

Vihaan grinned. "I have no way to answer that question."

She hopped in place. "I feel so thick and clumsy."

"Were you more graceful in life?"

"I suppose not," Theia laughed. "I'm not sure I like this. Solid just doesn't feel natural."

"Well, you don't have to stay that way all the time, just when you need to interact on the living plane."

"So, how do I... re-ghostify?"

"Well…" Vihaan rubbed his chin. "Noninvoked talismans usually react to the will of the wielder."

"Okay." Theia willed the stone out of her form. It popped out and fell to the floor. She sighed with relief. "That's *so* much better!"

She bent to pick it up, but her hand passed through it. She thought for a second, then lay down on top of it.

After a moment she got up again, still insubstantial. "No bonding and it looks like it can't be in contact with anything else to work. I can't solidify on my own."

"Well," Vihaan said as he picked up the anneal, "as long we're together I'm happy to help."

"That sounds like another sign."

Vihaan tossed the anneal back at Theia. "Take my hand," he said, extending his left hand while placing his right over the traject. "We'll traject to the antechamber and I'll show you the sky."

Theia took his hand. Vihaan shivered slightly; it was like holding on to an extremely lifelike ice sculpture.

There was a red flash.

Theia looked around in confusion.

Vihaan returned in a flash of blue.

"I guess I can't traject like this." She willed the anneal out again, and Vihaan caught it and put it into his jerkin pocket.

"What if we overlap?" Vihaan said, holding his left hand out again.

Theia extended her arm so that their forearms overlapped.

Vihaan shivered, then disappeared.

"Or perhaps not," Theia said to the empty hallway.

Vihaan reappeared and shrugged. "Perhaps we should just walk to the exit so you can see the sky again."

# DISCIPLINE

Vihaan met back up with his new ghostly companion in the first-floor parlor the next morning.

"So," he said, dropping down on what had become his favorite couch, "did you do any exploring?"

"Only here and the balcony." Theia shrugged. "I spent the night pacing while contemplating what to do with my afterlife."

"I wasn't thinking!" Vihaan slapped himself on the forehead and jumped up from the couch. "You can do what I'm doing!"

"And that is?"

Vihaan smiled. "Follow me."

He led Theia to the third floor and opened the door with a flourish.

"Welcome to my library!"

"Impressive!" Theia said with genuine glee. "I've never seen so many books in my life!"

"Most of them are in languages I've never seen before, but there's an elucidate on the table and I saw another one listed in the inventory."

Vihaan tossed Theia her anneal and, after stepping into its path, she headed into the room with a smile of anticipation.

She turned back to Vihaan, who was still standing on the landing. "Are you coming?"

"No." Vihaan smiled. "I want to start off my day with a little exercise, then some breakfast. I'll be back in a bit."

He started to leave but turned back. "If you find the history section, let me know. All I've found so far are novels and reference and spell books."

"Sure," she replied distractedly.

Vihaan left and, as he had every morning since finding the soul room, headed to the basement sword-fighting ring.

He was still impressed by how much it looked like the professional ones he had seen all of his life on the divulgate.

*Couldn't she have had just one divulgate associated with a news feed?!* Vihaan thought, not for the first time.

Leah might not have cared about the outside world, but Vihaan was starting to wonder if it actually still existed. He occasionally found himself half-convinced that he had died and was now living his eternal reward.

He pushed the thought away and formed the blunted practice blade that Dugal had introduced him to.

Then, picturing one of his earliest sessions with Dugal, he started to move.

"Parry, thrust." The memory-Dugal blocked the memory-Vihaan's thrust and made a slow one of his own. "Block!"

Vihaan closed his eyes as he recreated the moves, wishing that they had had more time together.

As he drilled his blocks for the fourth time, he felt a chill in his Hilt-arm, then heard Theia's voice. "Your block is weak."

Vihaan opened his eyes to see her standing in front of him, her hand held stiff through his forearm like a blade.

"Tighten up your arm so that the blade is steady." She mirrored his position, her hand cupped around an imaginary Hilt. "Your Hilt can guide you, but if you don't use it like an extension of your arm, you will never prevail against a skilled opponent."

Vihaan was so surprised that his Hilt retracted to neutral. "You know how to use a Hilt?"

Theia laughed, thrusting her hand out again so that her fingertips passed through his forehead—triggering a dramatic shiver. "And you're dead. You can't let yourself lose focus."

"How do you...?"

"In life I wielded a soul-iron Hilt."

"Just like mine!" Vihaan looked at his Hilt. "Can you help me use it better?"

"You'd better hope I can." Theia smiled kindly. "How long have you been bonded?"

"Since I was ten."

It was Theia's turn to be shocked. "And you can't even block?!"

"My brother was killed by a different Hilt on the same day. My parents made me promise never to use it offensively."

Theia sobered. "I'm sorry, I didn't realize."

Vihaan smiled weakly. "It's a very bittersweet memory."

"I would imagine so." Theia made a motion as if patting him on the shoulder, being careful not to actually touch him. "So why the change?"

"When Leah, the demon that I fought, attacked, I just froze. I couldn't make myself fight back. She nearly killed me while I was cowering behind a Hilt-shield in the corner!" Vihaan shuddered. "I don't want to be that helpless ever again!"

"Then let's get serious about this." She floated around him, nodding. "We can practice for two hours every day. It should be more—I put in eight hours a day when I was learning—but I'd like to spend my off-hours in your library and was hoping that you could help me catch up on world events during the day. Besides, it's not like we need to worry about attacks in this fortress."

"Palace."

"What?"

"I've decided to call it the Palace."

Theia looked around thoughtfully, then nodded. "I've never been in a palace, but I guess it wouldn't be any nicer than this."

They both laughed.

"How did you know where to find me anyway?"

"Sorry, I was spying on you," Theia answered with a shrug. "When my oddly hospitable benefactor handed me a shiny distraction and wandered off to parts unknown, I got a little nervous."

Vihaan nodded. "I guess that makes sense. I'll try not to be so secretive in the future."

Theia smiled. "If you get my anneal from the

library, I'll make it up to you with one of those practice swords."

Vihaan quickly trajected away. When he returned, he pulled the talisman out of his jerkin and tossed it towards her.

Theia stepped into it, then turned and walked over to the wall to pick out a practice sword.

"I've never seen a cuff like that one before," she said as she turned back. "Are holsters out of fashion here in the future?"

Vihaan started to answer, then stopped—he had never actually thought about how unique his Hilt-cuff was before.

"To be honest," he said after a moment, "I've never seen anyone else wear their Hilt like I do." He rubbed his hand over the cuff. "They took it away from me after my brother died. When they gave it back, it made a loop, then grew into this."

"So it was your own invention."

"More like it just happened."

"Nothing just happens with a Hilt." Theia grinned. "They answer to your will. Every aspect of them is a projection of that." She looked wistful for a moment. "My Hilt changed right after... right after I joined the uprising. It began to look more aggressive. The crossbar even grew vertical spikes after a while." Her expression grew sad. "But that's in the past."

She stepped forward and brandished her practice sword.

"Let's see how much you know."

~

They quickly fell into a routine.

When they weren't training, they were in the library, talking about the world or engrossed in its collection.

"That's not how they taught it in school!" Theia said one afternoon, setting down an old and worn novel.

Vihaan smiled absently, too absorbed in his own novel to reply. Almost all of the fiction presented a society with no unmet needs and plentiful magic—they couldn't decide if that was a reflection of the scribes' reality or their imagination. When Vihaan reached the end of his chapter, he leaned back. "We should be more organized about this."

"I don't know, I'm enjoying the thrill of discovery."

"Me too," Vihaan said, stroking the leather cover of the book in front of him. "Although I would be happier if I could find some history books." He thought for a moment. "I don't want to lose that, but I keep thinking that we should be documenting the world they write about."

"Even if it's not real?"

"We could note the similarities," Vihaan said, leaning forward. "I can't imagine that every scribe would come up with the exact same fantasy world."

"Unless it's a rule of the genre."

Vihaan groaned. "Still..."

Theia laughed. "I agree with you. But if we're going to be formal about it, we need to do the same thing with the reference works."

"What about just the spell books?" Vihaan said. "Neither of us actually understands half of the terms they're using in the rest of them."

"Then we document what we don't know."

"Fine," Vihaan said. "But how about we alternate? After each spell or reference book, we reward ourselves with a novel."

"We should cover one of each before we get a reward."

"Fine." Vihaan winked. "But one more novel after these before we start on the rest."

"Deal." Theia smiled and returned to her book.

Despite a persistent guilt over breaking his admittedly coerced promise to his parents, Vihaan was quickly becoming competent at using his Hilt as a weapon.

He was reveling in his new abilities and moved to block Theia's thrust, but his mood was shattered when the point of her practice blade came to rest against his solar plexus.

"Don't get overconfident."

Vihaan took the opportunity to step out of the ring to get a drink of water from the cold-cabinet in the corner.

Theia followed. "You're a quick study, but you're still prone to losing focus. I *know* you can block an impulsion thrust. Confidence grown into arrogance *will be fatal.*"

"I know, I'm sorry." Vihaan was embarrassed. "I won't let it happen again."

"Good. I think I know something that might help." Theia guided him back to the ring. "It's known as a cleft thrust, and it requires you to split your focus. It's not something that I'd recommend for battle until you have a lot more experience, but if you can learn to do it well enough while sparring, it will help your discipline."

"Show me."

"Okay, hold your blade up against mine." Their blades came together. "Now split your blade just below the point of contact, then use the top half to continue blocking my blade. Now use the lower half to strike out at me."

Vihaan split his Hilt-blade and smiled. "That's almost the same move I use when I'm splitting wood!"

"Of course." Theia nodded. "Many Hilt battle techniques are adopted from the tool's original uses."

*She actually understands!* Vihaan thought as a flush of affection filled him. "Most people today don't understand that Hilts were tools first and weapons later."

"I have a confession to make," Theia said ruefully. "When I was a Hilt-wielder, it was the other way around. I was the one trying to convince people that we could use them to fight back and being told that it was just a tool." Theia looked inward for a moment. "Have you heard of the Musawwir Style?"

Vihaan had to force his mouth shut. "I'm afraid not. Is that what you're teaching me? Wait, did you *invent* these battle techniques?!"

"No, no," Theia said with a hollow look. "My husband did."

"I'm sorry."

"It's okay," she said sadly. "Musawwir died years before I did, so the pain is a familiar one."

Vihaan remembered Gondefle and nodded.

"I hope people are still studying his creations." Theia brightened at the memory of her husband. "He was brilliant, but an introvert. He worked out the how and I brought it to the masses."

"And now to me," Vihaan said. "I'm honored."

"Don't be honored," Theia said, brandishing her practice blade. "Stop leaving your left side undefended!"

# EDIFICATION

Vihaan was looking through a shelf filled with spell books, trying to decide what to read next, when his elucidate translated one of the titles as *Healing Applications of Physical Transformations*.

"Physical transformations?!"

He took the old leather-bound volume down from the shelf and opened it to the table of contents. On the third page, he saw a spell titled "Physique Optimization Spell."

With as much speed as he could justify without risking damage to the book, he flipped to the spell, which was near the back, and inserted his elucidate.

Vihaan nearly dropped the book when he read the introduction:

Physique Optimization Spell

Designed to treat class-8 or higher trauma and restore patient to peak condition.

Requires: Level-3 certified practitioner, one soul (full-volume), 10 hours (assuming a single caster).

Alternate applications: gender confirmation, military conditioning.

*Gender confirmation!*

*Does that mean I could be completely male?* Physically *male?!* Vihaan's mind was spinning.

He skimmed through the spell, finally rewarded for paying attention in spell-work class.

"I could!" he exclaimed before he finished the practitioner's options section.

His elation evaporated.

*One soul.*

The soul room in the basement flashed through his mind.

"Absolutely not!" Vihaan murmured angrily to himself as he put the book back onto the shelf. "That's..."

He suddenly realized that, in the alcove beside the shelf, between the shelf and a large painting of a mountainside, one of the wall panels was discolored.

*Could it be?* Vihaan thought, remembering how he had discovered the assemblage.

He pushed the panel and a large section of the alcove wall, only slightly wider than the painting attached to it, silently slid back, then aside to reveal a room just large enough to contain a wide desk.

"Theia," Vihaan shouted, "I found something!"

As soon as he heard her answer, Vihaan stepped into the room—the desk was against the back wall and there were shelves built into the wall above it. Each was packed with thin, slightly uneven hand-bound books. The ones on the left side of the highest shelf were chipped and faded, each with a single symbol on the spine, while the ones on the right side of the lowest shelf were nearly new, with three stacked symbols.

He looked down at the desktop. An identical book was sitting neatly in the center with two pens beside it. He picked it up just as Theia arrived.

"Oooh, a secret room!"

"And I think these are journals!"

Vihaan held up the journal and opened it to the middle.

It was blank.

He started flipping pages towards the front cover until he arrived at a page partially covered by writing. He set it down on the desk and sat in the chair so that Theia could see the writing over his shoulder.

The page was filled with small, neat and tight text in the same language as most of the books in the library.

Vihaan fished his elucidate from his jerkin pocket and laid it into the journal's gutter:

8528-3-1: Chatter with Olen

Teivel has scheduled the next cull. He has decided that it won't just be Aurora either; it will be a wave through this half of Timor. Apparently, he's in one of his "uppity chattel" moods again. I'm looking forward to it!

"Cull!" Vihaan was outraged. "I've lived in fear of demon-attacks all my life and it's just... just... *wildlife management* to them!"

"Welcome to my world," Theia said, matching his anger. "Why do you think we rebelled?"

Vihaan suddenly pictured Amineh's father in the wilds around Hinter, his team being hunted down one by one—*for sport.*

"If these are really her journals and they're really planning a cu..." He paused. Even in anger, the word was too demeaning to repeat. "A demon-attack, we *have* to stop them!"

"I agree with the sentiment. But *how?*" Theia passed her hand through the desk in front of Vihaan. "I literally can't lay a finger on them, and all of my demon-related intelligence is rather out of date. I wouldn't even know where to start looking for them now!"

"I'll bet it's in here!" Vihaan grabbed another journal from the shelf and clenched it tightly in his hand. "We just need to find it!"

Theia nodded. "Then we need to make this room our focus from now on."

Vihaan relaxed a little and glanced down at the open journal. "But what's with the future date?" His eyes widened. "It looks just like the serial numbers in her inventory."

"Yeah, that date's not the future. It's written in a numbering system from the past," Theia said with a laugh. "She's using the old Zubizarreta calendar. I read about it in one of the banned history books that our scholars translated for the resistance in the early days."

"I've never heard of Zubizarreta."

"I'm not surprised. It was forbidden knowledge in *my* time. We were never sure exactly how old the book was. We only knew that it was ancient and claimed to have been printed in the year 5590. Some of us joked that the translator didn't know how to write the number two, so he put fifty-nine in the middle instead."

"Your bottle was labeled 6145."

"And, if memory serves, I died in 527." Theia floated off the floor as she did the math. "When you decanted me, you said that this was 2371, so I must have been bottled for one thousand eight hundred and forty-four years."

"Longer than that," Vihaan said. "Remember, our calendar dates from the end of the Demon War, which was around 540 in the old, or I guess middle, calendar."

Theia shrugged. "At my age, what's half a millennium anyway."

Vihaan laughed. "You don't look a day over a thousand!"

Theia put on a haughty expression. "I'll have you know that I'm the youngest-looking ghost you'll ever meet!"

"Probably true, even if you are from *before Liberation*," Vihaan continued quickly as Theia feigned offense. "So, to use *my* calendar, you died on 28 Anansin 13 BL. That means that your *ghost-day* is only a few weeks away!"

"We'll have a party." After a moment, Theia's smile turned serious. "Assuming we're not culled."

Vihaan shuddered. "Right, let's get started on these journals."

"If you could get my elucidate and anneal, we can read two at a time."

Vihaan pulled the oldest journal out, opened it to the first entry and laid his elucidate along the gutter. "You can get started with this, I'll be right back."

Theia met him halfway as he returned with her talismans. "Hurry, the first entry is huge and I need to know what happens next!"

Vihaan ran the rest of the way and dropped down roughly in front of the journal. "What does it say?"

"Ugh," Leah said, floating up behind him. "Read it for yourself, just do it quickly!"

5619-7-10

I finally know what happened to me, to my family, and need to write it down, to get it out.

I went to a gathering of other red-eyes and cornered one of the coordinators, a young woman named Rishu, before it started, demanding the truth.

She said it was a spell and that the only surviving caster is a red-eye called Teivel Alvah—I'm going to meet him next week. Apparently he's holding a press conference to tell the world what happened and how he was tricked into casting the spell without knowing the cost. He says that's why it failed and everyone wasn't changed like we were. He also says that our best way forward is together as a single society.

I'm not sure I trust him.

They call it the Split, and Teivel claims that it made us red-eyes immortal—which explains why my suicide failed so spectacularly.

The people they're calling "elves," who

turned red and grew pointy ears—the ones that everyone says were the cause of all this—are apparently just an unexpected side effect.

After the meeting, Rishu pulled me aside and made me promise never to repeat what she told me. When I demanded to know why, she said that there's a rumor that Teivel survived because he betrayed the other practitioners. That, after promising them they would all gain immortality, he used his position as lead to redirect the spell and kill them all.

Vihaan slumped back, stunned. "I'm a *side effect*?!"

"Turn the page!" Theia said anxiously. "No one remembered where the demons came from in my time. I need to know!"

Vihaan didn't acknowledge her. "It *can't* be true."

Theia passed bodily through him; he shook uncontrollably for a moment.

"Sorry," she said forcefully, "but I *need* this!"

Vihaan shook himself out of his consternation and turned the page.

Theia groaned angrily and lifted off the floor. "Elucidate!"

Still shaken, he had left the talisman in the book and had to turn the page back to retrieve it.

Vihaan quickly turned the page and again laid the elucidate in place.

But she doesn't believe that's why everyone died. Her brother is a practitioner and says that, for a spell with global reach, they'd have needed that many souls just to power it.

I believe her. I believe that they knew that half of the population would be killed. THEY KNEW!! It was part of their plan!

They wanted immortality at ANY cost! They didn't care about my family, or that anyone could lose everyone they love!

The man who ruined my life did it to power his greed, and I can't even kill him for it!

I need to find a place to hide this. I doubt that this will be my only entry.

"I can't believe this," Theia said, settling herself back down to the floor.

"*You* can't believe this, I'm just... *chaff*!" Vihaan was lost in the memories of everyone who had ever told him that he was worthless, that he was unnatural. If only they knew that they were *all* unnatural, *all* worthless!

"Vihaan!" Thea passed her hand through his shoulder to get his attention. "You're one of the kindest men I've ever known!"

Vihaan sobbed. "I'm not even that! I'm a fabrication in *every* sense!"

"Stop it! Just stop!" Theia slapped him, her hand passing through his face. He shivered again.

When he finally focused on her, she continued, "You need to break your rut, remember who you are, what you've overcome!"

Vihaan pressed his fists hard against his temples as if it might squeeze the knowledge back out.

After a moment, he dropped his fists and wiped his eyes. "You're right."

They were both silent for a while.

Vihaan looked at Theia again, his face full of sadness. "Sorry, I don't know what came over me." He paused, the sadness moving into anguish. "No, that's a lie. I know *exactly* what came over me. *Every* fear and doubt from my childhood that's been lingering in the back of my mind."

"Let's deal with the journals in the morning," Theia said softly. "For now, we should do some sparring—it will take your mind off this for a while, give you time to process."

Vihaan nodded and they headed down to the practice room. The door to Leah's journal room slid closed behind them.

On the way, Vihaan turned sharply into the kitchen. "One small detour."

Theia followed him into the garden and he led her to the bed of pilliate.

Vihaan gently stroked one of the leaves between two fingers. "When I was a child, I was fascinated by this plant. I always thought it was so pretty, so exotic. One of our neighbors found a pair of seedlings and got rich selling them." He paused, still stroking the leaves. "Having these here makes me happy, like looking at the picture on the back of my old chatter used to." He was quiet again for a moment, his eyes closed, his fingers slowly moving on either side of the waxy leaf. He opened his eyes and looked around. "I wish I knew what the rest of these were. Do you recognize any of them?"

"No," Theia said. "I was never very interested in plants. I'm surprised you never looked it up in one of your divulgates."

"There's no inventory map for this room," Vihaan said sadly.

"Did you ever look for a botany index?"

Vihaan slapped himself on the forehead. "It never even occurred to me!" He laughed at himself. "Enough plant therapy, I'll look up the plants later. Let's get to sparring!"

As soon as Vihaan finished breakfast the next day, he headed to the library to start back in on the journals.

"I realized something while I was waiting for you to get back," Theia announced as he arrived.

"You mean while I *slept*?" he asked with a bemused look. "Like every other living thing?"

"While you were wasting time? Exactly."

Vihaan rolled his eyes. "And your realization was?"

"That we need to move the journals out to the reading area." She pointed to a single journal sitting on her table. "The secrets room is shielded just like the outer walls of the Palace. Once you're gone, I can't get into it."

"I should have added you to the phylactery!" Vihaan said. "I'm sorry, I never even thought of that!"

"Oh, the burden of the deceased." Theia smiled. "We can do it at lunchtime. Nothing worthwhile happens then anyway."

"Okay, fine. We'll take care of it *just before*

lunch." Vihaan reached into his jerkin pocket with both hands. "But I found something in the inventory that will make this much easier."

With a flourish, he pulled out his hands and opened them to reveal a formulae talisman in each.

"Pick one and we'll start moving the journals to the big table."

Theia pointed at one of the formulae. Vihaan set it down on the table next to her anneal, which he picked up and tossed at her. As the talisman flew, he lifted his own formulae to his mouth.

"Invoke, Leah's Journals, Vihaan's Notes, Volume One."

"Volume One?" Theia, now uncomfortably solid, teased as she headed deeper into the library.

Vihaan smiled, sliding the formulae into his jerkin pocket as he followed. "I'm an optimist."

They both took as many of the journals as they could carry from the cramped room.

Just before he reached the big table, Vihaan stumbled over his own feet and dropped his stack, the journals scattering across the floor.

"Inutile!" he shouted at himself. "Now we'll never get them back in order!"

"Oh, my food-addled friend," Theia said, picking up her elucidate. "Let the spirit of experience guide you!"

She picked up one of the volumes and laid the elucidate's chain along the spine. The pair of symbols changed into 33.

"Okay, fine," Vihaan said mockingly. "I yield to the ancient voice of reason!"

Theia laughed. "Let's keep going."

Eventually they had all of the journals spread

out in neat rows, and back in the proper order, on the largest two tables.

Theia picked up the first one and opened it to the second entry. "Let's find out how her meeting with the head demon went."

They read together:

5619-7-18

Met the pustule Teivel today. He claims total innocence, but I'm not convinced. Rishu wasn't there. Neither were any of the others from the first meeting. He surrounds himself with sycophants who look up at him with awe.

He claims that he's no leader, but Olen, who everyone claims IS the leader, seemed quick to defer to his judgment. So, what's the difference?

I've thought about suicide every day since my last entry, even tried it a few more times. I jumped off the roof the day after the last meeting and drank every poisonous liquid in the house yesterday, but today I feel stronger and healthier than I ever have.

All I achieved was to repeatedly demonstrate that immortality is real.

I didn't choose this, but it looks like I'll have to find a way to live with it.

"We should split up again," Theia said. "It would be better if we aren't reading over each other's shoulders."

Vihaan nodded. "Sure, you keep going with this one and I'll start from the modern end. We'll compare notes when we meet in the middle."

"Do you know Grey's timeline format? It will make it easier to compile everything together later."

"Yeah, yeah," Vihaan replied, picking up the newest journal. "Even the food-addled remember our base lessons."

They took up positions at tables on opposite sides of the reading area and got to work.

Several days later, Theia gasped and looked up at Vihaan in shock.

"I think this next entry is about me!"

"Do you want me to read it first?"

"No, I need to know the other side." She beckoned at Vihaan with the same hand that held her elucidate talisman. "But I wouldn't mind if we read this one together."

Vihaan came over to her table and, once she laid her elucidate back down on the journal in front of her, read over her shoulder:

> 6145-4-1: Raid on Bantam
>
> Took out the cell that was giving Teivel so much grief. Passed the leader off to Kadherin but doubt she'll get any more out of him than she got from any of the other cell leaders. Harvested the rest and divided the spoils between us.
>
> Starting to doubt that we'll be able to keep this up. It seems like every time we squash one nest, five more spring up to replace it.

"Well," Theia said glumly, "at least we warranted a few sentences. Plus, now I know for sure that we *were* making them nervous."

"More than nervous, by the sound of it," Vihaan said. "The Demon War started just a few years later. As my favorite history book put it, 'After a decade of clandestine raids, the unseating of the demons finally turned to open warfare and Feracio's long-sought-after liberation was fully achieved a mere seven years later.'"

He grinned at Theia, but she was focused inwards.

"Perhaps we should take a break," Vihaan said. "Some sparring might give you time to process."

She focused on him. "That sounds like some vaguely familiar, and extremely wise, advice."

"Oh, it's nothing, I'm full of great ideas like that."

They laughed together and headed to the basement.

After a few more weeks, they were ready to compare notes.

"We're lucky she was so old-fashioned," Theia said as they settled at the largest table. "If she had put everything in blivet-secured formulae or protected lexicons it would have been lost forever."

"Small favors," Vihaan said over a pastry. "Since you had the beginning, why don't you start?"

"Okay." Theia nodded towards his snack. "It will distract me from that distasteful habit of yours."

"I can eat later if you prefer," Vihaan said, taking a big bite.

She smiled. "No need. As it turns out, she didn't hold the Split against Teivel for long. They were working together by 5701."

"What were they doing?"

"They called it 'cooperation' and told *the mortals* that they were offering the experiences of their extended lives as counsel. But really they were worming their way into the halls of power."

"So Leah was part of the government?"

"No, but it sounds like Teivel and Olen were tight with the local government of the day. He paired her up with another immortal called Kadherin for some special projects."

"The same Kadherin from that entry about you?"

Theia nodded. "The entries are vague at first—'making special potions for Teivel,' 'lending Teivel a hand' and similar comments—but eventually she admits that they were political assassins getting rid of anyone who stood in Teivel's way."

"So, demons haven't changed much over the millennia."

"Not at all," Theia said. "But they stopped pretending after less than a century and took over."

"Demon Rule."

She nodded again. "It took them a decade to establish, but yes. After that, Leah apparently checked out for a while. I guess there's no need for assassins when you can just openly kill your opposition. She moved in here—she claims that it's part of an ancient 'mountain city' called Catechi. And Catechi isn't the only one. They mention one called Bastion as well."

"I wonder," Vihaan said. "The foundry where I

found my Hilt was built into the mountain beside Hinter."

"Probably another one," Theia said.

"Antedil," Vihaan said. "They thought that Hinter was founded on the site of the lost city of Antedil."

"Lost *mountain* city of Antedil?"

"Let's not get distracted."

"Those are the highlights—we can cover the details after you fill in the other half of her story."

Vihaan took a breath. "First, I'm sorry to say that the village where you died was destroyed in a demon-attack in 7147."

Theia shrugged. "Aside from the obvious, I didn't have any attachment to it. It was just a convenient gathering place."

"Apparently it was quite the thorn in Teivel's side."

"I'll mourn it for that at least."

"Other than that, it was mainly cu... attacks." Vihaan shuddered. "So many died."

"Someday we'll bring the fight back to them."

Vihaan brightened. "Why wait?"

"You have a plan that I don't know about?"

"No, but Leah had contact with Teivel and a lot of other demons, or I guess immortals is more correct, all over the world." Vihaan gestured to the library around them. "There has to be *something* here we can use!"

Theia gazed around. "You could be right."

"I *need* to be right," Vihaan said. "I *need* to do something about these... demon-attacks."

"And the last chatter that Leah documented

was talking about a cull," Theia said, missing Vihaan's flinch.

"We'll need to go over the journals again and make sure that we've picked out all of the immortal interactions."

"You're right." Theia nodded. "And if we're really going to try to stop the next cull…"

Vihaan winced again.

This time Theia noticed. "Sorry, the next attack, I think you need to double your practice time."

"If I spend all my time practicing it will take forever to track down the rest of the immortals! I need to be working on a plan."

"A plan won't help if step one ends with you getting killed by a de… immortal who has millennia of hand-to-hand combat experience," Theia said gently, bypassing their usual teasing. "I'll research while you practice, checking in on you from time to time." She thought for a moment. "Even better, you can split your days, practice in the morning and research in the afternoon."

# DOCUMENTATION

*I wonder how many people would give anything to be reading this,* Vihaan thought as he reread one of Leah's journals over lunch.

He started, spilling soup down his chin.

*How many people...*

He stood, quickly wiped off his chin, and pulled out his traject.

In his excitement, however, he lost his grip and the treasured talisman flew across the room.

"I should go back to wearing it!" he growled at himself as he rushed over to scoop it up.

As he appeared in the library, he declared, "We can't keep this to ourselves!"

Theia looked up from her research. "What? Have you decided to open an inn?"

"No, the journals!" Vihaan paused. "And the library too, I suppose."

"Ah," Theia said, putting down her formulae. "I never thought that we would keep the journals secret. Won't we be turning them over to the authorities?"

"I've been thinking about that." Vihaan settled

into his usual seat. "Do you actually think that anyone would believe us?"

"I presumed they would," Theia said with a frown. "But I suppose I'm not really the best judge of the current mindset."

"No one is going to go after a de… an immortal." Vihaan thought of Dugal. "No authorities at least."

"So, we'll have to handle it ourselves. We could build a new resistance."

Vihaan shook his head. "I doubt we have time for that."

Theia was still frowning, a thoughtful look on her gray face. "And just getting the information out there wouldn't do any good—they'd just relocate and change targets."

Vihaan sighed. "I've been going over this a lot and I don't see any other alternative. We've got to deal with the threat, stop the culling."

Theia's eyes widened. "Us?"

"Who else?"

"What about…?"

After Theia's silence went on for a few moments, Vihaan nodded. "Yeah, I couldn't think of anyone else either," he sighed. "All my life I was told that members of my family should do what's right no matter what." He shut his eyes for a moment. "Although my parents never lived up to that with me and I've been disconnected from the Rumetre lineage—that instinct is still there. Believe me, coming face-to-face with another immortal is the last thing I want to do. But there *is* no one else who can do it and it *is* the right thing to do.

"But I know I can't do it alone and you're the one here who's actually a fighter."

"I never fought alone."

"You'll have me, and there's an arsenal in the basement."

"Will that be enough against an immortal?"

"Maybe not," Vihaan said with a shrug, "but it's all I can offer."

"Did you have some kind of plan or is this all theoretical?"

"I remember reading about the Demon War. My Delphi Press books said that they can be killed by soul Hilts. If we can find Teivel and confront him when he's not expecting it"—Vihaan patted his cuff—"I can threaten him with this while you catch him in a bulwark."

"And you have such a talisman?"

"It's in the inventory."

Theia sighed. "I suppose it could work."

"But"—Vihaan made a sweeping gesture encompassing the library and the notes from Theia's formulae that were currently displayed on the lucubrate—"if we go after Teivel and lose, no one would be able to access any of this! The world would never learn the truth about immortals!"

"I suppose that's true." Theia looked thoughtful. "I'm hoping that you bring it up because you have a solution rather than just as a casual observation."

"I do, I think." Vihaan bristled with excitement. "Do you have any writing experience?"

"I can't say that I have."

"That's what I was afraid of. I dreamed about becoming a scribe when I was a kid but never actually did anything about it. The closest I got was writing reports for school." Vihaan was crestfallen.

"And we can't just drop the journals off somewhere —no one would ever read them. It needs to be summarized, made digestible."

"Don't give up just yet." Theia smiled. "I did have to collate reports now and again when I was a government lackey. And, considering your age, you can't be too out of practice from school. I doubt writing a book is *that* much different."

Vihaan brightened. "Okay, then, where do we start?"

"We should start by listing what we hope readers will learn."

"Like I said, I want everyone to know the truth about these so-called demons." Vihaan leaned back. "And I think that would be easier if we could show them a clear timeline of everything that Leah experienced, especially those events that have been hidden from history."

"Good, then let's consolidate our notes. Do you have more formulae that we can use?"

"Sure." Vihaan pictured the formulae drawer in his head. "There were dozens there last time I checked."

"Get four more," Theia said. "I'll start putting together what I remember of Demon Rule history, you can fill one with post-Liberation history, and we'll consolidate that with what we've already gathered from Leah's journals."

Theia closed her eyes as she saw Vihaan reach for his traject, but her ethereal eyelids weren't enough to block out the red flash. She kept them closed until the blue flash marked his return.

"Okay," Theia said as she took the blank formulae from Vihaan. "We need to make sure we're both using the same index categories. I assume that we're already tagging everything by date."

"Of course." Vihaan rolled his eyes theatrically. "Even in Hinter they taught basic research!"

"Fine, then let's mark important events as 'pivotal' and anything that's no longer in the history books as 'suppressed.'"

They spent the rest of the day transferring relevant entries between formulae, then summarizing all of the major historical events that they could think of.

The next morning, they started back in on the journals.

Vihaan took his to Leah's secret room, enjoying being closely surrounded by books and the fact that he didn't have to listen to Theia dictating into her formulae.

"That's the third time Rishu has been at that same location!" He lifted his formulae again. "Mark this one 'immortal identifiers' and tag the location. Find all other entries for Rishu, mark those 'immortal identifiers' and tag the location as well."

He continued on to the next entry but stopped when he read:

Cozbi has successfully embedded in Luaidhe.

"Wait, what?" He lowered his formulae. "Nothing good can come from a demon-agent in the capital of Peregria."

*Cozbi, I know I've read that name before.*

Vihaan thought for a moment.

"She's an immortal!" He lifted his formulae.

"Edit last entry. Categorize as 'plants' and log the location."

"I can't believe that we're actually finished!" Vihaan said as he laid his second formulae in the fourth slot at the base of the library lucubrate.

"It was a long three weeks," Theia said. "Invoke, display consolidated timeline."

Four bars appeared on the lucubrate. One was colored blue, the next orange, the third green, and the fourth red. They shifted into a line across the width of the display, the blue and green overlapping each other only slightly while the other two colors spanned the entire width.

After a moment, the bars merged together into a single black line with a variety of different-colored ticks protruding from the top. Approximately dated items floated above the main line, each with its own blue line spanning its potential date range.

The display quickly became unreadable as the labels overlapped.

"Only display events marked pivotal or suppressed," Theia said.

Any tick not in red or orange faded.

Vihaan looked at it in awe. "All of Feracio's history!"

"Well, as much as we've gathered so far," Theia replied. "It has certainly given me more context to understand the entries."

"It gave me more than just context." Vihaan grinned and addressed the lucubrate. "Display supplemental timeline, populate with entries marked immortal identifiers."

A red line appeared above the black one. Each tick had a rune above it. There were larger green ticks, one for each rune, at the right end of the line. Beneath each of these green runes was a place name.

Theia gaped at it. "Are those *current* locations?"

Vihaan nodded. "As current as I could find."

"Why didn't you tell me about this?"

"I didn't know what I had at first." Vihaan shrugged. "I didn't think that they'd stick around anywhere long enough for it to matter, but I couldn't have been more wrong. Except for Teivel, it looks like the immortals that call the shots haven't moved in *centuries*."

"We can *really* do this!"

"There's more," Vihaan said. "Display supplemental timeline, populate with entries marked plants."

A blue line appeared above the red one with names of people and places and green ticks at the right end of the line.

"Immortals living among us." Vihaan tapped on the timeline. It expanded to cover the entire lucubrate. "I picked out every reference to them influencing events."

"We need to let people know!"

"It'll be in the book," Vihaan said, confused.

"That's not enough!" Theia shook her head and turned to the lucubrate. "Display entries marked as plants in list format with most recent location." She tapped on the list as it appeared. "We need to include them *just like this*! A timeline won't work, but seeing all of those names and places together will have an impact. We need to make it obvious that they're everywhere!"

"I get it." Vihaan nodded. "We can put it right up front!"

"No." Theia shook her head. "They need to understand the threat first. Maybe it should be the first appendix."

"And, once everyone knows who and where they are"—Vihaan grinned evilly—"their secret influence ends!"

"Now all we need is the actual book."

The mountain breeze was refreshingly cool against Vihaan's bare chest as he looked down at the Catechi Valley below him.

He moved on, hiking along the peaks back towards the one that contained the Palace.

As he walked, he absently ran his fingers through his chest hair and smiled in contentment.

He tilted his head to the sky and yelled, "I can't remember the last time I was this happy!"

"That's because you're finally being *who you are*," Gondefle said from beside him.

Vihaan sat up in bed, his hand shooting up to his chest, to his breasts.

He frowned and lay back down.

*Healing Applications of Physical Transformations.*

He rolled over onto his side and shifted his weight a few times until he was comfortable again.

The cover had been shiny, well-worn leather.

He rolled over onto his other side.

The spell *would work.*

He rolled onto his back.

*But it would require a soul!*

He could almost feel the book's leather cover in his hands.

He put his hands over his face for a moment and groaned, "I'm fine as I am!"

*I'd want it used against the demons, or at least for something worthwhile!*

Theia's voice echoed in his head.

"This is *not* what she meant!"

Vihaan sat up again.

"I will not waste a soul on vanity!"

*It hurt like demon-fire, but it was such a relief!*

Konnyr's words joined Theia's in the echo chamber of his conflicted mind.

He cupped his right breast in his hand.

A movement on his arm illuminated by starlight caught his eye.

The Rumetre family crest on his Hilt-cuff was fading away!

The disk was blank for a moment, then a sharp angular rune replaced it.

*Mount.*

Vihaan traced the symbol, running a finger up the lower side peak, through the highest central peak, them back down the other side peak.

*I need to talk to Theia.*

Vihaan showered and dressed in half the normal time and, after a quick traject to the storage subbasement to grab an ersatz talisman, he appeared in the spells section of the library.

*Healing Applications of Physical Transformations* was right where he had left it that fateful day, not quite fully flush with the volumes around it.

He took the book down and opened it to

the last section, then, using his elucidate to translate, flipped through the pages until he came to the entry titled "Physique Optimization Spell."

Gingerly he put the book on the floor in the center of a pool of light from one of the room's lucents. After making sure the elucidate was still translating all of the visible text, he pulled out the ersatz.

"Invoke, multiple captures."

He held it over the book so that the square marker of light that projected from the bottom of the talisman illuminated the first page of the spell. "Capture."

The light flashed off and on again.

He used the ersatz to capture all seven translated pages of the spell.

"Done!" he said softly, excitement filling his chest.

He pocketed the elucidate and ersatz, then returned the book to its place on the shelf.

He closed his eyes and traced the embossed text on the book's spine.

Vihaan lowered his hand, opened his eyes, and headed to the reading area.

"Sneaking up on me?" Theia asked when he appeared from the stacks and started towards the lucubrate.

Vihaan just smiled and rested the small end of the ersatz into the first unoccupied formulae slot. "Invoke, display captures."

"What's with you this morning?" Theia asked with a bemused expression.

"I need to talk to you about something," Vihaan

said as the pictures of the spell started appearing on the lucubrate.

"Is it about that new rune on your wrist?"

"Partly." Vihaan tapped on the first picture, which expanded to fill the front of the lucubrate.

"Do you know what this does?" he asked, stepping aside so that she could read it.

"I don't know much about spell-work."

Vihaan looked at the lucubrate, then sheepishly said, "Sorry, I forgot to capture the description page."

"So, what *does* it do?"

"It's a physical transformation spell. If properly applied, it would make my body just as male as my spirit."

"I never realized that you were unhappy," Theia said in surprise.

"Unhappy is probably the wrong word," Vihaan replied. "I feel more... *mismatched.*"

"Well," Theia said with a reassuring smile, "I'm on your side. If this is what you need, you have my full support. But I'm no more of a practitioner than you are."

"Thanks." Vihaan smiled. "But according to the introduction, it will take hours, and I will have to be unconscious the entire time."

Theia nodded. "You want me to bring you to the practitioner's and keep an eye on you. Right?"

"Right."

"Do you already have one in mind?"

"I do." Vihaan grew uncomfortable. "But first I need to talk to you about some of the other details..."

Theia looked at him with concern. "I've never

seen you this worried—are you sure you're ready to do this?"

"I'm ready. But"—Vihaan paused to collect himself—"this spell is too powerful for blood magic."

"Ah." Theia nodded in understanding. "You need one of the souls."

"It feels so selfish…"

"I meant what I said the day we met," Theia said gently. "If my soul was in that room, I would want you to use it for something worthwhile instead of storing it away forever." She smiled. "Especially if you could find a way to use it against the demons that killed me. And I can't think of a better way to do that than to help the man who's going to renew the fight with them."

"Really?" Vihaan said nervously.

"Don't make me repeat myself!"

"Thanks." Vihaan smiled. "But there's more. A dear friend of mine lives in Wove. I'd like to use another one so that she can undergo an alignment as well."

"An altruistic use," she continued in a formal tone. "I approve."

"I still feel awkward about it." Vihaan took a deep breath. "But this is something I've wanted since I realized I was a man, and I know it would mean just as much to Amineh."

"Stop, it's okay." Theia patted him on the shoulder. With her anneal active, it was like being tapped by a flexible piece of ice. "What about the practitioner?"

"When I was growing up in Hinter, anyone

deemed indecent was *persuaded* to move further out-loop to a village called Wove."

"Isn't that where your friend is?"

"Yes." Vihaan nodded. "But being partite is just one of a long list of things they considered indecent. People like my parents thought of Wove as a community so depraved that they would accept anyone. And, being so far from Akin, it drew outcasts from all over the area, especially those who couldn't play by the rules.

"I remember hearing stories about one practitioner from Akin who embarrassed the more established members of her cohort one too many times and got herself banished. She ended up in Wove."

"And do you think she'd cast it?"

"I think she would." Vihaan thought back to Hinter. "I was hearing new stories about her right up until I was sent away. She ran a place called Homestyle Potions and Talismans and was known to help people when they needed it."

"Do you have enough units to pay for work like this?"

"Not necessary! Most rule-breaking work is done under the table," Vihaan laughed. "At least that's how the stories go. There's an entire treasure room downstairs that we could use to barter for the service."

"I suspect that a soul would take care of the fee and be easier to carry."

"I would feel more comfortable using the treasure."

"Use the soul," Theia said firmly. "I suspect that you're going to have trouble convincing her to do something like this, no matter how helpful people say she is. A soul would be far more persuasive than treasure to a practitioner, especially a well-established one."

"I hadn't thought about it like that," Vihaan said. "But I'll bring some treasure along as a backup."

"Well, you'll be the one lugging it around, so do what you want."

"Ah." Vihaan smiled. "But I won't have to *lug* anything!" He got up and collected the divulgate from beside the door. "Show me the incessant bag."

An image of it appeared on the screen, and he set the divulgate down in front of Theia with a flourish.

"My new travel bag! There's an aggrandize bag down there too. I was planning to fill that with as much treasure as it can hold and store it, and anything else I might need, in my travel bag."

"Looks like you have everything figured out," Theia said with a laugh. "When do we start packing?"

# REEMERGENCE

Vihaan trajected down to the first subbasement immediately after breakfast the next day to collect his travel bag.

He reverently picked it up and placed his finger over the phylactery embedded on the front.

"Invoke, remove any current access and set this new individual as primary."

The talisman flashed red and Vihaan smiled.

*And I thought my jerkin pocket was convenient! Now I can carry literally everything!*

Vihaan happily transferred the contents of his jerkin pocket into the infinite storage bag one at a time.

After a few items, Vihaan pictured his grandfather's lucent as he reached his hand into the mouth of the bag. The lucent pressed into his palm.

"No more fishing around to find what I need!" he said happily as he released the lucent back into the bag.

He went to a nearby drawer and transferred an aggrandize bag, a limited version of the incessant, from it into his travel bag.

"Now for treasure!" Vihaan said as he trajected down to the treasure room.

He started loading treasure into the aggrandize bag one item at a time, alternating between gems and jewelry.

By lunchtime he had barely made a dent in the supply and the bag showed no signs of being full.

*That should be enough.*

He laughed at himself. The bag contained more wealth than he had ever imagined *existed*, let alone dreamed of having at his disposal!

He was about to traject up to the kitchen when he stopped himself.

*Just get it over with.*

Vihaan disappeared.

He reappeared outside the soul room and paused for a long moment before opening the door. When he did, he reached in and quickly grabbed three souls from the closest shelf before letting the door close again.

*One for me, one for Amineh, and one for the practitioner.*

He stuffed them into his travel bag, then disappeared.

He spent the rest of the afternoon trajecting around the Palace with one of the inventory divulgates in his hands, collecting anything and everything that he thought might be useful.

Finally satisfied, he invited Theia into the dining room to plan out their trip, but not before he set out a big going-away feast for himself.

∽

They had arranged to leave from the parlor the next morning.

When Vihaan arrived, he saw that Theia had brought her bottle up from the subbasement and placed it on one of the tables closest to the door. A clip had been attached to the mouth of the bottle with a leather strap. Her anneal was on the same table, dangerously close to the edge.

"Are we bringing that with us?"

"*We* aren't," Theia answered with a grin. "I realized while you were wasting the night away that people might get awkward if confronted with a ghost."

"You're right," Vihaan said with embarrassment, "I'm so accustomed to you that I never even considered how other people might react."

"I thought about how you were able to carry me around when I was in the bottle and began to wonder if that might be a solution to our trajecting problem." Theia floated over beside the table. "And after some experimenting, I discovered that I could do this."

Theia floated up into the air, then dove down at the bottle, her form compressed so that it passed easily through the bottle's mouth.

Almost immediately she flowed out of it again and reformed back in her original position.

"It's comfortable enough," she said to Vihaan's gaping look of surprise, "and if this works, I won't have to stay solid or need to *walk*." She said the last word with an exaggerated shudder.

Vihaan composed himself. "And you'll be okay in there?"

"It's better than the alternative." She smiled.

"And there's only one way to find out." Theia dove back into her bottle.

Vihaan picked it up, collected her anneal and willed himself into the dining room. "Still there?"

"Still here!" Theia replied from within the bottle.

"This will certainly make getting home easier!" Vihaan said as he trajected back to the antechamber. Then he walked out of the vestibule, clipped the bottle to his waistband and headed for Wove.

~

"Why are you stopping?" Theia asked from her bottle less than twenty minutes later. "We just got started!"

"I haven't been doing any cross-country walking while living in the Palace," Vihaan answered as he pulled off one of his boots and started rubbing his left foot. "I didn't realize just how worn out these boots had gotten."

"I had hoped that you'd changed your mind about trajecting."

"You know that I've never actually been to Wove," Vihaan said as he pulled a better pair of boots out of his travel bag one at a time; they barely fit through the mouth of the bag. "I'd have to traject to Hinter, then take the speedway. I'm not ready to face my old home just yet, not when I'm so close to actually having a body that matches my spirit-gender."

He took off his right boot and immediately started replacing it with one of the new ones. He winced partway through as he accidentally put his weight on his left foot for balance. He started rubbing his aching foot again.

"I guess I understand." Theia thought for a moment. "Perhaps, while we travel, we should focus on moving battle drills to keep your feet in motion."

Vihaan pulled on the second of the new boots with another wince. "I don't think that keeping my feet in motion will be a problem."

He stood and took a few test steps.

"Tolerable." He bent over to tighten his bootstraps a little more. "I should be fine until lunch if I keep it slow."

Vihaan sighed as he looked through the arch of the Wove speedway exit for the first time.

"We were supposed to do this together."

"What?" Theia's voice brought him out of his reverie. "I didn't think you needed me until we got to the practitioner's."

"Sorry," Vihaan said with a gentle tap on the bottle, "I was talking to myself. I once made a promise to Amineh that we would come here together after graduation."

"You could still see her."

"No," Vihaan said sadly. "I wouldn't be able to keep our plan from her and she'd insist on coming along. I won't put her life in jeopardy."

"I still think that's a mistake, but it's yours to make."

Vihaan sighed again, then finally walked into the village of Wove.

As Vihaan turned the corner into the main square of Wove Village Centre, his eyes landed on the trademark yellow consociate hub pillar that marked every branch of Chatter Warehouse. From where he stood, it had a green tint due to the number of blue consociate talismans that studded the path-facing side.

"First stop," Vihaan said quietly to himself, "a connection store to reengage with the world."

A representative greeted him before the bell above the door finished vibrating.

"Hello, my name is Biffie," she said with a smile, her hands stuffed into the front pocket of her worker jumpsuit. "How can we connect you today?"

"Vihaan Mount," he replied, the name feeling *so* right. "But first, do you barter?"

"We take all forms of payment at this location." She winked. "In Wove, you have to."

Vihaan pulled a small gem out of his travel bag and held it up. "Will this cover a chatter and divulgate?"

"And then some," she said, holding out her hand. "I'll take this to my manager and we'll convert it into a store credit for you. Feel free to browse, I'll be back shortly."

Vihaan walked over to the display of chatters. They weren't much different from his old chatter except that the beveled edges had the small reflective facets that had come into fashion in recent years.

He looked at the smallest version.

*Just like my old one*, he thought. *I'll certainly need something bigger.*

He picked up the largest version. His hand barely wrapped around it.

*That's too big!*

He picked up the medium version.

*Yeah, that's more like it!*

"Vihaan Mount?" Biffie said from the back of the showroom.

Vihaan turned, setting the chatter back onto the display.

Biffie came over and handed him a yellow specie with the Chatter Warehouse logo on top. "This is good at any Chatter Warehouse location." She smiled and gestured towards the display. "Were you thinking about getting the median model?"

"I think so, yes."

"New or used?"

"New," Vihaan answered. "Definitely new."

"Good choice, I use that one myself." She pulled out a formulae. "One median chatter, new, with starter recharge." She winked as she lowered the talisman. "The starter recharge is complimentary this week."

Vihaan nodded.

"And you said you were interested in a divulgate?"

"Yes, I've been without one for months and barely know what's happening in the world!"

Biffie smirked. "I spend so much time watching *Infatuation Diaries* that, even with my divulgate, I *still* barely know what's happening in the world!"

Vihaan laughed. "What do you recommend?"

"Well..." Biffie thought for a moment. "If you want one for home, you have to get the grand, but if you want to carry it around with you, the minute is a better choice."

"Can I take a look at the grand?"

"Of course." Biffie led him to a display with three sample divulgates.

Vihaan examined the width of the grand model. *Just narrow enough to fit in my travel bag!*

"I'll go with the grand."

"Very good," Biffie said with a smile, repeating his choice into the formulae, which she then handed to him. "Bring this up to the collector while I get your purchases from the back."

The collector's ledger had barely buzzed when Biffie returned with one large clear bag and one smaller one. Inside the bags were the divulgate and chatter respectively, each bathing in recharge potion.

"Once the potion is gone," she said, handing the larger bag to Vihaan, "they're ready to use." She held up the smaller bag and tapped on a red version of the Chatter Warehouse logo a fifth of the way from the top. The logo had red lines extending from either side. "When it gets down to here, you can start associating. I assume that you saw the consociate hub out front when you came in."

"Does anyone miss it?"

"You'd be surprised," Biffie answered with a wry grin. "You're welcome to try out the test units while you wait."

"Thanks, I'll take you up on that!"

He went back to the divulgate display, put his two bags down onto it, and picked up the grand model.

"Invoke, show me a content list."

He swiped through the list, looking for one of the news programs he used to watch, but stopped at the entry for *The Rajveer Chronicles*.

Vihaan paged back through the episodes until he found the first one that he had missed while living at the Palace. He tapped on it and was transported back to childhood as Cal burst in to excitedly reveal Rajveer's next mission.

At the end of the episode, Vihaan lifted the bag with his new chatter. Twice as much potion had absorbed as was necessary to start associating.

"Done," he said to the divulgate. He slid the new chatter into his travel bag as he headed out of the store.

"Enjoy your new toys!" Biffie shouted as the bell rang.

"Thanks, I will!"

Vihaan stopped at the consociate hub and shifted the divulgate so that it stuck out of the top of the bag just enough to expose its consociate. Each blue talisman on the hub had a small label above it describing the associated feed. Vihaan didn't read any of them as he methodically associated his new divulgate with every single one.

When he finished, his thoughts turned to Amineh.

*Would it really hurt to visit?*

His heart ached at the thought of never seeing her again.

*Don't be selfish*, he thought to himself. *You could be dead in a few days.*

He sighed and walked on.

# TRANSITION

Vihaan found Homestyle Potions and Talismans on the far side of Wove's Village Centre.

He paused in front of the shop and looked through the window. It was a small shop, with photos of satisfied customers on the walls and free-standing displays of available talismans and potions. An old human woman in a gray jumpsuit trimmed in practitioner-silver was sitting behind the counter, looking at something on her divulgate.

*That has to be Ulima.*

He pulled Theia's bottle from his travel bag and tapped gently on the side. "We're here. I'll let you know when I need you."

There was a muffled grunt of acknowledgment from within the bottle. Vihaan hooked it to his waistband.

The woman looked up as the bell above the door rang to announce Vihaan's entry. "Hello, I'm Ulima Hutchings, how can I take care of you today?"

Vihaan pulled out a formulae, walked over to

the counter and handed it to her. "I'd like to hire you to cast this spell for me."

She inserted it into a portable lucubrate that she pulled from beneath the counter and took a few minutes to read through the spell. Her eyebrows shot up repeatedly as she did so, and she glanced quizzically over at Vihaan twice.

"It's the most impressive piece of spell-work that I've ever read. But"—she shook her head—"I'm sorry, there's no way I can cast this."

She handed the formulae back to Vihaan.

"It's far too powerful for blood magic," she continued. "If I read it right, and I do, you would need *at least* five donors, each compensated well enough to put up with a year of malaise in exchange for a fifth of their soul. *Not* an easy thing to find. But it doesn't matter, I do a lot of things for a lot of people."

Her glance flickered to Vihaan's Hilt for a second.

She continued angrily, "But I will *not* harvest souls just to make you into the perfect warrior!"

"That's not what I want at all," Vihaan said calmly. "And I can provide the soul that you'll need for the casting"—Vihaan pulled two bottled souls from his travel bag and placed them onto the counter—"as well as another as payment for your services."

Ulima jumped off her stool, a look of horror on her face.

"Don't worry, I didn't harvest them." Vihaan smiled reassuringly. "They're from a defeated demon's cache, and I've made sure that there are no spirits attached."

Ulima didn't look convinced as Vihaan placed Theia's bottle, identical except for being filled with Theia's gray essence, onto the counter beside the souls.

She looked at it in confusion.

Vihaan grinned and tapped Theia's bottle. "Perhaps my friend can explain."

Theia's exit from the bottle left Ulima pale and speechless.

"I can vouch for him," Theia said as she settled down onto the floor. "I spent a few thousand years in one of these bottles and have personally verified that no one else is trapped like I was."

The practitioner was silent for a long moment, her eyes darting back and forth between Vihaan and Theia.

"Who *are* you?"

"Not who I was *meant* to be, not on the outside at least." Vihaan held up the formulae and shook it to draw her attention. "But *this* could change that."

Vihaan turned to the side and pulled the front of his jerkin away from his chest. The tight-shirt kept his breasts compressed, but without the jerkin to hide them, they were still obvious.

Ulima's anger faded.

"Ah," she said. "Sorry, I hadn't noticed before. You're looking for an alignment."

"No need to apologize," Vihaan continued with conviction. "But I've wanted an alignment for years. Until recently, I never thought it would be possible. Now that I have the means, I plan to give myself a body that matches my spirit-gender."

"I understand." Ulima was clearly moved. "I

take it this spell is from the same source as those souls."

Vihaan nodded.

"Did you really *kill* a demon?!"

"It was more of an assisted suicide," Vihaan admitted. "But still enough to claim victor's rights."

"I suppose that's true." Ulima nodded. "Not that those laws have gotten much use in recent history. But, back on point, I've done several alignments over the years." She glanced over at the formulae. "But those spells are cobbled-together, moderately difficult pieces of cosmetic spell-work—not much more advanced than a wart removal. But this... this is a *complete* transformation unlike anything I've ever seen! You'd actually *be* male, fertile and fully functional! I'm not sure I could—"

"I'm not claiming ownership. You'd be free to reuse the spell once we're done."

Ulima smiled to herself. "Isolating the pain-management sections alone would make this invaluable." An eager expression filled her face. "I haven't even seen any *proper* medical spells this advanced! *So* advanced..."

Her face clouded.

"So advanced that I should have an extra practitioner or two to share the load," she muttered to herself. "Someone to watch my back."

She paused and looked back at Vihaan.

"Unfortunately, I know for a fact that the other two practitioners in town will not participate in an alignment." She grimaced. "Even Wove has its bigots."

"Please," Vihaan said softly, "I've heard about

your work since I was a child. There's no one I would trust more."

Ulima looked at Vihaan, then down at the two bottled souls sitting on her counter, then at Theia.

"I have to warn you," she said slowly, looking directly into Vihaan's eyes, "from what I learned in theory class, I'm pretty sure that something like this will only work if your spirit is *truly* male."

"I understand." Vihaan smiled. "I'm more than willing to take the risk."

The practitioner sighed. "If you're certain."

"I am," Vihaan replied firmly.

Ulima nodded. "I'll have to spread it out over a couple of days and you'll need to be unconscious for the entire time." She frowned. "I'll have to bring someone in to keep an eye on you while I run the shop…"

"Don't worry about that." Vihaan pulled Theia's anneal out of a pocket and tossed it towards her. She floated into its path and dropped solidly onto the floor. "My friend can take care of anything that you need while I'm out."

The practitioner's eyes went wide at the casual use of such a rare talisman.

"But please try not to dawdle," Theia said with a grin. "I *hate* being solid."

Ulima sputtered for a moment, then finally said, "When did you want to start?"

"The sooner the better."

"Keep what we're doing in your quiver." Ulima put the souls beneath the counter. "Come back at closing and we'll start the casting."

～

Vihaan returned at dusk and Ulima hurried him into the back room, locking both doors behind them.

"You didn't tell anyone why you're here, did you?"

"No." Vihaan thought back to the cruel words that had been flung at him all his life. "I know how to keep out of view."

"Okay, I've got everything ready."

There was a cot in the middle of the room with a table on either side.

On the closest table was a shallow, faceted crystal bowl with a matching cover. One of the softly glowing silver souls had been decanted into it. Beside the bowl was a variety of vials, each filled with a premeasured amount of different-colored powders.

On the opposite table, a cauldron sat on top of a bask talisman, its contents just coming to a boil. A small talisman attached to a strap sat beside it.

Ulima went over to stir the cauldron. "I'm going to need a meal break about halfway through." She tasted a spoonful.

Vihaan pulled out Theia's bottle, shook it, and, as she emerged, said, "Did you hear? Dinner's cooking!"

Ulima looked surprised. "Ghosts eat?!"

"No." Theia feigned a cross look as she merged with her anneal. "He just likes to tease."

"Of course." Theia shook her head. "What have I gotten myself into this time?!"

Vihaan slipped Theia's bottle into his travel bag and sat on the edge of the cot.

He gave it an experimental bounce and grinned. "I'm ready to start whenever you are."

Ulima picked up the talisman and strap from the table. "I'm going to use this abeyance to keep you asleep while I perform the three stages of spellwork. The effect will be instantaneous once it's invoked." She handed it to him and he put it on. "Let me know when you're ready and we'll get started."

Theia stepped up to the side of the cot with a concerned expression.

"Sleep well." Her expression changed to a happy smile. "I might even stick around to watch." She put her hand onto the abeyance. "Invoke!"

Vihaan's world went dark.

It was nearly midnight on the third day when Vihaan's world brightened again.

"Did it work?"

"Can't you tell?" Theia asked mockingly.

Vihaan put his hand down there. "That's new!" He started laughing uncontrollably.

Ulima looked at Theia. "Is he always like this?"

"It's an emotional moment."

When Vihaan got control of his mirth, he smiled widely at the two women. "It actually worked!"

"I'm offended," Ulima said half-seriously.

"No offense intended," Vihaan replied with equal seriousness before his grin returned. "A body that matches my spirit-gender!"

"Are you just going to lie there all night feeling up your *matching* body?" Theia teased.

Vihaan jumped up and started walking around the room.

"Everything feels different." He ran his hands over his now-flat chest. "Everything feels right!"

Vihaan started jumping in place, laughing and crying.

"It's an emotional moment," Ulima said.

# APPRECIATION

"I'd have to say I'm satisfied," Vihaan said happily after he had finally calmed down and stopped bouncing around the room. "But I do have one more thing I'd like to hire you for."

"If the rate is the same, I'll do almost anything."

"I don't want to advertise my presence here right now, but there is a woman my age named Amineh Kamali who I'd like you to offer to perform the spell for."

"I think I know her," Ulima said. "Strong human woman with a booming voice. Right?"

Vihaan nodded fondly.

"She was in here a while back, just after I performed my last alignment," Ulima said with dawning realization. "When I asked her what she wanted, she said she was dream shopping and left."

"She's a dear friend. I owe her my life." Vihaan smiled at the memories of their time together. "I owe her this! Don't tell her who it's from. But please get in touch with her and see if she's ready."

"Do you have access to *more* souls?"

"Demons are unrelenting." Vihaan reached into

his travel bag. His satisfied expression faltered. "I only have one more with me! In all the excitement, I didn't think about paying for her alignment, just powering it!"

"You could always just pop home," Theia offered.

Vihaan put the soul onto the counter and reached back into his travel bag for his treasure bag.

"No need since I remembered this!" he said, triumphantly holding up the small bag, which appeared to be empty.

Ulima looked confused.

"Before we negotiate a price," Theia said, placing a hand just far enough into Vihaan's shoulder to get his attention, "I have a favor to ask."

"Anything."

"My bottle was better than having to walk, but it wasn't exactly comfortable." Vihaan flinched and Theia quickly made a consoling gesture. "Not your fault! I didn't realize it when we set out either."

"What's the favor?"

"Would you part with a small share of your treasure?"

"You can have as much of it as you need."

Theia turned to Ulima. "Here's where you come in."

Ulima looked surprised. "I don't know anything about ghosts or how to make them comfortable."

"No, but I took a look at the household talismans in your showroom while we were waiting for my snorey friend."

"I don't snore!"

Ulima ignored him. "Yes, most of my business is home maintenance." She shrugged. "They don't build nice houses this far out, so folks have to resort to other means."

"Would those means work on my bottle?"

Ulima turned thoughtful for a moment as Vihaan extracted the bottled soul from his travel bag and placed it on the nearest table.

"I don't see why not." She paused. "We'd have to forgo the usual assemblage and adhere the talismans directly to the glass..."

"Don't cover the label!" Theia said quickly. "I don't want to forget my ghost-day."

"Sure," Ulima responded, looking at the bag in Vihaan's hand with a bemused expression. "And how did you plan on paying for this?"

"Well," he said, brandishing his treasure bag, which flapped loosely in his grip, "Theia was being literal when she mentioned treasure!" Vihaan tilted the bag and poured out three large jewels, a gold ring and four gold pendants.

Ulima's eyes widened. "I take it these are from the same demon cache? Is that...?" She picked up one of the jewels. "Wow, I've never seen a fire opal this large!"

"Will this be enough to cover everything?"

"If I listened to my conscience"—Ulima placed the fire opal back onto the table and laughed—"I'd have to ask you to find a smaller opal."

"Then the opal is yours for your honesty." Vihaan smiled. "And as a thank-you for what you've done for me and what you're hopefully going to do for my friends." He gestured to the other items on the table. "And I'm happy to let you have everything else here as payment for the upcoming tasks. I can get more souls or any blood that you might need for permanent spell-work."

"Just in case you come to your senses." Ulima slipped the opal into a pocket and smiled. "Powdering that will give me almost a year's supply for my potion work." She paused, smiling nervously. "I have to admit that the two of you creep me out quite a bit. But it's an interesting challenge, and I like challenges. So I'll give it a try—if it doesn't work, I keep just the opal and return the rest."

Vihaan looked at Theia.

Theia nodded. "Fine with me, it's not my treasure anyway."

"Do you need anything to power the spells?" Vihaan asked.

"No, the... treasure will more than cover it. Besides, this is what I do," Ulima said with pride. "I have nearly everything we'll need in stock and plenty of blood-credit to cover the custom work."

"Okay," Vihaan said, putting his treasure bag away.

Theia smiled and Ulima pulled a formulae from her pocket.

"This should be fun. Invoke." She began speaking into the formulae. "Start with a standard new homeowner's package: phylactery, calefaction... wait." She looked up at Theia. "I usually include a calefaction and an algid to maintain a stable temperature year-round and an adit for public traject access. Would you need those? Uh, do ghosts even feel temperature?"

"We do a little, or at least I do. I haven't actually met any others." Theia shrugged. "But it couldn't hurt to have them."

"Okay." Ulima confirmed it into her formulae, then pulled a chatter out of her pocket as she continued, "I'll need to be able to let you know when it's ready or contact you with any questions."

Vihaan pulled out his new chatter and they tapped the right sides together, right at the point where the dark blue consociates were embedded. The chatters vibrated. Ulima pocketed hers, and Vihaan returned his to his travel bag.

"Now," she said to Theia, lifting the formulae again, "what are you picturing?"

"Several things." Theia rubbed her insubstantial hands together. "First, an aggrandize to turn it into more of a home—nothing too fancy, a dozen large rooms or so."

"No problem." She addressed the talisman in her hand. "Dividers for twelve—no, twenty-four—sections in two levels. Aggrandize." She winked at Theia. "I have half a dozen in the storeroom just waiting to be invoked."

"Second, something that will make it impossible for anyone to trap me inside."

"Some sort of escape route," Ulima said to the formulae before tapping it against her forehead. "Perhaps I could adapt a fissure like they use to force open doors when the owner has passed." She shook her head. "No, that would be too slow and would break the bottle..." She paused for a moment. "I'll have to think on that one."

"No problem, I'm sure you'll come up with something," Theia continued excitedly. "I'll also need a perdurable and a lodestar or two to make sure that my bottle doesn't get broken or lost."

"Got it." She spoke the two talisman names into

her formulae. "And a manifold," she said. "That will allow you to copy anything from out here"—she spread her arms—"into there"—she pointed at the bottle on the table.

Theia smiled for a moment, then her face fell. "But if I'm insubstantial, I won't be able to do anything with them."

"Fair point. But the spell-work for anneals is lost to history." Ulima was quiet for a moment before her face brightened. "I think I can do something about that! It's not something that I deal with much out here, but at school we covered asunder talismans. They use them when they need to handle dangerous or hazardous materials so that they don't have to get too close." She grinned. "My buddy Talib screwed up the spell-work during lab and only got a couple of inches of reach out of his. I'm pretty sure I can replicate his error and tighten it up even more so that it will be like wearing gloves."

"Two asunders," she said to her formulae. "No, two *sets* of asunders, internal and external." She addressed Theia again. "Anything else?"

"Not that I can think of," Theia said after a moment. "But feel free to make suggestions."

"I'll keep my mind open and let you know."

"One last thing," Vihaan said.

Theia looked at him with a questioning expression.

"Not about your bottle." Vihaan pulled a small sack out of his travel bag. It clinked as he held it out. "After we're gone, can you give this to Mosegi and Mbaziira over at Aligned Attire?"

"I don't think you'll need what they're selling anymore," Ulima said, looking at the bag.

"No," Vihaan replied with a grin, "but they were lifesavers for me at a time when I needed support and this is a little *anonymous* thank-you."

"Understood." She took the bag and set it onto the table with her payment. "I'll pass it along."

Ulima chattered them two days later, and when she saw them arrive in her shop, her face lit up. "You're going to *love* this!" She turned and hurried into her storeroom.

When Ulima returned, she placed Theia's bottle on the table with great fanfare.

The bottle was now opaque, as if filled with smoke, and there was a ring around the base with ten talismans permanently affixed and two strap-closed pockets, one full, one empty. The clip at the top was now attached to a fitted copper collar.

"In a fit of creativity I've added a consociate to the outside, connected to a chatter that I put inside. Also, I needed a way to make sure that the aggrandize was working properly, so I was using a quadrate to get myself in. While there, I thought it would be nice if you could invite in guests if you wanted to, so I permanently affixed it."

Theia laughed at the thought while she handed the cloak that she had used to disguise herself on the way over to Vihaan who slid it into his travel bag.

Ulima opened the full pocket and removed one of the two gray stones it contained. "This is your asunder." She poked the empty pocket with the stone. "And I figured it could come in handy to have somewhere to store that anneal of yours. That way you have both options."

Theia examined the asunder in Ulima's hand. "How does it work?"

"Pretty much the same as your anneal." She put the talisman down and gestured towards it. "Place your hand on the counter."

Theia willed her asunder out–Vihaan caught it in midair–then put her incorporeal hand down flat on the counter over the asunder.

"It's invoked by contact and I spelled it to map out the spirit-outline of your hand." She flexed her empty hand between them. "Give it a try!"

Theia lifted her hand. The asunder remained embedded in the center of her palm. She reached over and took hold of her bottle, lifted it and smiled.

"Fantastic, interaction without solidification!"

"Just remember"—Ulima tapped on her chest— "if you pick up a stack of boxes and try to balance them against your chest with these, they'll just fall through you."

"Good reminder." Theia placed her bottle back onto the counter and tapped it with her finger, enjoying the solid thunk. "And what about making sure that I can't get trapped in there?"

"That one was tricky." Ulima beamed with pride. "There are lots of ways to keep things in but very few that let you out without destroying whatever security talismans you're using."

"And?" Theia asked anxiously.

"I found an old trick called a liberation gem that constables use when they go undercover in a prison." She tapped on a green talisman attached to the bottle. "It allows the invoker to escape any secure location *without* compromising or disrupting *any* of the security talismans."

"No wonder I haven't heard of it," Vihaan said. "If it was public knowledge, nowhere would be safe."

"That's the beauty of it," Ulima said with a smile. "It only works one way—you can get *out* of somewhere but you can't get back *in*. Plus it needs to be associated with the phylactery of the location *by the owner* with the wielder *present*! There's no way to set it up in secret. Not that it will be a problem here since you'll be the owner *and* the escapee."

Theia was excited. "Can I take a look?"

"One thing first." Ulima placed a finger on the mounted phylactery. "Solidify for a moment—I'm not sure that the asunder will provide enough contact."

Theia dropped her new asunder on the counter and Vihaan tossed back her anneal. She stepped into its path, then laid a newly solid finger onto the phylactery.

"Invoke," Ulima said. "Remove all current access and set this individual as the household primary."

"Now?" Theia asked excitedly.

"Now," Ulima replied with equal excitement.

Theia ejected her anneal and dove in. Ulima had to scramble to catch it before it nearly struck her in the face then slid it into its new, dedicated pouch on the bottle.

Theia emerged again after several minutes, elated. "I love it!"

"I knew you—" Ulima was interrupted by a violent shiver. Theia had forgotten herself and attempted to give her a big hug.

"I'm so sorry!"

"No problem." Ulima smiled weakly. "Now I know what it feels like to be intimate with a ghost." She gave Vihaan an odd look. "You have peculiar tastes, young man."

Vihaan sputtered—the women laughed together at his discomfort.

# LEGACY

It was early afternoon when Vihaan walked into Tanner Leather Works, the bell above the door ringing loudly to announce his presence. He pulled his travel bag out of his jerkin pocket and clipped it to his waistband, then pulled off the battered garment.

*I feel naked!* Vihaan thought with a shudder.

A human woman walked out of the back room in answer to the bell above the door's summons. She was wearing a gray jumpsuit with thick clothier-tan trim done in leather. The jumpsuit was mostly covered by a leather work jerkin of a different cut than Vihaan's. Her jerkin was square at the bottom instead of tapered and there was an unfamiliar set of clips on each shoulder.

"Reetul Tanner," she said with a smile as Vihaan placed his jerkin on the counter. "Will it be repairs or replacement?"

"Replacement." Vihaan smiled back. "Same design but with a different rune on the front and some custom embedding, if you're up to it."

"Not a problem." She ran her hand over the

rough surface of Vihaan's jerkin. "As you might guess from the name, my family has always worked in leather. There's nothing we can't do for you." She checked a spot near where the side seam met the bottom of the jerkin and smiled. "Haven't seen one of these in a while. The Coiros shut down their works when I was a child."

Vihaan smiled. "I picked it up used when I was a boy."

"So"—Reetul grinned kindly back at him—"not long ago, then."

Vihaan laughed. "In the greater scheme of things, I suppose not." He reached into his travel bag and pulled out a formulae, then handed it to her. "This is what I'm looking for."

Reetul was still looking bemused as she slotted it into a small lucubrate built into the counter. A rough sketch of a new jerkin appeared with multiple notes connected to various points of its construction. After a quick glance, she spun the sketch to look at the back.

"I like a customer who knows what they want. Saves me all that time trying to sell them." She read through the notes and her eyebrows rose. "You must be one rich elf to gather so many talismans *and* be willing to lock them away in a single garment!"

"No." Vihaan paused. "Actually I suppose I am," he laughed softly. "I've been living an interesting life lately."

"You would have had to."

"So, can you do it?"

Reetul spun the sketch around again and tapped on the lucent mount.

"I'll need to call in my brother-in-law for the

copper work, but everything else we can do here in the shop." She looked up at him with a question in her eyes. "I've never embedded *this many* talismans... are you *sure* you want to lock them up like this?"

"Very sure," Vihaan said firmly.

She pulled an ersatz and a measuring tape out from beneath the counter.

"Can you take that bag off while I capture some reference shots of your old jerkin? I'll need to get your measurements."

"Sure." Vihaan unclipped his travel bag and laid it on the counter.

After capturing images of the jerkin's rough exterior, she inverted it and captured another set. Reetul inverted it again, set it down, then made her way around the counter. As she walked, she snapped the formulae into the set of clips on her right shoulder.

"This will just take a minute," she said, stretching out her measuring tape.

With quick, practiced motions, she measured Vihaan's torso, dictating each figure into the formulae as she worked.

She moved back behind the counter, unclipped the formulae and set it down beside the ersatz.

"You can put this back on," she said with a tap on his jerkin.

With a surge of relief, Vihaan settled the jerkin back into place. Reetul handed him his travel bag, and he stowed it.

"Anything else I can do for you?"

"I'd like a few bracelets with talisman pockets."

Vihaan pointed at her shoulder. "And perhaps a few more with clips like those."

"My brother-in-law invented these." She flicked one of the clips; it twanged loudly. "Thought they looked stupid at first, but they do come in handy. How many bracelets you need?"

"How about half a dozen of each type?"

"Okay." She pulled out a divulgate. "Let me tally up your order."

"Fine. I assume that you barter."

At Reetul's nod, Vihaan extracted his treasure bag and shook out a large gem. "Will this cover it?"

"Cover it," Reetul said after examining the jewel, "and make it my top priority."

"Then we have a deal?"

"We do indeed," Reetul said as she pocketed the gem and pulled out a chatter. They bumped consociates as she continued, "I'll let you know when it's ready. It shouldn't be more than a couple of days."

"Okay," Vihaan said quietly to himself a short while later as he stood in front of Wove Village Hall. "This is no big deal. It's just a formality."

He took a deep breath and walked into the lobby.

Along the lobby's right wall was a building directory with each department name listed with an office number and two stones beneath it. The stone on the left had the rune marking it as a manifold talisman and the one on the right was marked as a consociate.

Vihaan read through the names until he found "Registry of Persons, 4-7." He pulled out his chatter and pressed the two consociates together. His chatter vibrated after a moment, then he walked over to the benches on the other side of the room, sat down and lifted his chatter again.

"Invoke, get me Wove Registry of Persons."

*It's so nice to have a chatter again!*

A woman in black with light pink skin and rounded ears appeared. "Wove Registry of Persons. How can I assist you today?"

Vihaan was taken aback. Growing up in Hinter, he had never encountered a mixed adult before.

"Sir, can I help you?" she asked impatiently.

"Sorry," Vihaan said, "I was distracted for a moment."

"Okay, then what can I do for you?"

"Uh… I'm looking to record a name change."

"You can use the manifold to file our copy of the paperwork."

"I don't have the paperwork yet. I was hoping to come up, fill it out and file it in person."

"Fine," she said flatly. "We're on the fourth floor, room seven."

"Thank you," Vihaan said. "Done."

Her face disappeared.

Vihaan smiled as he ascended the stairs. "Time for Vihaan Mount to become a legal entity."

Vihaan's last stop for the day was Claes Saada's bookshop, located at the edge of town in the industrial district. The bookshop didn't have an official name and took up a corner of a larger building that housed Saada Free Press, Claes's print house.

Saada was widely known for printing books that the larger companies would never consider, and he had been kicked out of three villages for distributing "immoral publications" before settling in Wove.

Vihaan pulled out the formulae holding the final manuscript version of Leah's journals.

*At least if we fail, we'll have left something behind!*

He took a deep steadying breath and stepped through the door.

Behind the counter stood a late-middle-aged human, wearing a gray jumpsuit with the pale green trim of an information provider. He smiled in greeting. "Hello, I'm Claes, how can I help you?"

Full of nearly as much anxiety as he had been when he had faced Leah, Vihaan placed the formulae on the counter with a soft clink. "I have a book of research that I would like to get printed."

Claes's mild smile turned wry. "By your expression, I'm guessing that it's something that's going to make a lot of people unhappy."

"Not unhappy exactly"—Vihaan smiled weakly —"but it will force people to rethink things they'd rather not rethink."

"About...?" His smile faded.

"Our shared history, humans, demons and elves. How we got to where we are today. Who has been manipulating our history."

"So... little things," Claes said seriously before grinning again. "Relax, we're all friends here. I just need to know a little about where you got your information."

"I've spent the past several months living in the former lair of a so-called demon. Most of that time was spent going through her personal journals with a friend of mine."

Claes inserted the formulae into a small, battered lucubrate. The cover page appeared:

## True History
## Leah of the Immortals
## By the late Theia Ilham and Vihaan Mount

He looked up with a sad expression. "When did your friend pass?"

It was Vihaan's turn for a wry grin. "About six years before the Demon War."

Claes gave him an incredulous look. "Is that another set of journals or a pen name?"

"Neither," Vihaan said with a laugh. "She's a literal ghost writer."

Now Claes's look was simply confused.

"My late friend is a full-spirited ghost."

"Is that even possible?"

"She was involuntarily harvested by an immortal, and the reaper collected her spirit along with her soul."

Claes shuddered. "So why the 'late' if she's al... not dead?"

"She insisted on it." Vihaan smiled at the memory. "Seemed to get a kick out of it."

The publisher frowned. "Your story is getting more and more challenging to accept."

"I understand. But if you want proof, Theia is over at Ulima Hutchings's place." Vihaan thought of their combined teasing. "They seemed to be getting along quite well without me, and I wasn't much interested in their discussions about interior design."

Claes shook his head and grunted. "I'll chatter Ulima once we're done here. I take it that 'Leah of the Immortals' is the demon?" At Vihaan's nod, he continued, "Why don't you just say that in the title?"

"That's covered at length in the first chapter."

"How about a quick summary to convince me that this is worth my time?"

"That's fair." Vihaan crossed his arms across his chest. "Everything that we know about demons and Feracio's prehistory is a lie. The creatures that we know as demons are humans who sacrificed half of the world's population in exchange for immortality."

"That's quite the claim."

"Which is what brought me here."

"Fair enough." Claes gave Vihaan a hard stare. "And you stand by your work?"

"Completely."

He continued staring into Vihaan's eyes for a long moment, then nodded, satisfied.

"You're looking for a full print run?"

"And distribution, if possible."

"I can't promise sales, but I can get it into select stores all over Timor within a month."

Vihaan smiled. "That sounds great. Any international distribution?"

"Eventually, but they usually like to wait until

the second print run to make sure that it's worth their effort."

"That's fine." Vihaan pulled out his treasure bag. "Say when."

He started dumping out jewels one at a time. Claes's eyes bulged for a moment before he started carefully appraising them. "That's good," he said after the fourth one struck the counter.

"Okay," he added, gingerly placing the gems under the counter, "I'll have the proof ready in about three weeks."

"If I'm unable to get back to review it within a month"—Vihaan tipped another gem onto the counter—"please just move forward with publication."

Shaking his head again, Claes pocketed the gem. "Whatever you say."

# GEAR

A blue flash announced Vihaan's arrival in the Palace's library. Theia's bottle was sitting at her usual spot with a small pile of books beside it. Vihaan began impatiently, but still gently, tapping on the side of it.

Since they had returned from Wove, Theia had been spending most of her time in the comfort of her upgraded bottle, building her personal library with each transition.

Theia emerged and took shape beside him with an annoyed expression. "What?!"

"What do you think?" Vihaan asked, on the edge of giddiness, presenting the fresh new jerkin that he was wearing with a wave of his hands.

Externally, and aside from years of wear, it was almost identical to his first one, but the Rumetre family crest had been replaced with the Mount rune.

"Not sure it was worth rattling my bottle, but"—Theia floated around him—"it's certainly in better shape than the old one."

"And it will stay that way!" Vihaan tapped the

bottom right point of the Mount rune on the front panel. "There's a perdurable here"—he tapped the other bottom point—"an aegis here and..." He put his hand over the central peak of the rune and mentally activated the talisman beneath it.

He disappeared and reappeared briefly on the other side of the table before flashing back to his original position.

"No more dropping my traject!"

Theia laughed at his enthusiasm. "You're like a child picking out his first Yielding costume!"

"It's a garment worthy of Rajveer himself!"

Theia looked at him blankly.

He rolled his eyes. "You've missed out on *so* much!" he said with a laugh. "We *have* to watch the first episode of *The Rajveer Chronicles* tonight."

"I'm looking forward to it," Theia replied in a tone that belied her words.

Vihaan laughed again.

Theia smiled. "If you're done playing with your toys, how about you try doing something productive?"

"Got time to share thoughts?" Vihaan said a few days later, knocking gently on the side of Theia's bottle.

"I'm not sure I have any thoughts to share," Theia said as she appeared.

"I'm pretty sure I know where Olen is," Vihaan said.

"So, that makes the entire leadership except..."

"Except Teivel," Vihaan finished darkly, "the

only one that matters. Have you found anything better than 'remote trajecting to see'?"

"No." Theia shook her head. "Aside from that one reference in Leah's journals that said he 'actually walked' to one of their meetings, I've found nothing."

Vihaan groaned. "Even with the old speedways he could still be anywhere in three counties!"

"Let's go back to the beginning," Theia said after thinking for a while. "Perhaps if we can figure out where he came from, we can narrow down where he might have ended up."

The next day, Theia shook Vihaan awake. "I found something!"

He opened his eyes. It was still dark.

Groggily, he realized that she had *physically* shaken him awake!

He sat up. "It must be important for you to stay solid for the entire trip up here!"

"It is." Her anneal struck him in the chest. "Meet me in the library."

She sank through the floor, laughing.

"Finally!" Theia shouted when Vihaan strolled into the library a few minutes later, having deliberately taken the stairs instead of trajecting.

She was floating excitedly around the smallest of the work tables.

"Look and tell me what you see!"

One of Leah's journals was lying open on the table. Beside it was an old, faded picture.

Vihaan looked closer and realized that it was

the first of her journals and that it was opened to the second entry. The picture was of a man with red eyes standing at a podium, clearly midspeech. A man and a woman, both with the same eyes, sat on folding chairs behind him. There was a different rune painted roughly in white over the chest of each individual.

An elucidate chain was looped on the very bottom of the picture, revealing the title: "First press conference/5619-7-18."

Vihaan looked at Theia in confusion. "I don't get it."

"This was inside the back cover." Theia pointed at the journal. "Now, read these two entries again."

Vihaan placed his own elucidate into the gutter of the journal and did as she instructed.

He looked back at her with a shrug. "Can you just tell me what I'm supposed to be seeing?"

"The *date*," Theia said slowly, dramatically overenunciating the second word.

Realization dawned. "They're the same!"

Theia passed her finger through the symbol painted over the man at the podium. "This has to be Teivel!"

Vihaan smiled. "So we know what he looks like!"

"More than that." Theia smiled. "Toss me my anneal and I'll show you."

Vihaan pulled the anneal from a talisman pocket built into the inner edge of his new jerkin's front panel. He tossed it towards her and she stepped into its path.

Theia walked behind the lucubrate and came

back with a black gem, showing it to Vihaan with a flourish.

"It's a muster talisman," Vihaan said, confused. "I had one as a child, before I was old enough for a chatter."

"So did I," Theia said with a wide grin. "I got in so much trouble when I was five and traded mine with a friend who had a prettier one." They both laughed. "I didn't understand that they were part of a matched set until it started buzzing and I rushed home to find out what my parents wanted me for, much to their surprise. And much to *my* surprise..."

She spun the gem around to reveal the rune on the other side—it was Teivel's.

Vihaan brightened.

Theia tossed the talisman towards him. "The leadership must use them to summon their minions."

Vihaan caught it and bounced it in his palm before closing his fist around it.

"Now, we just need to pretend that Teivel is a lost child and key a lodestar to it!"

"Do we have one?!"

Vihaan reached into his travel bag with a grin. "Of course!"

He pulled out a lodestar and held both hands out to her, a talisman in each.

"Then we really do have a way to track him down!"

"Yes!" Vihaan put the two talismans on the table, with the lodestar directly on top of the muster. "Assuming he keeps the other half of the set close by and hasn't lost it." He placed his hand over them.

"Invoke, direct us safely and directly to the mate of this muster."

The lodestar made a soft chirp as it locked on to their destination. Vihaan closed his hand around both talismans with a look of triumph on his face. "We actually did it!"

"So, let's get going!"

"Relax, we'll leave in the morning," Vihaan said as he placed the talismans, one at a time, into his travel bag. "Besides, I need one more thing for the trip."

"Seriously?!" Theia said with mocking disbelief. "There's actually something in the Palace that you haven't *already* tucked away into that travel bag of yours?"

"There is one thing that just wouldn't fit." Vihaan smirked and gestured towards her bottle.

As soon as Theia retreated into it, he picked the bottle up and trajected down to the first storage room he had found in his exploration of the Palace's basement.

"Wow!" Theia gasped after she exited her bottle and examined the dark set of armor in the corner. "Our practitioners had just started working on aegis armor like this when I died."

"That's not aegis armor."

She looked closer. Her eyes grew wide.

"Do those runes mean what I think they mean?"

"They do. A full set of recondite armor!"

"I can see why it wouldn't fit in your tiny little bag."

"Don't mock my bag!"

Theia made an insincere placating gesture. "I

wouldn't dare. Will you be wearing it all the way or shall we take turns?"

Vihaan laughed. "According to the inventory, there's a porter's pack inside, so I'll be able to carry it until we get wherever we're going."

"Probably a good idea, it doesn't look very comfortable." Theia poked her head into the armor. "The bag's here!"

"There's one more thing that I think we'll need." Vihaan opened the drawer containing the bulwark talisman and pulled it out. "The net for our prey."

He moved over to a small drawer on the other side of the room and pulled out a tiny phylactery attached to a short chain. "And a lock to make sure that no one but us can release him!"

He held the loose end of the chain against the bulwark. "Invoke, associate these talismans."

The chain glowed white for a moment, then attached itself to the bulwark.

Vihaan handed Theia her anneal. She absorbed it and put a finger onto the phylactery.

Vihaan pressed his finger to the other side. "Invoke, remove all current access and set these individuals as primary."

They smiled at each other as Vihaan tucked the linked talismans into his travel bag.

Vihaan snapped his fingers. "I'll need one more thing from the bedroom."

Theia groaned theatrically. "Too spoiled to sleep without silk sheets?"

"Almost." Vihaan grinned and tapped the peak of the Mount rune on his chest. "But I think we need a countermeasure in case he has one of these."

Vihaan pulled another chained phylactery out of the drawer and trajected away.

Just after dawn the next morning, Vihaan stepped out of the Palace's vestibule, held the lodestone out in front of him and turned slowly in place.

When he was facing southeast, he felt a nudge.

*The adventure awaits*, he thought to himself in Rajveer's voice.

Vihaan tucked the lodestone into one of the many talisman pockets built into the inside of his new jerkin, choosing one of the innermost ones where it would be pressed firmly against his chest, and started hiking towards destiny.

The prompts from the lodestar led Vihaan through the countryside for three days before he realized where they were headed.

He tapped on Theia's bottle, which was sitting on a blanket beside the remaining half of his dinner. "It's leading us to Akin."

"I lived in Akin for a while," Theia said from inside the bottle, where she was relaxing in her plush private parlor. "I wasn't impressed. Nothing more than a few gropey farmers and the livestock that loved them."

Vihaan chuckled. "It's the capital of Timor now."

"So, no more farmers but, I would imagine, more gropey than ever."

They laughed.

Theia appeared from her bottle. "I just dropped the locus onto the Immure County map and it came to a stop about halfway to Akin."

"Since we're both in the real world"—Vihaan tossed her anneal towards her and began carefully pulling a practice sword from his travel bag—"Time for some sparring!"

They set camp a few days later just out of sight of Akin.

"I'm going to turn in early," Vihaan said after a practice session.

He pulled the armor's deterge talisman from the porter bag and invoked it.

Theia rolled her eyes. "There's a river just beyond those trees."

"But this is so much quicker," Vihaan said with a smile. "I feel like I just stepped out of a launder!"

"What time are we going to set out in the morning?"

"I want to be moving before dawn. I'll wear the armor."

The first soft glow of dawn was just brightening the sky as Theia finished helping Vihaan into the recondite armor.

She examined him. He was a striking figure in the black armor, the only relief from the dark coloring being his Hilt-cuff, which he was wearing over the armor's forearm, and his travel bag, clipped to one of the many loops positioned around the top of its faulds. She gave a few of the straps a final tug, then nodded.

Vihaan closed the armor's visor. "Invoke."

Theia stepped back, keeping her eyes locked on where Vihaan stood. She removed the leather wrist strap she was wearing. Inside the strap's custom-made pouch was a transfix talisman. She set it on a nearby stump.

As soon as she released it, the dark, imposing figure was gone.

"Have you moved?"

"No," Vihaan replied, tapping on the armor's chest plate.

"That was a stupid question!" Theia laughed at herself. "Without the transfix, I can't hear you either." She picked up the bracelet, and Vihaan reappeared. "Right where I left you!"

Vihaan pulled her bottle from his travel bag and set it down on the stump. "Just like we practiced."

Theia handed Vihaan the bracelet. It vanished with him. She willed out her anneal and it vanished from midair. Finally she dove into her bottle. A moment later, the bottle vanished.

Despite being very early in the morning when they arrived—three hours before the start of the usual business day—the paths of Akin were already packed with a mixture of humans, elves and mixed travelers.

The deeper they went into the city, the more crowded it became.

Vihaan's increasingly frantic dodging finally failed as a young human woman in a pocketless black administrative jumpsuit rebounded off him.

"Watch where you're going!" she shouted, shoving an elvish woman in gray who had stepped into the space that Vihaan had just vacated.

"I am!" the elf said angrily, pushing back. "*You* should sober up before going out in public!"

As they came to blows, the crowd condensed around them, unintentionally providing Vihaan a clear path forward.

"I'm not sure how much longer I can keep this up," he whispered to Theia.

"Maybe that armor wasn't the best idea," she replied loudly. "And there's no point whispering when the armor's invoked unless you're in direct contact with someone."

After three more fights and an overturned cart, Vihaan gave in and retreated into an alley.

"Finally taking my advice?" Theia asked.

"Don't rub it in. Done."

Vihaan set her bottle down against the wall of the alley. The porter bag and his travel bag quickly joined it.

Theia emerged and Vihaan tossed her her anneal.

She stepped into it and started helping him out of the armor, each taking frequent glances towards the mouth of the alley to make sure that they weren't observed.

Soon the armor was stowed and Vihaan slung the porter bag onto his back.

Theia stowed herself and he put her bottle into his travel bag, which went back to its usual place in his jerkin's large front pocket.

"This won't be a problem," he said to himself as he paused at the mouth of the valley. "There's no way anyone here will recognize me. I'll just fade into the crowd."

He followed the lodestar's nudging through the

city, drawing only a few glances from Akin's jaded citizens as he focused on looking nonchalant.

The lodestar directed them to an Ameliorates just inside the divide between the residential and commercial districts of one of the nicer sections of Akin.

Vihaan looked around, then headed for an inn just a few doors down on the opposite side of the path.

He walked up to the counter and smiled at the gray-clad human male behind it. "Do you have anything on the second floor with a path view?"

The keeper laughed. "New to Akin?"

"Very," Vihaan laughed with him. "I want to get a feel for the city!"

"No problem, we're barely half-full today." He pulled out a formulae. "Room for one, second floor, pathside." He lowered it. "How long are you staying with us?"

"I'm not sure." Vihaan wondered what would be less suspicious. "Why don't we start with a week, then see what happens?"

The keeper raised the formulae again. "One week duration."

He put the formulae into a ledger with three slots built into the counter. Vihaan reached into his travel bag for his specie, then cursed himself.

*Do you want to get caught?*

He pictured his treasure bag instead, drawing it just to the opening of his travel bag, where it couldn't be seen.

"Uh… do you barter?"

"Not officially"—the keeper winked—"but if I toss a little extra to my manager, he doesn't complain if I use my own specie now and again."

Vihaan extracted a medium-sized gem and placed it on the counter.

"Will this cover the week and any bartering fees?"

The keeper's eyes bulged very briefly before he recovered. "Just about."

In what appeared to be a well-practiced gesture, the gem vanished and a specie appeared in the ledger.

After the ledger buzzed, the keeper took out a dull-gray stone and inserted it into the third slot.

The ledger buzzed again, and the keeper picked up the stone and handed it to Vihaan.

"You're in room three on the second floor, and this patron is good for a week."

"Thanks, I'm looking forward to my stay."

The keeper smiled and patted his pocket. "So am I."

Vihaan had half-turned to leave when a thought occurred to him. He turned back to the keeper.

"Do you know anywhere nearby where I can set up an anonymous specie?"

The keeper smiled and held out his hand.

Vihaan placed a small gem into it.

"I know just the place."

His room was easy to find, directly in the center of the second floor with an oversized 2-3 painted across the door.

In the wall beside the door was a slot just like the ones he had seen on the third floor of the Palace. He held the patron talisman against it, then pushed open the door.

Vihaan slid the patron into one of his outer talisman pockets, dropped the armor onto the bed, then rolled his shoulders, grateful to be relieved of the armor's weight.

Next he pulled out Theia's bottle and gently tapped on the side. As Theia materialized, he made his way over to the window and opened the curtains just enough to look down at the path below. Theia came up beside him.

"The lodestar is locked on that Ameliorates," Vihaan said, opening the curtains just a little wider.

Theia looked out the window. "The king demon is hiding in an apothecary?"

"Well, it is a chain." Vihaan shrugged. "Not a completely inappropriate place for the greatest evil of our time."

"Watch your mouth," Theia said. "My parents ran an Affables when I was growing up."

Vihaan shrugged. "Never heard of it."

Theia closed her eyes and made a happy sound. "The best steak sandwiches I've ever had."

"I'll leave you with your fond memories," Vihaan said mockingly.

He stepped away from the window and the curtains fell back into place.

"The innkeeper gave me directions to a place where I can pick up an untraceable specie. I'll double-check the location on my way back." He stretched and groaned as his tight muscles protested. "But first, I'm going to rest for a while."

# COVER

"Are you sure you should go out like that?" Theia said as Vihaan finished getting dressed after his nap.

Vihaan looked down at his beloved new jerkin. "What's wrong with it?"

"Rather conspicuous, don't you think?" She poked her finger through the Mount rune, causing Vihaan to shiver. "Not really what you want when picking up a legally dubious specie or scouting out an enemy stronghold."

"Fair point." Vihaan removed his jerkin and, after setting it on the bed, looked down at his worn tunic in embarrassment. "Perhaps I need to find something a little more presentable."

"Or convince everyone that holes are the new fashion." Theia looked at his wrist. "And an elf with such a visible Hilt will stand out too, you know."

Vihaan's Hilt-cuff slid up his arm.

Theia watched the bulge in his sleeve until it stopped on his bicep. She rolled her eyes. "I'm sure that the tailor won't notice that."

"I can barely remember the last time I deliberately went out in public without it," Vihaan said as the cuff made its way back down his arm until it slid off and landed, flattened, on the palm of his left hand.

"You *can* put it in your travel bag."

Vihaan grinned sheepishly and followed her suggestion, then clipped the bag to his waistband.

"I'll be back as soon as I can."

Vihaan stepped into the path in front of the inn, feeling naked and vulnerable.

*Theia was right,* he told himself firmly, *your Hilt is there if you need it. Besides, you wouldn't have been able to traject anyway!*

The keeper's directions led him to the far side of Akin's large City Centre and to a storefront with no signage other than the glowing word "open" just visible through a frosted window beside the door.

*My dad would be so furious if he knew where we are!* the memory of Amineh's voice pointed out.

Vihaan nodded to himself—it did feel a little like Shant. Despite his unease, he stepped inside.

The small store was lined with closed cabinets along the walls. An elderly human woman in a threadbare gray jumpsuit sat behind the counter. She looked up at Vihaan and put down her divulgate.

"What service are you looking for today?"

"I... uh... need an anonymous specie and... uh... I was told I could get one here."

She nodded and, with a groan, stood and walked over to one of the cabinets. After removing a gray specie, she shuffled back to the counter and gratefully lowered herself back onto her stool.

"Transfer or trade?" she asked as she inserted the specie into the ledger built into the counter.

"Trade," Vihaan said, extracting several pieces of jewelry from his treasure bag. "I'm hoping that this will be enough for a week's expenses here in town."

She grinned, retrieving a formulae from under the counter. "After my fee it should be enough." She lifted the formulae to her mouth. "Six hundred units."

She placed the formulae into an oversized slot in the ledger. After a moment, it buzzed and she handed the specie to Vihaan.

"If anyone asks, you are Amon Agadhi, born in the Chichi neighborhood of Akin on 1 Kadherian 2350."

Vihaan groaned inwardly.

*Did she just pick the first names and date she came across?*

"Any other services today?"

"No, thank you."

Vihaan quickly exited, relieved that no one had caught him inside the shady establishment. Just as quickly, he headed back towards the more respectable parts of Akin.

The manager of Akin Business Attire quickly suppressed his look of dismay as Vihaan stepped through the door.

He needlessly pulled on his pocketless gray

jumpsuit by its thick clothier-tan trim. "Can I assist you with something, sir?"

"I'm starting at Akin Central College next week and need to pick up some jumpsuits."

"Ah, an academic. I should have known." He smiled insincerely. "Please come this way. Do you know your size?"

"No, I'm afraid not," Vihaan answered.

The administrator's smile grew more strained. "I'll have one of our clothiers measure you." He gestured towards an elf at the back of the store. "She'll take care of you from here."

The female clothier approached, her jumpsuit's tan trim far thinner than her manager's. The manager turned and quickly walked back to the front of the store.

"I'll just need to take a few measurements," the elf said nervously as she pulled out her tape measure and formulae.

"No problem." Vihaan smiled reassuringly. "I'm Vihaan."

"Tayla," she replied without meeting his eyes.

She began, softly dictating his measurements into the formulae.

"Well, Tayla," Vihaan said during a pause, "do you get a commission for your sales."

"Yes, but"—she glanced up with an embarrassed look—"Manager Abimbola only sends me the basic jobs."

"How much would a full work-set cost?"

Tayla brightened. "A standard set would be two hundred units plus fitting fees."

"And a premium set?"

"Twice that."

"Well, today's your lucky day." Vihaan grinned. "I'll need a full work-set with the premium fabric."

Tayla's face filled with a genuine smile.

She was still grinning when she finished dictating his measurements. "You're almost a perfect men's size seven."

Vihaan felt a flush of pride.

"It will only take me about twenty minutes to get them fitted." Tayla gestured to a lounge behind Vihaan. "Just take a seat in the waiting area and I'll bring them out to you as soon as they're ready."

Vihaan pulled out his divulgate and spent the next twenty minutes savoring the fact that he could once again browse the newsfeeds at his leisure.

Tayla returned from the back room, proudly carrying a stack of green jumpsuits. "Akin Business Attire is proud to provide you with the best professional wear in the city."

"Thank you, Tayla, it has been a pleasure."

"Thank *you*!"

She smiled and returned to the back of the store.

Manager Abimbola was at the checkout when Vihaan set the six carefully folded jumpsuits onto the counter.

He smiled unconvincingly and picked up his formulae. "Academic, work-set." He put his hand on the top one, then looked down at the pile in surprise. "Premium fabric."

"Tayla was *extremely* helpful. You should be proud of your staff," Vihaan said pointedly, looking the manager directly in the eyes.

"Yes," the manager replied in a strained tone,

"she is one of our best." He lifted the formulae again. "Full commission, Tayla Aasim."

Vihaan cringed inwardly when the ledger showed the total: four-hundred seventy-three units.

*At least I can refill it anywhere and don't have to go all the way back to that crack in the wall.*

He handed over his new specie.

The ledger buzzed a moment later.

"Do you have changing rooms?" Vihaan said as he accepted his specie back. "Clothier Aasim did such a nice job, I'd like to put one of these on right now."

"Yes, sir, changing rooms are behind the green door beside the waiting area."

"Thank you for your assistance today!"

Vihaan entered the first available changing room and began to unfold the top jumpsuit. A small piece of paper fell out.

He picked it up and saw small, neat handwriting:

> Vihaan,
>
> Thank you for your kindness today.
>
> If you ever need anything else, please ask for me. They don't like me bringing it up, but store policy guarantees customers the right to pick their clothiers.
>
> With gratitude,
> Tayla

Vihaan grinned and changed into the jumpsuit.

"Now that's nice!"

He looked at himself in the mirror and felt a lump in his throat.

*A perfect fit and it feels just like one of Gonde-fle's old jumpsuits!*

Manager Abimbola's eyes followed Vihaan as he left the store in his new jumpsuit with the others and his worn old clothes tucked under his arm.

Vihaan made sure to stroke the silky fabric and make an appreciative noise as he passed him by.

"Have a good day, sir," Manager Abimbola said tightly.

"Thank you," Vihaan said, opening the front door. "I'm sure I will!"

# CONFIRMATION

*No sense lugging all this around,* Vihaan thought to himself when he was alone on the path. He looked around. *I don't want to make a spectacle of myself.*

He stepped into a dark alley and quickly transferred his new and old clothes into his travel bag.

Relieved of his burden, and comfortably anonymous, Vihaan stepped back onto the path and made his way towards the Ameliorates that held Teivel's muster.

*It's on the next path, so I'll start scouting here,* Vihaan thought as he approached an intersecting path.

He reached into his travel bag and, at his thought, the lodestone pushed against his hand. He closed his fist around it and turned down the intersecting path.

The lodestone tugged towards the first alley. As he passed, Vihaan looked down the alley and saw that it went all the way through to the next path. He smiled and continued walking.

As he walked, the lodestone tugged towards every path and alley that would lead him back to the path where the Ameliorates was located, stronger and stronger as he approached the spot parallel to the apothecary's location, then weakening.

Vihaan looped around the end of the block and for the first time noticed that the apothecary was on Sovereign Avenue.

*The king of the immortals indeed!*

He walked slowly past the Ameliorates and, after making sure that no one was paying attention, followed the lodestar's tug into the alley beside it.

It kept tugging gently forward until he got to the back half of the building, where it started tugging towards the side—tugging towards a window, presumably opened to let in the day's breeze.

After a glance back at the mouth of the alley, Vihaan looked quickly through the window—it was dirty, but he could still see a brightly lit storeroom on the other side of it.

He walked towards the back of the building, the lodestar continuing to tug back towards the open window.

Vihaan walked around the back of the building and into the alley on the other side. The lodestar began tugging towards another open window.

*That confirms that the muster is here,* he through as he put the lodestar away. *Now we just need to figure out how to determine whether Teivel is here too.*

He stepped out of the alley and casually headed across the path to share his findings with Theia.

~

"The muster is definitely there," Vihaan said as soon as the door to their room was closed.

"And so is Teivel!"

Vihaan's eyes went wide. "You're *sure*?!"

"As sure as I can be from up here based on one old, faded image."

"How do you know?!"

"He went out for lunch."

"And no one noticed?!"

"He must be using an ephemeron to hide his eyes."

"Just like they did when Orang Hemshil retired from *The Rajveer Chronicles*." Vihaan nodded. "But why hide just his eyes?"

"Vanity, I would assume," Theia said with a smile, "and I think he's the store's only employee!"

"Really?!" Vihaan was shocked. "I would have expected him to surround himself with lackeys. How do you know?"

"I saw a few people try to get in while he was gone," Theia replied. "Perhaps, when you have all of demon-kind following your orders, you don't feel the need to bring your lackeys home."

Vihaan laughed. "I need to be sure. I have to see for myself."

The next day Vihaan stepped out of the inn, wearing his academic jumpsuit and a distracted expression, just as the proprietor left the apothecary. As he shut the door, he pressed a small talisman against it for a brief moment before sliding it into the pocket on his plain gray jumpsuit. He stepped onto the path and headed to lunch.

Vihaan nodded absently at him as he passed to disguise his examination of the potential immortal's face.

He had to fight the urge to draw his Hilt.

Even with those brown eyes, there was no doubt that they had found Teivel.

His heart pounding, he returned to the inn, where Theia was waiting.

"It's him," he said forcefully as he unconsciously willed his Hilt-cuff back to its usual position.

"Are we going to traject in tonight?"

"No—even if he doesn't have an occlude, we can't risk a passing constable seeing the flash."

"Did you set the other lodestar?"

"No, I didn't want him to see me before he left." Vihaan's heart was pounding again. He imagined striking Teivel down in the street before stopping himself and taking a deep breath.

*I need to calm down!*

He put his hand on his Hilt-cuff, expecting it to be warmed by his rage—it was no warmer than the skin beneath it.

"I'll head out after I'm over the immediate urge to cut him down on sight."

Two hours later, Vihaan, still in academic green, stepped through the door into Teivel's Ameliorates.

He forced himself to ignore Teivel, who was at

the counter talking with a customer, and stroll calmly towards the back of the store.

On his way, he made a point of pausing at each rack of potential impulse buys as if drawn in by the bright displays.

When he got to the back wall, he saw that the door to the storeroom was two aisles to his left, just beyond the display of recharge potions.

He walked over and slowly made his way across the potion display, randomly picking up bottles, which he pretended to examine, before setting them back down on the shelf and moving closer to his objective.

Finally he was standing beside the door.

After a steadying breath, he raised his hand as if to scratch his right temple and whispered to the spare lodestar in the band fastened around his fore-arm, just behind where his Hilt-cuff usually was. "Invoke, lead us safely to the other side of this door."

The talisman chirped softly and Vihaan re-leased the breath he hadn't realized he had been holding.

He thought of the immortal at the checkout.

*Would it be suspicious if I just walked out with nothing?*

He sighed to himself and grabbed the closest bottle of potion before heading back to the front of the store.

"Ah," Teivel said as Vihaan handed him the bottle. "Old Hat"—he smiled—"my father used to swear by it."

Vihaan tried to grin back. "Mine too."

He put his untraceable specie into the slot in the ledger.

"Old Hat brand recharge potion, one bottle, ten percent first-time customer discount." Teivel was still smiling as he slotted his formulae into the ledger. "Ameliorates is always happy to welcome new customers."

The ledger buzzed and Teivel handed over the potion and specie. "I hope we see you back real soon!"

"You will," Vihaan promised.

"He did something weird last night," Theia said as Vihaan blinked away sleep the next morning.

"What did he do?"

"After he closed the shop for the night, the entire building stayed dark for two hours before the lights in his apartment came on."

"Could he have been taking a nap in his office?"

"I don't think so," Theia said. "The more I mulled it over, the more I thought about the Palace."

"You think he has a palace of his own?"

"Why wouldn't he? And, since I didn't see a flash, I think it's underneath the shop."

Vihaan looked thoughtful. "I suppose it's no more difficult to dig under a city than into a mountain."

"So, if he's not in his apartment when we get there, we'll know where he is, generally speaking."

"So you're good with the plan?"

"You keep him occupied." Theia smiled. "I'll package him up!"

It was three nights later when their nightly check of the lodestar finally resulted in a positive vibration.

"I'll check it out," Theia said and passed through the window.

Vihaan watched her float across the path, willing it to remain empty.

She floated into the alley beside the Ameliorates and moved out of his field of vision.

It wasn't long before she reappeared and floated back across towards their room.

Vihaan sighed with relief as she passed through the window.

"What did you find?"

"There's an open window into the storeroom." Theia smiled. "And there's no occlude, at least not on the apothecary building."

"We leave in an hour," Vihaan said, his voice full of anticipation. "He should be asleep by then."

# CONFRONTATION

"Are you sure you don't want me to leave you somewhere safe before I go in?"

"No," Theia laughed as she stood beside him on the path in front of the inn. "I have confidence in you, but only to a point." She grinned to take the edge off her words. "And unless you've come up with a new plan, you can't pull this off on your own. Do you have it?"

Vihaan returned his friend's grin as he reached into his travel bag and removed the bulwark.

Theia took the talisman in her fingertips and lifted it up to eye level. The phylactery swung beneath it from its short chain. "This thing still makes me nervous. I spent far too long locked away and have no interest in repeating the experience."

Vihaan flicked the phylactery, causing it to swing back and forth.

"You know as well as I do that we're the only people who can control it."

"Intellectually, sure," Theia said with a forced shudder. "But the thought of returning to the abyss is still terrifying."

"We've taken every precaution."

"Except for staying home."

"I just gave you that option." Vihaan stowed the bulwark back in his travel bag and pulled out the lodestar that was set for the storage room door.

"Yeah, more the fool am I for not taking it."

They laughed quietly, nodded to each other, then started across the quiet path.

The lodestar directed them to a window at the very back of the Ameliorates—Vihaan quietly slid it all the way open.

Theia willed out her anneal, then she stepped through the wall as Vihaan caught it.

He tossed the talisman to her through the open window before hoisting himself through.

Once inside, Vihaan pulled out the lodestar set for Teivel's muster.

They followed its prompts to a well-preserved antique cabinet tucked under the stairway against the alley-side wall of the storeroom. The cabinet was simple in appearance but had an ornately carved cornice on top with several gems embedded into it that appeared to be a more recent addition.

"Well," Vihaan whispered as he pocketed the talisman, "we know where he stores his musters."

"Right by the stairs to his apartment," Theia whispered back. "Let's seal this place and head up."

They turned to the shelves behind them and Vihaan pulled the occlude from the Palace's assemblage out of his travel bag. A phylactery swung from a chain beneath it. "Invoke," he whispered, "seal this structure against intrusion and isolate the second floor."

The talisman pulsed once and he set it on the middle shelf.

They both nodded. Vihaan handed Theia the bulwark, then moved silently to the foot of the stairs. The pair cautiously ascended towards the back of the building.

The stairs led to one end of a hallway that spanned the full width of the second floor.

Theia paused a few steps below the landing as Vihaan continued, stepping softly into the hallway.

"You're going to get so much more than the family silver," a firm but warm voice said from the darkness.

Vihaan rolled open the lucent-cover on his chest and the room filled with its silvery light.

Teivel, wearing nothing but a pair of night shorts, was standing at the midpoint of the hallway, glaring at him with his red eyes.

"I'm not after your wealth, *demon*!"

"Ah, so 'recharge potion' was casing the demon's lair!" Teivel laughed. "Is it revenge or a righteous quest? I suppose it doesn't matter, I'll kill you either way." He laughed again. "I'll be honest, I would have killed you no matter what. It almost feels weird to have a reason—other than you breaking into my home, of course."

Teivel stepped back into the closest room. A lucent inside flicked on.

Vihaan rushed through the arching entrance to the room and found Teivel waiting for him with a large double-edged sword, its crossbar studded with a variety of small gems.

"I haven't bloodied this in centuries," he said with a cold grin.

Vihaan's Hilt snapped into place, and a matching blade extruded from it. He smiled as he caught a momentary flicker of doubt pass across Teivel's face. He took advantage of the moment and launched an aggressive attack.

Teivel blocked it, but not fast enough to stop Vihaan's blade from clipping his arm. He leapt back and watched the wound turn black and the surrounding skin start to flake away.

"You're not as innocent as I thought!" He ran his hand over the wound. "There's more than just the souls of a few red-tip slaves in that Hilt!" He looked at Vihaan with malice. "You've taken an immortal's soul!"

A flash of guilt passed through him, but Vihaan stood firm. "The soul was not taken, it was given."

"Nonsense. No immortal would volunteer to die—it defeats the purpose!"

He started to circle Vihaan just as Leah had.

"I have nothing to fear from you." A sneer filled Teivel's face. "I was there to witness the birth of your untoward race and I will be there when its last member crumbles to dust."

He leapt forward, shifting his attack at the last second and catching Vihaan by surprise.

Teivel's blade pivoted expertly against Vihaan's and the tip stabbed hard into his chest.

Vihaan gasped from the pain but quickly recovered and struck at Teivel's unprotected side.

Teivel looked at him in surprise as he blocked the well-placed thrust. "Common misperception about the aegis talisman…"

He swung, and their blades clashed together loudly.

"...while it provides ample protection against magical assaults"—he struck again—"it only blunts physical ones"—and again. "If I hit you hard enough, the blow will still kill."

"Then I had better keep my guard up!" Vihaan replied as their blades scraped apart.

From the corner of his eye, Vihaan saw Theia slip into the room, the bulwark held out in front of her, the word invoke forming on her lips.

Teivel must have noticed his gaze flick towards her, because he suddenly leapt back, spinning as he did, and slashed through Theia's torso.

It was a supremely lucky strike.

As Teivel finished his spin and faced him again, Vihaan saw Theia's anneal bounce away, rolling unevenly towards the door. He never saw the bulwark land.

He thrust at Teivel but was met by a strong riposte.

As they clashed, he saw Theia desperately trying to retrieve her anneal from the floor.

*What do I do without the bulwark?!*

After blocking another blow, he nearly smiled and started shifting position, carefully maneuvering Teivel to where he would be able to see Theia futilely scrabbling for her talisman by the door.

Thinking that she was a third intruder, Teivel spun again. His blade passed through Theia and, not facing the expected resistance, continued on until it sank deeply into the wooden framework of the entry arch.

Theia and Teivel looked at each other with

equal surprise as the immortal struggled to free his sword.

Vihaan swung for a decapitation just as Teivel wrenched his blade out of the framework with a loud crack, a large fragment splitting off and passing through Theia ahead of the blade.

Vihaan's Hilt-blade opened Teivel from shoulder to shoulder as he rose, the wound blackening his entire upper back.

Teivel spun, a look of fear in his eyes.

Then he grinned and placed his thumb against a brown stone on the side of his sword's crossbar. His brow furrowed for a moment, then he looked at Vihaan with renewed respect.

"Not as stupid as you look, are you?"

"We came prepared."

"Not prepared enough!"

Teivel attacked with a renewed ferocity.

Vihaan was barely able to hold his own. *He was toying with me!*

He retreated and lost his footing, quickly forming a Hilt-shield to protect himself as he stumbled back against a bookshelf.

The bulwark spun away from beneath his sliding foot.

Teivel advanced with fury in his eyes.

Still off-balance, it was all Vihaan could do to block the blows.

He regained his footing and counterattacked, succeeding in pushing Teivel back towards the opposite side of the room.

He stopped his advance when he saw that the wall was covered by a selection of weapons—he let Teivel push him away from the wall.

Vihaan's chest was burning—despite all of his training, his stamina was no match for the immortal's.

As he steadied his arm after a particularly vicious blow, Vihaan remembered his final sparring match with Dugal.

He took a wild swing, then retreated—Teivel smiled and advanced with a flurry of strikes.

Finally, Teivel's blade slashed horizontally towards Vihaan.

Vihaan blocked the blow and started twisting his Hilt-blade around Teivel's.

The immortal shifted his weight and Vihaan moved forward.

His strike was true, the tip of his blade slipping smoothly between Teivel's ribs.

With a final burst of will, Vihaan extended his blade all the way through Teivel's torso, widening it as it advanced.

It tore through the other side with a sickening crunch, leaving an exit wound three times the size of its entry.

Blinking sweat from his eyes, Vihaan looked at Teivel.

A look of shock was frozen on his now black and cracking face.

Vihaan closed his eyes just before the blinding flash of light announced his victory. He opened them again to see the final silver remnant of Teivel's soul disappearing into his Hilt-blade.

Vihaan doubled over, gasping for breath.

It was over.

~

The blinding light of the demon-flare was seen all across Akin—bright enough to pull half of the city from their beds.

Those closest to the fight emerged onto the path, still blinking away purple afterimages, and discovered a glittering yellow crystal encasing their local Ameliorates.

# EPILOGUE

**Mount (primary): mountain**

# CLOSURE

Vihaan steeled himself at the sight of the painfully familiar rockslide covering the Hilt foundry that had so radically altered the course of his life.

The only thing that had changed, aside from a new selection of the spindly shrubs, was a shiny brown stone now adhered just to the right of the entrance.

Vihaan pulled his annul from its dedicated pocket in his jerkin and held it out in front of him. "Invoke. Suspend the spell that blocks my entry."

The rocks shimmered. He returned the talisman to its pocket and rested his hand over the Mount rune on his chest. Just as he was about to close his eyes to picture the foundry's main room, a glint caught his eye.

*It can't be!*

Vihaan stepped into the entrance. Leaning against the wall where the passage turned sharply was a copper Hilt.

*It is! They just tossed it away so they didn't have to think about it anymore!*

It was the Hilt that had killed Gondefle.

Vihaan reached into his travel bag, pulled out his magic-proof gloves and put them on. He knelt, gingerly lifted the deadly relic and slid it into his travel bag.

After a moment of silence, he closed his eyes and pictured the foundry's main room. Flashes of red, then blue bled through his eyelids.

Opening his eyes, he reached into his travel bag again and removed a long, thin sack. He untied the mouth; it was full of premade tags, each with a loop of string at one end, and a scribe talisman.

Vihaan moved to the exposed Hilt display and methodically copied each inscription from the wall onto one of the tags, attaching it to the associated exposed Hilt and placing the Hilt into his travel bag.

When he got to rume, he willed its former occupant to form a short, tapering blade, then carved the piece of stone containing the inscription from the wall. He pulled out a red velvet bag, with rume and a copy of the date already embroidered onto it, and placed the cube of stone inside. After holding the bag for a moment, he slid it into his travel bag.

Long after darkness had arrived that first night, he trajected to the small park in his old neighborhood. He quietly made his way to the least-visited corner, just between the two oldest trees, where he had buried his preserval trunk full of Delphi Press books, and started digging.

It wasn't long before his Hilt-spade struck the top of the trunk.

*They're still here!*

Vihaan soon had the trunk excavated and trajected it back to the Palace's vestibule. He carried it through the antechamber and into the parlor, where he had to fight the urge to open the trunk and lose himself in the books within.

*Keep on task. They're safe now and you'll have plenty of time later.*

After a fond pat on the trunk's corner, Vihaan returned to the vestibule, then trajected back to the foundry, where he fell asleep on the same bench where he had first bonded with his Hilt.

After collecting all of the exposed Hilts, he started processing the workrooms.

It was early afternoon on the third day when Vihaan arrived at the room where Gondefle had died. His eyes filled with tears as he reverently placed his late brother's torch into his travel bag.

His mood brightened when he stepped into the next room down the hall. It was a small room, barely large enough for four adults to gather on either side of a low central counter that extended out from the back wall below a domed ceiling that began at waist height.

*A resonance chamber!*

Just like in the pictures he had seen in books, the chamber's dome was tiled with square crystal panels, each a shade of foggy green, which covered the surface all the way up to a single red crystalline disk at the apex. Unlike the pictures, the apex disk was cracked, with a chunk missing from one edge, and the green tiles that hadn't already fallen to shatter on the floor were similarly ragged.

*It's still beautiful*, he thought as he panned his lucent-light around the room, where it reflected back at him from the remaining crystals.

He spent the rest of the nights sleeping on that

work counter, wondering if it was this chamber, the most intact of the four he found in the foundry, where the spell-work that had created his own Hilt had been cast.

During the days, he worked his way through the rest of the foundry, logging and removing every artifact.

When his traject finally returned him to the sunlight outside the foundry, he smiled to himself.

*If I ever run out of library books, figuring out how I survived should keep me busy for a few years.*

He pulled out his annul again and turned back to face the rockslide.

"Done. Restore the suspended spell."

He tucked the talisman away and turned towards the valley.

"Now, it's time to confront my past."

Instead of trajecting again, Vihaan decided to honor Gondefle by walking the route of their final trip together.

It wasn't long after he made his first step into the village that he started hearing whispers:

"It's the Mountain Warrior from the divulgate!"

"The one who made the Demon Crystal!"

"The one who drove every demon away from Akin!"

Unlike the voices that had haunted his childhood, these were filled with awe.

Vihaan cursed himself.

*Of course, there are security remembrances all*

*over Akin! I should never have taken off my armor!* He remembered how many accidents wearing the armor had caused. *Okay, the armor was a bad idea for entering a city, but I should have removed my jerkin too!*

After a barely noticeable hesitation, he continued on towards Hinter Village Centre.

A crowd started to gather in his wake, most talking excitedly into their chatters, but none of them approaching or attempting to start a conversation.

Surreptitiously Vihaan reached into his travel bag, focused, then pulled out one of his freshly printed copies of *True History: Leah of the Immortals*. The thick volume barely fit through the bag's mouth.

When he approached the Village Hall building, Clerc Grimaldi, the current village manager, was waiting at the bottom of the steps, flanked by several constables in yellow armor.

"That's close enough," he said. "Who are you and what are your intentions here in Hinter?"

"I am Vihaan Mount." He folded his arms around the thick leather-bound book against his chest and smiled. "And I'm here for a homecoming of sorts."

"I don't know of a Mount family in Hinter, or *anywhere* for that matter. What *home* are you returning to?"

"That's the *of sorts* part. I was disowned by my parents and had to claim my own name."

"And what makes you think you're worthy of a *primary* rune?!"

"You'd have to ask my subconscious"—Vihaan

lifted his arm to show his cuff and the Mount rune that dominated the top of it—"or my Hilt."

A rustle passed through the manager's security detail. One constable reached for his own potion Hilt, but in the end they maintained their positions.

He glanced back over his shoulder and smiled.

"But perhaps the crowd behind me could provide some additional justifications."

Manager Grimaldi's eyes flicked towards them.

"So, you *do* claim to be the Mountain Warrior whose Demon Crystal protects the city of Akin."

"No," Vihaan laughed, "I hadn't heard either of those terms before today. While 'Demon Crystal' is a surprisingly accurate description, it's really just a bulwark."

"So," Manager Grimaldi laughed derisively, "the Mountain Warrior is a lie."

"Not quite. I did confront and kill Teivel, the leader of the so-called demons."

A look of fury crossed Manager Grimaldi's face. "I've seen the pain that demons can inflict first-hand! Only a fool would be so *arrogant* to label them 'so-called'!"

"I say 'so-called' not to minimize the danger they represent but to acknowledge that they are not the supernatural creatures that we've been led to believe."

"Fantasy!" Grimaldi snorted with disgust. "I find it unlikely that a *single elf* could kill *any* demon, let alone their leader."

There was an angry buzz from the crowd.

"You should be careful with specist comments like that out here."

Grimaldi started to reply, but Vihaan continued

loudly, "Despite what we have been taught, the divisions in our society are not the way things are *supposed* to be! Despite what we have been taught, we are all more alike than we are different." Vihaan tossed the book at the manager's feet. He jumped back in surprise and his guards all drew their Hilts and extruded blades.

Vihaan continued, "That book is a summary of the life of Leah, the former Beast of the Mountain, taken from her own journals. You can expect to see more books like this one documenting our lost history." He turned to address the crowd. "We called her a demon, she called herself an immortal. She was not some mystical being, she was a human who was changed by an atrocious spell they called the Split."

There was an incredulous grumble from the crowd and many faces were turning angry.

"The practitioners who cast it," Vihaan shouted over the increasing crowd noise, glancing back at Grimaldi, "the *human* practitioners who cast it, wanted immortality at any cost! And they were more than willing to kill half of Feracio's population to get it!"

Vihaan started to pace between the crowd and the village manager.

"They cast their spell but didn't all get what they expected. They created immortals all right, but elves too."

Both Manager Grimaldi and the crowd tried to shout him down simultaneously.

A few of the bravest, or angriest, elves from the crowd moved forward with menace in their eyes.

Vihaan calmly lifted his right arm over his head, his Hilt snapping into his palm and forming into a fierce-looking serrated blade. He swung it casually in the direction of the advancing members of the crowd.

Everyone went silent and the advancing elves quickly retreated.

Vihaan's Hilt returned to neutral. He released it and it snapped back under his wrist.

"It's true, they drained the souls of half the world's population to get what they wanted!"

The crowd made an unhappy noise but maintained their distance.

"But they were betrayed by Teivel, the lead practitioner, who didn't want to share his power. As half of the world was dying, he willed the spell to kill his associates. I doubt he intended to create us, but we're here and we deserve to be treated as equals."

The crowd roared with mixed emotion.

When they finally quieted, he continued.

"For a while the immortals worked with us, claiming that they were building a new, better world. Then they took over and created a new world, but not a *better* one—not for any of us at least. They created a world that served *them*. Have you ever wondered why we know so little from before Demon Rule? It's because they outlawed history! They purged anything that stood in their way!"

Vihaan paused to scan the increasingly hostile crowd.

"But, as you know from the history that remains, our spirit was too much, and we—humans *and* elves—rebelled."

There was a unified angry grumble from the crowd.

"I know." He glanced back at Manager Grimaldi. "The humans turned on us the day after Liberation."

Grimaldi flinched as the crowd roared again.

Vihaan made a calming gesture. "I've spent a lot of time with the ghost of a woman named Theia Ilham, one of the dissidents who started the movement that became the revolution that ended their rule. While going through Leah's journals, we realized that, although Demon Rule ended, *the Demon War never did*!

"Everything we've been taught has been part of their ongoing campaign to keep us in line! To keep us so afraid of them—and each other—that we don't even dream of fighting back!

"Some of these immortals even live disguised among us—quietly influencing our leaders towards what's best for them, towards anything that will maintain our divisions! They keep us so busy fighting each other that we leave them alone!

"The large-scale demon-attacks that we face every generation are organized cullings!"

He nearly choked on the word but knew that it was necessary.

The crowd protested, but Vihaan continued even louder.

"We are culled to provide the blood and souls that fund these immortals and their hidden society. But it's not just the culls. Anyone who might cause trouble for them is disappeared." Vihaan continued over the noise of the crowd, "Who among you hasn't suffered a demon-loss?

"But it doesn't *have* to be this way! Things *can* change! *People* can change! I should know, I've changed more than most."

Vihaan steeled himself.

"I was born as Aadima Rumetre, a man trapped in a woman's body."

The crowd murmured with uncomfortable recognition.

"I was miserable until I figured that out and never truly happy until I was free to live my true life. The majority of you disapproved, tried to deny who I am. My parents were first among you, eventually disowning me and pushing me out into the world as soon as I came of age."

Vihaan scanned the crowd again. Many of the faces were familiar, but few would meet his gaze. Of those few, most were angry, hateful or scared, but his heart swelled with hope when he saw that some were filled with understanding.

"I plan to help this world change for the better, and ask you to do the same. The first step is to challenge yourselves to be more open, more accepting. To let people be who they *really are*, not what you *want* or *expect* them to be."

There was a sound of disapproval from the crowd, broken by a few faint cries of support.

"I don't expect miracles. I don't expect you to lay down generations of bigotry and hatred on just my words. My next step will be to provide all of Feracio with the history these immortals took from us so that we can all profit from that knowledge."

Vihaan gestured towards the book that lay untouched at Manager Grimaldi's feet.

"I will share the evidence that I uncover in

books like this one. My partner and I are still sorting through hundreds of pre–Demon Rule books from an immortal's private library."

Vihaan felt a weight lift from his shoulders, and he smiled at the crowd.

"When I was a child, I craved your approval. Now that I'm a man, I no longer need it. The only thing that matters to me, and the only thing that should matter to *anyone*, is being true to yourself. I know that I am who I was meant to be and I know what I need to do with my life."

Still smiling, Vihaan put his hand to his chest, focused on the vestibule of the Palace, and disappeared in a flash of red light.

*The Man of the Mountain*

(forthcoming)

Vihaan Mount and the late Theia Ilham have settled into a life of research, safe in the belief that they cut the head off the immortal threat. But, as their second book meets stiff resistance from the entrenched mindsets of Feracio society, the threat resurfaces.

Suddenly it's clear—they didn't kill a snake, *they wounded a hydra!*

# AFTERWORD

I hope you enjoyed this novel, and that you'll stick around for the upcoming sequels. I'm already hard at work on the next volume, *The Man of the Mountain,* and have written several scenes for the third book in the series.

If you're sticking around, and would like to help others find this book, please leave a review at the store where you got yours or on *Goodreads.* Thanks in advance!

If you're interested in keeping up to date on my upcoming releases, consider:

- Following me on Facebook:
  facebook.com/DanielJLyonsAuthor
- Joining my mailing list:
  dansformers.info/mailing.php

You can also learn more on my website *Dans-Formers.info.*

# ABOUT THE AUTHOR

Daniel J. Lyons is a lifelong fan of science fiction and fantasy, especially Star Trek and the works of Isaac Asimov, who grew up along the East Coast of the US as a Navy brat before settling in Massachusetts. He started writing fan fiction in high school, then earned a degree in journalism with a minor in creative writing before unexpectedly focusing on a career as an IT professional, eventually specializing in web and mobile communication.

# OTHER WORKS BY DANIEL J. LYONS

*Severed*

A science fiction novel:

Five hundred years in the future, humanity has exhausted planet Earth and moved out to live "on the stars."

With your closest neighbor light-years away, the "on the stars" lifestyle guarantees a level of privacy unmatched in human history. But even ultimate privacy doesn't need to come at a cost when modern technology can whisk you instantly back to civilization.

But when that modern technology is taken away, three private vessels find themselves completely unprepared for the isolation that follows. The three crews have very different strategies to cope with a radical change to the status quo.

Will they have the supplies and wherewithal to survive the weeks and months that it will take to get back to civilization?

*The Infinitesimal Collection: Bureaucracy, Stuffed Bears and Alien Duels*

A short story collection including:

"A Visit to the Licensing Department"

A science fiction story about what life might be like if human lives were cheapened to the point where they could be taken legally as long as you have the correct permit.

"The Busiest Workday"

A speculative fiction story told by a midlevel angel that attempts to answer the question "will bureaucracy ever end?" by documenting the heavenly aftermath of the apocalypse.

"Come Around Here Often?"

A science fiction story told by Captain Wilson Banski, who, after an enemy attack destroys his ship, deals with misadventure and cultural misunderstandings after his escape pod lands on an alien planet.

"Best Friend Bears"

A fiction piece told by Sarah about growing up with her best friend Ann and their special pair of stuffed bears.

Visit *DansFormers.info* for a full bibliography.

* 9 7 8 1 7 3 5 5 9 5 7 7 1 *